The Aviation Girls

A HISTORY OF FLIGHT IN STORIES

NINE CHALLENGING YA ADVENTURES

by Tom Durwood

From H. Barber, "The Aeroplane Speaks" (1917)

Commentary by Michael Quetting, Paul Glenshaw, Jennifer Ghilani,

Cameron Smith, Sezail Adilm, Anne Millbrooke, and Tim Grove

Paperback ISBN 978-1-952520-41-9

EMPIRE STUDIES PRESS

MEETING D'AVIATION
NICE
10 a 25 AVRIL 1910
Grasset

REVIEWS

Brilliant, engrossing stories …

--Karan Thakur, Goodreads reviewer

Profound, provocative and eye-opening … strong, beautiful writing and a sense of deeper emotion.

-- Isha Singh, Good Reads

Mathematics NEEDS to be taught in a way that conveys its wonder and its awesome beauty. If this book can contribute to that kind of a goal and that kind of education, then more power to it. What a GREAT idea!

Hurrah for The Geometry Girls!

-- Paul Weiss, Goodreads

Exciting ... ambitious

An exciting and ambitious work of historical fiction for young adults.
-- *Marta Cheng, SPR Review*

Clever ... deeply realized characters

The construction of Durwood's stories is complex, but the messages they carry are straightforward: Durwood's focus stays on the relentless struggles for identity and self-discovery.

-- *Books Coffee's Reviews*

Wonderful reads ... happy to recommend!

-- *Diane Donovan, Editor, Bookwatch*

Stellar . . .

Richly detailed ... Durwood strikes gold.

The unique and captivating artwork in this series brings Durwood's prose and historical knowledge to life.

Brilliant, engrossing ... 5 out of 5 stars.

I enjoyed Mr. Durwood's beautiful writing. Always found myself reading for longer than I planned to ...

So many layers; it's hard not to become addicted. It is profound, provocative and eye-opening ... all unified with strong, beautiful writing and a sense of deeper emotion that covers a wide range of the human experiences throughout time.

Written with a skillful hand and with the kind of attention to detail that will grip an ambitious teenager.

Young readers will crave more details about the workings of the key solution in each story.

The MLK story ... an excellent story with a crucially important message for young people in modern Western society. **The mathematics is simple but elegant.**

This was the first time I've seen Bayes' rule used in fiction, let alone in a captivating way! A very enjoyable narrative.

Both the codebreaking and astronomics content are approachable, not too technically heavy. I especially enjoyed the ending ...

Refreshing .... **there is a special youthful ambition about the whole thing.**

-- Graham Van Goffrier, third-year PhD candidate (Theoretical neutrino physics)

CONTENTS
AVIATION GIRLS

Within all of us is a varying amount
of space lint and star dust,
the residue from our creation.
It is strongest in those of us who fly.

– *K.O. Eckland*

TOM'S WELCOME

Hello!! I am very happy you are here. I hope you like the stories.

Girls drop out of STEM classes at an astonishing rate when they turn 14.

Please stop doing that.

"Women make up only 34% of the workforce in science, technology, engineering and math (STEM), and men vastly outnumber women majoring in most STEM fields in college," reports the American Association of University Women. "Girls and women are systematically tracked away from science and math throughout their education, limiting their access, preparation and opportunities to go into these fields as adults."

The collection of adventures you are holding is my contribution to the effort to correct the mass migration of teenaged girls away from science and technology. These adventures are not for everyone. I tend to drive all of my stories through some region of

How Things Work. If you aren't willing to learn a little about electromagnetic pulses and astrobotany, then you won't appreciate "Murder on Moon Colony Saraswati."

I am hoping that you will be so interested in Rupa's family-tugboat drama that you will happily engage with her in a risk analysis of zeppelins.

* * *

I have taken a few liberties with aviation science and aviation history in my tales, so I have asked several experts to provide you with the real story. You will find their commentaries right after the stories.

I hope you get the chance to look up these scholars and delve more deeply into their work – Michael Quetting, for example, tells the true story of his adoption of seven goslings in *Papa Goose*. Tim Grove and Anne Millbrooke have written entire histories of flight, and Cameron Smith looks at establishing a science of human space settlement in his recent book, *Emigrating Beyond Earth.*

* * *

All of your teachers and I ask just one thing of you young readers:

Wake up.

Begin to understand how a mortgage works. What's the catch? Who is Stanley Milgram? Why do electric cars *not* need oil? How are *Hamlet* and *The Lion King* the same story? What is Pi? How do monarch butterflies reproduce? Why does it matter? What does that dream you had last night really mean? What is the deal with that lithium thing, anyway? How does a fourteen-ton C-17 Globemaster bomber actually fly?

What your teachers and I know that you don't know is this: Either you figure out how the world works, or you are a permanent victim. Critical thinking is what we have. Try to understand everything. Only by doing that will you have a chance to succeed in this complex modern, global civilization we live in.

Bernoulli's Law. (The answer to the C-17 Globemaster question.)

Critical thinking is what we have. Try to understand everything.

I am currently working on a story about that lithium thing. The next collection of adventures should be ready soon ...

Read on.

Your pal,

www.theaviationgirls.com

THE ADVENTURES OF RUBY PI AND
The Aviation Girls

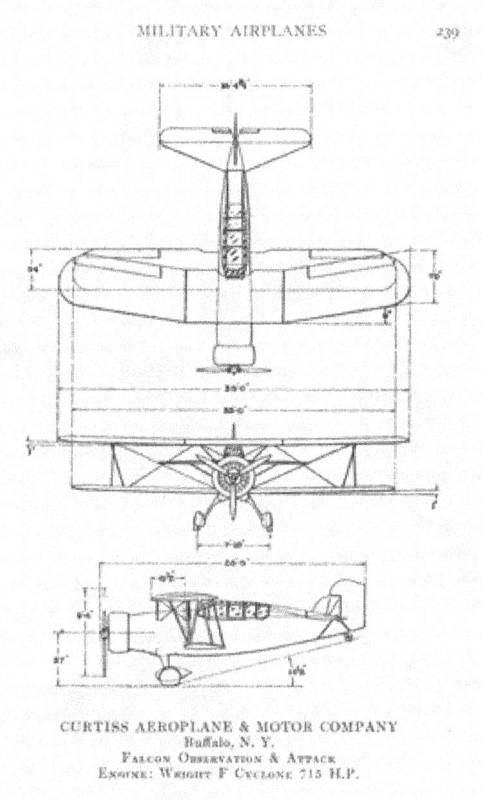

A HISTORY OF FLIGHT IN STORIES

1. How Birds Fly

A fable about causation.

Is the Tanager right?

ACT ONE: A LOST BABY

When feathery therapod dinosaurs launched themselves into the air roughly 160 million years ago, they were limited flyers, fluttering only over short distances or in tiny bursts. But with only a few exceptions, the more than 10,000 species of birds descended from those dinosaurs have evolved into extraordinary flight machines ...

-- Samik Bhattacharya

Ayaeeewueeiioooo --

It was a Capuchin.

So much pathos showed in the baby monkey's face, having suddenly become aware of its helplessness. She called for her mother.

The pitiful infant was stranded high in the top branches.

She was lost. Helpless. Terrified.

EEEeeiiioooooo ahuhahuahu ...

The high-pitched trill came out in short bursts.

It repeated, worse this time.

The baby had tried to find and touch the pretty lights in the sky and gotten lost in the process.

Disoriented, too many trees away from home and scared, the baby Capuchin called again and again for its mother. Her distress was unbearable to hear.

A storm gathered in the mountain beyond. Raindrops plunked in the foliage. Strong winds bent the branches to and fro.

AYowwww ahuhahuhahuh WAAH!

Far below her, near the first branches up from the ground, a panther crept, silent and stalking.

He was a figure from a nightmare, a walking embodiment of death.

The Capuchin wailed pitifully.

She tried to call out her tormenter's name, so as to more properly demand help.

"Demon!" It was the only word she could think of.

"Demon! Oh, someone save me. Mama! *AAaaagghhh --* "

The baby monkey's cries were lost in a compound sequence of crashing thunders.

The storm moved closer.

Mesmerized by the way the cat's powerful muscles moved beneath a blue-black gleaming coat of fur, the baby monkey made no effort to hide.

The Panther's eyes looked around. He blinked and caught some small movement in the growing storm winds.

The panther stared upward.

He locked eyes with his prey ...

ACT TWO: A KETTLE

Birds can completely alter both the aerodynamic characteristics that govern how air moves over their wings and the inertial characteristics of their bodies that determine how they tumble through the air to complete fast maneuvers.

– Yasemin Saplakoglu

In that very same, storm-riven grove, three trees over, a pair of starlings fluttered, let their wings luff a moment, and alit adroitly on the thick oak branch.

"Go away!" shrieked the baby Capuchin in the adjoining tree crown, to its unseen hunter.

"Help! Help! Help!"

"Has anyone seen that baby monkey?" asked the younger of the two Starlings, with some urgency.

"Yes," replied the Owl, on a branch higher than the others. "She seems to be trapped in the top of that alder."

"AYowwww ahuhahuhahuh WAAH!" cried the Monkey, begging for mercy.

The birds were perched in a natural circle, or gathering, formed by interlocking tree limbs, partially shielded from the rain. It was a council, or informal meeting-place of birds. An amphitheatre among the sturdy branches of beeches, araucaria, nothofagus, Patagonian oak.

A parliament. A congregation of birds.
A *kettle.*
Thunder rumbled ominously.
This particular kettle took place in that part of the world where the Valdivian forests rule, in the shadows of the Grand Concourse, sometimes called the Andes. The kettle included a mix of local and migrating birds – two rough-hewn Gulls, a giant-sized Condor, a Scarlet Tanager (a migrator), an oddball Wren, an Owl and now the two Starlings.

"Something's closing in on that poor thing," added the Starling's older sister, worriedly.

"She's in big trouble," echoed the Starling.

"Just a baby, sounds like," added the Starling's Sister.

"So what?" asked the First Gull.

"It's nobody's business, that's what," commented the Second Gull. "Baby monkeys are hunted down every day."

The Owl fluffed her neck feathers. She tilted her neck until it made a cricking sound.

All seemed to agree, except for the Starlings and the towering, hunched-over Condor, who was busy grooming. Condors have a frill of white feathers which surround the base of the neck, and the feathers here are meticulously kept clean by the birds. This Condor was young, and not so jaded as the others. He glanced around innocently, as he groomed.

Thunder rumbled, not so far away now. Lightning flashed after four beats, meaning the storm front was closing in.

"I'm going to help her," announced the Starling, preparing to launch --

"You can't, Dear," instructed the Owl from her perch (higher than the others). "You're too small. Too light. That monkey would grip you tight and strangle you and you'd both crash."

The Starling stopped.

"You could," said the Starling.

She was looking at the Young Condor.

"You're big enough."

"*Ba-wang*," said the Wren.

* * *

The Young Condor seemed surprised to be singled out in this manner.

"No, he couldn't," corrected the Scarlet Tanager.

"Why not?" demanded the Starling's Sister. "He can fly. I see his kind fly, every day -- "

"He can *soar* but he can't *fly*," corrected the Tanager politely. "Not every bird flies the same."

Tanagers themselves are skilled flyers, long-distance flyers, as well as songbirds. At the approach of the lightning storm, this Tanager had thought it prudent to pause on her journey northward.

"'Soar but not fly'? What's that supposed to mean?" asked Second Gull.

"*How do we fly at all?*" asked Young Condor, as though it was a question that had been bothering him for some time. His voice was raspy and foreign-accented, like a Spanish songbird, but with a sore throat.

Well, not every bird flies the same.

This sudden and much larger question caught the group off-guard.

"Well, we fly because we're chosen," explained First Gull.

"*Wrong!*" cried Wren gleefully.

"We fly on the sins of the Deese Mal," stated the Owl." By that term, known among birds, the Owl meant to indicate all walkers – lions, turtles, snails, the entire animal kingdom, all fish in the seas. All non-birds. Every being that is unable to fly.

"The stupidity and evil of the Ten Thousand curse the universe," the Owl continued, speaking plainly and kindly, as a teacher might. "We are the universe's reward. The world delights in seeing us."

"I think everyone *knows* that -- " commented First Gull.

Now, in the western horizon, the long, low rumbles gave way to violent thunderclaps and light displays so bright and so thorough that they illuminated the mountain ranges.

Air within the storm clouds was displaced. An imbalance in the contrasting temperatures generated low, titanic noises and bursts of electricity. Continual inversions spurred rolling peals, thunder which began in the highest peaks and picked up speed as they came down the hills and crescendoed over that deep and moody mountain body of blue water which humans of the region call Llanquihue.

The storm was almost on them.

* * *

The Panther advanced its careful climb up the staircase of slick-bark branches.

Soon…

"Faith," replied the Starling's Sister. "We fly because we believe we can. If we ever doubt it, we crash. Destined to crawl with the *Tinamou.* All the walkers."

"That's not true," objected Scarlet Tanager. "That's not how we fly."

"Then how, Finch?" asked First Gull, 'finch' being a rude thing to call a tanager. "Why don't you tell us?" challenged Second Gull.

"Really? Is everything a fight with you?" said the Starling to the Gulls.

"Pretty much," First Gull replied.

"I saw a *gannet,*" declared Second Gull.

"I saw a gannet once, fly circles around a pair of sea-hawks," he continued, "and then dive 200 feet straight down into the deep blue ocean. And swim like a penguin! And she stayed under!

"Expert flier. Swims like a fish," added Second Gull, to clarify. "Did you ever think about that, hey?"

First Gull shivered, as though the very thought of such a thing rattled his entire belief system.

"*Ba-wang!*" said the Wren.

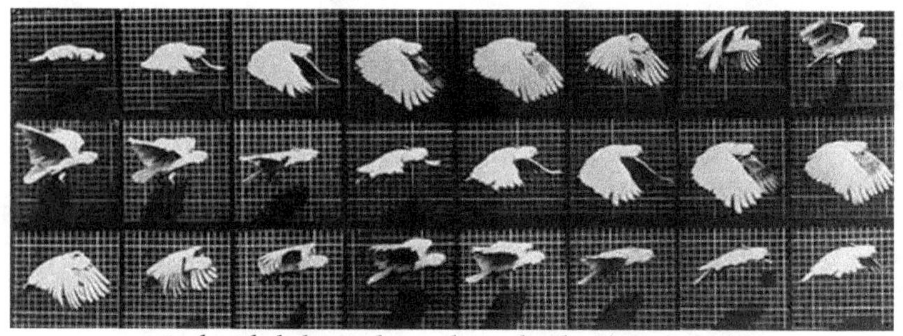

Bird in Flight by Eadweard Muybridge (circa 1896)

ACT THREE: CLASHING THEORIES

Evolution has created a far more complicated
flying device than we have ever been able to engineer.

-- Samik Bhattacharya

"Can you stop saying that?" demanded the Owl of the Wren. "It's not at all helpful. What does it even mean?"

The rainstorm had arrived, in its full force.

"The truth," declared the Scarlet Tanager, "the truth is that our Young Condor friend can't save that baby monkey because he can't fly that way."

"What way?" asked the Starling.

"The big Starling, you might have a chance," continued the Tanager. "You can hover."

"What do you even *mean*?" asked the Starling. "We can all *fly* ..."

"Yes, but the Condor doesn't fly in a manner that would allow him to do any good," answered the Tanager. "Do you not realize that? Right away?

"He's meant to flap, slow, like this, and glide, in the upper middle sky. Not hover low, among the tree crowns. You've seen how ponderous it -- it's the opposite of what you'd need. A wasp. A flying *ant*. A dragonfly. That's more like it."

She added a melodic trill from the Tanager songbook -- of the *chick-burr* variety, you would recognize it -- for emphasis. She repeated it. The unexpected beauty of the musical call changed the mood (slightly) in the kettle.

"We fly by Magic," said the Owl, hoping to assert a different way of seeing things.

"*No, we don't*," said the Tanager.

"We can fly because the forward motion of our wings displaces air. That way, the upward force, the *lift*, can win out," stated the Tanager. "Over the drag.

"Our bones are so light," continued she, "that, with propulsion from our chest muscles, our wings flap, with just enough force to keep us aloft.

"That's how we fly."

All eyes had turned to the migrating songbird.

Finished talking for now, she groomed her wing feathers, in the front, along the edges, giving the others time to digest what she had said.

"*Uh huh*," said First Gull. "Great. That's great. And what is 'air'?"

"Air is what surrounds us. We breathe it." The Tanager demonstrated.

"I can't see any 'air,'" said the Second Gull. "What does it look like?"

"It's invisible," answered the Tanager.

"What?" asked the Starling. "It's *what?*"

"Okay," said First Gull to the Tanager. "I get it."

He scuffed his talons on the branch where he stood, as though he were making an effort to be patient.

"So you've invented an invisib -- "

"What about bumblebees?" asked Second Gull, peeved. "Have you ever seen one of those things fly? I mean, up close?"

"What about *gliding?*" protested the Starling, belatedly. "That's done on stiff wings. How does 'air' figure into *that* -- ?"

"That doesn't count," said the Owl. "That's *flying* as in a 'flying' squirrel -- "

"Ba-*wang!*" said the Wren, laughing.

* * *

"*Must you?*" The Owl turned and displayed, and did so at full extension, talons and all – making as if to attack the Wren, who cowered. Owls are, appearances aside, among the fiercest of raptors.

"Some birds have a fantail, so they can hover," the Scarlet Tanager said, trying harder to explain. "They can maneuver. Like a butterfly. Ever seen a godwit?"

"Have you been eating some of those fermented berries or something?" snickered First Gull, of the Tanager.

"Well, if we don't understand how we fly, we certainly

can't help that little monkey," replied the Tanager. "If we don't understand how we fly, we can't -- "

"All right, we get it!" snapped First Gull and Second Gull in unison.

ACT FOUR: RESOLUTION

Modern aircraft can't do that.

-- Christina Harvey

Chackerchackerchacke

The baby monkey was way past panic.

The panther stepped onto the very branch where the baby Capuchin cringed, shivering with terror.

Where was the Mother?

A lightning flash caught the white fur along the front of the creature's face.

Raw terror -- beyond mere fear – now crept into the baby capuchin's voice. It was a caterwauling tone which every living thing larger than a microbe recognizes: the banshee shriek of violent death. A succession of liquid sounds poured out of the monkey, as though emptying his body – howls, wails, hollers – begging, pleading, weeping, demanding help from any living mammal or reptile who could show some morsel of pity.

The new lightning bolt was forked. Its partnering thunder peal crashed right with it, its sound having changed from a cloth-tearing sound to a cannon-shot.

Now again, thunder and lightning struck and sounded as one.

The storm raged, bending the tree branches to and fro.

"We are alive for a reason," stated the Starling. She clenched the branch beneath her.
She vaulted straight upward.
Young Condor vaulted after her --
His mighty leap shook the heavy, wet branches and shivered all the leaves.
"Hey! Wait!"
The others scrambled to follow –
At the top of the neighboring arbor, the drama played out.
Any number of things happened at once.
The panther arrived to claim its prey –
The brave Starling dipped at too high a speed to help the monkey and narrowly missed the panther's outstretched claw –

Young Condor tried to luff and shout and scare off the panther, but his wings were too big, too heavy, and he could not properly unfurl them.
He fell earthward into an awkward roll and half-tumbled.
"Whoa! Hey --"
Then the two Starlings attempted to mob the cat as his face pushed through the foliage –
The open spaces were too small and their wingspan ratio too large, too clumsy, and the Starlings, too, lost stability and spun out, squawking --
First Gull recklessly flew directly at the big cat --
Second Gull sought to strike from the panther's blind side –

Young Condor reappeared in an ill-advised hover.
He could not sustain the flutter --
He tumbled once more --
It was the Scarlet Tanager who adroitly caught an upward

swell and glided left, then outward to the right, in a long curve ...

Now the monkey's Mother chittered in the branches just below --

The Panther ducked First Gull and batted Second Gull away --

Suddenly a predator from above dove down, talons open, vying to seize the monkey as a prize for itself --

It was the Owl.

The Starling clacked her bill in fury at the betrayal and attempted to shield the baby monkey --

The Tanager made a tight, smooth circle and pounced --

The Scarlet Tanager transported the baby Capuchin across the gap to the neighboring tree, where Mother Monkey grabbed it and skittered down the trunk.

The nimble Panther, in a motion too quick to see, stuffed the Owl into its open jaws and clamped down hard --

The Owl screamed in protest --

"Hey!" cried First Gull.

The panther bounded off with its mouthful of struggling fowl.

He disappeared into the lower branches ...

And was gone.

Lightning seared a new pattern across the sky. Brocades of thunder rolled, seeming to understand what had just taken place.

The storm passed to the East and mostly the South, perhaps on its way towards those less civilized latitudes, the archipelagos, and the complex shorelines of the Lands of Fire.

\#\#\#

Tom's Story Notes

Any consideration of aviation needs to include birds -- the best flyers in the known universe. We share the planet with 50 *billion* of them. A bird's flight is so uncanny and complex that it makes human flight look one-dimensional. Slightly ridiculous.

Every year, the small, slender Arctic Tern migrates from its Arctic breeding grounds to the Antarctic Circle, a round-trip journey of 18,000 miles.

Biologists and engineers are currently using geometry and biomechanics to explain how birds evolved their maneuverability. Humans connect with birds: recent research suggests that seeing—or even just *hearing—birds is beneficial for mental health.* One ornithologist recommends bird watching as the cure for the current epidemic of teen mental health problems.

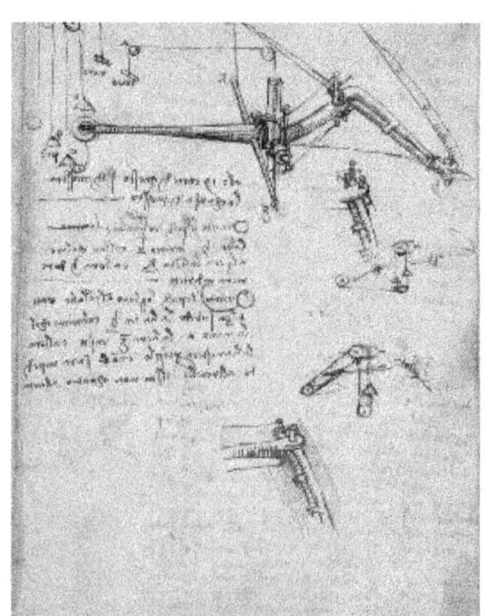

Da Vinci's Codex on the Flight of Birds (1505)

COMMENTARY by Michael Quetting

Tom's fable "How Birds Fly" illustrates the constant threat and the associated need to act together against common enemies. This dynamic reflects the reality of human communities, where cooperation and solidarity are crucial to overcoming challenges and ensuring security.

Birds represent one of the most diverse groups of animals on our planet. With over 10,000 species existing in almost every habitat, they offer a fascinating range of colors, shapes and behaviors. But what makes them stand out is their unique ability to fly.

Bird flight is a complex process made possible by a number of anatomical features and physiological mechanisms. Feathers are of central importance. They serve not only as protection against the elements, but also as flight tools. The shape and arrangement of the feathers generate lift and enable the birds to stay in the air.

Another important feature is the hollow skeleton of many bird species. These cavities reduce the weight of the skeleton and thus facilitate flight. In addition, birds have a high metabolic rate and an efficient respiratory system to meet the energy requirements for flight.

There are different types of flight, which vary depending on the bird species. Most birds use wing flapping, in which they move their wings up and down to generate lift. The way they fly can vary greatly: Hummingbirds are masters of fast flight with a rapid wing beat, while birds of prey tend to specialize in long gliding flights.

Some birds use thermal updrafts to cover long distances with minimal energy expenditure. Albatrosses are a remarkable example of this. They skillfully soar on the uplifts created by solar radiation and dynamic wind, thus saving energy for long flights over oceans.

The diversity of birds and the mechanisms of their flight are a fascinating example of the evolution and adaptability of living creatures. Their flight has always fired the imagination of mankind and inspires researchers, artists and dreamers alike. Bird flight remains a wonder of nature that deserves to be further explored and admired.

2. The First Manned Flight

Anke makes a daring attempt to save her sister. Rickety battle-kite flies and crashes into forest tower stronghold.

PROLOGUE

Is it not by the depth of his wounds

that one takes the measure of a man?

    --Melisa Gode

"Clean your room," commanded Romy, careful to stand just at the doorway to her little sister's bedroom.

She wore an apron. She carried a laundry basket on her hip.

Anke lay prone on her very unkempt bed, reading a book, Gibbon's *Decline and Fall.* The tall window's wooden frame cast a pattern in the sunlight that fell on her patchwork quilt.

"You're such a slob."

"Well," countered Anke, "you're like some farm animal. Which is worse?"

She turned a page in the book.

"I'm sick of it!" said Romy. "It may be one of my chores to do the laundry around here, but I'm not your maid." She switched the basket to her other hip. "Anke."

"I'm not listening to you," the younger sister, Anke, who was a brat, replied.

"Okay then, live like this -- "

"I WILL. I WILL LIVE **EXACTLY** LIKE THIS."

"You have a very high opinion of yourself, Princess High-Flier. The boys treat you like you're so special -- "

"I AM SPECIAL! Mom and Dad certainly thought so -- "

"Dad did," said Romy cryptically.

This comment signified a new and deeper phase of the argument.

Anke looked up.

"What is that supposed to mean?"

"It means you have to CLEAN YOUR ROOM once a month. *Kannst du dir vorstellen?*"

"No, but why did you say that thing about Dad?"

"You keep thinking I'll do all the housework but you're mistaken, Miss Anke Mobelbauer -- "

"Don't mention them! It upsets me! You COW! I HATE YOU!"

Anke got up from the bed and slammed the door to her

bedroom with such force that the echo of it reverberated throughout the house.

I. THE VIEW FROM THE SKY

Your air-widget thing doesn't work.

-- Charlotte Sanson

The first flight of a manned, fixed-wing aircraft was short, unplanned, and violent.

Its pilot, a thin, moody girl named Anke, initiated the chain of events leading to that flight with a call for more freedom.

"Let out the ropes," said the voice.

The sentinel moved silently across the skies above the forest landscape.

From that height, everything looks very different.

Seen from above, the familiar ground-level arrangements of matter are new and remarkable. Cliffs and canyons and tree groves did not look deep or tall, when seen from above, but flat shapes and minutely distinct patterns of color. Earthbound blacks, grays, and browns collided with vibrant red, orange, yellow, green, blue, indigo, and violet. It was not only form or color being captured, but it was time, a moment of life, a moment of a life.

Humans do not usually experience that perspective reserved for high-flying clouds and griffon and geese.

"Let go the ropes, Uwe!" said the voice.

"Let me fly!"

* * *

The Forest Marcynian, in the state of Baden-Wurttemberg, sometimes referred to as Baar by the Romans, is a region of tall trees among high mountains and sharp ridges.

It is a land of ghosts.

There, winding roads lead past abandoned castles long overgrown, carved arches, lighting-shattered stone staircases. The phantoms of the centurions of the Salain emperors still line the mountain passes under fluttering lances, so they say. Slumped skeletons in their finery yet sit on broken thrones in the buried mountain halls and forgotten courts of pagan kings. King Theudebald once quashed revolts of the younger stem duchies here, and here the stout warriors of the Alamanni met their fate at the hands of Saxons.

The Forest Marcynian is a haunted, restless land of secrets. Its old-growth forests had seen their share of fairy tales unfold -- sleeping princesses, magical elves, kindly tailors and such -- fairy tales, yes, but also darker stories, stories with less-than-bright endings.

Marcynian's geography gives rise to sail-winged birds and other flying things which take advantage of unusually strong and constant updrafts.

You may know it by another name:

The Black Forest.

2. ANKE'S SANDWICH

I wasn't mad until just now.
– *Babak Amvari*
"'No mustard,'" Anke said to the plate.

The white ceramic platter sat innocently on the wood surface of the courtyard's dining table, under the trees.

"I'm pretty sure that everyone KNOWS that I don't like mustard."

No reply was forthcoming from the plate, or the sandwich on the plate.

The excellent sandwich on the platter was piled high with bread, lettuce tomato, sliced beef cheese, all topped by a healthy dollop of yellow mustard.

"This beef sandwich right here," insisted Anke. She paused. "Can't you see, can't you *all* see that yellow color?"

"I see it," said Stan.

Anke, the skinny and highly particular second daughter of the woodworking Mobelbauer clan, glared at her food.

"I always say '*No mustard.*' Don't I always say that?"

The Mobelbauer children were gathered at noon, in the courtyard of the family compound, between the house and the workshop, beneath the leafy oak tree, near the gates, across from the barn and paddock.

"Yes, yes, Anke" replied her older sister, Romy, broad-faced and radiant.

She spoke in a sunny voice that only served to madden Anke more. "We all know your little demands."

"But you've put a TON of mustard on it," said Anke bitterly.

Anke folded her hands on her lap to make it clear to the world that she would not be eating this sandwich.

The soft clatter of silverware and pitchers pouring liquid into mugs continued as before, seeming to ignore Anke's sulk.

Everyone was hungry. Delivery of the Town Court benches contract was three days hence. There was so much to do. They had been working since dawn.

Now Anke folded her arms.

"I sure wouldn't like that," offered her brother, Uwe, his mouth full. "Who would? Who would like that?"

"Here," offered Stanislas. "Dake mine, Prinzess. No mooster. See?"

The two plates were exchanged.

"But you already *took* a bite," groaned Anke. "I can completely see your teeth marks! Stan. Are you kidding? Stan? Tell me you're kidding ..."

This heartfelt complaint lingered in the air above the table as everyone but Anke continued eating. Uwe refilled his cup from the pitcher.

"Please tell Anke," said Romy to the table at large, "that we're out of bread and for that reason, I can't actually make another sandwich just to please Her Highness -- "

"Please inform the heifer at the end of the table that I don't care what she says," replied Anke. "Fair is fair," she added. Father used to say that.

A cuckoo in one of the upper branches of the oak tree called out, hoping a mate might be in the vicinity.

"Don't mention them! It upsets me! You COW! I HATE YOU!"

"*Age quod agis*," commented Jakob, the eldest, as he entered late from working on the lathes.

"NO! YOU do what you're supposed to!" replied Anke.

Jakob came over and plucked his little sister out of her seat, so he could hug her --

"Stop that!"

She shoved him and broke away.

"How can I do all that I do, if Romy does such a TERRIBLE job at cooking?

"*Was zum teufel!*" Anke added angrily. "Try making furniture without the wood I provide!"

"You don't actually provide the wood, little girl," Uwe reminded her.

"It's *dangerous*, what I do!" Anke huffed. "And I do ten other jobs that no one gives me credit for. I feed the livestock -- "

"Stan feeds the livestock -- "

"Not always!"

Jakob, the eldest, stood and switched out Anke's platter for his.

The sandwich on the new platter had extra tomato, a fat pickle on the side ... and no mustard.

The cuckoo, thinking he had heard a faint reply, redoubled his song.

"At last," said Anke, acknowledging the new plate and its untouched sandwich. "*Thank* you."

A bell rang among the lathes. marking the cycle end for the Stenross, the steam box oven. Jakob rose to change out the steamer. That more pliable wood would be used for the bench-end handles ...

"We love you, *gliebten*," said Jakob.

"I know," Anke replied. She took a bite of her sandwich. She nodded, satisfied.

3. DARK WINDS IN THE WOODSHOP

Those who speak the same language ... belong

together and are by nature one and an inseparable whole.

– *Johann Gottlieb Fichte*

Just then, the gate at the top, or street-side wall, of the courtyard opened.

Three strange men entered, to the accompaniment of wind chimes.

"Is this the shop of the Mobelbauers? The woodworkers?" asked their leader.

"Yes," answered Uwe, rising.

They were young and wore city clothes. The leader was a stocky man with a speaking voice that was a little too loud.

He wore a city coat of brown leather, with copper buttons down the in front, and on the sleeves.

The others had groomed mustaches and scented hair.

"Yuuur from Strasbuuurg ..." ventured Stanislav.

"Seebach."

"Same difference," said Uwe.

"We are aides of Count Vilnius," declared the lead city-man.

This statement had no effect on the listeners.

"The poet."

"Like Schiller?" asked Anke. "*An die Freud --* "

"My client needs a large circular piece," said the aide. "Carved of your finest wood. It shall be an insignia."

One of the men from Seebach removed a rolled paper. He spread it on the table.

High in the oak, a female cuckoo made a long, sincere, four-toned answering call. She was considering the offer.

"Vat is dis?" asked Stanislas, eyeing the design on the paper.

"An eagle. Wings spread. He holds gathered arrows in his talons, as you see. They represent our freedoms."

"It looks like war," said Anke.

"A republic, Cousin," replied the Seebacher. "And yes, one that is ready for war, if war is needed.

"It announces the combined power of the fiefdoms. A modern Germany. The New Order. The Count attracts good Germans wherever he speaks -- "

"I don't think you and I are cousins," said Anke.

"We will all be cousins! Soon!" replied the aide. "You'll hear for yourself. Count Vilnius visits your town. His message will resound like pealing bells across the uplands -- "

"We need this proud wood-carved insignia behind him on the stage. You should be honored. "

"What kind of Count is he?" asked Uwe.

"*Sonderweg*," replied the aide. "One who will lead us to our special destiny."

"And let me guess," offered Uwe. "Highway tariffs and service in the militia come next ..."

"And a t-treaty with Proosha," added Stanislas.

"When do you need this insignia?" asked Romy, pretending she was in charge.

"Friday. For the *Volksfest* -- "

"That's in three days!" exclaimed Uwe.

The city man tossed a bag of coins on the table.

"We're prepared to pay a premium."

Jakob came through the swinging doors from the lathes. He wiped his hands on a towel.

"Gentlemen. I am Jakob Mobelbauer."

He went to each of the three visitors and shook hands firmly.

"What can we do for you?"

He listened carefully to their proposal and admired the eagle drawing.

"I'm sorry," concluded Jakob. "We are at capacity, and

then some."

He turned, just slightly, to face them squarely. Anke noted something in Jakob's posture, the tensed lines of his legs and shoulders ...

"They want to pay a premium," said Uwe.

"Perhaps later in the summer," said Jakob.

In the trees above, the cuckoo, not having received the desired response from a female, repeated his offer to mate.

"We are most disappointed," said the Seebacher. He spoke slowly, as if he were leaving out something really important. "We heard you are the best."

"You are most civil," said Jakob. "Join us for a beer before you go."

The visitors demurred. The Number One Seebacher rolled up the eagle drawing. The trio took their leave, leaving one of their illustrated posters on the table.

"*Dark winds blow tru dis foress,*" muttered Stanislav once the city men were gone. His features had gone grim.

"Dis Count. I seen ones like dem. In my village. It's de auld empire."

He meant the Austria Hungarian Empire, heir to the Holy Roman Empire, only recently disbanded in these remote regions of Marcynia.

Now that they could look closely, they saw that a woodcut illustration of Count Vilnius decorated the poster which the visitors had left behind. The Count seemed to be a giant of a man, with blazing eyes beneath a tousled beard and long, black, unkempt hair.

"Looks crazy, if you ask me," commented Jakob.

Anke read the text beneath the illustration:

Deep into that darkness peering,
Long we have stood, wondering, fearing.
No god but evil; no light but darkness
No hope but doom.
Our banners sway and fall in the haunted gloom.
The gleaming basilisk eyes come for us
Where we lay. Dig me no grave.
We can only flourish together.
Brothers! We are the safeguards.
Sisters! Breed an army!
To beat back the shadow tides.
Let the bells peal
From the Meuse to the Neman,
From the Adige to the Belt,
A Fatherland will rise!

"'Breed an army'!" exclaimed Romy. "What's that supposed to mean?"

"I don't hear any bells pealing," snorted Uwe.

"That is the world's worst poem!" said Anke. "Our mule is a better poet ..."

4. FLIGHT

Within all of us is a varying amount of
space lint and star dust, the residue from
our creation. It is strongest in those of us who fly.

> – *K.O. Eckland*

"Am I a FROG? Trapped in a *basket*?

"Am I some Chinese BUG in a CAGE?"

She slapped and shook the ropes which tethered her to the slow-walking donkey below.

"Yah. You are," came the reply.

"Three more and we'll call it a day."

Skinny Anke floated high above the terrain, on the big

kite, and shouted out when she saw the particular elm, or fir, or beech that they needed.

They were scouting trees.

Stan and Uwe and the sanguine donkey, Leo, and a cohort of curious mountain goats trailed far beneath her. The entourage followed the erratic paths on the forest floor, mirroring Anke's smooth glide above.

Anke searched carefully among the trees. The best wood tended to hide from her.

"Faster!" cried Anke from her perch thirty meters above the rugged terrain.

There was a mix of trees at this elevation – oak and birch in the valleys, fir and pine and spruce higher up.

"Agh!! Let the tethers go, Uwe!" she urged. "I can fly it on my own -- "

The trees of the Marcynian forest murmured amongst themselves. Their roots mingled in the lower realms, out of man's sight, and away from his limited ken. They clucked at the girl's impatience. They had seen it before.

The family of woodworkers needed the best wood, and this high perch was a good way to find it.

"Three more," shouted her brother, Uwe. "Find us a nice, big-waisted spruce, Anke. A hard fir."

Anke rode thirty meters high above the earth in a floating perch. This most unlikely aircraft was a *Kriegsdrachen* a kite-like antique war device. They had found it years ago, in a hidden cache of war bounty, in a high cavern, a cache of swords and lances and mailed gloves, artifacts of a forgotten campaign of some time-lost war. The high lookout aircraft had been designed to elevate one person above the battlefield, to better see the enemy, to better plot deployments and tactics.

Now Anke and Romy and their brothers used it to hunt wood. A most awkward-looking contraption, with its double-frames, the vessel floated surprisingly well in the forest updrafts. Fabric stretched over a light wood frame reached a span of ten feet, wings jutting out from a cramped sling or pilot's nest. A second section tethered above the first added to the contraption's capacity for lift, so that a small man (or a teenaged girl) could crouch in the berth and float high over the earth below.

"Dark winds blow tru dis foress," muttered Stanislav ...

"There! Stop, Stan! Stop!! There is a white birch! Two!! Do you see them?"

It took a while for Uwe and Stanislas to scramble over the rocks at her beckoning and climb up the slope until they saw the birches.

"Yes, these will do," called Uwe. "These will do very well!"

Uwe shot an arrow with a red ribbon, sinking it into the tree trunk.

Anke marked her map, making sure they would be able to find their way back to it.

5. SISTERS BICKER

As a German citizen ... I hold it my right but also my moral duty to take part in the shaping of our German destiny.

-- Kurt Huber

"Improving your kite, as ever, Little Sister," commented Romy that afternoon as she folded laundry on the big table.

Bang! Clang!

Anke sat at the smaller lathe, smoothing a wooden blade that would eventually become a rudder on her flying crow's nest.

"You call attention to your bustline, as ever," replied Anke.

"You're just jealous," said Romy.

"You can NOT wear that dress," remarked Uwe, who stood at the small forge, banging with a hammer on red-hot horseshoes (which he held with tongs).

"Well, you'll attract the attention of every male within ten leagues," said Jakob, at the work bench.

Bang!

"That's the whole point," said Romy. "I am seventeen. A rose in bloom."

The hammer once again struck the anvil.

"A rose with no dowry and only one offer of marriage," continued Romy.

"I need to shake the tree ... "

"Marry Stan," suggested Anke.

"His is my one offer," replied Romy.

Bang! Whang! went Uwe's hammer.

Patting the stacks of folded laundry, Romy turned to go.

She wrapped a shawl around her shoulders.

"I will be circulating. At the fair."

Once the door had closed, Jakob gestured to Uwe to follow her.

6. ROMY GETS LOST AT THE FAIR

Hounds follow those who feed them.

-- Otto von Bismarck

Late that afternoon, Stanislaus escorted the livestock back into the pens for their dinner. The cows swerved when they saw Anke coming.

"Dey shore don't wan' see dat Angry Prinzess come close," chuckled Stanislav. "Leo, he 'member that kick you give him las' week ..."

"He deserved it," replied Anke.

"Did you see my new wings?" She showed Stanislas what she had fashioned for the *kriegsdrachen*, which lay spread out on the table. "They fold out from the kite's frame. See?"

"You need a centerboard," suggested Jakob from the furnaces.

"Almost done," answered Anke.

Without warning, Uwe burst into the courtyard --

He was breathing hard, disheveled from running.

"They took her! They took Romy!" Panic made his voice tremble oddly.

"She's been kidnapped!"

"Who?" demanded Jakob.

"Those Seebachs!m The Count was with them -- "

"I was watching the orchestras and then I saw them -- "

"They took her into the Hohenzollern -- the Tower –" gasped Uwe.

Jakob lay down his tools and gathered a jacket and a crow bar --

"How could I be so stupid -- "

Together, Uwe and he ran out the gate back to the village square. Anke tried to stop Stan from following, but it was no good –

The Tower was Tower Hohenzollern Citadel, a weird and foreboding structure at the edge of the village square. Designed by some eccentric, long-forgotten talent, its architecture was remarkable for two things – broad balconies in the treetops and a base that was impregnable.

If the Seebachs had kidnapped Romy and retreated with her to that Tower, then the only way to save her was from above –

Anke turned and ran as fast as she could in the opposite direction -- towards the high flat clearing where the float was tethered.

7. FLIGHT TO THE CITADEL

The first aspect of flight student pilots must grasp

is the concept of aircraft axes: that flying an airplane is a three-dimensional task.

– *Matthew Johnston*

One of the Hohenzollen outposts, the Citadel had been designed by its architect to be virtually unassailable from the ground. Once the steel gates closed, it was impregnable.

The only entry, Anke knew, could be from the sky. She knew the parapets and broad balconies from glimpses on her scouting sorties. She had seen a broad patio, high up on the Citadel's tower. She could land there.

* * *

The first manned fixed-wing aircraft flight was a short and violent affair.

Yet it shared all of the components and concerns of aircraft as we now know them – speed, yaw, pitch, roll, flight path, trajectory, landing. She would resolve one of these forces, make clever progress on three others, and wholly neglect the fifth.

Once aloft, Anke let go of the mooring rope too fast.

Anke flew upwards -- way too high, too fast. Without Stan and Uwe and the mule Leo to anchor her, she let the up-winds carry her skyward too fast.

The earth fell away at a sickening speed –

I'm going to crash in the northern ravines –

Lift was one thing the young pilot Anke had figured out. By floating the old war kite into the updrafts, she had given the craft lift. Lift is the force that opposes weight, or gravity, pushing a balloon or bomber up into the atmosphere.

She leaned forward, pushing the wings outward at a fierce angle, to catch air and force the kite downward.

With a great struggle, she straightened the trajectory of history's first manned aircraft.

She flipped out the two new wing extensions that she had designed. Her rise slowed. The extensions helped hit enough air so that she could control her flight path ...

She crashed through the upper crowns of twin birch trees.

Two crows and a squirrel leapt out of her path --

Below, the mountain goats looked up from their foraging. They bleated at the sight of Anke passing –

Then Anke mistook gliding for actual flying. Anke had no propulsion, beyond that of sheer planetary gravity.

She was not flying the way a bird flies, up and down, turning and wheeling freely. She was falling to earth at a manageable rate.

She assumed she could stay on an even flight path, when in fact she was on a progressively downward trajectory ... with little to brake her berserk momentum.

One wing snapped off.

Gamely, the young pilot grabbed it and tried to use it as a sort of extension.

Was that the Tower she glimpsed?

If only the damn branches would move out of the way --

Gravity. It is what pulls you back down when you rise from sitting. Things fall to the floor. Gravity is the reason why.

A planet – any planet – draws all things to its center, using gravity. It is the invisible force that keeps you on the ground, the power that makes things fall. Anything that has mass has gravity. Objects with more mass have more gravity. Gravity is not the same everywhere. Gravity on the moon is much lighter, weaker force than it is on the earth. Anke knew very well that gravity would end her flight and quickly crash her in spectacular fashion.

Gravity was about to annihilate young Anke, smashing her little aircraft mercilessly into the stone tower that loomed ahead.

Romy needed her.

The pilot Anke held out the former-wing at arm's length, in an attempt to create drag.

Drag is friction. A counter-force. It refers to the surfaces where the aircraft interfaces with the medium through which it moves – an oar through water, an aircraft through air. Drag was of little consequence to Anke, since her flight was so short, and mostly sharply downward, so that she would crash very quickly, with or without drag.

A planet – any planet –
draws all things to its center.

As to Direction, Anke had none. By leaning, by changing her center point this way and that, she hoped to influence the craft's direction. She grabbed onto passing branches, to no avail.

The fifth dimension of flight – thrust -- Anke ignored altogether.

The ground approached at a frightening rate.

She was now crashing through the heavy branches of the lower trees.

For a long moment, time stood still –

The Citadel snapped into view --

Resolute, she yanked back on the wings' levers with all her might, holding to her course, battered to and fro --

There! There it is --

Stone and green grass went by in a rush below her.

Where is the landing?

Anke lost control altogether. She put her hands up to cover her face --

The war-kite landed on the broad balcony with a clatter and crash, skidding, sending tables and furniture flying –

8. A DEADLY CLASH

Hard pressed on my right. My center is yielding.

Impossible to maneuver. Situation excellent. I attack.

– Ferdinand Foch

The girl Anke rose from the wreckage of her aircraft.

Blood marred her view. She could not feel her left arm.

She saw two figures struggling on the far side of the balcony --

"Romy! Romy!"

The Count – familiar to her from his image on the poster -- held Anke's sister in a vulgar stranglehold.

Romy was waving her arms piteously. Now the Count grabbed her hair.

Romy's body seemed to go limp --

Hefting a length of heavy rope from the wreckage, Anke rushed across the balcony space --

She struck like a cannon ball.

The Count, eyes wide with surprise, swung out mightily at the intruder ... and missed. Holding his captive with one hand, he swung again, and again it was done too clumsily --

This left him in an open stance, defenseless --

Anke kicked him savagely, in the stomach.

Romy fought to free herself.

Anke stuck a second time, and a third, even more savagely, kicking him along his right side, where the liver resides --

Count Vilnius winced and doubled over --

Romy spun away, gasping for air --

Seeing the Count wobble, Anke advanced with a ruthless blow to the stomach, then a foot to the throat.

These efforts sent the Count convulsing, staggering, trying to turn away from his attacker –

"They usually don't fight back, eh?" muttered Anke, as though she and Count Vilnius were old friends.

Anke pounced.

The mad poet fell against the parapet and raised his arms, as though gesturing for help --

---

"They usually don't fight back, eh?" muttered Anke.

"Mercy!" cried the Count. His voice was deep and thick, feral, and strangely accented.

"Sure," said Anke –

Anke took full hold and slammed the man's head on the stone parapet so hard that it bounced backward.

"Oh!" she cried. "You're hurt! Here – just lean your neck -- "

Dexterous Anke wrapped the hemp rope around the man's neck. *Twice, three times* –

She secured the truss in an instant with a strong double-eight knot of maritime origins.

"Let me -- "

Romy joined in.

The sisters lifted the Count onto the low battlement wall. Much grunting ensued, followed by sisterly curses, as they grasped and groaned against his struggling --

They shoved him off the parapet.

He fell through space.

The hemp tugged hard.

Something snapped.

A heavy weight lolled and swayed at the end of the rope.

* * *

It was long rumored that the poet Vilnius had been snatched by a coven of trolls and kept in caves, and that he was eventually reincarnated as the Russian madman, Rasputin.

His body was never found, only the empty noosed rope.

The trees, members of an ancient brotherhood of Marcynia, those discreet sentinels, yet remain.

The tall trees watching over the Black Forest murmur amongst themselves.

Their roots mingle in the lower realms, out of man's sight, and away from his limited ken.

They have seen much.

They keep their secrets.

In the annals of the Black Forest, the site of so many strange occurrences over the ages, nowhere is it recorded whether Count Vilnius was able to consider, in his final moments, the properties of a maneuverable aircraft in a crowded-airspace trajectory ... or the savage strength of a sister's devotion, a thing that knows no bounds.

###

COMMENTARY by Jessica Ghilani

The hard-headed girl Anke in this story is determined to fly on her own. In that, she is similar to so many of the early aviation pioneers. Inventors who engineer new technologies share an important trait that helps them find success: they are not afraid to try and fail and try again. Through these numerous trials, often referred to by engineers as iterations, the aircraft that animated early aviation history were able to pave the way for the many developments that followed. These developments over time have enabled all of us to bear witness to the marvel of flight.

The dream of pursuing flight with the help of a balloon is hundreds of years old. Hot air balloons rely upon the fact that hot air is lighter than colder air. You may have heard of the idea that heat rises. This concept helped guide the inventors who were instrumental in "ballooning," the sport or pastime of flying in a balloon. The first successful human

carrying flight occurred via hot air balloon in Paris, France, which may help put into clearer context the geographic location for this story. It occurred on November 21, 1783, thanks to aviation pioneers and brothers, Joseph-Michel Montgolfier and Jacques-Étienne Montgolfier. The Montgolfiére-style hot air balloon was their invention, and it was able to carry Jacques-Étienne in what is credited as the first confirmed piloted ascent by humans in 1783.

We all can admire the persistence, creativity, and ambition of the many inventors who – like Anke -- helped marshal forward the marvel of aviation due to their shared dream of flight.

3. Kites Or, Red Blue Blue

A bridge collapse summons the

latent powers of the Middle Kingdom's villagers.

A daughter of the Yunhe clan, an odd young Regent

Prince, and fleets of silk kites all play their parts.

PROLOGUE

The kite is an intermediary between heaven and earth.

— *Ben Ruhe*

One wants to say that the English bridge at Jiazhuo collapsed 'without warning.'

But it wasn't. Without warning, that is.

It was the cofferdam that failed, not the English bridge itself.

The designer of the English bridge at Jiazhuo knew his craft well, as did its chief engineer. The structure, completed, would have proven to be most sturdy, in itself.

But nothing exists in itself. We are all figures in a larger field. And these craftsmen knew little about hydraulics -- the greater system of waters and water forces, especially as they applied to this location.

They should have built the bridge forty yards south. There, the stream was broader and shallower. Here, the current was deep and the gulley narrow.

The waters changed too much. After two days of heavy rains, water rushed down the tributary creeks like rapids. In a drought, as dry as a desert sand-bed. Even a quick review of the topography would have given them warning of this.

While the cofferdam – the temporary dam, that is, the structured box which allows workers to complete the project without drowning – looked as if it were serving its purpose, it actually was not. The pillars and braces of the cofferdam had been sunken into highly solvent red soil, or latosol, and not the heavier irrigation silt and clay.

Red soil will not hold. A local farmer could have warned the bridge's designer of this.

The waters now swirling in the confined space brought new flow patterns and new pressures at new angles on the coffer dam walls.

Gradually, at first, then all at once, the force of the waters grew.

Fissures opened beneath the waterline, until -- with a smashing earthen and wood sound -- the first row of braces cracked. Dislodged by winds, a heavy dredging bucket swung down dramatically on its chain and crashed into a caisson panel.

The panel snapped in two.

Then all of the seals exploded.

The extended protective wall buckled.

Nothing exists in itself.
We are all figures in a larger field.

In a vivid scenario, a tableau from a nightmare, the entire bridge fell in on itself. Three English laundry women, six English soldiers, two carpenters, and a pair of English quarry-wagons (and their draft mares) were lost, either crushed by the weight of the stones or drowned in the floodwaters.

All that was left was the echo of the victims' screams -- the whinnying, panicked horses, the bleating of the sheep, braying mules, screams of the laundry women and soldiers' bellowing...

It was a spectacular architectural failure.

Within the hour, a string of kites bobbled and danced in the strong winds above the river, reporting to the countryside what had happened that day to the Scottish Bridge at Jiazhuo. There were black and white disc-like kites, and kites fashioned after ships, and cranes.

One particular color combination dominated the middle section of kites – *Red, Blue Blue.*

I. THREE MINISTERS MAKE THEIR DEMANDS

Chinese have never looked at foreigners

as human beings. We either look up to them

as gods or down on them as wild animals.

  -- Lu Xun

Oh! Steaming mutton, conger on yellow rice, fragrant braised partridge in a bed of roasted spiced potatoes. A third platter followed, featuring an array of Sirloin of Beef cuts, smothered in brown gravy and dressing.

Were those freshly baked cherry cream pastries, for dessert?

The foods on the English platters had been lovingly prepared. Much thought invested, much care taken.

The tastes of the two young monarchs of China's Butterfly Throne were widely known.

"The English King's proposal," announced the English emissary. He placed a scroll down, discreetly, away from the victuals.

It was the morning of the Day of Applications.

The British Ambassador made no mention of the collapse of the bridge at Jiazhou.

"The pressures on His Serene Highness are many," he murmured.

"As you say," agreed Zang Tu, Prince Regent.

He took the platters and handed them to a servant, who placed them on a long side table, for display.

"No, no. Show them to my Sister first," fussed Zang Tu.

The royal luncheon would begin soon.

"I'm not, you know," blurted Zang Tu.

"Excellence?" inquired the Ambassador.

"Serene. I am not *serene*. How can I be?"

"Ah. It is the human condition," offered the Englishman. "We await the Throne's wisdom,"

Next, the German ambassador, the young aristocrat Wachenhut, offered the Regent and Queen-to-be, Sizhen, volumes of sauerbraten, brown bread and venison, surrounded by schnitzel and cabbage, offset by currants and sugared oranges and cranberries.

He would no doubt be requesting an expansion of his nation's interest in Kiautschou Bay.

The Regent Prince Zang Tu nodded, admiring the arrangement, insisting again that it be shown to the girl next to him.

"The sweet with the savory, Liege," smiled Wachenhut, a sunny and seemingly carefree young man (for an ambassador). "In Food. as in Life.

"Our application."

He lay down the scrolled document He bowed handsomely.

Young Zang Tu and his even younger sister, Queen-to-Be Sizhen, seemed most pleased.

The French ambassador, Cercy, presented a plate of sliced turnips, toasted millet with pungent herbs, roast turkey, snipes, and duck in fruit sauce.

"The edict cannot come soon enough for France," he said, nodding slightly.

"The brave men and cultured women of France -- true friends of China – anticipate the terms of our partnership.

"The Reading is in only three weeks."

"We appreciate the reminder," said Zang Tu, Regent Prince, Protectorate of the Realms of the Middle Kingdoms, temporary keeper of the Butterfly Throne, co-ruler of All China. "Do we not, Sister?"

"Aye," said Sizhen. "That we do. The, um, the throne, does acknowledge the Francaise. Truly."

Younger even than the German ambassador, Zang Tu was not a monarch in his own right, but a proxy, or regent, or place-holder, for his twelve-year-old sister, Queen-To-Be, Sizhen. It was she who sat dutifully beside him, occupying a separate throne.

Zang Tu saw his sister remove one shoe and rub her toes. "It is the acid crystals, collecting in your bloodstream," he opined. "Crocus root," he instructed his First Minister, Cheng, with a clap of his hands.

The crocus-root ointment was brought and carefully applied.

"Is that better?" asked Zang Tu.

"Yes, Brother," replied Sizhen.

Turning to his guests, Zang Tu proclaimed, "We thank you, gentlemen.

Our bounty this day is surely without equal. Due to you.

"Our ruminations are deep. The calculations are most

devious. The considerations are many to balance. And consider.

"Most challenging.

"Your loyalty to China will be rewarded," he concluded. "Together, we will build a new, worldly kingdom. Beneficent to its subjects.

"We meet again soon."

"*Zhufu zhe pian tudi!* Bless this land. *Wansui!*"

"*Wansui!*" echoed Sizhen, the young Queen-to-be.

"*Wansui!*" echoed the three ambassadors, as they departed.

2. THE SAILOR GIRL

A kite makes use of an opposing force.

A kite cannot fly on its own. It needs

strong winds pushing against it.

– Sally Schildhauer

"'*Sphere of influence*'? Is that what you said?" asked the insolent Sailor Girl.

She was the morning's final visitor.

"Yes," replied Zang Tu.

"And you're referring to yourself."

"Just so," replied the Prince Regent.

"Yes. I do. I do refer to Myself," he sought to clarify, "and, by implication, the Empire as a whole."

He was most vexed, a fact that seemed to escape his visitor.

"But I fail to see – as you seem to do -- any irony in my usage."

The recording secretary made small pen-and-paper sounds as she scritched.

The Sailor Girl returned the Prince Regent's gaze flatly. She had no visible or audible desire to explain herself.

In contrast to Zang Tu's dazzlingly colored robes, embroidered with rainbows of dragons, she wore a simple white cotton tunic, belted, as was then (and is today) common among the working classes. Her hair was pulled back. Her face was smudged. Yet around her wrist was a band, and at her neck was a necklace, both of unusual color and distinctive design, indicating that there might be more to learn about her.

A chair was carried in by a silent servant, an elderly man, so the standing visitor could sit.

"Ho!" exclaimed the Regent Prince to the servant. "What are you doing? *Stop*, I say -- "

Then a second servant, a woman long in the royal employ, brought in an ottoman, so the Sailor Girl might rest her feet comfortably.

"What? Am I no longer Regent Prince?" cried Zang Tu. "Am I not speaking? Are my commands – *Agh!* What is the meaning of this?"

He motioned for the recording secretary to ignore that outburst.

"'Sphere of influence'? Is that what you said?" asked the insolent Sailor Girl.

The Sailor Girl thanked the servants. She sat.

"Did you somehow request a chair and ottoman?" demanded Zang Tu of his visitor.

"I did not," replied the Sailor Girl.

"Then why have my servants -- "

"Perhaps they respect the working man."

"I *am* a working man. I work for a living."

"Well, working man, you may call me Le Lang. And if you interrupt me one more time, I'll leave."

"*Gah!*" exclaimed Zang Tu, Regent Prince of All China, Proxy to his minor sister, Soon-To-Be Queen Sizhen of the House of Bahe, occupier of the splendid Butterfly Palace.

"Is this some CONFUCIAN EXERCISE? Or have I wandered into a *madhouse*? Aacchhh! Did I miss the signage?"

Zang Tu looked at the recording secretary, in the corner, and bugged his eyes, as if for confirmation.

His words echoed down the adjoining hallways and rebounded among the hard surfaces of the tile floors and smooth-stone walls. The celestial designs in the ceilings looked down with amusement. They had seen charades like this before.

"You asked for this meeting," said the Sailor Girl. "Not me."

"You are the most irritating person I have ever met."

"That's because I talk back."

"And very rudely," huffed Zang Tu.

With an effort, the Regent Prince composed himself. He shifted his weight on the throne. He rubbed his knees. He took a deep breath.

"A month ago, you wrote a letter, to the Magistrate of the Seventh Prefecture. About the new bridges," he said to the Sailor Girl.

"You specifically warned about the impending collapse of the Scots bridge. Is that not so?"

He held up the letter.

"I wrote that to protect the folk who live and work up and down the river," replied Le Lang, the Sailor Girl. "The good men and women of China. They needed to know. I do not take pleasure in the failure of others," she added thoughtfully. "Even *wai guo ren.*"

"Yes, but how did you know the Jiaxhuo bridge would collapse?"

"Have you ever seen it?" asked the Sailor Girl.

"No."

"Aren't you paying for it?" she challenged.

"Yes. Yes, I am paying for it. It is an investment," added Zang Tu, hoping to save face. "A rehearsal. For a much larger project."

"My ways are inscrutable," he reminded his guest.

The recording secretary refilled her pen with ink.

"No citizens were present at the bridge's collapse," said Zang Tu. "Only *lowai.*"

"Yes."

"And just how were you able to warn the populace" the Prince Regent demanded. "How could you get word out so widely?"

"How do you think?" asked the Sailor Girl.

"I don't know, I'm sure," said the Prince Regent. "That is why I'm asking."

"Kites," replied his visitor.

The recording secretary asked Le Lang to repeat what she had said.

"Kites," said Le Lang.

"Do you mean," asked Zang Tu, "do you mean the silken and paper kites which the children fly ... in the schools and parks?"

"Yes," came the reply. "They are seen up and down the Canal. Ask any villager. Ask a farmer."

"I see. How singular," commented Zang Tu.

"The German bridge. And the Francaise? Will they fail also?"

"See for yourself," said Le Lang. "I can show you. I can tell you what I see."

"I do not wish to go and *see* for *myself,*" chuffed the Prince Regent.

The Sailor Girl Le Lang was unmoved.

"I rarely leave the palace, Crude Peasant. If you must

know. In honesty, I am a creature of the indoors. Somewhat of a hermit. You may now realize."

Le Lang's gaze remained level.

"Are all the river-folk as block-headed as you?" asked Zang Tu.

"More so."

Le Lang rose to leave. "Excellency."

The recording secretary made a series of furious hand signals to someone outside the Throne Room's entryway.

"Tomorrow," decided the Regent Prince.

"You and I shall spend the morning. We can inspect the bridges together."

3. ONE EYE CLOSED

For every three years during which the people ploughed the soil, surplus sufficient for one year was put in storage. When a store of three years surplus had been accumulated, the preceding nine years labor was called a 'Rising Period.'

— *Robert Eno*

Water is the driving force of all nature.

— *Leonardo da Vinci*

China prospered.

Yet danger surrounded her.

The population was stable, and well fed from three successive years of bounty. The New World crops – sweet potatoes, peanuts, tobacco – thrived in Chinese soils.

Yet district managers could scarcely contain and govern the burgeoning midlands. Rebellions had cropped up in prefects where foreigners controlled too much trade, and bought up too much silk and poppies and tea to take home to Europe and Japan.

A hawkish Mongol King stood impatiently at the northern frontiers, demanding a place at the table for his people. The Spanish traders and their warships crowded the treaty ports, defying local laws, testing the firm hand of the Crown. Western missionaries infiltrated the countryside, and gained a growing foothold in the lands of the Red Dragon.

Japan encroached in the east.

England wanted China's tea.

France coveted her opium.

Germany lusted for her ports, and the bushels of wheat which Chinese ships transported.

The Koreans needed millet and spices for their armed legions, helping to check Japan.

Ambassadors and emissaries of the warlords vied for treaties, alliances, trade routes, franchises, permissions, waivers of tariffs, and more.

England wanted China's tea.
France coveted her opium.
Germany lusted for her ports.

All were granted something, of course. It was a delicate dance; a balancing act. A complex scheme of concessions to offset one foreign power from another. Loyalties could be bought.

The January Edicts were the Emperor's way of controlling the many and varied affairs of China. The Day of Applications was the opportunity for each nation to make its argument for favor before the Edicts were announced.

* * *

"You will forgive me if I am clumsy," said the Regent Prince Zang Tu to the Sailor Girl, early that next morning.

They had met at the Palace's western guardhouse and taken horse and cart to the Jinsui Stables, by the wharfs, along the waterside.

"I am a creature of the Palace," confessed Zang Tu. "Of furnished rooms, of ledgers and desks. Ho!" He almost slipped as he boarded the *kakam*, a trim, well-built, mid-sized sailboat.

The Hermit Prince wore a hooded and voluminous robe ... not that anyone would recognize him.

They shoved off. "*Agh!* Good luck to us!" exclaimed Zang Tu.

* * *

"How is it that you have not mentioned my girth?" Zang Tu asked Le Lang as the vessel moved out into the center current.

"My enormous weight. The boat can scarcely contain me, or float on an even keel."

Their *kakam* rounded a barge full of bleating sheep and cows.

"I did not notice," said Le Lang.

They passed under a bridge. The air had gone still. No breezes filled their sails. The boat luffed.

Their pilot, a broad-shouldered *cohong* girl, a daughter of the guild of merchant mariners whom you often see along the wharves, handed Zang Tu a paddle.

"Stroke deep, my lord -- "

All three of them paddled. The Pilot switched sides while tending the rudder.

Cows grazing along the grassy banks watched as Zang Tu dug his oar too deep, almost falling in.

Every tenth stroke or so, Zang Tu muffed his oar-stroke, threatening to capsize the boat. Each time, his two river companions restored the vessel's balance, seemingly without effort.

They nearly bumped gunwales with packet boats, with their stern-mounted rudders, coming down from the springs of the Yuquan Mountains.

"Huh! Now! Put your shoulders to it ..."

The boat caught the current. Their sails filled out.

* * *

They entered the main channel.

They passed close by junks carrying salt barrels from Yangzhou, and treasure ships, *baoshan*, escorted by quick dhows. From a distance, they saw a 12-sailed ocean vessel, bristling with archers and cannon to discourage pirates. They could smell Turkish coffees offered by the tented brothels.

Soldiers stood guard at the Garrison flash locks.

They shared the river with clusters of colorful houseboats, some ornately decorated with stelae and comets and names of ancestors.

A stoic herd of water buffalo watched them pass.

A gaggle of black and white disc-shaped kites flew in the distance.

4. A DAY ON THE RIVER

No man ever steps into the same river twice.

It is not the same river, and he is not the same man.

   — *Heraclitus*

The German bridge at the Nandong Gate featured a long, slanted causeway and a modified center arch, with buttresses on either side.

Of a pretty design, and an ambitious one, the structure seemed to capture a bit of the geometry of the stars and planets so cherished by the Chinese elite. Artisans were already busily fashioning heavenly carvings into the stone.

"Well thought-out, is it not?" asked Le Lang. "Yet it has little to do with its surroundings. Better suited for an offshoot of the Egyptian Nile. Or some sheltered harbor. This is a busy location. The Imperial Road is close by, the warehouses just there. See there, the roofs ... "

They floated under the bridge, stopping beneath the joists where the causeway met the arch on one bank.

Le Lang pointed with a baton to the support beams. "Mismatched. See where they have used straw and mud smashed together, without waiting for one layer to dry before applying the next? It will eventually clump and fall, like a ball of muck ..."

The Regent Prince took stock of the work which his own Treasury had subsidized. The plans had been lovely to see ...

"Function," said Le Lang.

The underside of the German Bridge at the Nangong Gate showed ugly spans and trusses slapped together without thought. Missing planks and a half-buried flagstone spoke ill of the engineers.

"Even the buttresses won't save it, I'm afraid," said Le Lang. "You see this with certain midland granaries, where the villagers do not know enough to sequence the construction properly ...

"It will be washed away with the first spring flood," she concluded.

* * *

To see clearly the Bridge at The Ferry at Bien Shu, being

constructed by the Francaise, they had to leave the boats and walk around the battlements.

Using a design meant for smaller distances, the French bridge consisted of flat spans of granite supported by sunken wood and schist beams. A horizontal stone design called for connected slabs mounted on vertical stanchions and pylons and piers.

"It is a clapper bridge," said Le Lang. "A clapper times ten. But their girding will never support it.

"It looked good on someone's drawing board," she added.

As they strolled the site, a giant apparatus, a double-towered *polypastos* crane of the kind the Romans once used, loomed over them. Suspended on the crane's many cables was a stone slab so heavy that it seemed to bend the arms of the crane.

"*Eh, abruti!*" barked the gruff crew chief of the French installation.

He was a burly red-faced Frenchman whose muscled arms rested for the moment on a thick staff with an iron hook at the end.

"*Perd-toi d'ici!*" he suggested. He pointed back to where they had come from.

The crew was engaged in an ongoing effort to lower the great slab squarely onto the pylons and stone supports that had been prepared for it -- a job that was far above their skills, if it was even possible at all.

From the looks of it, they were about to find out ...

"*S'en allez! Tu m'entends?*"

"*Attendez m'sieur,*" answered Le Lang in a most friendly way, "*s'il vous plait ...*"

This angered the man. He advanced towards the unwelcome visitors –

A French mason -- noticing Le Lang's left wrist, and the baton that had appeared in Le Lang's right hand -- tugged at the Foreman, telling him to let it go.

"*Abruti!*"

With a roar, the Foreman rushed straight towards them, staff raised in one hand --

With no thought to his own safety, Zang Tu grabbed the French brute and jumped off the bridge –

The two figures fell together in a short, neat arc --

A mighty splash sounded. As the others looked over the ledge, the two men stood, wet and sputtering, in the shallows.

"I thought he was going to hurt you," explained Zang Tu to Le Lang, when they pulled him out.

5. GRANDFATHER'S VISION

Without the Grand Canal, there is no 'China.'

-- Sally Schildhauer

They stopped to eat at a waterside embankment, where roasted chestnuts and corn on the cob and braised meats shared a long fireplace dug in the soil.

Zang Tu's clothes were hung to dry on the low branches of a chestnut tree.

Over a fire, Le Lang composed a rambling, robust song to

Zang Tu's brave deed. She attempted to rhyme 'Regent Prince' with 'ever since.'

When lunch was done, the Sailor Girl carried the plates and cutlery to wash them in the river.

"How does she know so much?" Zang Tu asked the *cohong* Pilot as they   prepared to sail back to the stables near the Palace.

"Do you really not know?' replied the Pilot.

Zang Tu shook his head. "I do not."

"Your travel companion is a member of the inner Yunhe family," said the Pilot. "The Navigators. Unofficial wardens of the Canal. Beloved by very many.

"The wristlet. The necklace. Both signify.

"Her true name is Cai, and few would rank higher, if rank mattered to the Yunhe."

* * *

"There is a reason for my commissioning these three bridges," said Zang Tu to Le Lang as they sailed, smoothly and evenly this time (since they were before the wind), on their way back to the Stables.

"There is a purpose.

"My Grandfather," explained the Regent Prince, "had a vision. He sought to remake the Great Canal. To widen it. To connect it to the sea. To extend it, in the north to Zhuozhuan, in the West to the mountain springs and Luoyang, in the South as far as Yuhang, and all the way to Shangyang in the East.

"He imagined a complete water system to serve the people, in all seasons – irrigation for plantings, flood plains for the monsoons. Ships for the southern grains, freight for the guilds. Dikes and levees. Dams, with spillways and gates and locks, to go up and down slopes. Bridges. A truly Grand Canal.

"For all China."

"That would be a mighty legacy," said Le Lang thoughtfully.

"Aye. It is ... generational," said Zang Tu, although he meant more than that. "It could change the lands of Cathay forever.

"So five of the European powers are bidding for the charter," he continued. "That is what these first bridges are –a test run. But which do I choose? It vexes me no end -- "

"The French design was clever," offered Le Lang. "Perhaps they can improve their engineering."

* * *

When they had returned to the Stables and mounted the Regent Prince in his cart, one of the horses came up lame.

"She has a hoof that needs a new shoe," announced the driver.

Zang Tu volunteered, saying that he had never shod a horse, but that he could learn quickly. He climbed out of the cart to see. He insisted on helping. It proved to be a more difficult process than he imagined.

6. ONE EYE OPEN

The thief became so reformed that when he saw

someone drop his sword in the road he stood guarding it till the owner came back to get it.

— *Wang Youpu*

People with good memories are liable to be

crushed by the weight of their suffering.

— *Lu Xun*

"Sire," began First Minister Cheng Tun, with some concern. He stood at the dining table, midway between the two young, gobbling royals.

"Sire, you slept an entire day and night after your outing. Now I see that your hands are bandaged -- "

"I *shod a horse*, Cheng! It took *hours*."

This proclamation was met with a silent lull. No one knew what to say. The very young Future Queen's fork scraping her porcelain dish could be heard in the absence of words.

"Ah! A horse," replied the Minister finally.

"And I took the boat's rudder!" continued Zang Tu. "I single-handedly guided us through the dangerous maze of wild river traffic. *What ho!*"

"Brother!" exclaimed the girl Queen-to-Be Sizhen, from her place at the far end of the table. "You didn't!"

"Yes! Expertly, so I was told. And I got into a fight! With a Frenchman! We both fell into the water!"

Sizhen clapped her hands and stomped her feet.

"I flew a kite!" continued Zang Tu. "With a song that we composed! A song about me!

"Sister, we must get to the roof, to see if my message has been answered."

This last prospect was almost too much, causing the Future Queen to spill her platter of scrambled eggs (garnished with cheese, herbs and Polish sausage) from the buffet.

"Friend Cheng," said the Prince Regent to his Minister, "you once lived in a village -- Shen Zhou, was it not? Do you yet know of kites? Your son knows, perhaps?"

* * *

A kite has three main components -- wings, tether and anchor. The wings, or body of the kite, are created by stretching fabric (such as silk or cotton or paper) over a frame, usually in the shape of a cross, and usually made of light wood. The tether attaches it to the ground, where the kite-flyer can maneuver it. A bridle can align the face of a kite to the proper angle in the wind for lift. Struts are the pieces of dowel or bamboo which reinforce the frame.

A kite flies most efficiently when the three forces – lift, gravity, and drag (air resistance) -- are balanced at an imaginary point, known as the center of pressure. The face of the kite should allow air to flow around the kite, not hold air in its shape. The kite is seeking the path of least resistance, a calm spot in the atmosphere's turbulence.

"Shen Zhou, was it not? Do you yet know of kites? Your son knows, perhaps?"

They come in hundreds of shapes and sizes -- flat, bowed, cellular (box), air-inflated, rhomboid, sled, snakes, birds. Some kites are built with an airfoil, a surface especially curved to make air flowing across it provide lift. A dihedral is a V-shaped kite, where the face is divided into two planes.

Burmese fishermen trail lures from kites attached to the sterns of their boats. Soldiers tie messages to kite-tails, and use them to measure distances on the battlefield. The cotton kites of Bali mark a good harvest. The enormous pinwheel kites of Sumpango, Guatemala announce the arrival of Spring.

A Japanese kite-master once made a 100-foot-long centipede kite.

Some kite lovers believe. that kites represent our spirits' urge to reach the clouds, that is, a higher world, where Earth meets Heaven, and that the thrum in the ropes is the hum of living nature itself.

Kites flown by the Yunhe often made use of semaphores, the mariners' code, a set of symbols known to sailors. Some of the symbols had more than one connotation. The combination of colors could carry meaning, as well. Proficient kite-masters can hold conversations in the sky with any number of correspondents.

7. TIME WITH THE YUNHE

Planetary systems evolve by instable steps

until they find their final peace.

– Alessandro Morbidelli

Let there be you, let there be me.

Let there be oysters under the sea.

-- Ian Grant

After that eventful day on the river, Zang Tu postponed the Edict Reading.

He decided that he and Sizhen would make a pilgrimage to visit Le Lang and the Yunhe.

* * *

Sizhan's time with the Yunhe changed her.

She pulled the ferry ropes when the rains washed sediment down the slopes and knocked out the swinging bridge. She helped dig out the docks from the mud.

She waved to the ships.

Yelu was Le Lang's aunt. Normally dour and taciturn, Yelu took Sizhen under her wing, and spoke to her patiently, and showed her how to swim and how to sail and how to fly a kite.

Yelu helped Sizhen learn to cook, and to design the progression of sluices and locks which would fill up and transport dhows and small boats and cargo up and down the hillside.

"You can't design a sluice if you have never walked that ground, and canoed those waters," Yelu told her.

So 12-year-old Sizhen walked, and boated in the dugouts and dinghies. She learned and practiced. She explored caves and cliffs and underwater cinques. She saw how the Yunhe had constructed closet-granaries and cupboard storehouses under the river cliffs – storehouses of grain that would serve the Canal cantons during the four-year famines.

* * *

"Now," urged Yelu crossly. "Hold it with your gloved hand and walk towards the kite ...

"Reel it in slowly, *jeijei*. Slower! *Sha!* You're going to – wait. Your clothes are too big! Look. You can't keep shoving up the sleeves -- "

"*Ta made niao!*" replied Sizhen. "You are impossible!"

Yelu laughed at her young student's retort.

The session was not going well. The delta between what Sizhen thought she was doing and what she was actually doing would not abate.

"You're talking too much," announced Sizhen. "I can't focus."

"Ugh! Now you have too much slack!" called Le Lang, who was watching.

"What's wrong with you?" asked Yelu. "Can you not see with your actual eyes what is happe -- "

"What's happening is that your bad instruction is ruining my kite-flying." Sizhen adjusted her stance.

"Moderate winds. Moderate. *Hei.* So you reel it in slowly," instructed Yelu. "Obey the rules, palace girl! High winds give you a hard-pulling kite. Now, you want to walk it down.

"AH! There! That's it. You finally decided to listen to me, eh?

"Now, *congming de tuzi*, if you ever see the color combination Red Blue Blue, you come get me."

"Why?"

"That means the message is special. It's important."

* * *

While her brother went back and forth to the capital, Sizhen apprenticed with the artisans who sold their wares in the shaded markets terraced along the hillsides above the Canal.

By hand, she helped dig out the viaduct from when a monsoon brought mudslides.

She learned how to recognize the categories of wind.

Smoke rises vertically. Smoke drifts yet wind cannot be felt. Leaves and twigs in motion ...

One morning, Sizhen dove in and almost drowned trying to rescue a pair of lambs when they fell off a Khaifang barge.

She accompanied Le Lang's father when he boarded a moored handsome ten-sailed junk bound for Shanghai with his men and their swords and confiscated trunks of opium.

One day, everyone else was away building irrigation trenches for the village gardens of Linhe. It was a modification of the *Dujiangyan* scheme, and required many hands to install. Left all alone, Sizhen single-handedly impounded a Dutch-made *fluyt* which claimed to sail for an Eastern Warlord but actually turned out to be tea smugglers from the Jade Belt.

She helped repair the blue-with-white-trim canvas which, tied to a trellis-like frame, sheltered the larger boats in the cay.

She took to inventing new designs for the kites.

She delighted in communicating with far-reachers in the Yunhe network. Other Navigators. She traded recipes. She organized and labelled the jars of heirloom seeds kept in the Navigators' wives' shelves.

She helped Le Lang's mother design the gated canal that would one day connect the Yangtze to the Hulon.

* * *

"My most excellent brother," began Sizhen.

"Dear brother."

Zang Tu's blood froze at these words. Sizhen had never spoken in such a way before.

"How much you must love me."

Sizhen's hair was combed differently. *Why had he not noticed that before?*

"All the troubles you have shielded me from," she continued.

"I can never repay you."

They sat in the Yunhe longhouse, in the large chairs by the bay window overlooking the vista of spillways and docks. She had made them tea, and properly so, served in a correct order, mindful of the 8's and 9's. The great window offered a panorama of waters, rushing and calm, deep and shallow. The dark-azure-blue-with-white-trim canvas boathouses were visible.

"I abdicate."

Zang Tu's eye fell on the near shoals below, the close-by pools and shoreline. If you look closely, if you had seen them before, you could see through the water, and pick out the richly-colored pebbles in the streams' rock-beds, like beds of little sculptures, only shimmering.

"I renounce all my titles," she said.

"I will remain here. I'm happy here."

Sizhen's palace clothes were way too large now, so she had borrowed from Le Lang and Le Lang's older cousin.

"The bad dreams are gone," said Sizhen. "The twisted stomach. The gout.

"The gluttony ..." she began. "It ... it masked ... " she struggled to complete the thought. "Wounds. Wounds better healed here. Outdoors. In the skies."

"You are the true monarch, Brother. You have always been. You are most kingly."

She folded her hands in her lap. "Eccentric, but kingly." She smiled.

The blood had drained from Zang Tu's face.

He did not look kingly.

Gazing at the slender, tan, vibrant young woman his sister was growing into, Zang Tu could muster no counter-argument.

He could only nod.

Oh, the kites would fly that evening.

7. RED, BLUE BLUE

The string tethering it to the ground was

what kept the kite flying. Without its connection,

it would never stay aloft.

– *Nancy E. Turner*

The January Decree was announced in a flurry of food and concerts and dances. Many flags fluttered. The ceremonial music competition played in full force.

The kites signaled *Red, Blue Blue.*

German merchants were granted trade rights in all five of the treaty ports.

The French were granted permission for Christian missionaries to propagate their faith.

An indemnity of 200,000,000 taels would be paid to Japan in regard to the Ryuko Islands.

Russia would have jurisdiction over the lands north of the Amur River.

The Dutch were granted a year's passage through South China Sea.

The English were awarded jurisdiction over the Dagu forts at the mouth of the Hai River, well-trafficked by the opium trade.

Any decision as to the Management of the Canal was suspended for a year, in light of the bridge at Jiazhuo's failure.

The chart of tariffs was reconfigured, giving more leeway to those ethnic cousins of the Crown to the North and East, the Mongols and Koreans.

On and on.

It was very much. It was not enough.

Bitter complaints and threats rumbled in the corridors and courts of the Butterfly Palace.

Yet somehow, open warfare did not break out.

Negotiations began anew.

Wheels turned. Daily life continued. The regime shambled onward.

* * *

It was a week later when young Wachenhut, the German envoy, paid a visit to the Butterfly Throne.

"I am leaving the Beautiful Grandness, Liege. I will miss you. And China.

"The new emissary, Schulz, is a good fellow. He can tell a tale or two.

"Your edict, sire.' The smart young German envoy paused. "One important clause is buried deep inside. In the Appendix. Note 71.

"This is a virtual grant of the Canal stewardship to the Yunhe.

"It is innocuous-sounding, yet revolutionary in its effect. The Yunhe will control the waterway at the heart of the Divine State. In perpetuity. They can even raise their own funds.

"They will reign forever," the envoy concluded.

"I believe I am the only one among the consuls bored enough to notice that particular clause. The others do not read as carefully as I do.

"Not yet. But sooner or later, they will."

Aristocratic young Wachenhut thwacked a coin on the royal podium. A heavy Prussian coin. It was gold, with silver inlay. It depicted a lion with raised claws and teeth bared, and bore a motto.

The motto read: *Unicuique suum.*

"May all get their due." Zang Tu smiled at the motto's wording.

"A bit of equity for you," said Wachenhut.

"Equity. That is a Western idea."

"If you accept Western moneys, you'd better get used to it. But you don't need my advice. You are smart." He used the Chinese term *congming*, which included 'sly' as well as 'smart.'

"You never know where life will take you, Zang Tu. Germany is a good friend."

He bowed. "Farewell, Sire."

Zang Tu grunted. He bowed in appreciation. He would remember.

The kites would bring the message.

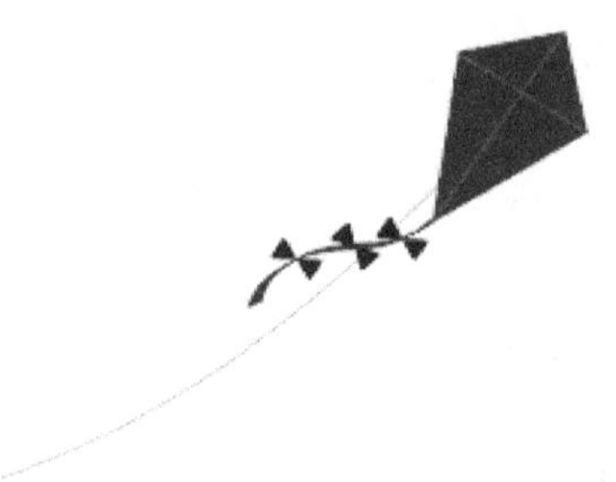

Tom's Story Notes

Along with mainstream or more traditional history-of-aviation stories like my X-1 and Zero stories, I wanted to include something offbeat for my reader ... a different aspect of flight, not so much about the mechanics, but the philosophy and spirit of flight. Specifically, kites.

I liked the idea of a young monarch issuing edicts when I ran across the mention of the 16-year-old Kangxi Emperor issuing a Sacred Edict, in 1670. This edict consisted of sixteen maxims, each seven characters long, instructing citizens in how to live.

The original title of this story was *How the Yunhe Were Granted Fill Control of the Grand Canal in the First Place*, since that excellent clan of Canal Keepers and Navigators appears throughout my adventures.

Three books about China that I can highly recommend are *Blockchain Chicken Farm*, by Xiaowei Wang, Peter Hessler's excellent <u>*River Town: Two Years on the Yangtze*</u> and Evan Osnos' *Age of Ambition.*

Commentary Essay: Kite Cultures

The Global Tapestry of Kite Flying: A Cultural Celebration of Unity and Tradition

By Sezai Adilm, Ph.d

As Tom's story suggests, kite flying is much more than a child's pastime.

Kite flying transcends geographical boundaries, weaving a vibrant tapestry of cultural traditions that span continents and centuries. From the bustling streets of Istanbul to the serene parks of Japan, the act of launching a kite into the sky resonates with symbolism and shared experiences, enriching communities with its timeless appeal.

In Turkish culture, kite flying holds a special place, especially during the spring season. As the vibrantly colored kites dance against the backdrop of clear blue skies, families gather in parks and open spaces, embracing the arrival of warmer weather and the promise of renewal. This tradition is deeply intertwined with the celebration of Nevruz, the Persian New Year, a time when people come together to welcome the arrival of spring and celebrate the triumph of light over darkness. Kites soar overhead, adorned with intricate patterns and symbols, serving as tangible expressions of hope, prosperity, and the enduring spirit of the Turkish people.

In Arabic cultures, kite flying is steeped in history and symbolism, resonating with echoes of ancient traditions and spiritual significance. During Eid al-Fitr, the festival marking the end of Ramadan, families across the Arab world take to the skies, launching kites adorned with crescent moons and stars. This symbolic gesture heralds the end of a period of fasting and reflection, ushering in a celebration of community and faith. Beyond religious observances, kite flying is embraced as a cherished pastime, bringing families and friends together during holidays and special occasions, fostering bonds of kinship and shared enjoyment.

Across Asia, kite flying takes on diverse forms, reflecting the rich tapestry of cultural heritage and regional variations. In China, where this story takes place, kite flying traces its roots back thousands of years, the practice is infused with mythology and tradition. Elaborate kites, inspired by legendary creatures like dragons and phoenixes, adorn the skies during festivals and celebrations, symbolizing power, luck, and prosperity. Meanwhile, in Japan, the annual *Kodomo no Hi* festival sees families flying *koinobori*, carp-shaped kites, as a gesture of love and protection for their children. Against the backdrop of cherry blossoms and ancient temples, these colorful kites embody the resilience and strength of the Japanese spirit, inspiring awe and admiration.

In India, kite flying takes on a particularly vibrant and competitive form during the festival of Makar Sankranti. Rooftops and streets come alive with the sound of buzzing kites and the shouts of enthusiastic participants engaged in friendly battles. This tradition fosters a sense of camaraderie among neighbors and friends, who come together to celebrate the onset of spring and the promise of new beginnings. With each kite that takes flight, adorned with intricate designs and vibrant colors, participants honor age-old customs while embracing the joyous spirit of the occasion.

In Western societies, kite flying is often embraced as a leisurely pursuit, offering a serene escape from the demands of modern life. From picnics in the park to beach outings, individuals of all ages find solace and joy in launching a kite into the endless expanse of the sky. As the wind catches the sails and the kite ascends gracefully overhead, worries melt away, replaced by a sense of wonder and awe at the beauty of nature.

The global culture of kite flying serves as a testament to the enduring power of tradition. It taps into a deeper, universal language of joy and creativity. Whether in the bustling markets of Istanbul or the tranquil gardens of Kyoto, the sight of a kite soaring overhead evokes a sense of wonder. It bridges continents and generations in a shared celebration of life's simple pleasures. As we look to the skies, may we be reminded of the rich tapestry of cultures that unite us and the boundless possibilities that await us, soaring on the wings of imagination and tradition.

4. Gia Finds a Love

Gia, a young mathematician, leaves her close-knit Italian family in Lower Manhattan to pay a pivotal role in one of the most overlooked yet consequential battles of WWII. A most remarkable aircraft.

A most determined girl.

PROLOGUE: THE PILOT J.J. HUBBELL

The first aspect of flight student pilots must grasp is the concept of aircraft axes: that flying an airplane is a three-dimensional task.

– Matthew Johnston

A fortnight after the landmark Battle of Midway, a pair of American Curtiss P-40 Warhawks chased a lone Mitsubishi A6M Zero across the top of the world.

The three warplanes left thin, deadly contrails in their

wakes, lines to delineate where the hot engine exhaust froze in the arctic atmosphere above the vast and barren landscapes of the islands of Kitsack and Attu.

"Easy money," said J.J. Hubbell, pilot of the lead Curtiss.

He sounded nervous.

J.J. Hubbell, the pilot of the lead Curtiss, was well-liked among the American contingent. A friendly young California aviator with dark-blond hair, Hubbel knew how to fly. He was all of 21 years old.

But flying an airplane is a three-dimensional task.

And J.J. Hubbel had neglected one of the dimensions.

"Let's leave Zeke a souvenir," said Hubbel loudly into his radio. "Then we can light a shuck ... "

"Copy that," chuckled his companion pilot, Robbie Reed.

Easygoing J.J. Hubbell from California glanced down at his instrument panel to check altitude and bearing and fuel, preparing to fire on the Zero and return to home base.

Hubbell banked the P-40 into a skidding turn, so he could line up the enemy craft –

A sudden *Thump!* along the plane's left flank jolted him. It was followed quickly by a "ping" --

But I only looked away for a moment -- thought Hubbell.

"Where did he -- "

A sudden, deafening barrage violently shattered the Curtiss' fuselage and half its left wing.

The Zero had somehow circled and curled and repositioned himself. The A6M was now directly behind the two American aircraft –

"The hell --" exclaimed Reed over the radio.

Hubbel immediately sank his plane.

He cut speed.

He dove almost straight downward -- as tight a descent as the Curtiss could make, tighter than anything you could hope to see in one of the training flights over Goose Bay.

He swerved furiously, hoping to shake the Zero. Not only was the A6M not shaken, it had gained ground on its American rival –

Whomp! Whomp! Whomp!

A thunderous burst from the Zero's 20-millimeter wing cannon blew a man-size hole in the Curtiss.

"Jayjay! " cried Reed. It was already too late.

Flying an airplane is a three-dimensional task. J.J. Hubbel had neglected one of the dimensions.

A merciless strafe of the Zero's 7.7- millimeter machine guns sent long, lethal bullets zipping and pinging across Hubbel's vulnerable cockpit, smashing glass and metal and flesh.

Then a second pass, so fast and precise as to be surreal.

J.J. Hubbell died instantly. His upper body shook and torqued like a puppet gone mad, contorting in a grotesque dance of death. The bullets continued to strike.

The Zero broke off., leaving Hubbel's Curtiss P-40 Warhawk to trail smoke and flame in its sickening death spiral. Metal shards whined and whipped as the aircraft fell.

Both pilot and plane were gone before the trailing debris struck the freezing waters of the Bering Sea.

The Japanese pilot, Daichi Yamada, of the village Biei, on the island of Hokkaido, watched the Curtiss airplane fall.

An efficient sortie.

Daichi was a most talented pilot.

He was all of 22.

Daichi took no pride in killing a fellow aviator. Young Daichi did, however, take a great deal of pride in fulfilling the mission protecting his beleaguered homeland.

He decided that he would let the second Curtiss survive. Its pilot could tell the others what he had seen. How easy it had been.

Pilot Daichi spoke briefly to a photo of a lovely young woman which adorned his dashboard.

In the photo, she was standing by a fence, in a garden.

Her smile was shy but genuine.

* * *

The Aleuts' wooden boats rocked on the sea.

Along the beach, where the Cinder River meets the Bering Sea, the day was ending.

The tribe's hunt had been a good one.

The girls and women along the shore sang to Silla, the Sky God, as their sons and brothers and husbands harvested the day's catch.

The song gave thanks that all concerned had gone unharmed. The second verse called out to the fish, seals, and otters who were giving their lives so that the Atabask could live.

The tall boy, Tay, with the red neckerchief and shaggy mane of black hair falling over his collar led the effort to beach one of the three open-faced big boats, the fifty-foot sailed *umiaq.*

Two more *umiaq* were being unloaded along the docks. A dozen smaller *baidarkas* waited patiently to transfer their sea-lime baskets.

"Dip your oars," the women sang. "You're almost there. Almost home safe."

Follow the waters' light

Dip, dip and swing

Dip, dip and swing her back

Hexa coli misha woni

Sulli makes all things right

The Northern Lights will shine tonight

Tay pulled the red neckerchief from his face, so that it fell around his neck.

He looked up at the moving sheets of clouds. He listened closely.

He fixed his gaze on the western horizon. Nothing appeared.

He returned his attention to unloading the big boats.

He made sure his rifle was within reach.

* * *

A world away from the frozen lands of the Bering Sea, in Lower Manhattan, ten months after Father's passing, the landlord, Fitzgerald, stopped Gia on the second-story landing, a floor above the familiar bustle and commerce and neighborly chatter of Sullivan Street.

Fitzgerald had a cigarette in one hand and an envelope in the other.

"Rent's goin' up," he told Gia, eldest daughter of the Tomasso family.

Warily, she took the envelope.

"Your father left some serious debt," explained Fitzgerald.

Gia opened up the letter inside the envelope, her hands shaking slightly.

It was on thick paper, paper with a watermark and an ivory finish. 'Sweeney, Doyle and O'Callahan, Attorneys at Law' announced the letterhead.

"That's a twenty per cent hike!" exclaimed Gia.

Fitzgerald took a drag on his cigarette.

"You can't just raise th -- " she protested.

"Yes, I can," stated the landlord. "My lawyer says."

She re-read the letter. She recognized her father's signature on the bottom.

"The store rent, too?" she asked.

"*Vigerish*," shrugged Fitzgerald. He extinguished the cigarette.

"Call the lawyers. You make sure it's on the level."

Oh, she surely would do that--

"Bill's come due, kid," he concluded. "Starting Friday."

PART ONE

We're going through a period when nothing
can be left to chance.

-- Yasmina Khadra

The samurai looks insignificant beside
his armor of black dragon scales.

-- Tomas Transtroner

The season of snows was preferred,
that I might experience the pleasure of suffering.

-- Estwick Evans

I. HIGH COMMAND

The Pacific Theater from 1941-1945 was desperate, dark, and bloody...
-- *Stacey Anne Baterina Salinas*

"We're squarely behind the Eight Ball, gentlemen," said Admiral Durden. He added a colorful expletive for emphasis.

"George Patton," said Durden. "Omar Bradley. Eisenhower. Montgomery." A few guffaws sounded at this last name.

"Plenty of military leaders in the European Theatre are bringing glory to their cause.

"But not us. Not us. We are the ones *losing* the Pacific War ..."

An image came onto the wall-mounted screen behind the admiral.

"And here's why."

It was a blurry black-and-white photo of a ghostlike Mitsubishi A6M aircraft. *The Zero*. Its image had been enlarged many times.

"We know almost nothing about it," said Durden gravely.

He wrote this on the blackboard:

12:1

"Not a mistake," declared Durden.

"Twelve to One. Twelve of our Warhawks and our Hellcats crash and burn for every Zero we manage to shoot down.

"At *fifty thousand American dollars* per plane, that is quite an expensive habit we have. Sending our boys to their deaths against these devil planes."

No comments came forth.

"All espionage had failed," he continued. "The Japanese allow in only Japanese. Our data on this aircraft is almost nonexistent."

"The entire Pacific Theater is aching for a shred of information on the Zeke," he urged, as if somehow the point was not obvious.

"The floor is open for suggestions, gentlemen ..." Admiral Durden's fury was scarcely contained.

"I might have something, Sir ..." ventured one of the meeting's attendants, a bespectacled junior-grade analyst named Egan.

"An operation, actually. The Math boys came up with it."

A charged silence took hold in the tightened atmosphere of the conference room. Chairs shuffled on the tile floor.

Egan squirmed slightly.

"I just don't know who we could get to execute it ... "

2. SULLIVAN STREET FIRST VIEW

Look well to each step; and from the beginning, think what may be the end.

-- Edward Whymper

Gia Tomasso studied the problem on the chalkboard.

The girl's features were open, friendly, warm, even comfortably readable.

Her eyes were not.

Her eyes, sharp and evaluating, assessed all that they took in, both in their general aspect and in their details. Gia's gaze was set at odds with her easy manner.

The face gave away the teenager's caution, and a little of her depth of understanding as well. She was almost-grown, almost-womanly. Her smile – a flash of white against dark curls and strong eyebrows – was quick and genuine. Beyond that initial smile, her respect needed to be earned.

She raised one hand.

"Eleven point two," she volunteered.

"Yup," said the Instructor. "Now can you walk us through how you got there …"

After class, the Mathematics teacher approached his star pupil.

"Gia, some of the military types have set up a war-time Math Council," he told her.

"Up at Columbia. Morningside Heights.

"You might be just what they're looking for."

Before she could say No, he added: "Pays pretty well."

"Uptown Line stops right at 116th Street," he pointed out.

Gia Tomasso looked up. Her features were still friendly, but now her eyes were fully engaged.

* * *

"'*Homey*,' is what I said," corrected Gia's nosy Aunt Chiara as she helped Elena with dinner.

"*Homey*. Not '*homely*.'

"As in a homey, nice, stay-at-home kind of girl," Chiara explained, digging herself a deeper hole. "Home-maker."

"As in good cook," added Elena, Gia's mother. "As in my Angel."

"She's actually sitting right here, as you're discussing her," observed Dario, Gia's uncle, the two women's younger brother.

"Gia is an angel," agreed Chiara. "An un-married angel. A stay-at-home-forever angel. All respect."

"She presents herself like a comfortable sofa. Is all I'm saying."

"You're full of it," Dario told Chiara. "You got a mean streak, you know that? Don't listen, Gia."

Leaning on his cane, Dario walked across the crowded kitchen to clear pots and pans from the crowded tabletop where Gia was working. He carefully made space for her books and ledgers.

"So. Gia! Would it hurt to apply a little make-up? Show

yourself off a little?" asked Aunt Chiara. "I don't see the boys flocking--"

"The boys are occupied. It's called World War Two," corrected Elena as she stirred the sauce and tasted.

Chiara looked out the window onto Sullivan Street. Shoppers were buying ingredients for dinner.

"A nice blouse, sweetheart," continued Chiara, "long-sleeved. Give you a slimmer look --"

"Maybe you can see that I'm doing the books," replied Gia evenly.

"Books for who?" asked Elena.

"Baker. Then the Barber. Then inventory," replied Gia.

"That one," commented Chiara disapprovingly.

"Rent's due Friday," replied Gia. "We're short."

"Your father, he could always sweet-talk the landlord," said Elena to Gia. "He could sweet-talk anyone alive."

Elena stopped Chiara's hand as it started to sprinkle something into the pot. "Smidge," explained Chiara. Elena allowed it.

"Your Mother and your late Father, now they had a love," Chiara told her industrious niece, not for the first time.

"And it wasn't an accident," continued Chiara. "Your Mother got up an hour early every day of her married life.

"He never saw her without her make-up. True fact. A woman's gotta present herself -- "

"Don't you peddle that true love hogwash to Gia," objected Dario. "Don't listen, Gia. Love ain't a con game."

"Love isn't always perfect," warned Chiara.

"Love is the reason to live," said Elena.

"Love rules," said Luca, nine years old, just home from school.

***

A full year after Father's death, a light snow was falling on a bustling Sullivan Street when someone called her name.

"Hey, Gia!"

Gia Tomasso leaned her head out the third-story window of her bedroom.

It was Morant, the superintendent, an honest man.

"You got a visitor, sweetheart."

A figure stood beside him on the stoop

Gia walked down the three flights of stairs.

There stood a short-ish woman wearing a fur collar. Gray-blonde hair protruded from under her woolen hat. She carried a big black purse.

"Gia?" asked the woman. "Gia Tomassi?"

"Yes," said Gia.

"You look like him."

The woman reached into her big black purse.

"You got his eyes."

Up close, Gia saw that the woman was in her forties. Good-natured wrinkles suggested that she was a person who was used to smiling.

Her right hand held a pair of gloves. Her left was adorned

with a modest wedding ring.

She handed Gia a large manila envelope.

Gia opened it.

Out fell a black velvet case.

Gia carefully opened the case.

It was a golden eagle, wings spread, a fierce expression, and feathered arrows grasped in its claws. Around the eagle was a circle in a deep blue, the border lettering spelling out, *The Distinguished Service Medal.*

"Here you go, hon. I could never keep this. I only took it to make him happy."

Gia stared at the medal, then back at the visitor.

"I looked it up," said the woman. "It's legit. It's for 'Exceptionally meritorious service ...' Battle of Cabrai.

"He called it his good luck charm."

"Love isn't always perfect," warned Chiara.
"Love is the reason to live," said Elena.
"Love rules," said Luca, nine years old.

The woman shrugged, and shook her head kindly.

"How did you know my Dad?" asked Gia after a long, long moment had passed.

"From the hospice. Down the Shore."

The woman clicked the big purse shut. She put on her gloves.

"And before."

An entire conversation between the two women unfurled, in silence ... yet certain important information was exchanged.

On Sullivan Street, a vendor pulling a cart swerved to avoid a car and almost spilled his load. He caught his balance. The cart rolled on.

The woman looked at Gia and smiled.

She stepped off the stoop.

"Awright. *Molto bene*," she said. "*Cose buone*, dear."

She merged into the bustling throng of people and carts moving along Sullivan Street.

"Who was that?" asked Mother from the third-floor apartment's narrow laundry room.

"Friend from school," replied Gia.

"A boyfriend, maybe?" commented Aunt Chiara, *sotto voce*.

"Rent's due Friday," reminded Mother.

"I didn't forget, Ma," replied Gia.

3. JAPAN'S RADICAL AIRPLANE

So formidable was the Zero that the official

American strategy for pilots attacked by the

Japanese fighter boiled down to this: *run away.*

    – Elizabeth Hanes

It weren't hate, boy. More like... pride.

– Calvin Clements

When the Japanese High Command issued a Request for Proposals, in early 1937, the four major Japanese manufacturers declined. The Emperor's demands for a new aircraft, one so advanced that it would out-perform any warplane in the skies, was impossible to achieve.

No plane could do all that. *It cannot be done,* they said. *No, they said, such specifications cannot be met.*

Jiro Horikoshi had disagreed.

This resourceful aviation engineer had been thinking. The IMF 10 experimental model had failed in flight tests, yes, but he felt he could fix it. He had in mind the creation of the world's fastest, lightest, and most acrobatic aircraft.

Now, ten months later, the fruits of Jiro Horikoshi's labors rolled off the assembly lines. The vision had come to life.

Up close, the A6M Mitsubishi Zero was most impressive. Graceful form and lethal function wedded. The A6M looked like a pure-bred hunting dog, always at the ready. Eager, upward- and forward-leaning, the Zero was prepared to engage.

"Every possible weight-saving measure has been incorporated into the design," said Haru, the young engineer, to his friend Daichi.

The two boys stood in the cavernous Mitsubishi Heavy Industries Factory in Nagoya. The assembly bay was that area where the paths of the various subassemblies – engine, wings, tail, landing gear -- came together.

"Horikoshi used the new material -- all extra-super duralumin alloy – for the frame. Fanatical," continued Haru. "He cut holes in the rear struts just to gain an ounce.

"Spitfires need long, pristine runways. The Zero can launch from the surface of an aircraft carrier.

"The Focke-Wulf needs a great deal of maintenance: 16 hours per hour of flying time. The Zero only needs 3 hours maintenance per hour of flying time.

"Fourteen-cylinder engine. Eleven hundred horsepower. Top speed 565. Cannon up top, guns alongside, bombs underneath the wings.

"Look! *Louvered*," admired Haru.

Haru showed Daichi how the panels behind the cowling had been layered. "Of Chinese design," he bragged.

"She weighs 5200 pounds. Two-thirds the weight of a Messerschmidt ..."

"Stalling speed below 110. Nothing like it has ever been seen. An aircraft to match your skills, Pilot --"

Daichi was one of the Air Combat Group's most-decorated young pilots, with nine verified kills. He had recently been promoted to *Teishin Shudan*, the Dash Forward, the Emperor's Raiders.

Nothing like the A6M Zero
had ever been seen.

Yet the aircraft's underlying reality could not be disguised: the Zero was all offense.

In every design detail, the aircraft clearly cared nothing for its pilot.

All manner of protection for the cockpit had been removed. The American planes were not like this. They seemed to cradle the pilot, to cherish him. The young pilots of the Japanese Imperial Air Corps had heard rumors of thick armor to protect their American counterparts, ejection seats, parachutes, food rations, maps for the downed Allied aviators ...

Japan's admirals had botched Pearl Harbor. There had been one chance, one clear shot to destroy the Americans' Pacific fleet, at Pearl Harbor. And they had missed. Half the attack force had simply turned around without engaging. After that debacle, everyone thought that surely the government had in mind some diplomatic measures to avert all-out war. But none such were forthcoming. Worst of all, the Japanese had misunderstood their enemy. They thought America would be slow to respond, and that its soldiers' level of zeal would be low. *Wrong.* After Pearl Harbor, America mobilized ... and fast. Young men and women joined the military in huge numbers. New agencies like the War Production Board hyped the manufacture of a new air fleet, and mighty battleships. America's industry shifted into high gear. Its military capacities grew by the day, and so far seemed limitless. Japan was shoveling her boys to slaughter. Was no one sane in charge?

A portrait of Emperor Hirohito graced each aircraft's dashboard, as a reminder of the *bushido* code. It is a powerful force.

But, so is the will to live.

"Banzai!" said Haru, enthused by the presence of both the master pilot and the thoroughbred A6M.

"Ten thousand years!"

* * *

"There," said the young man, Daichi.

In the camera lens, he could see the familiar figure leaning against the wooden fence of the paddock. Green fields and the famous lavender meadows beyond spread beyond and behind her.

"Smile, Mei."

The young man took his girlfriend's picture.

They had been quarreling all morning, even as they pulled weeds from the vegetable rows.

The hill people of Hokkaido did not have the same reverence for the Emperor Hirohito as others within Japan might. The Ainu had been growing crops in the fertile fields and hunting the green Hokkaido forests long before there was a Japan. Concerns of Empire seemed far away from these villages.

So it was not surprising to Daichi that his girlfriend, Mei, opposed his volunteering for the Emperor's Air Combat Corps.

At Daichi's request, the girl Mei stopped and posed, rake in hand, by the fence on the pretty farm in the village of Biei.

She smiled as Daichi searched for the just-right angle. Her expression was most genuine, for she loved him completely, as he did her. They had picked out a carriage house on her family's farm compound, the home where they would raise their children. Mei had opened a savings account for them, and was collecting wallpaper and dishware for the day they moved in.

The moment as this misguided war was over.

Daichi's camera clicked. It was a fine portrait, with lavender fields and the mountains of Furano in the distance.

"I'm scared," said Mei, still holding the rake. "Promise you'll come home."

Daichi promised.

Nothing would stop him from returning to Biei, he told her. Nothing could.

* * *

"*Long live the Emperor,*" said the stern Air Combat Chief Instructor to begin the pilots' briefing.

He could care less about the Emperor, thought Daichi,

"You pilots are the crown princes of our forces," continued the Chief Instructor. "Now. You have all seen the subassemblies. Each aircraft is a treasure. A miracle, almost. Each holds secrets.

"You have seen some of the sacrifices which your brothers and sisters have made to bring us to the brink of victory.

"The same is expected of you.

Heard it before, Daichi remarked to himself.

"If your aircraft is downed, you will have a choice," said the Chief.

Ah, noted Daichi. *This. This is it. This is what he cares about* ...

"You have done good work for the Emperor. But failure is part of life. Failure must be planned for.

This ... this was new.

"If your aircraft is downed, the enemy must not find so much as a centimeter of it intact."

"If your aircraft is downed, you will have a choice," said the Chief.

Daichi cast a covert glance towards the pilots nearby ...

"Each plane has a flare. Use it to immolate your aircraft. Down the gullet. Explode the gas tanks. Destroy the plane. Outwit the Americans."

Wait, thought Daichi. *Could that flare not be used to signal to our comrades, so the pilot could live to fight again* ...

A suicide directive. The *Samurai* code. Or a long life on the family farm with the ones you love.

Quite a choice.

4. ON THE COLUMBIA CAMPUS

Every time you need something to be optimal, there's going to be some mathematics at play.

-- Hannah Fry

The **SRG** was a group of incredibly intelligent experts in statistics that was assembled to solve military-related problems during WWII.

– *First Aero Squadron Foundation History*

Walking along the path through the green lawns of Columbia University, past Low Memorial Library and the students carrying their shouldered book bags and the statue of Alma Mater, Mia came to the brownstone on the south side of 116th Street. Ivy climbed the building's brick walls.

She hit the doorbell. A voice asked for her name. The gate-like door buzzed and opened.

There in the bright lobby, sunlight fell on the floor tiles, where some 19th century tile artisan had created a mosaic of full sails, tides, boats, oars, and whales.

* * *

"Hi, Gia. I'm Sheila Atwater."

The self-possessed young woman in the khaki blouse and skirt descended the staircase and introduced herself. They shook hands.

"Heard good things about you."

They climbed the staircase.

They emerged into the busy, humming open office floor, spacious, with high ceilings and slanted sunrays on oak tables and ladders leaned against stacks and stacks of bookshelves. Morningside Park was visible through the tall windows.

"A small group of us are convinced that we can use mathematics to win the war," said Shiela. "Save the world.

"We're called the Statistical Research Group," Sheila continued. "SRG. We're part of the Applied Mathematics Panel. Both initiatives are privately funded."

"Privately funded. So you're not part of the Army or Navy," said Gia.

"Right. We coordinate with all of the Forces, we wear the uniform, but

we 're independent. We are our own chain of command. It makes a difference.

"You'd wear the WACS uniform. Like mine."

"A small group of us are convinced we can use mathematics to win the war," said Sheila. "We are our own chain of command."

They passed posters of bombers and schematic diagrams of submarines, with red circles placed around the fuselage.

They entered an office with half windows all around.

They sat down at a conference table. Displayed on the walls were sea charts and maps of Europe.

"We try to contribute close statistical support where it will mean the most.

"Our intention is to place a mathematician at every military base and installation with a personnel count over six.

"We've had some successes. Three bridges at Beta Fromm were built within a day. With our help. Tank fuel projections at Graveney Marsh proved to be useful. The critical-path mapping for the Messina Convoy. That sort of thing. The hard part is reading the database. You'd be surprised how much really good information can do.

"Your security check came up clean. Your Dad was at Cabrai, huh? That couldn't have been fun."

Gia glanced up in surprise.

"We pretty much know everything," explained Sheila. "You'll like it here, I'm hoping."

She pointed through the window, towards a far corner.

"See that guy, he looks like Akim Tamiroff, standing under the African maps? That's Arthur. He's the head honcho. He recruited me and Milt. And Abe.

"We would like to get to know you. See if you might be a fit.

"We can pay two thousand dollars for five hours of your time, helping me with research and reports, here in the offices, three days a week, for a month.

* * *

It was at the end of her third week with the Statistical Research Group when Gia was called into one of the big offices.

Walnut paneling. Lamps with green shades. No windows. The heavy door closed.

Arthur Lamb sat beside a thin, owlish woman whom Gia only knew as Leigh. The expressions on their features gave away only that they were intently engaged.

Tacked to the bulletin boards behind them were plans for the new bomb sights whose performance Gia had been monitoring through all the forward-base reports. Notes in Gia's neat handwriting dotted the charts.

Gia closed the door. She sat.

"I'm putting together a team," said Sheila. "Wondered if you might want to join."

Gia nodded. Gia was suddenly aware that she had pencil stuck in her hair. She removed it.

"High Command wants very badly to capture a Mitsubishi A6M aircraft. Intact.

"We think we might have found a way."

* * *

"You'd be my Second-in-Command," said Sheila. "We've never had anyone score as high as yours. We feel you can handle yourself in a forward-base setting.

"So, there are two stages to our operation.

"First stage, we have to help crank the Dutch Harbor base up to par. The bombs they drop all miss their targets. They should have built another seven miles of paved road. No radar. No early warning.

"Their C.O. is gun shy -- only three sorties in the last month. He shows no capacity for imposing discipline or attacking the enemy. A new one should be in place in two weeks.

"The supply chain is FUBAR. It looks like the capitalist spirit has taken hold in the Pacific Northwest. Base full of slackers. Low morale. Looks like there is a small criminal element, too."

Gia questioned closely until she understood every aspect of the assignment.

"A colony of Aleuts share the base. They've been pretty much abandoned by us. It's almost criminal."

Gia looked at Sheila.

"Aleuts. Aleutian Islanders. *Unangax*. The Indian tribe native to the Alaska atoll. Like Eskimo cousins. The war has been nothing but bad news for them.

"Now they have their own complex, on Siska. A prison, really. The Japanese killed half of the settlement on Attu and sent the other half to prison camp."

* * *

"The second stage is where it gets interesting," Sheila told her apprentice. "We will execute the plan to capture a Zero.

A Zeke, as the Navy would say. That plan has a lot of moving parts. If you decide you're interested, we can go over it in close detail.

"Now." Shiela stuck a pencil behind her ear. "Abe has cleared this mission for hazard pay ... and that is quite a multiplier. Your upgraded salary ..."

Sheila wrote down figures on a notepad and showed it to her apprentice.

"Per month?" asked Gia.

"Per week."

Leached sound came floating into the chamber. A hubbub arose through the glass concerning some kind of a new weapons system from out West.

"A third member of the team will meet us there. A pilot."

"Meet us where?"

"Top of the world."

She nodded towards a large rectangular map that had been pinned to the bulletin-board wall.

The map was an unusual, pretty blue, almost turquoise. It depicted the lands we call Alaska.

A graceful arc of islands curved into the deep ocean waters, beckoning Asia.

The archipelago looked like it could be Hawaii, or Fiji in the tropics, where you can walk on the sand out into the calm ocean waters.

Except that it represented not the South Pacific but the deep arctic waters of the Bering Sea.

"They say you can see the Northern Lights," Sheila added.

* * *

"I'm in," said Gia two days later. "I believe I can help you get this done. But I have one request."

"I'm all ears," said Sheila.

A few sentences into Gia's plan, Sheila smiled. Six sentences in, she gave a laugh.

"Yes," said Sheila. "We might be able to make something like that work ..."

5. ON SULLIVAN STREET, SECOND VIEW

Let's stop pretending that something else is going on.

-- Kirk Webster

It was a small Tomasso family meeting.

It took place in the laundry room, across from the long kitchen. The door was closed. Towels hung on the hooks on the back of the door

Gia, young Uncle Dario and third-grader Luca were in attendance.

Gia wore her military-brown WAC uniform, her unruly waves of chestnut hair pinned down.

"Dad left us over four thousand bucks in debt," said Gia.

"Damn!" Dario pounded his fist. "I *knew* it-- "

"That's why our rent went up so high," continued Gia.

"Now, my new assignment qualifies as hazard pay. So, I consulted with my boss. She's a banker.

"We been meeting with lawyers and a couple of banks. Seems that our landlord, Fitzgerald, is in deep in arrears. He has liens against the properties, from all the back taxes.

"Our family now owns the building."

Cars honked below, on Sullivan Street. A dog barked twice. A pedestrian complained. The incident passed.

"What, we own this building?" asked Dario.

Gia nodded. "Two Twenty-One Sullivan Street."

She held up the deed and loan document. The seal stated quietly, 'Vienna Charter Bank.'

"This third document clears our debt to Fitzgerald." She held up a letter from Attorneys-at-Law Sweeney, Doyle and O'Callahan.

Dario took the documents and read them.

"Is this for real, Gia?"

"Been working on it some time," she answered.

"But how ...?"

"I've signed over everything -- my monthly pay, my life insurance, my hazard bonus. This means that my loan is backed by the U.S. Government. Banks favor guarantees like that."

"What about Ma?" asked Luca.

"I talked to her already."

"Bet that went well," remarked Dario.

Gia raised an eyebrow. *"Chi lavora mangia."*

"Oh, *doctor*," laughed Dario. "Good," he said. "Good for you."

"Fitzgerald has exited," continued Gia. "John Morant is staying on as Super. He will make sure all the rents are current. When I'm gone, you deposit them in the bank each month. He'll fix the pipes, pay the bills."

"What about the store?" asked Luca.

"You're not working there anymore. We own that space now. Morant thinks he can rent it out for a good price.

"You focus on school full-time, Luca. That's what. You're gonna be an engineer. Like Dad."

"I'm scared," said Luca.

"I'm scared, too," replied Gia. "Furthest away I've been from home before now is Dad's hospice. Beach Haven.

"His gambling debts were going to sink us, kiddo," said Gia. "That's a fact. Even with my two incomes.

Luca looked like he was going to cry.

"I'll only be gone a year," said Gia. "And when I get back, my boss has a couple of banks who want me. Imagine that. Me on Wall Street."

"Where," asked Dario, rallying, "are they sending you? The planet Jupiter?"

Gia smiled. She did not answer the question.

PART TWO

Modern armies had never fought before
on any field that was like the Aleutians....

-- Corporal. Dashiell Hammett

There are two kinds of Arctic problems, the imaginary and the real.

Of the two, the imaginary are the most serious.

– Vilhjalmur Stefasson

I can't go on in simple compliance.

From now on I must struggle with the world.

-- Osamu Dazai

6. WELCOME TO THE ARCTIC

Certainly my death at this point does not seem beneficial to God's plans as perceived by me.

-- Linda Bishop, per Rachel Aviv

Tents are not boats, and grassy fields are not the Bering Sea.

– Karen Hesse

"What did you do before this?" Gia asked Sheila over the drone of the aircraft's engine.

The cargo space of a B-24 Liberator is not built for passenger comfort.

It is not built for passengers at all, but for tanks, and Jeeps, big metal objects.

The too-spacious, slab-sided cargo areas were nicknamed 'flying boxcars.'

Benches, stools and assorted chairs that might decorate a fraternity basement provided seating along the bomber's bare fuselage walls.
Corded nets and parachutes hung down from hooks in the ceiling.

Area rugs only served to emphasize how slippery the floors were.

"I was a banker," answered Sheila. "I stepped in as head of Vienna Charter's New York office.

"When the war shut down the Paris and Amsterdam markets, stock prices limits were locked in.

"No one wanted to buy. So we bought. It didn't take much foresight to see that as soon as the war tilted and markets reopened, prices would shoot up.

"By Ardennes, prices had tripled. By the end of Stalingrad, times seven."

* * *

Each patch of our earth has lived many lives.

Every flower-filled pasture was once an undersea canyon, or mountain cliff, or the stage for deadly combat among

129

warm-blooded predators, man or other.

Now, these frozen, barren lands which Gia Tomasso of New York City saw below her window ...

Had these lands once housed the spires of Sunda, or the craggy citadels of Golcond? Might the final resting place of Prince Helig ap Glanalawg and his loyal, doomed army lay deep in this permafrost, their blank eyes yet staring upwards? Had the green meadows now silent and still beneath this tundra once seen the sunlight of fabled Adria and time-lost Kerguelen, or the treasured libraries of Lemuria, in those brief days when men sought knowledge and not bloody victory? Had the rippling shadows of the flying horses of Gansu once graced these terrains? Had wooly mammoths roamed the glacier-cut vales on older days? Did Sultan Giyas al-Din Mohammed Öz Beg Han here fight the final conflict of that bitter, decade-long war over a marriage?

* * *

A garrulous red-headed oceanographer from San Francisco, their onboard companion, filled the time with descriptions of glowing lantern-fish among the coral reefs, and jet-black damselfish who farmed their algae gardens on pastures of the Zhemchug Canyon floor, deep beneath the Bering Sea, alongside single-cell zooxanthellae.

He told them war stories. One was of a young British concert pianist, a prisoner of war at Nong Pladuk, who played concerts on a broken-down Steinway for the jungle elephants of Thailand. He was so gaunt and sick he could barely hit the notes, but the elephants loved the music, so he carried on until one morning he was found slumped over the keyboards. The elephants especially liked Debussy's "Sunken Cathedral," maybe because it was so sad.

* * *

"We haven't seen a sign of life for over an hour."

Leaning out the window, Gia could spy only wastelands below, clouds and featureless terrain. No roads, no lights, no wolf packs, no structure, no sign of man.

Humans are affected more deeply and in more ways by geology than we have any idea. We absorb certain profound signals through our subconscious senses, ancient truths of life and death and survival that do not register in our waking minds.

The expanse of empty-of-all-walking-things terrain over which they flew triggered that deep fear and doubt which each of us carries.

Gia had not known it would be like this.

They had not seen so much as a wild horse or snowshoe track since Vancouver.

How can any place be so forlorn?

She wanted to call it 'barren' but the word needed to be a thousand times stronger.

This must be what Sullivan Street looked like a million years ago ....

She had never understood how much she had taken for granted in her life, such as Western civilization.

Why did I agree to do this? How could I have done something so stupid?

She sat on her hands, so Sheila could not see how badly they were shaking.

Can't we just turn the plane around? Gia wanted to ask. *Maybe I could just work out of the Seattle warehouse ...*

The expanse of empty tundra over which they flew triggered that deep fear and doubt which each of us carries.

A sudden fusillade brought her to her senses.

The bullets made a supernaturally loud *Whiirp!Snap!* sound when they struck the metal of the aircraft's armor plating.

"Take cover! Enemy fire!" called the pilot over the intercom.

The Liberator banked and swerved, way too steeply, trying to dodge that torrent of fire. Such a big airplane was not built for evasive maneuvers --

The Liberator's turret and waist guns revved to swivel and aim --

The pilot changed altitude downward, again too radically --

Sheila was thrown violently from her seat. Gia could see her friend's neck being wrenched twisted in a weird angle --

Sheila slid across the floor -- and slammed into the bulkhead

"Sheila!" cried Gia. She moved to unbuckle herself so she could help her friend --

"Stay in your seat!" warned the copilot, looking back from the cockpit.

"Take cover until the danger has passed -- "

The Liberator's turret and waist guns let loose blazing salvo upon salvo --

Seated in the plane's waist, Gia and a mechanic from Spokane tried to shield themselves. They lung onto the netting which decorated the walls.

At length, Gia listened as the Curtiss Wildhawk jets escorting them drove the enemy aircraft away --

"Sheila! Sheila! Hey!"

Why won't she wake up ...

The red-headed oceanographer lay jammed between the artillery skids and the bulkhead, his neck broken.

It was then that Gia saw the widening pool of red spreading beneath her friend and commanding officer, Sheila...

7. SOUTH HANGAR TWO

With the Mark 15 bombsight, I can drop a bomb into a pickle barrel at 20,000 feet.

— *Carl Norden*

The reasons of the world are not exactly your reasons.

— *Eugenio de Andrade*

"But all this extra work," complained Petty Officer 1st Class Jeanie Wasson, Acting Quartermaster.

Gia rubbed her temples.

"Think of it as capitalism," she explained to Wasson. "You are part of a marketplace. So every time you order, you are in competition with all of the other military bases – Pacific bases, West Coast bases – for these goods.

"If you don't make a convincing argument for those eggs at 50 cents per dozen, they're going to Portland or Pearl Harbor for 70 cents. Or, worse, they'll send you a palette of ball bearings, or three dozen bicycles. None of which you need, or asked for. Get it?

"You vet *them*," exhorted Gia. "You're vetting *them*.

"Question their methods. Question their reports.

"They need to look good to the Quartermaster General's Office. Prove that giving you the goods you need multiplies the benefits to the U.S. Army.

"Double-check all their bills of lading. Earn their respect."

"Yes, Ma'am. I'll do my best." Wasson saluted and took her leave.

Unlike the other Quonsets, South Hangar Two had been divided into a variety of interior spaces. Across from one end of Runway 7, South Hangar Two opened to the Aleuts complex, with the Longhouse, or Lodge, with its chimney and smoke and fragrant smells. Beyond the structures, towards the foothills, stood a corral and barns. In the expansive space of the aircraft hangar, Gia had arranged partitions for separate functions. Standing screens and half-walls and portable shelves divided spaces decorated with molding to hang pictures, potted plants, rugs in warm colors, couches, table and chairs. Gia had ordered from the Seattle warehouses horizontal files with wooded drawers for her charts and work-spaces.

"You're the Texas pilot," said Gia to the skinny woman in

the pilot's suit.

"Tessa Smith," the woman drawled. They shook hands. "Sorry about your friend."

Tall and somewhat gawky, Tessa Smith was older than Gia. Beneath a bushel of dirty blonde hair were clear eyes and a steady gaze

"I got the bombardiers next," Gia said to Tess from Texas.

"I'd appreciate it if you can sit in. Just 'till Sheila gets back."

* * *

"What's CEP again?" asked Bombardier #2.

"Come on, Louie," moaned Bombardier #1

"*Focus*," said Gia. "It stands for 'Circular Error Probable.' The diameter of your strike zone. Get it?"

"Do you get what it is now?" repeated Bomardier #1.

"Just look at the photo," said Bombardier #3 to #2.

Three glass-and-copper devices sat gleaming on the big table.

They looked foreign, like they had come from another civilization, perhaps advanced relatives of the ancient Greek Antikythera.

The four young bombardiers craned to get a close look at the new bomb sights.

"Used correctly," said Gia, "these new Norden sights have a CEP of seventy-five feet. The median CEP for Navy bombers over the month of June was twelve hundred feet."

"You gotta be kiddin' me," breathed Bombardier #1.

She had spread out on the huge conference table that dominated one section of South Hangar Two. Photos and instructions were spread out around the three bomb sights which Shiela had managed to tear away from the engineers at Sperry.

"I don't get it," said Bombardier#2.

"What's CEP again?" asked Bombardier #3.

"Circular Error Probable," replied Tess. "We just said that. Focus, Kenny. Jesus!"

"But you only have three bombsights," complained #4. "There's four of us,"

"Each of these things costs eight thousand bucks," Gia told him. "USAAF doesn't like giving them up -- "

"Look," she continued. "With the equipment you're currently using, the vector bombsights, the calculations you need to make are taking too long. The stabilizer systems could not engage. You can't keep the target in range for long enough."

She looked around at blank faces.

"Look. Guys. When the plane is not on a level trajectory, the bombs don't fall straight," reiterated Tess.

Nothing. No response from the men.

"Half of all your bombs are missing their targets altogeth ..."

When the plane is not on a level trajectory, the bombs don't fall straight. Half of all your bombs are missing their targets.

"Okay." Gia stopped herself.

"You know what? It doesn't matter. The history of bomb sights, all that, who cares? Just make sure you know how to use 'em."

Gia dismissed the four bombardiers.

She walked to the bay doors to vent her frustrations. In Italian.

This isn't working…

She held her head in her hands, as she had seen her father do from time to time.

This is never going to do…

One of the old Aleuts women sewing, rocking in her chair on the lodge porch, across the way, waved in an encouraging manner.

Maybe if Shiela were here…

Gia saw the tribal woman in the rocking chair and waved.

Early Norden Bomb Sight (Maxwell Air Force Base)

* * *

"*Qagaasakung*," said Gia to the petite Aleutian woman who came to the door of the Aleut Lodge, or longhouse.

"Hah!" chuckled the woman. "That's for later. At the end. You mean *Ukudigal*.'"

"*Ukudigal*," said Gia. "I've got four new water heaters for you. Where do you want 'em?"

The woman looked behind Gia to see two white trucks with soldiers standing by, ready to install.

"Oh! One around back, for sure. Thank you!"

"You might put one tank in your greenhouse," recommended Gia. "Sink it right in the middle of the rows."

"Okay," said the Aleut woman, stepping around to see the water tanks being rolled on dollies.

"My name is Gia."

"I know. I'm Elisapie."

"I know. I got this for you, too -- "

A tiny girl in a bright purple parka tugged at Elisapie's skirt. The Aleut woman answered in sign language.

"This is Gia, a new friend. This is Meriwa,"

"Howdy," said Gia.

Gia turned to wave in the men in the second truck.

They unloaded a big pallet. On it were buckets and Army-issued paint rollers and what looked like netting.

"This is for your roof," explained Gia to Elisapie.

"Our roof? The longhouse roof? What you got?"

"Camouflage. Paint and patterns and canvas and rope. All the Army buildings have them. You should too. So the Japanese bombers can't pick you out."

The little girl in purple signed a question. Elisapie signed an answer.

"She asked me what is that big thing you mounted on a pole over by the Depot."

"It's radar," answered Gia. "And a siren. Early warning system.

"If you hear it go off, take cover. The kids, everyone. It means enemy planes are coming"

"Thank you, Officer Gia. This is ... this is, ah, exceptional. *Assagutasdaq.*"

The Aleuts chieftain gave her visitor a most genuine smile and a bow of the head.

"*Qagaasakung.*" Gia turned to go.

Across the way, she saw that boy again. He looked like he was departing on a hunting trip. He mounted a pack horse, rifle in the saddle's scabbard.

"Who is that?"

"My little brother. His name is Tay. Tayra. Tayra Tulimaq. He's the tribe's lead hunter. He is named after the wolverine."

"Yesterday, he asked me if I knew what your name was."

Gia nodded Hello to him.

He seemed to smile, but she wasn't sure.

* * *

At one side of the open South Hangar bay, two uniformed officers stood respectfully at attention. They had been waiting for her. She recognized the gold caduceus insignias on their lapels. Physicians.

They introduced themselves to Gia.

"Sheila Atwater succumbed during the night," one of them said. "She's gone. We – we tried everything.

"We just couldn't -- " said the other.

"Her head wounds were too massive, ma'am. I'm sorry. We all are."

8. PREPARATIONS

An airplane by its nature wants to fly ...

A helicopter does not want to fly. It is maintained in the air by a variety of forces and controls working in opposition to each other.

— *Harry Reasoner*

"Jesus," remarked the nurse pouring coffee in the makeshift buffet sideboard they had set up for food and drinks. "What is *that*?"

The Aleut children had gathered on their lawn to watch ...

Tess was practicing her landings in the Vought Sikorsky.

The new, ungainly, experimental aircraft, the helicopter, represented a new way to fly. Where an airplane gets its lift from its wings speeding into atmospheric resistance, the helicopter's rotary blades spin around and around in a circle, like spinning blades on a beany cap. The rotary blades allow the helicopter go straight up and down, and to maneuver deftly back and forth, or hover like a bumble bee.

A helicopter moves along short trajectories that would snap an airplane in pieces.

It requires no runway. It takes off and lands vertically.

The helicopter represents a new method of manned flight. It took off and landed vertically, not moving very fast in a horizontal fashion. It was nothing like an airplane. Helicopters can remain stationary in the air. They can move in all directions, while an airplane can only move in one direction. A helicopter has no wings, only thin rotors, which spin around and around like a ceiling fan, on a central shaft.

The Vought-Sikorsky 3000 model was small, with room for three passengers. Delicate machines, the early helicopters were mostly metal frame and canvas, as light a construction as could be imagined. A skeleton of aluminum connected the main body to a rear rotor, which helped stabilize the copter. The pilot, equal parts artist than mechanic, controlled the V-S 300 with a stick.

"Wouldn't want to see that Bug coming over the rise ..." said the nurse as she stirred her coffee.

Next to the sleek Warhawks and sculpted, muscular Liberators, the VS 300 was a neglected puppy. Powered by a single three-blade rotary 75- horsepower (56 kilowatt) engine, it existed somewhere between an ingenious toy and fighting aircraft.

Pilot Tessa tilted the machine, testing gravity with dangerous angles and sudden swoops, seemingly inches above the asphalt. She seemed to lose her bearings twice. She hovered ten feet above the tarmac. She turned the Sikorsky on its axis like an ice dancer. Overconfident, she accelerated upward in lurches, close to out- of-control.

"Looks like she's getting the hang of it," commented Gia.

* * *

"Let's fix that salute of yours, Brooklyn Girl."

"Lower Manhattan," corrected Gia.

"Same difference. Give it to me, girl. Look sharp, now."

Tess got in Gia's face and made a crisp salute, tucking in her thumb, moving her hand at right angles to her brow and then slickly downward.

Gia returned the salute.

"That's *weak*," pronounced Tess. "That's pathetic."

"You're a hick," replied Gia. "A Texas hillbilly. What do you even know?"

"I know that your new celebrity status is gonna keep you busy for a month or two."

She motioned behind Gia, along the hangar wall.

A line had formed in the gaping open maw of South Hangar Two.

"Your petitioners," chuckled Tess.

"Wasson's been telling everyone how wonderful you are," she continued.

"Everyone's noticed all the upgrades. The doctors and nurses pretty much worship you ..."

When the two women returned to South Hangar Two, they found bags of fresh meat waiting ...

Gia looked around for that boy, that hunter, the one named after wolves. Or was it wolverines? She could not see him anywhere ...

9. VISIT FROM THE AIR COMBAT GROUP

Another twelve large fuel tanks containing aviation fuel were constructed on the hill overlooking the valley, used to refuel the seaplanes that soared in the Aleutian skies.

An estimated capacity of 15 million gallons of diesel and aviation fuel and thousands of 55-gallon drums of motor gasoline combined for a massive gas station in the middle of the Bering Sea.

– Julia Pinnix

A day later, the tall Aleutian boy named after wolverines stopped moving.

Eliasena and two other women were chaperoning recess activities on the bug grassy lawn in front of the Lodge.

The horses had heard it first. Tay had heard the horses.

The loud and animated gaggle of children were laughing and calling out names as they played 'One foot high kick.'

Three dots had appeared in the sky, north of them ...

Something entirely different from recess was about to happen ...

Now Tay was looking up at the western sky --

Tay reached for his rifle.

The radar siren adjacent to South Hangar Two sounded, a nose to strike fear.

"*Amangudagan!*" Tay shouted to the children. "Yonder! Under the eaves! Like we practiced -- "

They continued playing. Several stood watching the dots in the sky get bigger and bigger ...

A figure appeared from within the hangar, racing across the landing strip. Running hard --

It was Gia, coming straight for the kids –

"They've got the wrong valley!" shouted Gia. "They're after the fuel tanks -- "

"Get under the trees!" shouted Tay.

A trio of Mitsubishi A6M Zeroes were coming straight at the Aleutian compound.

The *Hiko Sentai*, the Emperor Hirohito's 11th Air Squadron, had decided to pay a visit.

An east-blowing wind had deceived the children and their keepers. The marauding planes were much closer than they sounded --

Now came the ripping, cruel slams of volleys of bullets strafing the compound. Death-dealing machines had arrived at the nursery school.

"They've got the wrong valley!" shouted Gia. "They're after the fuel tanks -- "

"Beneath the roof!" cried Gia. "It's camouflaged -- "

Having missed the valley with the fuel tanks, the Zeke pilots had decided that someone had to pay ...

The enemy aircrafts' thin, high drone thickened into an eerie, distinctive roar, well-known among combat aviators, a mean, hunting sound somewhere between a jammed throttle and a medieval dragon.

Now pings whipped the ground.

A sharp sequence of explosions let them know the clay pottery along the benches had burst.

The three Zeroes' 77-calibre speeding shells sank with a *Thunk!* into the Lodge's wooden walls.

In the barn and pens, horses and mules and chickens bleated and whinnied and rose up in panic. One mule hurled himself against the cattle pen in sheer disbelief at the turn of events, and the closeness of death ...

Gia ushered the children under the Lodge eaves. The women carried them inside.

Those toddler figures across the way huddled beneath a canopy of trees, hoping the foliage might protect them from whistling death.

But too many of them were still out in the open --

No American planes had yet scrambled to meet the marauders. Now it was too late.

Gia watched as two of the Zekes continued straight south, headed home.

One turned for another pass ...

Gia looked up as the third airplane climbed and turned for another pass.

"Dal cure fredo!" cursed Gia.

On one knee, under the branches, across the lawn, Tay took aim with his rifle and let go six fast salvos at the incoming Zero --

Seeing fear and mobbing among a nearby cluster of confused toddlers, he threw down the rifle and scrambled to herd them into the pine grove --

At the same moment, Gia saw two little figures in parkas standing, oblivious, on the near side of the lawn. One of them was Meriwa, the little girl in purple –

They're deaf –

As the third Zero lowered and settled into its lethal strafing run, Gia swept the two girls in her arms.

Gia watched as two of the Zekes continued south, headed home. One turned for another pass. She cursed bitterly.

He's flying right at me ...

Bullets tore through the lawn and lined up speeding straight towards them.

Zip and thud sounds surrounded her, then an impossibly loud roar.

It was as though the diving Zero knew her, and wanted to kill her specifically.

Gia could smell the soil being thrown into the air. At the edge of her vision, she glanced a tall figure running across the lawn towards her --

Gia got a glance at the plane's underbelly. The Zero seemed to wave the wings as he passed, in some kind of mirthless salute ...

Gia stumbled –

She shielded the two toddlers with her own body --

Then she felt Tay land on top of her, knocking her breath out --

The Zero roared --

The livestock panicked and whinnied and slammed into walls and stall cubicles. A mule burst through the corral fences --

A woman cried out –

Gia felt the impact of the bullets as they struck Tay --

Ugh!

She tasted iron in her mouth.

The Zero zoomed and swept up and away, so close above them, letting loose a monstrous engine-call of victory.

Now Gia could hear the girls crying.

How did they get so far away...

Strong hands reached to lift her. She heard his voice --

Now she was falling backwards ...

Gia's world went black.

* * *

The young Aleutian hunter, Tayra, named for wolverines, awoke in the infirmary.

Soft sunlight through the window fell across his face. He ran one free hand through his hair, to get it out of his eyes.

Gia sat sleeping beside him, slumped in a big chair. She was wearing a regulation U.S. Air Force anorak, a bulky parka two sizes too big.

Tay blinked his eyes, getting used to the light. He studied her features. Her cheekbones, her skin. Her breathing. The way her hair framed her face.

Gia's left hand was holding his. Next to his, her fingers looked delicate and slender.

Now she stirred. Her eyes fluttered open.

"Hey!" said Gia.

He tried to get up. He fell back with a wince.

He glanced at the corner of the Infirmary room, where a giant pile of paper flowers and carvings and whalebone good luck trinkets and well-wishers' cards had been neatly arranged. Many were written by children,

"You've been out for two days," said Gia. "You've had visitors."

He took a drink of water, through a straw.

She removed something from the pocket of her jacket.

She showed him two 77-millimeter bullets. From the Japanese planes. The long, lethal cylinders caught the light.

"You were hit twice," she told him. "And you still carried me twenty yards to the longhouse.

"*Why did you do that?*" she asked him. Her eyes welled up with tears.

"You saved those kids' lives," said Tay. "You didn't even think about it ..."

A knock sounded on the door.After a pause, the door creaked opened. Seeing the patient awake, two nurses entered.

They set to changing his bandages, clucking and fussing over him.

Gia turned away, wiping her eyes with a handkerchief. The tears would not stop.

10. THE PLAN

"Do you know what it is?"

"No. But it's coming closer..."

 – *Frank Schatzing*

Supposing I were to ask you, as a stranger
going to the West, to seek that which is lost.
What would you say then?

 – *The Man Who Would Be King*

"*Ukudigal*," said Gia.

"Ukudigal," said Tay, smiling.

The young hunter arrived at supper time two days later. One of his arms was in a cast and sling.

"What is this?" he asked, when the main course was served. "What do you call this?"

"Spaghetti."

Tay looked at Gia.

"It's pasta. Wheat, made into noodles. The sauce is mostly tomatoes. Onions, peppers. Some herbs. Like that."

"How do I eat it?" he asked.

She showed him, twirling strands of spaghetti on her fork.

He tried.

Tay tried again, blocking the spaghetti up against the heap of vegetables. He tried to use his wounded arm to spin the strands.

"It's Italian," explained Gia.

"I don't know what that means."

"Italian. As in, from Italy. How could you not know that?" she laughed.

"This is good," he responded.

"Why would I need to know that?"

"Well. My people are Italian, that's why. Don't eat so fast. It hurts the stomach."

"My sister tells me the same thing," replied Tay. "Is there more of this?"

She served him a second plate of spaghetti with red meat

sauce, including this time a bunch of the grapes she had been saving for him.

She placed a warm basket of bread sticks beside his plate.

"I've scammed you, right here," said Gia.

Tay grinned. He finessed another bite of spaghetti onto his fork.

"I asked you over here so I could get your help," said Gia.

"I figured," he replied, through a mouthful.

She placed a heavy contraption on the table.

"This is a tree-mounted motion detector camera. The lenses finally came in last night."

"*Ihagee Kine* Exakta," continued Gia. "Thirty-five millimeter. Single-lens reflex. These are pretty rare."

Besides the cameras and lenses was an activity counter and wind-and-weather- instruments, all to be mounted on the camera's housing. Wires connected the camera and apparatus to a bulky battery pack.

"We need to install a system of these cameras across the islands. So we can get a good look at those *dannazione* Zekes.

"With this data, our boys will have half a chance. When we send our planes up."

"How many of these are there?" asked Tay.

"Nine sites, in all. You can see here ..."

She showed him the maps, well away from the food.

Tay left his seat to look closely.

"I know where those are," he concluded. "I can get us there. But it's a lot of distance to cover."

"Tess can get us to these outlying ones," said Gia.

"In that flying thing?"

"Roger that," she answered. "It will save us days of travel."

Gia brought out an oversized book. The cover was brown leather. She put it on the table and opened it.

The title page was a single sepia photograph, enlarged, with white title lettering proclaiming *Motion.* The photo showed a crowd of Manhattan commuters, mostly men in coats making their way walking across a plaza in Manhattan. The figures were blurry, but the buildings around them were clearly defined.

"This is by a photographer named Edward Muybridge," explained Gia.

She turned the page. "He set out to capture how things move." She flipped through pages of photographs showing a motion-studies taken of horses galloping, birds flying, in dozens of sequences.

"This is what we want. This kind of breakdown for the Japanese planes."

"Ah," said Tay.

He looked closely at the horse sequence. It seemed as though a secret was being uncovered.

"Look," commented Tay. "The horse never has all four hooves in the air at once. One is always touching the ground. I never knew that ..."

He turned the pages, finding similar studies in motion -- a man running, an ostrich.

"Okay. I understand."

He closed the book and looked at Gia.

"When do we leave?"

11. STATIONS

It must have required many ages to discover that a brace of pheasants and a couple of days were both instances of the number two.

  -- *Bertrand Russell*

Kutkh is a raven god, or spirit, important to Siberian and North East Asian shamanic tradition ... a link between the worlds of the living and the dead.

  --*Rick Clarke*

A vast silence reigned over the land ... it was the masterful and incommunicable wisdom of eternity laughing at the futility of life and the effort of life. It was the Wild, the savage, frozen-hearted Northland Wild.

  -- *Jack London*

Two horses with riders and then, after them, two pack horses walked the gangway of the gunboat *Casco* and set out into the broken landscape of the Aleutian island of Shemya.

The last three stations, clustered along the north-west side of Sweepers Cove, were inaccessible to the helicopter.

Tay and Gia would have to find and equip the observation sites on foot.

"We should be good," said Tay. "Two things. One: critters.

Stay clear. Move slow around them. Two, river ice." He had explained this several times on board.

"It's a nice outlook. Last time there was a hot springs."

"We might surprise a few moose or snow hares or even a family of wolverines. But they're not hunting us."

"Doesn't your name mean 'wolverine'?"

"Yup. But the wolverines don't know that."

* * *

Before long they fell into a rhythm. The horses gradually became convinced that the snowy landscape did not hide leaping cougars or clawed dragons, and fulfilled their roles in the portage steadily.

"That book you showed me ... what was that?" asked Tay. "All those men in coats, in the pictures. In the city. Where were they going?"

"Offices," explained Gia. "Every day they go into those tall buildings. Rooms with tables and chairs and windows and telephones"

"Huh," said Tay. "And what do they do, indoors like that, all day?"

"I don't know. Different things. Insurance. Stock brokerage. Hold meetings. Talk on the telephone. Make decisions. They set their companies' budgets. They supervise construction of dams in Egypt, or shipbuilding in Holland, so the men who work under them are good to go."

The Aleutian hunter squinted in the Arctic distance, nodding his head, slowly, thoughtfully.

* * *

Arctic rivers are treacherous little ice creeks running along the tops of much larger rivers. These grander rivers flow beneath the surface in ways you cannot imagine.

Aufeis is a term for unpredictable sheet ice. River water flowing underneath a frozen surface can come up through cracks and form new layers, treacherous to any walker. *Aufeis* ice can spread out along the sides of a river channel.

Arctic rivers are much more than they seem.

Twice they dismounted, so Tay could walk each horse across such streams. He made his way slowly over every one, suspiciously, so he knew exactly where their safe path forward was. He carried Gia across.

They followed a trail along a gulley.

Arctic rivers are treacherous little ice creeks running along the tops of much larger rivers.

They saw the wild horses, remnants of the herds of Russian horses from eons since. The herd followed its lead stallion pass along a ridge to the south of them. Gia said she had never seen anything like that.

A small avalanche fell in the horses' wake.

"How much money would it take," Tay asked, "to fly from Juneau to where you live?"

"I don't know. Maybe eighty dollars."

"That seems like a lot," he surmised.

The leather of their saddles creaked as they rode.

"I used to sell beaver pelts, over in the markets," said Tay, as though he had just been asked.

"In Nome. Sold salmon, too. Elk meat. Before all this, you know. So. I have some money."

"Smart," said Gia.

"Elle, my sister," continued Tay. "She keeps the money for me."

"She seems responsible," said Gia.

Tay grunted.

One of the pack horses, a nervous young Percheron, balked at some phantom threat. Tay went back to soothe him.

* * *

By late morning, they arrived at the Sweeper Cove site, where the last three stations – 7,8, and 9 – would be installed.

The campsite was a small clearing beneath a bluff, facing the stream, and Sweeper Cove beyond. It overlooked a shallow fjord, or Alleyway, that Sheila had noticed on the maps way back in Morningside Heights. Others had been there before, providing to them a big timber lean-to and a ring of stones for a fireplace.

A large-basin hot springs was tucked into the bluff,

bubbling and steaming. Gia climbed up to take a look at it and laughed. Those same faults that allowed the entombed arctic rivers to seep upwards allowed thermal bubbles to emerge from deeper in the earth's crust.

Stands of fir trees across the stream blocked part of the expansive view of Sweeper Cove.

They unpacked. They needed to install three stations, 200 yards apart, one pointed due west and one pointing almost all the way north.

Tay set up a tent and a fire. Gia began drilling in the ice with the hand auger, as she had seen him do. It was hard work. The ice did not give way easily.

Tay fed and watered the horses and put them in blankets, underneath the stone overhang.

Tay took over the augers while Gia set up each of the three cameras.

The first station took over an hour. The second and third went faster.

Gia loaded the film and adjusted the mounts carefully, looking through the lenses to make sure they lined up. She swiveled them to make sure. She swore when Camera Two clicked accidentally.

Tay sunk the poles deep into the ice. Working together, they wrapped and attached each component, going one by one until all three cameras were secure, primed, and ready for action. The battery cables were fussy in the cold.

* * *

Gia was walking back from the southern station, on the

far side of the stream, when the mother wolverine showed her face from among the trees.

She made no sound.

Wolverines do not retreat. Wolverines do not back down from a fight. They seem to be quite aware that the rest of the animal kingdom underestimates them.

Gia froze where she stood.

"Tay," she said, calmly.

She was close enough to see the animal's sharp teeth and long claws. The fur around the wolverine's neck was standing. She seemed ferocious and ready to fight, striking from low to the ground.

Tay bolted the rifle.

This distinctive metallic sound gave the wolverine pause.

Wolverines seem to be quite aware that the rest of the animal kingdom underestimates them.

No animal picks a fight they don't need, especially with a big, strange enemy.

The mother wolverine turned. She walked back into the snow and pine trees.

They waited in the stillness until the animal sounds had receded.

Relieved, Gia crossed the stream –

She instantly slipped.

Her head bounced on as she fell heavily. The hidden *aufeis* ice sheet cracked and gave way and Gia Tomasso of Sullivan Street was being swept downstream by the powerful hidden river beneath, sucking her downwards even as it raced her away, downstream, toward the sea.

Tay leapt into the arctic waters.

He had to swim hard among great shards of ice to catch up with her –

Twice she slipped from his grasp.

At last, he pulled her, drenched and spitting water, out of the arctic stream. He quickly carried up the stone steps her to the hot springs.

The springs were a portal to those fathoms-deep, volcanically heated regions of the earth's mantle, typical of many such hot springs in the Far North. Smaller than most, this one had a wide shallow deck around a deeper-water circle or cinque in the middle.

Tay seated Gia on stone benches so she was seated, yet most of her body was under the warm spring waters.

She removed layer after layer of her ice-laden clothing.

He climbed down, to give her privacy.

Tay, equally drenched at his companion, stoked the little fire.

Gia threw an angry fit at him, insisting he would freeze that way. She rose and pulled him into the hot springs.

"You're too skinny," Tay told Gia at some length.

"You mean it," she remarked, shivering. "You think I'm too skinny."

Steam rose as the thermal waters continued to bubble and steam, striking the cold air.

Gia pulled Tay closer to her, there on the stone bench.

* * *

Two nights later, it was an odd task force that made the midnight sortie. Seven kayaks, three barges towed by six tugs, and the gunboat *St. Louis* picked their way silently through the arctic concourses and mazes of inlets on the way to the very furth or narrow inlet which Sheila had identified all those weeks ago.

It was there they would make their gambit.

Alley 761, on the unoccupied island of Akutan.

Akutan Alley 761.

At the terminal point of that inlet, they mounted a gigantic trap, complete with tilt-up wood frame, jute nets and wire cable riggings, sandbag counter-weights and pulleys, coils upon coils of woven sisal hemp. Struts kept every component in place, according to Gia's meticulous drawings.

12. ONE STEP BACK

I see you, fingers splayed, counting on your fingers.
I know what you're counting.

— *Paavo Haavikko*

"You can't do that," Gia said, without looking up.

Icicles seemed to form on her words.

"You can't just leave like that," Gia told the young hunter, trying to stay calm, when Tay appeared in the bay one morning, after hunting.

Two days and three nights hunting.

"We were looking for you," Gia told him accusingly. "To gather the cameras. Tess and I had to do it ourselves. We just got back.

"It took *a day and a half* without you -- "

Tay cupped his hands around his mouth and called out. "*Fiteen fitty* naow. Toosday, Monday, Sat'day! *April!* Repote. Repote. Tin four! *Tin faw!* Oh-nine! Oh-niner! Oo-rah!"

"*Che diavolo!*" exclaimed Gia, moving menacingly towards him even as Tessa came between them.

"I hunt for my family," stated Tayra flatly. "In Baku. Thirty of my cousins and aunts and uncles. If I don't hunt, they don't eat."

"Your first fight. This is excellent!" said Tessa encouragingly, arms extended as if to embrace them both. "What we have here is a healthy exchange of viewpoints...

"Aloots time, military time," she refereed, "that's all it is. Just different *senses* of *time* -- "

"*Come ahi potuto farmi in cosa del genere* --" said Gia darkly.

"She's a little high-strung," Tess said to Tay. "She's been working around the clock -- "

"I'm right here, you know," Gia reminded Tess.

"*Clock,*" said Tay.

"C'mon now!" Tessa urged Gia. "Today's the day. Isn't that

the SRG motto? Today's the day.

"Let's *get 'er done!*" exclaimed Tess. "Git this show on the road, Gal! Work to do! Whattayasay ..."

"Fiteen fitty naow. Toosday, Munday, Sat'day! April! Repote. Repote. Tin four! Tin Faw. Oh-nine! Oh-niner!"

Tempers cooled. Tess carefully laid out and then labelled each station camera.

Two lenses had cracked from the cold. Camera six had frozen altogether.

Most had survived.

* * *

Around midnight, Tess looked up.

She sat on the hangar floor, disassembled rotors surrounding her.

"Hey," said Tess.

"Pep talk," said Gia.

Gia sounded dejected. Her shoulders slumped in exhaustion. Dark circles framed her sunken eyes.

Tess put down her wrench. She cleaned her hands on a rag.

"Lady," she began. "As hard as the road is now, that's exactly how glorious it's gonna be when you succeed.

"Nothing good ever comes easy. *Nothing.*

"This is *exactly* what you're equipped to do. You've been *trained.* No one else can do this.

"You are a Smart! Young! American! Woman!" Tess ticked off three adjectives and one noun on her fingers. "With all the modern means of production at her right hand. A Sikorsky. Fourteen Warhawks. A dozen of American's finest pilots. Omigod.

"You're a pioneer. OF COURSE it's hard. *Yeah* it is! You are like Amelia frickin' *Earhart.* Cut from the same cloth. Uh huh.

"Sheila would want you to do this right. The way you know it has to be done, Girl.

"Tess has your Six.

"Today is the day.

"You are the one.

Gia nodded in agreement with this train of thought.

Tired, she stared at an upper section of the wall, as if considering some far-off phenomenon – white-tailed comets and meteors in their elliptic orbits, perhaps, or crocodiles in swamps, bright eyes gleaming just above the surface, or maybe those far-off lagoons in the southern seas, where jet-black damselfish farm their algae gardens alongside single-cell zooxanthellae, quietly building coral reefs like rainforests.

"You're right," Gia surmised, rising to her feet.

"*I got this.*"

* * *

Inside the closet she had converted to a photo-developing lab, in the dimmed light, Gia muttered to herself.

She held one of the brown-glass bottles up to the light-box.

She checked the thermometer.

The timer dinged.

Standing over the large developing tank, Gia carefully probed the blank sheets of photographic paper floating in the chemicals, using oversized tweezers, waiting for an image to appear.

She had practiced it so many times ...

Why is it still blank?

Had she diluted the solvent developer too much?

She re-checked the charts.

Reels hung from the cords along the wall over the sinks. Beakers were stacked on shelves behind her.

So many of the shots had misfired. Those few which had operated as intended had yielded odd, useless imagery.

All that effort, for nothing ...

Then she had seen Station 5, Roll 3, Frames 22-26.

Then she had seen Station 9, Roll 1, frames 1-7.

Now, why wouldn't this new image resolve? *What had she done wrong?*

Was it 3 parts to 2, or 5 to 3??

Then she saw it.

Something appeared on the giant photo sheet.

It was a face.

It resolved slowly, as though by magic ...

It was a photo of Tay. He was watching over Gia. They were walking in a forest.

His eyes shone fiercely through the dark mop of hair that falls across his forehead. His gaze and his aspect suggested a fierce attention to detail, the kind of attention a father wolf might show as he shepherded his family in a land full of murder and danger, hearing the rustle of enemies in the woods.

12. JUST SWELL

Airplane pilots are open, clear eyed, buoyant extroverts. Helicopter pilots are brooders, intro-spective anticipators of trouble. They know that if something bad has not happened, it is about to.
--*Harry Reasoner*

"Just ... " said Gia. "Swell. Just swell! Isn't it?

"It's not working. Is it?" she demanded of the tabletop. "It's not GOING to work.

"I can THINK I'm making progress, but when --

"You're tired," Tess interrupted Gia's self-blame failure ritual. "You haven't slept for two days.

"Hey!" Tess turned. "Look who it is!"

A tall figure approaching in the light dusting of falling snow. Tay. He carried two heavy bags, a cache of fresh meat.

"To replace that cat-food you eat ..." said Tay.

Gia put her pencil down. She smiled. She went to open the bags.

More and more of the nurses had been eating in the kitchens of South Hangar Two.

Gia carried the meat and deposited it in one of the banks of refrigerators. Tess took the second bag. When she returned from the coolers, he was still there.

"I wanted to show you something," said Tay. "It's just up the hill. There."

"Okay." Gia pulled her hair back and pinned it. She grabbed her gloves.

Tess watched the two of them make their way through the snow, falling heavier now, moving towards the lodge and perhaps beyond.

They fell in, walking close together, in rhythm, like a couple.

* * *

"Is this a date?" asked Gia.

He hesitated, unsure of the word's meaning.

"Yes," replied Tay. "Yes, it is a date."

They could see, through the darkening sky, a slip of the Northern Lights flickering.

"You're not married, are you?" asked Tay.

"No," replied Gia with a laugh. "I'm not married. Are you married?"

He shook his head.

"Why are you laughing?" she asked.

"You would have known by now," he replied.

They walked past the longhouse, past the stables, past the barns. Horses looked them over.

They turned onto a path that led into the pine forest and up into the foothills.

They came to a clearing and stopped.

There, in a clearing among the pines, raised on a bluff, sat a cabin. Chimney smoke rose from a chimney. Rocking chairs waited on the porch.

"This is my place," said Tay. "For when I have a family of my own."

The cabin was not that far from the tribal longhouse, but because it was around the bend and protected by fir groves, it seemed like a world apart.

The cabin looked small from the front, but if you moved several steps left or right, you could see that it extended and expanded.

"I've been building it for two years," he told her. "It's private," he added.

"I see that," she said.

He walked off a square on the little house's eastern side, leaving a line in the snow as he walked.

"The mud room goes here. The dining room over ... here.

"See that red string? The plan is for a second bedroom over

... here. I think a closet would fit."

They entered the cabin. A fire crackled in the living room, under a high, angled roof.

They warmed their hands.

"I found some of the white birch for the floorboards," said Tay. "From Umitak. Two islands over. She's pretty solid." He stomped on the floors to demonstrate. "Took two days to portage."

Gia took off her gloves and bent down, to run one hand along the smoothed wood floor planks. She murmured her appreciation. Care had been taken in laying that floor.

A staircase led them up to a trap door in the ceiling and then to the cabin roof, which was laid out like an observation deck.

Tayra of the Wolverines had arranged two oversized wooden slat chairs on the roof so they could watch the skies, with blankets on their laps.

The Vikings thought the phenomenon of the Aurora Borealis -- the Northern Lights -- was light reflecting off the armor of the Valkyrie. As it turns out, the Aurora Borealis is formed when energized particles from the sun slam into Earth's upper atmosphere. Our magnetic field protects us by redirecting the particles towards the northern and southern poles.

Tay descended and returned to the rooftop with two cups of steaming tea. They sat together.

"You know, there's a store over there in Juneau," said Tay at some length.

"It's like a grocery store."

Tapestries of blue and red and mostly green played out

above them.

"They sell spaghetti, I'm pretty sure," he added.

Now the lights refracted through the distortions in light from the falling snowflakes.

"Yes," replied Gia. "Yes, I'm sure they do."

Now it was her turn to figure out what he meant.

This, all of this, on his part, she concluded, was as close to a proposal of marriage as a man like Tay might make.

Gia felt a dam burst within her. Tay's gesture, his unconditional acceptance of her, had released powerful emotions within Gia.

Above, the lights shimmered a particularly bright shade of blue-green. Now violet, at the edges. Now traces of indigo.

Gia had been too busy to properly mourn Sheila. It had been a horrible, violent death. The images of that scene came rushing back to her – and so did the sickening feeling of being all alone. Gia felt as if for the first time the profound strangeness of this lonely place. It was all so sad.

There had been too much to do, so she had packed away all these feelings, all these unprocessed experiences.

And now this arctic forest wolf-boy was offering to share his cabin, and his salmon, and all he had, or ever hoped to have, with her. A steadfast young man wanted to live his life with Gia Tomasso, her and no one else. He had already proven his deep devotion to her. Twice.

Tay listened to her. He wanted to understand her. He seemed to be level with anything she said, or did.

She could feel his loyalty like a physical force, like gravity.

This, it occurred to her. This must be love.

Gia placed her ungloved hand on his.

"I liked that hot springs," she said.

"Me, too," he said.

Later that night, she would teach him dances she knew, the *Hokey Pokey* and the waltz and more, on that little roof deck. She would hum, *It's Always You* and *This Love of Mine*, trying to sing like Sinatra.

But just now, the Math Girl from Sullivan Street in New York City and the young Unangax hunter were happy looking up, sharing all of this, seated in oversized chairs on the roof of a well-built cabin in a pine forest on an island in a string of islands, beneath the luminous veils of color.

The lights undulated slightly, back and forth, hanging in the night sky.

13. BEYOND THIS DUSK

We strain our eyes beyond this dusk

to see what ... we shall step into.

-- Charlotte Mew

Always carry a firearm east of Aldgate, Watson.

-- Sherlock Holmes, "The Creeping Man"

The next night, Tommy Dorsey came on the radio in South Hangar Two.

Dusk had long come and gone.

A lone figure stood amid pools of light at the work station.

So worried over every detail of the plan, so consumed that every calculation be tight and triple-checked, so sleep-deprived was Gia that she did not notice the trio of uniformed men.

"Glad to see you're not wearing that parka," said a voice.

Gia looked up from her charts.

Three soldiers stood in the hangar bay.

"We're on night patrol," one of them said.

Something in the way they stood screamed 'Menace' ...

They walked towards Gia.

A long-bladed hunting knife glinted in the moonlight.

"Bring her over here," sounded a low, guttural voice. "Behind the barrels -- "

A tall figure emerged from of the shadows ==

Tay jammed his rifle butt into the first soldier's knee –

Aaagghh!

The man staggered and fell, his knee having been snapped

--

The Unangax hunter swung his rifle and the second soldier went down, blade clattering to the concrete floor.

The third man drew a pistol and pointed it at Tay –

A shot from across the bay rang out. The soldier with the pistol screamed and grabbed his hand --

Tessa advanced, keeping the Colt single-action handgun aimed at the man's head.

This was a serious firearm, the 1914 model, for many years

the preferred weapon of the Texas Rangers. Tessa Smith and the pistol seemed well acquainted.

Tay swept up the hunting knife and jammed it into the groaning *segundo's* leg.

Loud trucks approached. Running steps clattered towards South Hangar Two.

The Military Police --

Tay was gone.

"Nobody moves," ordered Tessa Smith.

14. NEW COMMANDANT

I don't want to get any messages saying,

"I am holding my position."

> *— General George Patton*

Mathematics endures. When the ancient Babylonians worked out how to solve quadratic equations ... their result never became obsolete. It was correct, and they knew why. It is still correct today.

> *— Ian Stewart*

The red light bulb was ON above the door of the South Hangar Two storage closet which Gia had converted to a photo developing lab.

A soldier walked up and made a sudden pounding on the door.

"*What!!*" shouted Gia from inside the closet. "Can't you see that RED LIGHT BULB -- "

"Yessir," answered Private Wasson, her voice shaky. "I mean, Yes Ma'am –

"The CO asked me to come and get you. He wants to meet you."

"I am NOT in his chain of command!" replied Gia, through the door. "I do NOT follow his orders." A string of colorful warnings, in Italian, echoed the sentiment.

Twenty minutes later, the closet door opened.

Gia emerged, tearing the plastic gloves from her hands in disgust.

"*Porca miseria! Bafa--* "

"Got it, got it," interrupted Tessa, who had been waiting. "You're unhappy. How can I help?"

"Well," replied Gia, smoldering.

"I'm out of Diafine. The 35 mm paper is blistering, for no good reason. The overhead projector doesn't work. It needs those special bulbs and there's not enough time to order them from -- "

"No sweat," said Tessa. "I can make shadow puppets, with my hands ... see that?"

Suddenly a Jeep swerved the corner and entered the generous spaces of South Hangar Two ...

The tires squealed as the Jeep braked in the open bay. The lettering on the Jeep's windshield announced, "Mama Tried."

An officer stepped out.

"Thank you, Sergeant," he said to the driver who held the Jeep door.

"Peter Ord." He reached out to shake hands.

"I'm the new C.O."

He was a bearish man, with a booming voice and a personality that seemed to want a larger body. An orange-and-black insignia on his shoulder showed two bars and crossed swords.

"You the Math Girl?" he asked Gia.

* * *

"Sorry I haven't come over here sooner," said Ord. "Now, what the hell is that?" he asked, noticing the helicopter.

"'Vought Sikorsky 300,'" answered Gia.

Ord shook his head. He would leave that discussion for another day.

Tess brought tea. The three of them sat at the big table

"How did you know what we needed?" Ord asked Gia. "How are you getting us all these first-class materials?"

"Supply chains have their own logic," answered Gia. "They were sending you all their spare parts to make their ledgers balance. At the Statistics Group, we had access to all the western bases' data. We could see what was happening.

"So I spent four days with the Seattle warehouse. So we're best friends now."

"Much obliged," said Ord. "It's making a big difference. Morale is up.

"Now. Tell me about this Muybridge operation of yours ..."

"*Banzai*, sir."

Gia pulled out a thick set of plans from the topmost vertical drawer and plopped them on the table.

***

"I see," said Peter Ord at some length.

They had shown him an overview of the location of the 9 stations in relations to the Japanese installations, and the enemy ships *Arare* and *Nenohi*, as well as detailed schematics of what they had in store at the base of Inlet 65.

"And that's where you came in," he said to Tess.

"Yessir. Three months wrangling whirlybirds down in Austin have prepared me.

"Gotta say. Without Gia, we never could ever have planted and then gathered all those cameras," Tess told Lieutenant Ord. "All of this is due to her."

Peter Ord listened carefully to every aspect of the operation plans.

"This is monumental work," he concluded. "*Exceptional*," he proclaimed. "They'll be teaching this in the War College -- "

"My boss, said Gia. "Sheila Atwater. She designed all this."

An assistant spoke in his ear.

"Will it work?" Ord asked Gia.

"Yes, sir. Using Lanchester's Law, your chances of success capturing the Zero 6MG, without all this, is 11.9 of 100. ... and if you initiate the action, with present resources, your chance of success goes up to 33.9%."

Young Commander Ord stood to take his leave.

"So, three in one."

"That's about right, sir."

"Outstanding. To think you were sitting in a high school math class a year ago, eh?" He shook his head.

"I've got some arrests to make. I'll be back tomorrow. We'll go over it all again. Then we'll bring in the pilots for an all-day briefing. Just them.

"Then we're a Go."

He saluted, smiling when he saw Gia's returning salute.

He paused as he climbed back into the Jeep.

"Let's get us a Zero."

15. BIG MEETING TURNING POINT

The trigger doesn't release the hammer.
The trigger holds the hammer back,
until an intentional force arrives.

 — *Saul Dubinsky*

Zoologists have found chimpanzees intuitively follow *Lanchester's Square Law* before engaging another troop of chimpanzees. A group of chimpanzees will not attack another group unless the numerical advantage is at least a factor of 1.5.

 — *Randy Kryn*

"*At ease*," ordered Lieutenant Peter Ord.

"All right. Take your seats. All right. All right.

"We're taking the fight to Hirohito. In the next forty-eight hours.

"An air assault.

"As of now, the base is closed. No communications in or out. You are all confined to the Green Zone."

Base Commander Peter Ord gave a toggle signal.

Twin doors swung open. A column of unhappy-looking soldiers marched sullenly across the floor of the big room. Included were all three of the men who had hoped to pay a late-night visit to Gia in the South Hangar Two. Two of them limped.

The small group exited.

"As you know," continued Ord. "Part of our commission is to develop four of the eastern islands and prepare them for occupation by the U.S. fighting forces. My predecessor fell behind on this directive.

"My name is Gia Tomasso. I'm with the Statistics Group. We've collected some information on the Zero that your XO thinks might be useful ..."

"These volunteers you just saw will be developing sites on the islands of Akutan, Greater Sitkin, and Sand Bay. They will be laying paved roads, building landing strips, generating stations, railroad tracks, shelters and boathouses. All valuable to the American cause. We salute them."

This, everyone knew, was as close to a death sentence as one could draw. In the frozen and unforgiving landscapes of the arctic, the elements will kill you long before a Japanese round.

"Anyone who would like to join them can step out now.

"No? No takers?"

A mild hubbub went through the uneasy group ...

"To clarify. You are either Gung Ho -- all in, on task -- or you are paving roads in Sitka."

A scuffle broke out. Something heavy thudded on the floor.

"The second part of our mission is to kill the enemy. Disable his arsenal.

Here's how we're going to do it."

He clicked a switch and an overhead projector whirred to life.

"Miss Tomasso."

* * *

"My name is Gia Tomasso. Some of you know me. I'm from Sullivan Street in New York City. I'm with the Statistics Group.

"We've collected some information on the Zero that your XO thinks might be useful.

"Five points in particular -- "

A cat call came from the back bench of seats –

"Weston! Sanborn!" barked Commander Ord in response. "You're volunteering. Enjoy Atu."

He nodded to a group of MP's. The two offenders were dragged out.

"Over the past month," continued Gia, "we installed nine motion-capture cameras throughout the atoll.

"We wanted to get any data we could on the Zekes. Most of the cameras did not work. Bears, moose, freezing rain.

"This one did. Lights, please."

Click.

An intake of breath could be heard among the pilots. An unusually clear photo of a Mitsubishi A6M Zero appeared on the screen. It was static shot, like portrait.

"*Point One,*" said Gia.

Click.

There on the oversized screen, as clear as day, they saw an entire Muybridge-style sequence, composed of phases – only instead of a man or a horse or an ostrich, the figure in motion was a Mitsubishi Zero A6M aircraft. You could count the fuselage's rivets, and see reflected light in the cockpit bubble.

These were from Station Five, Roll 3, Frames 22-26.

Gia clicked forward, to whoops and whistles from the audience.

These were the images she had salvaged from Station 17,

Roll 1, frames 1-7.

A second Zero, in fine full focus.

"Look close," said Gia. "What do you see?"

She ran the pointer down the length of the fuselage, along the top of the aircraft.

"No antennae. *No radio.* The pilots in these Zeroes are cut off from one another.

"The Japanese surely hate their pilots ... there should be a wire here... from mid-wing to the tail fin. Ending in an insulator.

"So whatever we do, however we can surprise them, they can't warn one another. They cannot adapt during an aerial encounter."

* * *

"*Point Two,*" said Gia.

"The Zeke carries an extra gas tank. An *external* extra gas tank. See it, right here, along the flank.

"Hit it and either it explodes, or it leaks and you cut their range in half.

"*Point Three.* Twist Inside.

"Here's how they downed your friend Hubbell.

"From Reed's description, we think they used this maneuver – they call it *hineri-komi.* 'Twist inside.'

"This is a diagram we got from Naval Command, of what the Japanese pilots have been using on you. *Hineri-komi.*

"Starts with a steep climb to into a half-loop ...

"Right rudder ... *Click*

"Yaw ... *Click*

"Side slip ... *Click*

"Right here – at the top of his loop – when he is inverted -- this is your chance, and if you miss it –

Click

"Aileron ... *Click*

"Rolls aircraft ... *Click*

"Right rudder ... *Click*

"Twist ... *Click*

"Elevation ... *Click*

"And he's behind you.

"*Booyah.*"

* * *

"Point Four. The Zeke has only 66 rounds. You have twice as many. Once he has shot 66 times, that's it.

"Point Five. Thach Weave.

"A Navy pilot named Thach has come up with a way to counter, or at least blunt, the Zero's air superiority. He calls it the Thach Weave."

This appeared on the screen:

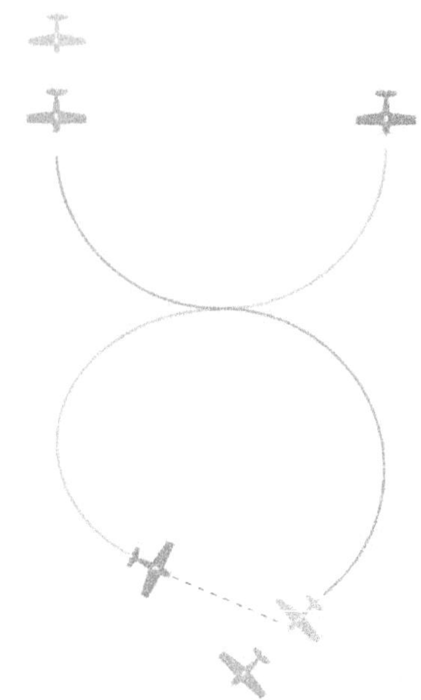

16. CLIMACTIC DOGFIGHT AERIAL ASSUALT

War is a series of catastrophes

that results in a victory.

> — *Georges Clemenceau*

Things seem to be falling apart at a berserk pace.
> — *Stuart Heritage*

To tell you the truth, your death was not

anticipated by the Spirit World.

   — *Yoshihiro Togashi*

Seven Curtiss P-40 Warhawks and seven pilots -- Reed, Piersall, Curry, Little Bobby Hayden, Anspaugh, Jones, and the XO from Hartford, Peter Ord -- flew calm and steady through the early arctic morning skies, ten thousand feet above the Aleutian atoll.

The American squadron had a plan.

Flying at 210 knots in a combat-ready jet over beautiful, purely desolate land- and sea-scapes offered a moment one could remember for a lifetime. If a painter were illustrating the tableau, she would have to use abstract shapes for the turquoise- blue sea and the charcoal-brown lower islands and dawning skies and cotton clouds, juxtaposed with detailed cross-hatching of these very particular, magnificent, man-made airplanes. Feathering at the edges of the airplanes might suggest the human component, unseen but pervasive, for only man would think to ruin the atoll's unparalleled aesthetics with mud roads and rockets and gasoline fuel and entire operations meant only to destroy. The trick would be for the painter to tie it all together, to somehow echo or evoke the meaning of the undergirding shapes that poke through the image's surface, to give viewers a sense of structure. A clever contrast – the flat grey metal surfaces of the aircraft set against the deeper and more painterly, scumbling rich colors of nature, seen in haunting natural light – might reveal some shard of the human condition.

As soon as they passed Akutan Harbor, a quartet of Mitsubishi A6M Zeroes from the Imperial Air Combat Unit rose to meet the American planes.

They must have detected the American flight squadron somewhere around Atu's western coast, when they crossed into what was traditionally Russian territory.

Bbbrrram! Blamblamblam!

The Zero leader let go an opening volley.

Now two American bombers -- one Liberator and one Dauntless – hidden by the escort of Warhawks, broke off, rising to 30,000 feet, an altitude the Japanese would not recognize, since traditional bombing took place at much lower heights.

The Americans intended to use their new bombsights to blow the aircraft carriers *Ryujo* and *Jun'yo* out of existence.

Seeing this new development, the lead pilot for the Zeroes -- the decorated young Daichi Yamada from the farmlands of Haikkado -- broke off to intercept the American bombers.

The Liberator and Dauntless had left too much time and space between point of contact and their target.

Now Daichi would make them pay ...

The big, fat bombers could not maneuver. They would never reach the Japanese carriers.

No sooner did airspace show between Daichi and his wingmen, Warhawk pilot Curry (on the left wing of the formation) swayed off at a sharp angle to give chase.

Two more – Anspaugh and Jones -- did likewise.

Hayden, who had been hit, was still functional.

* * *

One of the Zeroes chased down Hayden, the least experienced U.S. pilot.

Ord moved in to shake the Zero off of Hayden. He let go a short burst in the hopes it would discourage the Zeke, making him break off. It did not.

The Zero climbed and banked, preferring to come at his prey from high and behind, then climbing in a steep vertical to recover, as is typical.

Refusing to quit, Ord came straight at the Zero, firing button depressed., rather than moving to evade or ducking under the enemy aircraft.

The Zero strafed young Hayden. Flames licked his underside.

Ord let loose on the Zeke. Recognizing the external gas tank, he concentrated his fire –

The Zero exploded and spiraled downward to the sea.

But Ord had not seen the second Zero sweeping down to avenge his comrade.

Blazing fire riddled Ord's Warhawk.

He was gone from the skies.

Curry and Piersall turned in a broad arc to face the remaining Japanese squadron in a modified Thatch Weave ...

* * *

Seeing the Americans' weave begin, the northward Zero slipped down, like a knife-cut.

Curry barreled down on him.

The Zero, delineating a smooth scrawl beneath the dramatic cumulous backdrop, lost him.

Curry pulled out of the trajectory –

185

He made a mistake, and was too slow in his turnout --

The southward Zero jumped on his tail and shot him down.

"*Sixty!* That's sixty!" screamed Piersall, who had been watching --

"He's empty -- "

Piersall gave chase recklessly, without concern for his or his plane's safety ...

The Zero could neither return fire nor radio for help ...

"THAT'S SIXTY!" screamed Piersall. "Bud, you are OUT OF AMMO ...

"*Banzai,* f—"

The rest of the Warhawk pilot's battle cry was lost in the curtain of heavy sounds from the aircraft's engine.

The Warhawk struck at full speed into the Zero.

Both planes went down in a spectacular collision.

* * *

Pilot Daichi Yamada, trailing the two American bombers, saw the two Warhawks behind him.

He made a steep climb into a half loop. *Nose up, full throttle and 240 knots and picking up speed fast. Daichi* applied his right rudder to yaw the aircraft ...

Reed recognized the maneuver -- *Hineri komi* -- that Gia had outlined.

"Right rudder ... *Click*

"Yaw ... *Click*

"Side slip ... *Click*

By the time the Zeke had side-slipped, Reed had caught him inverted and helpless. He aimed ahead in the Zero's trajectory -- at the loop's vertical plane -- before the aileron and reverse-rudder could do their work.

But Reed missed.

Daichi spiralled momentarily and then leapt towards the pair of U.S. bombers --

* * *

Now both Reed and Hayden, his plane wounded but still functional, were close on Daichi.

In a sweeping turn, Daichi foiled the attacking fire by ducking into a fjord that appeared on the on Atu coast -- a sort of broad gulley or causeway where he sought to hide from the Americans.

Akutan Alley 761.

Too late, he realized he had been set up ...

The Warhawks split and banked to either side of the causeway.

Daichi was effectively walled off from his comrades.

He had been lured and tricked ... into an alleyway.

And now the light bombers appeared above him, trapping him under a roof.

No outlet above.

Only blue sea below.

Daichi tied to turn, at least enough to open fire –

He missed, but not because the Americans were taking evasive measures, only because the airspace was too cramped.

The Warhawks were not shooting back. They were willing to sacrifice themselves in order to force the Zero ever lower ...

Now Daichi saw that the inlet was narrowing ...

Daichi dipped his aircraft downward, radically down, now flying almost at sea level ...

He saw the nets when he cleared the snowy berm.

The gigantic wooden construction loomed across the furth. Framed gigantic hemp-and-cable spiderwebs, like some rodent trap set by titans. Daichi could see pulleys, rigged thick hook cables, sandbag counterweights and long, thin runouts woven into the mesh.

This behemoth mousetrap was the centerpiece of the plan. This was what had taken Sheila and the Statistical Research Group at Columbia so long to assemble correctly.

Daichi tried to yaw and then to side-slip, but even he could not avoid the netting --

---

Now tracers zinged past the Zero's belly –

Now sandbags fell and pulleys raised the great nets and

their frames of corded hemp. More counterweights zipped upward --

Daichi tried to yaw and then to side-slip, but even he could not avoid the netting --

Daichi rolled hard right and blasted his guns at a crease in the nets --

So excellent was young Daichi Yamada, so skilled a pilot was he, that the Zero almost escaped the nets.

He found a seam between one set of stanchions and the pine trees.

If only the helicopter had not been there,

Without warning, the Vought-Sikorsky 300 rose like some Harpie in a nightmare, tipping, ungainly, hovering over the berm to block the Zero's escape –

What is that thing! Is it actually flying?

Daichi's instinct saved him. He was somehow able to dodge the alien-looking flying craft --

But having done so, Daichi was forced to land the Zero on a gentle bank in the snow meadow.

The helicopter crashed into the trees. Not built for combat, the Vought-Sikorsky crumpled on contact and crashed awkwardly.

Two figures flung themselves into the snowbank –

The helicopter's gas tank exploded --

The magnificent Zero shivered and shimmied slightly on impact, then settled, coming to rest. Its engine revved, squealed, and sank, cutting off.

Aside from smudging along one wing and several bullet holes. The aircraft was untouched.

Gia ran straight towards the plane's gas tank, visible halfway up the exposed fuselage.

"*Gia!*" cried Tess, struggling to stand beneath a pine tree. Her entire left side showed red --

Tay, having been thrown clear, rallied –

One of his legs buckled. He toppled onto one side, into the snow.

Events unfolded in muffled silence, in slow motion ...

The Zero's cockpit popped open –

Several things happened almost simultaneously –

The pilot Daichi, reeling, one arm useless, stood and switched the flare gun from the hand of his broken right arm to the left.

He spotted the plane's gas tank. He took aim --

Gia, knowing the samurai code, threw herself forward to protect the Zero --

Daichi let go the flare gun --

Tay, barely upright, fired a volley at the Japanese pilot --

The rifle made a loud cracking sound.

The flare hit Gia in the stomach and seemed to explode –

"GIA!" screamed Tess. "NO!"

Daichi was spun around from the impact of Tay's bullet --

Tay bolted the rifle and fired again --

Daichi was knocked backwards --

"*Gia!*" yelled Tay.

Listing terribly, Tay reached the Japanese pilot – glass-eyed, now – and kicked away the flare gun.

Daichi spoke. The words were too soft to be heard.

His hands tried to pluck the letter from around his neck, so it could be seen, and delivered, to his home village.

Daichi shivered and seemed to shut off, like a motor that just runs out of gas.

Gia had fallen, partially aflame from the flare, sprawled, against the Zeke.

Tessa shoved snow on her friend furiously, so the uncanny blue-and-red fire would stop its terrible fizzing and burning --

"Today's the day," said Gia optimistically, looking up at the sky.

Her voice was already sinking ...

"Yup. Today's the day."

"Hang in there, sweetheart -- " Tess could not stop crying.

"Actually, maybe tomorrow is the day," said Gia, removing her hand from the red stain which was fast spreading over her parka.

"I'm – I'm not gonna -- "

She added something, in Italian.

Tay held her gently.

"*Stay.* Stay with me," he told her.

Tears rolled down Tay's face.

"We did it," said Tess. "You did it, girl ... "

Gia tried to look over her shoulder at the Zero, nestled like a bird in the snow, legs tucked under ...

"You ..." said Gia Tomasso, recently of Sullivan Street, to

her beau, the taciturn Aleuts hunter.

She smiled.

"*You --* "

Her dimming eyes, once so bright and lively, would not leave Tay's face.

She squeezed his hand.

Above, the witness clouds moved briskly, as though hoping to miss that terrible heartbreak. In the distance floated the dwindling sounds of aircraft engines.

They would find the hero pilot Daichi Yamada with a powder-blue envelope on his chest ... neat, clear lettering. It was addressed to a young lady in Haikkado, that same young lady as seen in the photo on his dashboard.

EPILOGUE

The capture of the Akutan Zero was a prize almost beyond value to the United States.

   — *Jim Reardon*

She is still at my side. She carries her kit of colored threads.

   — *Mei Yao Ch'en*

Historians disagree.

Some say the capture of the Akutan Zero shortened the

war in the Pacific by a year, saving thousands of lives, both American and Japanese.

Others say that its impact was even greater.

The engineers at the Naval Air Station in Patuxent River, Maryland who were dismantling the beautiful Akutan Zeke were awed by Jiro Horikoshi's work.

They made sketches, and took photographs, at every stage of the process.

"Look at that," whispered one of them as the cockpit cowling was removed.

The best design is a conversation, an ongoing dialogue between the user and the designer.

The poets hold that beauty is truth, and truth is beauty. So it was, in that noisy assembly bay by the Chesapeake, among the members of the brotherhood of aviation. Over the weeks, they would discover fully the great care which had been taken. They would experience the full beauty of the Zeke.

* * *

Gia's funeral was held at the Church of St. Anthony of Padua, on Sullivan Street, two blocks down from the building she had bought for her family.

The pews were filled with all manner of people, including members of the High Command who came in from Washington and Virginia. Those self-contained gentlemen mixed uneasily with neighbors and a high school Math Instructor and brainiacs from the Statistics Research Group.

Luca received his big sister's posthumous awards, and the flag at the cemetery. The eulogies were glowing. Specifics of her accomplishments were notable for their absence.

* * *

The girl Mei watched the military vehicles recede along the hill road among the lavender fields, beneath the Haikkado skies.

She was halfway up the stairs. Something was obstructing the third-shelf irrigation, causing a backup; a rodent, perhaps.

The officials had said only that he was missing. They did not know where Daichi was. They didn't say he was dead. *"Unaccounted for ... "* they had said, not *"Dead."*

Daichi had promised to return.

Mei would wait.

She would prepare faithfully for his homecoming. *That would be a day!*

She walked with purpose up the stairs.

She would find and clear the obstruction on that upper level. Water would flow properly once more.

TOM'S STORY NOTES

The Akutan Zero can be seen today at the National Naval Aviation Museum in Florida. You can read the actual story of its downing on History.com

* * *

It is rare for a story of mine to absorb so much effort and thought as this one did. I remember the story "Ulysses S. Grant in China" unfolding easily, like it had already been written. With "Gia Finds a Love," which gestated over a period of six years, each new turn of the wheel seemed to force me to create a new character, and to give that character a new, original contribution to my mini-epic.

One example is Sheila. Once I understood that this person, Gia's boss at the Math Council, needed to be more than a cardboard cutout (like Morant, the building super), I had to step off the Zero-narrative treadmill and give Shiela her due. When I came across an account of European stock markets during WWII, I understood who she might be … and I was able to lend some depth to the Gia-buys-out-her-crooked-landlord episode, as well. Then, as Sheila and Gia shared the same space, the two characters naturally connected. Readers could only find Sheila's sudden death meaningful if they think she is a character who is going the distance, as Gia's sidekick.

I had a romantic triangle ready to go with Peter Ord as the third party (with Tay). Again, no room to take that detour without the main capture-the-Zero storyline losing velocity.

* * *

"World War II" is a misleadingly simple term.

What we now call WWII spans continents, and includes scores of theaters of war, a thousand battlefields, a hundred categories of battles, from feuds over a water well to transcontinental amphibious assaults, from tiny and almost inconsequential events to massive and world-shaking ones.

When I was teaching at Valley Forge Military College, I invited a Vietnam veteran, Joey T., to speak to my class. He fought in the battle of Ia Drang, and he told my class that any time his regiment holds a reunion, the stories never match up. It's like a thousand different battles were being fought in those three days, not just one. Spread across the length and breadth of the Ia Drang valley, everyone's battle was different.

Every war is that way, I think. That is part of why we keep re-telling these war stories, to get all the parts connected, to see some sort of larger pattern.

* * *

Beneath such an event as the capture of the Akutan Zero exists the clash of five cultures -- Aleutian, American, Japanese, Italian, and that of the U.S. Army. I am glad I was able to include at least a little of the Japanese and Aleutian side of things. These points of view are not as common as that of the Americans.

* * *

In the timeless *Saving Private Ryan*, Captain Miller's troop comes across a shell-shocked pilot, sitting in the wreckage of his plane. He explains that the General he was flying had insisted on adding an extra steel plate along the aircraft's bottom, for protection against flak, not realizing that the added weight would throw off the plane's balance so badly that it crashed immediately after takeoff.

The Zero makes the opposite trade-off: master designer Jiro Horikosh tossed away layer and layer of protection to gain speed and maneuverability. Surely it has something to do with devaluing the lives of the pilots .... *bushidos* were sacrificial pawns in the game of empire. Pilots in the U.S. were protected.

* * *

After I block out the pillar scenes of an adventure like this, I try in a second draft to 'see' the dialogue in isolation. I want to make sure the character's conflicts and lines of motivation are clear to the reader. Then a third draft gives me time to figure out the staging of each particular scene -- how the action (and the readers' understanding of it) should unfold. Then I grapple with what the scene is actually about, as opposed to what it appears to be about. My final go-through identifies where to add description and where to leave it alone.

COMMENTARY by Paul Glenshaw

Tom's story *Gia Finds a Love* centers around the efforts of a young mathematician tasked with trying to capture a Mitsubishi A6M Zero in the far Pacific Northwest during WWII. It is based on a true story. One of these top-secret, highly feared aircraft was captured after a crash landing in 1942. Keeping top-secret fighter planes out of the hands of the enemy is as old as aerial combat itself.

It began in World War I, with the first airplane to be able to fire a forward-facing machine gun through the propeller—without shooting it off. A French pilot named Roland Garros mounted steel wedges on the back of his propeller that would deflect the bullets that struck it while the gun was firing. It was crude, but deadly, and Garros quickly racked up the kills. When Garros was shot down, he tried to burn his airplane to keep the secret safe but was captured before he could light it ablaze. The Germans discovered his secret, and developed an even better system, which paused the gun from firing each time a propeller blade passed in front. This was even deadlier.

During WWII, the fighter plane's role was diverse. They were used to protect reconnaissance aircraft, but also to escort bombers and conduct bombing and strafing attack missions on their own. Pilots had to learn how to use their particular fighter to its best advantage. The P-40 Warhawk was designed before the war began and was much slower and less maneuverable than the Zero, which could easily outclimb and outmaneuver it. But the P-40 was much more rugged and could dive a lot faster than the Zero, so American pilots would try as often as possible to attack from above, and dive away, and hopefully outrun the Zeroes.

Fighter aircraft designs took many forms. Some, like the American P-47 Thunderbolt, were extremely heavy and could withstand a lot of damage but needed a huge engine to make it fast and maneuverable. Some had two pilots, most just one. Some had special radar systems to allow them to fly at night, like the P-61 Black Widow. That airplane, like so many others, had great names, like Spitfire, Lightning and Mustang. By the end of WWII, jet fighters, and even some early rocket-powered airplanes had been introduced.

It goes back to the origins of the fighter plane in WWI. The opposing sides of the First World War used airplanes to fly over enemy lines to take photographs of troops and artillery emplacements—so they would know where to aim their soldiers and cannons. These airplanes were unarmed at first. Other aircraft were sent up to shoot these observation airplanes down. Then others were sent up to protect the observation airplanes by shooting the shooters down. It quickly became a race to design airplanes that could outmaneuver whatever the other side was sending up. The advances in design and technology were so rapid and the competition so fierce that secrecy was of utmost importance.

Today, the weapons, guidance, and control systems of fighter planes are extremely advanced, and a single aircraft can perform as much as what took much larger groups of airplanes to do in WWII.

5. Salvage

An only child worries that her family is splitting up. Three eccentric new friends join Sarra in her quest to fly. Rome takes notice. Can Sarra salvage her family Sunken ships and early balloons in First Century Tunis.

PROLOGUE

One parent port, another starboard:
an only child keeps the rocking boat from tipping.
It is a never-ending task.

   – *Sally Schildhauer, A Brief History of the Navigators*

I'm going to say some things.
I'm going to use some bad words.

   – *Robin Green*

"What do you mean, '*It's not ready*'?" asked the Lion of Judah.

Father stood in the kitchen doorway.

A stocky, big, distinguished man, Hiram Ben Yijou was one of the toughest and smartest salvage operators along the northern coast of Africa, if not the entire Mediterranean.

Behind him, the crew of divers took seats around the dining room table, ready for a robust noon meal after fighting the blue waters of the Port of Tunis all morning.

They were ravenously hungry.

"You've been busy writing letters," he said to Mother.

She removed two trays from the oven.

"*Woman ...* " began the Master Salvager.

"Don't you dare 'Woman' me -- " warned Mother. "You had her in the water *all morning!* You *promised,* Hiram!"

"And nothing happened!" rejoined Father. "Look! Look at her! She's fine!"

"And what if she weren't? What then?"

"Then we'd have an injured child AND a late lunch -- "

"My fault!" interjected their daughter and only child, Sarra, age 15.

"It was my fault, Father! I got behind!"

Sarra shoved a bowl of freshly-washed pears and peaches and apples into his hands.

The idea of Sarra being to blame for a late lunch was, everyone knew, absurd, since Sarra was the salvage crew's First Hand, and had been diving the wreck all morning, alongside the *sabah,* the crew of divers.

Her hair was still wet, her fingers still wrinkled.

Hiram glared at his wife, then shook his head, just a little.

Everyone knew what came next.

"Don't the *Philippians* have enough to worry about today, without your sermons riling them up -- "

"They're not *my* sermons, Hiram -- " corrected Mother.

This, Sarra knew, would only lead to a larger, longer argument.

"Start on the pears," Sarra assured her Father brightly. "They look good today -- "

The Lion of Judah reluctantly took the bowls from his daughter.

"*Go* -- " The daughter tried to shove the Lion of Judah back through the doorway. He was too big and heavy. "*Fruit.*"

"*Wife*," he intoned, "it's time for you to make a choice.

"Who do you love more? These *m'tupash* letters, or your own family?"

"Got it, Father, thank you," urged Sarra, before the appearance of the term 'Wife' ignited a new round of bickering --

"Lunch is almost here!" urged Sarra. "Five minutes!"

Sarra managed to shove Father back into the dining room before the argument could continue.

"Four minutes! It's coming! Get your forks ready, boys!"

I. THE WRECK OF THE AGULHUS

What works is different from what people think.

— *Emily Guskin*

Stop hiding, nephew.

It only prolongs the pain.

   — *Ten Rings*

"They had another fight last night," announced Sarra. "He slept in the barn."

Sarra and her best friend, Cyrine, walked among the shrubs and dwarf trees and bushes of the karst, following ancient footpaths, back behind (inland, that is, from) the villa. They hunted berries.

The donkey, Esme, trailed behind, pleased to be outdoors.

"Mother thinks I'd be better off among the Christians and letter-writers, I'm sure," said Sarra. "She thinks salvage is dangerous."

"She's right," replied Cyrine. "It *is* dangerous."

The two girls wound their way past half-intact stone walls and ruined iron gates that were old before Hasan Ibn al-Numan defeated Tiberius at Carthage.

The overgrown trails and grassy cover led them through long-abandoned orchards and gardens and ponds of earlier Tunic eras.

"My Dad thinks your Dad is a genius," said Cyrine. "Says he can find the pivot point on any salvage ship with his eyes closed.

"He also says most geniuses die broke," she added.

"I just wish my parents would stop fighting. Come on, girl." Sarra gently tugged at the rope to pull Esme along. You can graze later, that's right. I promise."

Humid sea winds all the way from France combed the complex landscape of limestone and meadow grass.

Sarra and Cyrine searched for fruits among the yellow, blue and red berries, the sea holly, juniper, and ceretonia.

They came to a hillock overlooking a small ravine.

"My brother says he saw some gypsy wagons out here." Cyrine shaded her eyes and looked out over the northern horizon. Beyond -- further north-west, that is -- lay ancient migratory trails across the wind-swept valleys of the Maghreb.

"I don't' see any gypsy wagons," observed Sarra. "Are we stopping now? Is that it?" She addressed the donkey, who had found a grouping of ripe plants. The girls picked berries and dropped them into their buckets. Sarra could already smell the pies ...

"Which of your parents likes the other more?" asked Cyrine.

Sarra began to answer, then stopped. "I don't know."

"With mine, it's my mother," continued Cyrine.

"Definitely," agreed Sarra.

"She sees him coming and poses against the windows," said Cyrine, shaking her head.

"She thinks if her hair catches the sunlight just so, it will make her look like Cleopatra. It never does. It's sad."

"It's my Father, is the answer," admitted Sarra. "Father likes Mother more. I just didn't want to say it."

"I know," said Cyrine.

"I wonder if *he* knows," said Sarra. "That everyone can tell that about him."

"Well, it's not really a bad thing ..." offered Cyrine.

The mule brayed, frustrated that they had sped up. She had found more berries. Couldn't they see that?

"Do you think your parents would ever actually break up?" asked Sarra.

"Naw," said Cyrine. "True-love Cleopatra would never leave. Or let him leave."

"I'm never getting married," proclaimed Sarra.

"*Yooo-ah*," replied Cyrine, who sometimes preferred sounds to words.

A south-bound wind, all the way from France, bent the grasses.

* * *

It was the flagons that gave Sarra the idea.

Sarra had been underwater, on the *Agulhus* salvage, when she had seen the row of flagons, and saw what they could do.

They were glass tankards, like wine flagons only five times the size, half a dozen of them, very large glass decanters, and they were lined up in a row on a shelf. Narrow necks, strapped snug in place. Each must have been tightly sealed, for no trace of bubbles could be seen.

The wreck was a decade old, by the state of the wood, and well away from shore. The hull had been breached – it was an almost impossible job to re-float it. But times were hard, they had to give it a try.

Whatever was inside those flagons – simply air, perhaps – gave them remarkable buoyancy. On their own, they were holding up the wrecked ship's entire starboard side, even as the damaged vessel listed like a drunken whale.

Painstakingly, she removed the tankards. Each time she moved one, she felt the wreck shift. These tankards were not for liquid storage, but for buoyancy.

Sarra always tried to reclaim something from a wreck. She felt that she was rescuing a bit of that water-born catastrophe from oblivion.

The *Agulhus* salvage would end in failure.

But Sarra would not forget those flagons.

They meant something.

She did not yet know what that might be, but she would find out.

2. ROME ANNOUNCES A CONTEST

During the first three hundred years after Jesus' death, there was neither an organized Christian religion nor a central authority or book.

— *Laurence Galian*

"Is mercy ours to give, sweetheart," Mother asked Sarra as they prepared a half-dozen berry pies two days later. "Or is it God's alone?"

The family's home had once been a small villa, built a century earlier by Berbers. It sat on a bluff overlooking Tunis harbor. The city of Tunis was visible, in the west, from the kitchen and from the deck.

"I don't know," answered Sarra. "You're making my head hurt." She sat at the kitchen counter, dicing fruit with a sharp, serrated knife.

Click, click.

The cutlery blade hit the cutting board.

"Ours, I suppose," she said. "Mercy is ours to give."

"That's what I would have said," commented Mother. "But this new letter says that only God can give mercy."

"How about Jesus?" asked Sarra. She had finished the fruit. She reached for an onion to slice, for the roast. "Wouldn't he handle that, too?"

"No, I don't think so," replied Mother. She turned her attention to arranging the barley and chickpeas and corn and tomatoes and peppers and carrots in a very large, smoke-scarred pot.

"As far as I can tell, his main contribution is his sacrifice. For all our sins, you know. I don't imagine Jesus can be bothered to deal out specific mercies."

She added potatoes to the pot. She added a half-handful of parsley.

Mother was a very good cook. Whatever ingredients she found -- pomegranates, grapes, figs, carobs, orchard fruits, walnuts, hazelnuts -- she could make a *kaak warqa* to remember, with layers of flour and a sesame wrapping.

"Who wrote this letter?" asked Sarra.

"The engineer from Tarsus. Saul." Mother lifted the pot by its handle and carefully placed it on the fire grate, well above the coals. It would cook all day and be ready by sunset.

She added water to the pot.

"Maybe ask the Lion of Judah," suggested Sarra, nodding towards the boatyard where her father was working, visible through the kitchen windows. "He has strong opinions."

Sarra carefully scraped the sliced onions from the cutting board into the pot.

"Too strong, I'm afraid. We'd just get in a fight.

"Oh! Listen to this!" continued Mother, reading from the letter. "Saul writes:

"Now enflame us faith, hope, and love, these three. But the greatest of these is love."

"It's almost poetry!" exclaimed Sarra.

"Such a pretty idea," said Mother as she re-arranged the coals. "But ... shouldn't it be something else? Some other verb. Love and faith don't really burn like flame ...

"Shouldn't it be ... 'These three *exist*'? Isn't that better?" asked Mother.

"'Abide.'" suggested Sarra.

"Now abide faith, hope, and love, these three," tried Mother. *"But the greatest of these is love."*

She set down the iron bar they used to stir the coals.

"Yes! That's better. *Abide.* Hah! Now *that* is poetry -- "

"Can you just change the wording like that?" asked Sarra.

Before Mother could answer, they heard someone open the iron gate in the front yard. Now they heard someone shut it.

They looked to see a familiar figure coming up the pebbled walk. Sarra called Father in.

It was Daiyu, friend and harbor-master. He brought a large section of lamb, barter for Father's work in repairing Daiyu's fishing boat. A curved-hull boat, it had needed the attentions of Father's fine tools – adze, mallets, augurs – to fashion a working keel.

"Lamb! We'll add it to the *tajine!*" exclaimed Mother. "Sarra, help me -- "

* * *

The call to adventure arrived in the form of a contest.

"Rome is holding a salvage competition," Daiyu told Father.

"In five weeks. A contest. Each port sends its champion salvage team to raise a wreck. Rome wants their sunken ships back, and to assess the talent that can do clean-up for add to their Navy, I'm guessing.

"First prize is five hundred denarii.

"Plus, the winner's home port gets extended rights-of-way. Turkish sea lanes. Routes into the Greek harbors. It would benefit all Tunis!

"Rome is holding a salvage competition," said Daiyu one day.

"The new prelate is most ambitious. He knows that promotions up the ranks await anyone who found ways to recover the Admiralty's sunken treasures ...

"All the families want you to go, Hiram. To represent us."

Hiram, the Lion of Judah, was pleased, although he tried to hide it. He thanked his friend.

Above the charcoal fire, the lamb-fortified *tajine* bubbled in its pot.

The lamb broth was beginning to produce that particular and pungent aroma ....

3. THE MYSTERY OF THE VAPORS

Nine out of every 10 atoms in the universe are hydrogen ... the other 10 percent of all atoms are helium.

— Sam Kean

Sarra held the bow sideways, low, in front of her pelvis. An arrow was notched.

Father liked meat.

The *Thalia* salvage had yielded little in the way of treasure, the same with the attempt to refloat a Greek merchant ship, despite Father's clever use of screw pumps. With four strong horses – as other salvage families had – it would have been easy.

Business was slow.

The family could not afford to shop at the butcher stalls among the markets, so Sarra was on the hunt.

She had seen wildebeest among these foothills behind

their property, a rare sight, migrating this far north. Perhaps a small gazelle.

She came to the stone hillock. The ravine below ran along a narrow creek, halfway up a craggy talus slope. Here and there the path dipped through bracken and gorse and curved around a corner.

Again, she led the mule, Esme, over the grassy paths. The two had been toddlers together, grown up together, and Sarra knew that the mule much preferred light conversation and the irregular fissures, half-buried streams and sinkholes of the karst to the silent, fragrant-free walls of her lone stall.

"Come, donkey -- " she muttered as they rounded the path out of the old orchards --

BaBOOM!

A loud sharp crack made the earth shake.

A second deep and booming explosion knocked Sarra off her feet.

What the --

She saw an upshot of dirt and rock.

Two big seahawks – osprey – who had been circling above that spot abruptly plummeted from the sky --

She heard the roar of rushing waters.

That can't be – there is no river there –

An extraordinary sight greeted Sarra as she came over the ridge --

Where once stood a hillock and small cliff overlooking grassy meadows, there was now a rocky outcropping – great broken blocks of talus in a declining slope. Through the raw rock formation now ran a ravine filled by a rushing stream, a combination of strong currents. A gorge had been formed. An entombed river had burst forth into the open from some nameless cavern or riverbed.

A second deep, booming explosion knocked Sarra off her feet.

Now Sarra saw that two women flailed in those swirling waters. They were waving and calling desperately for help --

The girl shucked her bow and arrow and dove in –

Powerful strokes practiced over years of sea-salvage carried Sarra directly to the first woman, who was small and apparently unskilled in waters.

Sarra felt her legs being caught in a whirlpool-like current that sought to take her downwards, into the earth, into some abyss.

With the woman on her back, Sarra swam this way and that. She grabbed for overhanding branches from an olive tree, but she could not reach them.

Sarra called for Esme.

The mule heard her, and came to the edge of the hillock, so that her reins trailed into the waters. Sarra wrapped them around one wrist. With the small woman clinging to her neck, Sarra gripped hard and shouted for the mule to pull, as if this were another salvage operation –

The mule knew to hold fast. Esme stood her ground, even backing up ...

This helped bring Sarra close enough the shore to grab several dwarf pines and rugged shrubs. The sturdy plants held her weight. Sarra pulled harder.

She climbed out of the torrent.

She lay the heaving woman on the grass riverbank and dove back in –

A second swimmer, a larger woman than the first, was weakly treading water at the lip of the whirlpool.

Sarra reached her quickly. Turning her over, Sarra was able to float and kick, pulling her ward toward safety.

Yet they could not break free of the circling clutches of the pool –

A youth dove from the shore to help and quickly disappeared down the cinque, which appeared more like a cavern entrance to the sunken flow.

Two of his friends dove in to save him –

Below Sarra and her companion, downstream, a series of violent rapids and sharp jutting rocks awaited --

Panicked shouts rose from the riverbanks in various tongues.

With a grunt and renewed push, Sarra swam upstream and to starboard. She was able to cross wide, laterally, against the current, towards calmer pools on the far shore --

Many hands pulled Sarra to the grassy berm --

"Hail, girl of the waters!" she heard someone proclaim.

4. THREE NEW FRIENDS: LING NA, GUDRON, AND SATYAVATI

Writings of the society have been traced back as early as Hanno the Navigator, a Carthaginian mariner of the fifth century B.C.

— *Sally Schildhauer, A Brief History of the Navigators*

Three women, three new friends, hovered over Sarra.

"Several faults come together in this basin," said the small, odd Bharat woman as she carefully dried and straightened all her jewelry.

The inside of the big cart was warm and colorful. Walls were opened to show tents and other wagons assembled in a glade. Magnificent horses were being groomed next to a large lean-to.

"The Kasserine, the Rifo-Tellian chain, the Sbiba," continued the Asian woman. "When clay is stacked on sandstsone, interbedded with foraminifera, it all needs to settle. From time to time. The fault lines must have shifted today, and released that accused underground river -- "

"I don't understand a word of what you just said," replied Sarra brightly, toweling her long hair.

"But I have seen a pair of osprey drop from the sky. Earlier today."

Sarra twisted the towel into a bun around her hair.

Sarra looked around. She found herself in a very large, open-walled wagon, in a glade bordering the new river.

"I don't understand a word of what you just said," replied Sarra. "But I have seen a pair of osprey drop from the sky."

A fire crackled. Smoke rose through a chimney in the wagon's roof.

Outside, she could see around several campfires were gathered wagons and tents -- sewn-leather tents, flat-top shades, tents with pentagonal panels and geometric shapes which Sarra had not seen before. Labeled jars of seeds lined one set of shelves, and maps of seas and stars hung above the shelves.

Esme nibbled at flowers outside, nearby.

"So, you went to investigate -- " the woman from India continued, "and you came upon our friends."

"Yes yes!" said the woman who had almost drowned. "Lives were saved this day!"

"Praise Allah! Tell us your name, river-girl."

"I am Sarra. Who are you?" Sarra replied, trying to be polite. "How do you come to speak my language?"

"I am Satyavati. I am a Bihari. This wet rat is my friend, Ling Na. And this poor, coughing thing is my friend Gudron. From Iceland. You saved them both!"

"We three are mapmakers," explained Satyavati. "Navigators. Navigators' wives."

"We speak most tongues," said Ling Na.

She offered Sarra a cup of hot tea.

"We are currently following the wildebeest," said Gudron, the third of the women, whose accent was the thickest. "They usually migrate far south of here. We were curious."

"We are all in your debt," said Satyavati.

"A lifetime's debt, I will say," added Ling Na.

"Those vapors you were chasing, that which felled the two birds – that was helium," said Satyavati. "An ancient gas, from the eons before mankind. Lighter than air, as you saw. Poisonous when breathed directly. Its sudden release must have caused that explosion. And felled the two osprey.

"Pytheas, of Massalia, wrote about it. He found a field of it in the Rift Valleys, far south of here."

"The helium must have been released," conjectured Ling Na, "when the entombed river broke through."

Sarra proceeded to tell the women of her interest in the rising vapors, and the tankards from the *Agulhus* salvage, and how she might somehow help Father in his salvaging.

A long, thoughtful silence ensued.

"Those vapors you were chasing, that which felled the two birds – that was helium," said Satyavati. "An ancient gas, from the eons before mankind. Lighter than air, as you saw ..."

Sarra looked around in specific, taking note of the variety of fabrics which adorned the wagon – silk, canvas, fine Egyptian cloths. She saw instruments a surveyor might use, and an astrolabe. She saw tankards similar to those on the Thalia, packed in long carts.

"Yes," said Gudron. ""I think we can help."

5. DIVORCE

Divorce diverts you, taking you away

from everything you thought you knew

and everything you thought you wanted.

— *For One More Day*

The arguments in the Yijou household worsened.

Father's preparations for the Roman contest dug the family into debt. He carved out more and more time for fishing and for ship-repair jobs, but it did not seem to help. There was always another winch and pulley set to purchase, more feed to buy for the draft horses, feed that they could not afford.

Mother sold her pastries in the markets, sharing a stall with her sister. She continued to serve as scribe for the Christian apostles and would-be apostles. News reached them of flare-ups among the Christian cults vying for primacy in the settlements along the Phoenician coasts.

"You're dragging us into trouble," Father growled. "You're dragging us into debt," Mother would reply.

Even worse than the bursts of vitriol were the long stretches of angry silences.

Sarra was caught between. She adored both her parents. The wretched prospect of the family breaking up kept her from sleep. She gave up trying to reason with either of them. Attempting to referee their fights always ended in disaster.

* * *

"But... but it's just a pivoting *lever*," said Sarra, disappointed.

They were nowhere near ready for the salvage contest.

It was less than three weeks away.

She had heard so much about *tripastos*, and how one of the devices could make all the difference in a hull-hoist. But now that she saw one, it was just a single beam jib, a lathe, and a rope connected to a block of three pulleys.

"Is this it?" complained Sarra. She was expecting something more intricate.

"Don't worry, my girl," urged Father. "It will help. You'll see ... "

"Not half what Esme alone can do," Sarra muttered.

They had been working steadily since hearing of the Roman salvage contest. Other teams had more money and more horses.

Father invested in a treadmill crane.

Sarra watched the road for signs of a messenger from Ling Na, Gudron, and Satyavati, the three women of the caravan. *Had they abandoned her?*

Father and the crewmen built a floating dock – a moored

flat barge, almost – which they could use to dock alongside the wreck and anchor the cranes.

Mother cooked and baked and roasted in the kitchen constantly. She insisted on bringing her husband's crew, the *sabah* divers, Berber coffee and fruit drinks for their loyalty and good efforts.

Father borrowed money from Daiyu to pay for crew hours. They needed to practice the timing of each phase of the Roman salvage. Mother and Sarra and Cyrine wove coils and coils of rope from the sturdy hemp growing in the back.

Father stayed up late at night, tinkering on the pulleys so they could be collapsed and re-struck when needed, so a man could pull several times his weight.

He redesigned the two-man wheeled crane.

"Mighty is the Lion of Judah," said Sarra one midnight, lantern held high, yawning. "But he needs his sleep."

Where are those Navigator women? Sarra wondered.

We should hear from them soon…

Had they been making it all up?

* * *

The Salvage trade is built on someone else's shattered dreams.

The Salvage trade is an all- or nothing- proposition.

The Law of the Find allows for the mining of past disasters, but there is no reward for trying, no stipulation for close misses. The Salvage Master risks his or her own time, money, and effort. Only if a viable marine vessel (or its parts) emerges, or a cache of rubies discovered, is there any reward.

Salvage is a process of problem-solving. One must try to salvage not only the wreck, but the story of the wreck, a reliving of the chain of mistakes which caused the tragedy to come about.

Sarra tried to solve the helium puzzle on her own.

We are going to need the lifting power of those pontoons. With or without the Navigators' help.

How could it work? Sarra asked herself.

How could she capture something that is invisible, and possibly poisonous?

Sarra worried. She tossed and turned at night. There were too many unanswered questions.

* * *

The answers came on the eleventh day.

Two of the colorful, bannered wagons from her three new friends drove up to the gates of her home.

The wagons were driven by two young Egyptians, brother and sister. Well-schooled (at Alexandria) and deft, they stayed an extra day in order to help Sarra and Hiram assemble all of the crates' contents and working parts.

Elaborate instructions from the three Navigator women showed them to run hoses into the thermal pools to access and then close off the trapped helium, explaining that this is how Pytheas of Massalia had done it.

The glass tankards were ugly, but functional. The helium hoses and collars were almost impossible to make work, and the air pumps even worse, but when the full apparatus took its test run, Sarra was much pleased. She had never seen anything like it. No one had.

Most impressive were the two great pontoons. Trunks opened to stacks and stacks of folded silk and canvas. She had never worked with water-tight, air-tight fabrics, and the needles and threads balked, at first. It took Sarra and Mother a day to get the hang of it (it had everything to do with the angles at which the needles were held).

Once sewn and laid out on the back lawns, the pontoons were gigantic – twelve meters across, and seven meters tall. One was pure burgundy and the second depicted two gigantic, brightly colored stars against a blue background.

Sarra, her mother, and her friend Cyrine sewed and re-sewed the layers of silk.

How does it work? wondered Sarra. She found her answer in a note from Gundar:

Heating a gas increases the kinetic energy of its particles, causing it to expand. Warmed as it merges into sunlight, the helium exercises its buoyant or upward force. Hot air pushes out on the air around it, and thus becomes less dense. It weighs less than the air it displaces. The balloons rise.

We now call this Gay-Lussac's Law

* * *

The Navigators' two young messengers also unpacked three dive lights, spear-mounted glass bulbs with magnesium powder on the tip. They might last less than a minute, cautioned Ling Na in her instructions, but they might be useful.

Another carefully-packed crate contained resin, naptha, quicklime, sulfur and reed tubes -- the ingredients for a thing which Gundar in her notes called 'Greek fire.' Sarra read it with great interest.

Over and over, they showed her the procedures for capturing the gas.

"Helium is a powerful form of magic," warned Satyavati. "It can lift an entire ship, if deployed correctly. Yet, like all magic, it brings, it carries deadly danger ... as perhaps those mariners aboard the *Aghulus* found out."

Helium is a powerful form of magic. It can lift an entire ship, if deployed correctly. Yet, like all magic, it carries lethal risk ...

At the end, after inviting Sarra to join them in Alexandria in October, Satyavati wrote this:

Best to keep your pontoons out of Rome's sight. Caesar will misunderstand.

* * *

Sarra injured two fingers of her left hand on practice dives.

"She can't even *write* now, Hiram. See what you've done?" said Mother bitterly.

"I know how much you love her," she continued. "But you are no longer capable of keeping her safe.

"I'm taking her with me. To my family's home," declared Mother. "As soon as this Roman contest is over.

"You can hate me all you want, Hiram. But she'll be alive."

6. THE SALVAGE OF THE LITTLE SYRACUSE

The marine salvage sector has always been

a perfect storm of commercial pressures,

technical complexity and uncertainty.

— *Chad Furhmann*

In their love for the theatrical, the Roman port commissioners had fashioned a single-day contest. Dawn to dusk.

The bells to mark the start of the salvage rang just at sunrise.

All across the port, salvage teams scurried to their assigned wrecks. Shouts and cursers of the crew chiefs filled the morning air. Mallets pounded so oars could be stroked in unison. Sails strained. Hulls creaked. Prows split the waters. Anchors splashed and sunk, cables and ropes were belayed in knots to be slung around cleats. Cranes swung into place.

* * *

Rome had saved a special salvage for Hiram.

Resting on a narrow shelf sixteen meters deep, at the base of a cliff, The *Little Syracuse* was a loose replica of its namesake, one of the premier vessels of an earlier age. Criss-crossing the Mediterranean carrying cargo to feed supply lines to support garrisons of the ports and lowlands as well as the Rhine corridor and, even further north, Gaul, the transport ship was thirty-five meters long, fourteen wide, and twelve high, propelled by sail and oar.

Her pilot had sought to shorten the trajectory on his way to Carthage. In so doing, he encountered the little-mapped shallow shelf beneath cliffs of Tunis. There the fine ship *Little Syracuse* was stuck, its hull mostly intact.

The first job was to map the wreck. While Sarra dove all around the submerged vessel, Hiram and his crew were wheeling winches and pulleys into place and assembling the cranes, which would lift *Little Syracuse* up and out.

"*Oyoyoya!*" ululated Cyrine, in the spirit of encouragement.

"Swim, Sarra!"

Cyrine and her parents and a handful of their neighbors watched from the bluffs. Her mother combed her fingers through her hair nervously.

* * *

Each shipwreck has its own personality.

Each diver is a detective, trying to understand what happened, where the storm struck, where things went all wrong: the story of the wreck. Who did what, what weakness brought about this tragedy.

Blindly yanking on ropes is never the answer. One needs to understand how the ship was built, and exactly how and why it sank.

Using underwater torches – thick-handled sticks with magnesium caps at one end – supplied by the Navigator women, Sarra was able to create a schematic.

Hiram's dive crew gathered around. Sarra drew a picture of the wreck, circling the pull points and marking out the rope-placement positions.

Cranes braced on the twin barges which had been pulled alongside the wreck.

They installed screw pumps.

Blindly yanking on ropes is never the answer. One needs to understand how the ship was built, and exactly why it sank.

They drilled holes in the uppermost, starboard side of the hull.

A storm approached from the north. High winds caught the cranes and the upper deck of the ship.

The *Little Syracuse* shifted in its placement on the shelf.

How stable is it? Sarra worried.

* * *

On the shore, next to one of the barges, Sarra's *sabah* diver-brothers unscrewed the collars to inject the helium into the pair of stitched silk pontoons.

The great silken globes took shape – slowly, at first.

The cranes and pull-horses needed to apply an equal force, so that the great ship's hull was lifted evenly.

They let the pontoons fill out, rising, taking the port side of the wreck with them.

"I don't like it, girl -- " worried the Lion of Judah.

They were being forced to take certain chances.

Hiram gave the whistle for the first pull.

"NOW!" called Father sharply. "PULL!"

A crewman hit the gongs –

Cyrine and the crowd of onlookers cheered.

The mules and horses dug in – the starboard side had to be lifted at the same pace as the port (or pontoon) side, or the hull would collapse.

Father warned his crewmen clear. The risk was not theirs, he reminded them.

The cranes tightened and the lines strained, creaking --

The men in the rotary cranes pedaled fast.

One of the winch reels immediately jammed. A diver, shouting, fell from the high platform. He landed safely in the water. Swarming over the winch, the *sabah* cleared the snag.

But the damage had been done.

The momentary knot had caused slack in the lines --

Two of the cables came loose from their hooks.

Now two of the port-side struts slipped their clamps and went flying.

Seeing this, Sarra dove in, over Father's protests --

Now the force of the pontoons' lift was out of whack. Too much.

The balloons worked too well, and lifted the one side of the wrecked ship too quickly, and too hard –

The port side lurched --

The *Little Syracuse* was knocked ajar –

*　*　*

Sarra needed to try and re-hook the pontoon lines to the mounting struts of the salvagers' wood frame.

Eerggghh!

It was too much. The distance was too great, and increasing with each passing moment.

She grabbed the errant cables.

She fought the pull of the water as well as the tension of the ropes.

If Sarra could not replace the cables, the ship would go lopsided and tumble from its perch into the deeper waters of the Bay of Tunis.

She tugged them back towards their hooks.

It took all her strength –

They moved, but just barely.

The wreck's starboard side was rising --

Why isn't Father stopping? We practiced this --

She yanked three times on the bow line –

The starboard side stopped rising.

Aaagghh !

This gave Sarra the chance to slip the port-side hooks back onto the struts.

She strained every muscle. She bent her knees, and shoved hard against the keel.

Moving in water ...

Father appeared beside her. He took hold of the cables and pulled –

With a last surge from the two of them, she felt the hook go over the clamp.

The hook clicked.

She retuned to the surface, gulped air, and dove back down --

Somehow, they managed to move the second hook until it clicked.

The helium, thrilled in its every molecule to be released from its earthly prison, raced upward to fulfill its destiny alongside neon, argon, radon and the other noble gases, in earth's stratosphere, where it could bask in the sun's pure light ...

The gases expanded.

The fabric contained.

The ship floated.

The Law of Gay-Lussac ever holds.

Gas cannot be denied from rising.

The helium was successfully constrained by the canvas and silken barrier. The gas gained strength and muscled upward with the force of all natural phenomena – water falling down a ravine, an avalanche, a volcano erupting in rivers of lava, the glaciers' advance.

Like magic, the helium-filled pontoon lifted the great seacraft *Syracuse* with it. The two shapes rose, in synchrony.

But a loop of cable had caught Sarra's left arm.

She was being pulled upward by the force of the helium rising --

Wriggling back and forth, Sarra could not escape the rope around her leg.

Now she was vaulting upward, too fast, like a sandbag counter-weight --

Hiram kicked to gain momentum so he could free his daughter –

His foot accidentally snapped one of the cleats –

The hooks caught Hiram and tore into his side. Blood stained the waters.

Still, he gripped the hemp rope that held Sarra prisoner, holding tight, slowing her mad ascent --

Father and daughter were shot ten meters into the air before Hiram was able to free Sarra's arm from the balloon cable –

Both figures fell and slammed to the barge deck, quickly

tumbling off and splashing into the waters of Tunis Bay --

Mother leapt into the water –

Mother could not swim.

Three divers followed.

Sarra caught her mother and swept her upward.

Father and the two divers broke the water's surface --

Sarra held both her parents in a tight embrace, and whether it was from the water or relief or joy, tears burst forth.

The good ship *Little Syracuse*, salvaged.

Sarra's family, salvaged.

* * *

Behind them, and then above them, the majestic pontoons rose, powered by helium, floating in the atmosphere, looming over the hull of the Roman shipwreck.

The assembly clapped and shouted.

Incredibly, all of the Navigator women's instructions had worked.

Such a sight had never been seen along Tunisian shores. The twin balloons moved skyward steadily, surely, smoothly, implacable, effortless.

Towed upward by the pontoons came the intact hull of the wrecked ship, her barnacle-covered underside dripping, robed in kelp and algae.

Clanging bells and shouts and whistles and cheers rose

from the port. Cyrine shouted the last line of a Phoenician sea-chant, using the *can'ani* phrase for "conqueror."

One of the Arab ships let off rockets.

The balloons were let to go high ... too high.

They slid up against the cliffside. They rose until their vast twin contours broke the cliff-face skyline.

Sarra's balloons were proudly silhouetted for all of Tunis and all her fishing boats, barges, and dinghies to see.

They had forgotten Satyavati's warning ...

7. ROME'S PRELATE STOPS FOR LUNCH

Leave the situation, change the situation, or accept it.

All else is madness.

— *Eckhart Tolle*

I am Titus Flavius Virulis, Commander of the 9th Legion.

We have come here looking for a fight.

— *Neil Marshall*

Sarra was grooming Esme when the mule perked her ears up.

Sarra looked to see two men walking up the path. On the road, she saw a *pilentum*, a fine Roman overland carriage, which had carried them up the hill.

Horns and whistles and bells sounded across the port in celebration of Master Hiram and his crew.

The man in front smiled and waved in a friendly fashion. He was stout and sturdy and wore a woolen cloak pinned at one shoulder. The second man was a youth, his hair tinged with gold in the sunlight. He wore a tunic and belt and stayed three steps behind.

"May we approach, daughter of Tunis?" he called out.

Sarra replied that they could indeed approach. She called for her parents. She walked down the path to meet the visitors.

"I am Marcellus, of Corsica: Roman Prelate; Deputy Commissioner of the Southern Ports," said the man in front.

He was a dapper, clever man.

"And you must be Sarra."

"Yes, I am. You can eat lunch with us, if you would care to. I hope you like *shorbat frik*."

"What is your name, brother?" Sarra asked the second visitor, a young man not much older than she.

"I am Quintillus."

"Aha. Sit with us. My Mother sets the finest table in these parts.

"Are you a slave?" Sarra asked the young Roman.

"Quintillus is a former slave, recently manumitted," answered Marcellus. "A *libertus*."

"May he speak?" asked Sarra.

"Ah. Of course," said Marcellus. "My manners ... "

"What news from Rome?"
Mother asked Marcellus.

Father entered from the back and washed his hands.

"I am Hiram."

Introductions were made all around.

The Yijou family and their two guests sat down at the table.

"Business first," said the Prelate Marcellus.

"Here is your purchase price for the *Little Syracuse*. Rome happily purchases it from you. The price, you will find, is generous."

Quintillus removed two boxes from the heavy bag he had carried with him.

The boxes were filled with gold coins.

"And a contract," added the Prelate. "Per the Law of the Find." The boy Quintillus placed a scroll on the table.

Father handed the contract to Mother to read.

"And here is a separate award," said the Roman. "For your innovations."

"'New Methods in Salvage,'" explained Quintillus. "At Caesar's pleasure."

Marcellus then brought out two large carafes from a

separate satchel. He set them on the table.

"Falerno wines," said he. "From the Campania."

Father bowed his head, and all at the table bowed, too. *"Baruch Ata Adonai, Eloheinu Melech Haolam, shehechiyanu, v'kiy'manu, v'higianu lazman hazeh.* Blessed are You Eternal Spirit who has given us life, sustained us and allowed us to arrive in this moment."

Mother's prayer came next:

"In Christ's name, we gather. We are thankful for our guests, who have come so far. Each day is a momentous arrival. Love is all. Let us never miss the miracles that are right in front of us."

Marcellus was last with his prayer, quite different from the first two.

"Goddess revered, O Earth, of all nature Mother, we pray for good weather, so our ships may carry honest merchants' goods, to feed the families of our empire, from Carthage to Cumbria.

"Bless the one. Bless the many. Show favor on our brave soldiers, who bring protection to the imperial house. Smile upon the hardworking craftsmen -- such as these here in this house -- who bring security and prosperity to the *empire.*"

The prelate snapped open his linen napkin with a laugh.

"Hah! A Jewish prayer, a Christian prayer, and a Roman prayer," laughed Marcellus.

"We have a synod!"

* * *

"One spouse is Jewish and the other Christian? What does that make you, my girl?" asked Marcellus once Sarra had taken her seat at the table.

"Christians are part of the Jewish community," corrected Father, before Sarra could reply.

"Christians are Jews. Jews who are exploring some new ideas."

"Of course," apologized Marcellus.

Sarra served the lunch in bowls, with ladles, steam and fragrances filling the room. Sarra set down a heavy platter of rustic bread.

It turns out that the two visitors did indeed like *shorbat frik*, as well as large numbers of Mother's *makroudh*, fat diamond-shaped cookies stuffed with dates, nuts, and almond paste.

"My wife is a fine scholar," said Father. "She knows the Septuagint. She writes, too. She writes in a beautiful script. Rabbis across the Maghreb and Egypt and Babylon await her letters.

"Her father trained with Callimachus."

"Is this lamb? Are those chick-peas?" exclaimed Marcellus in a jolly tone. "Qidra style! Most unexpected."

"What news from Rome?" Mother asked Marcellus.

"Your empire is hard at work," he answered. "Her faithful servants are building roads, beating back the pagans.

"The wars in Dacia and Germania drain our coffers.

"The expansion to Britain is made thorny by the irascible nature of those tribes. Now we are drawn into the Armenian wars of succession, against Parthia.

"The madman Tacfarinas gains ground – and followers -- in Africa.

"Unrest in the South. More military actions in the North. Traitors from within. *Pax Romana* is threatened on all sides ... and from within, I am sorry to say.

Rome needs all her citizens.

"Which brings me to your magnificent pontoons. Every ship saved is worth a small fortune to Caesar. Your triumph will be Rome's glory.

"But the flight of those two balloons we saw over the Tunisian cliffs yesterday ... they well may qualify as a minor miracle for Rome.

"Your raising of a ship like the *Little Syracuse* is no small thing. Our people say it was the largest salvage, the most complete -- no lost turrets, no split hulls -- and the most complex.

"But is among the birds, not the fish, where the true potential of your pontoons lies.

"I'm not sure you fully understand your own creation, Hiram. You haven't reinvented pontoons for salvaging sunken ships. You have invented manned flight; ponderously slow, elegant, manned flight.

"These balloons of yours could carry our centurions high over the fields, across oceans and mountains. Rome rejoices! A fleet of such instruments of war will give Rome a great advantage. An imperial advantage, like no other.

"It is not a *diving* device but a *flying* device!

You have invented manned flight. These balloons of yours can carry men high over the fields, across oceans and mountains. Rome rejoice!

"Yesterday will be recorded as a moment in *aviation* history, not in the history of maritime salvage.

"A new age of flight for whomever masters the skies ... as you have done.

"Caesar must hear of this. Such an innovation will prove most valuable to the Admiralty, in particular -- "

Father folded the napkin on his lap.

"With your permission, Master Salvager," said Marcellus, "we would love to see the balloons.

Father made no motion, nor did he speak.

Ah, thought Sarra ... *I did not understand.*

"May we impose? To learn how you prepare them. What is inside them, that gives them lift? How do you insert your mystery vapors into the globes? What is the system of pulleys and rope by which you guide them? Without these answers, the balloons themselves are of little use ..."

"We must decline," answered Father.

The air in the dining room had gone thick.

Silence.

Sarra touched a bowl with a metal spoon. She put the spoon down.

"We shall not impose more than minutes, sire, no more," assured the Roman.

"No, seigneurs," said the Lion of Judah, and there was no mistaking his meaning, or the tone of his voice.

Hiram spread his hands in apology.

"But we are fellow Romans -- " protested Quintillus. Again, an almost unbearable, heavy, hostile silence ...

"If we could just *see* the balloons," cajoled Quintillus.

"I'm afraid not," answered Father.

"Perhaps," urged Marcellus, "perhaps Sarra could just explain about the vapors she -- "

"Just a peek," echoed Quintillus. "It would be most appr --"

"*What my husband says,*" interrupted Mother in a steely voice, a voice unfamiliar to even her husband and daughter ...

"*Goes.*"

She was looking directly at Marcellus, in the deadly, tensed manner of a cheetah, or a flat-eyed leopard, whose shoulders are primed, whose claws are out and flexed, who has just identified his prey from across the veldt.

Mother rose from her seat. She extended her hand to her guests.

"Good afternoon, gentlemen. Thank you for stopping by."

EPILOGUE

When you become comfortable with uncertainty, infinite possibilities open up ...

— *Eckhart Toll*

They came for Sarra and her family the very next day, but they were too late.

All that remained was a single silk balloon, stitching removed, an empty shell, laid out almost as a gift.

Three days later, an incident was reported from the road to Alexandria. Two very large balloons, flying creations from some vision, or dream, had demolished a Roman garrison seeking to detain them.

The two balloons had been gliding on easterly winds, a trajectory that would take them towards Alexandria, and Jerusalem beyond that.

Survivors remarked that the balloons dropped on the legionnaires a hellish incendiary similar to what the flame-huddled chemists of Constantinople call Greek Fire.

\#\#\#

TOM'S STORY NOTES

This story was built around the last two scenes, the lunch with the prelate and the ultimate use of balloons in warfare.

I wanted to surprise my readers by starting far afield, in the salvaging-shipwrecks trade, and lead in a winding way to the revelation that this is a landmark in early lighter-than-air flight. I felt that I had to build backwards to make the story in any way compelling.

The earth's supply of helium, the only element on the planet that is a completely nonrenewable resource, is very much an issue in our own time. To the relief of naturalists, a rare and gigantic concentration of helium has been recently discovered deep in Minnesota's Iron Range. The helium concentration was measured at 12.4 %, which is unusually high.

6. Murder on Moon Colony Saraswati

Two high-flying teen astro-botanists find a cadaver in the Moon Colony gardens. The official investigation stalls. The pair play detective ... only to find corruption at the Colony's highest levels. Will the dramas of space fall along the same colonial lines as on Earth?

PROLOGUE

Because the Moon is a rich source both of titanium and of aluminum, it is likely that these metals will be used extensively in the colonies.

— *Gerard K. O'Neill*

The nations which build the first space colonies will wield immense power ...

— *T. A. Heppenheimer*

In the shadow of the Moon, the music settled over the sleeping gardens.

Plants favor music. They grow taller and healthier with music.

This piece was a classical version of the *Raaga Bhairave*. It is supposed to be played in the early morning hours, but the Moon Colony's rows of lentils and duckweed seemed to like it just fine overnight.

Three human figures – two male, one female – skulked along the garden paths, among the many plant rows.

They ran low and fast.

Suddenly the lead figure fell.

It was just at Row 31, Section 7, between where the Winona strawberries ended and the Minnesota Hardy began.

He slumped heavily, face forward.

His two companions ran to see what had happened. *Had he been shot?*

The second figure shook the fallen colleague, trying to wake him ... but he had been dead the moment he hit the ground.

The raga's improvisational section ended. The players returned to the main melody.

The high fans clicked on.

I. TEEN BOTANISTS AND A SHOCKING DISCOVERY

Science has thus, most unexpectedly, placed in our hands

a new power of great but known energy.

— *Benjamin Silliman*

The gods grow jealous of too much contentment

anywhere, and they show their displeasure all of a sudden.

— *R. K. Narayan*

"You know them as India's rising-star gardeners, daring young Botanists bringing their Gregor-Mendel-style wizardry to outer space as they generate new species -- "

"No," pronounced Dhruv on himself. "That's lame."

"*Wincing,*" I added.

"Super phony." offered Saanvi.

Dhruv started again.

"Teen lunar botanists Mahi Jaat of Uttar Pradesh and Saanvi Yedev of Chhatisgarth can now add '*Aircraft Inventor*' to their remarkable CV's -- "

"*No,*" said Saanvi.

" -- Thanks," continued Dhruv, " -- thanks to their invention of a new form of flight! Incredibly enough, right here on Colony Saraswati, magnetic flight is a reality -- ”

"*Terrible* -- " groaned Saanvi.

Then the beam detectors went off.

"That's weird," I said aloud.

Both Saanvi and I checked the panel monitors.

I switched the detector alarm off.

* * *

The whole chain of events began the morning that our irritating pal, Dhruv, was trying to interview us, like we were celebrities.

Dhruv and his nosy editor, Parvati, needed content for the lame Colony daily newspaper. And I say 'newspaper' to be polite.

Saanvi and I were busy at our stations in the Botanicals headquarters. It was a Wednesday, so we had quotas to meet. We wanted to check the data on the Botanical Gardens' produce, grains, and orchards before they went out. A bank of LED's told us the status of the vertical gardens and sprawling territories of the Farms. We shared our live data with not only the other Colonies but several Earthside collaborators. The Americans were very, very interested in our new zero-grav-derived hybrids.

We had a Wisconsin Simon zoom meeting scheduled for noon.

"Your reporter Dhruv Masal here, amidst the special soils and legacy seeds for which my two friends here are renowned ..."

The alarms came back On.

"What is *that*?" asked Dhruv.

'Shut up, *glitch!*" I told the machine. I checked the connections in the back of the consoles. All secure. I switched the main power off, then on again.

The alarm went silent.

A bank of LED's showed that the signal had originated in the lower lettuce rows, between Orchard Ten and the Southern vertical farms.

* * *

"Okay, well this part of my profile of you two is pretty easy to resolve," said Dhruv.

"I say you have altered the history of aviation. You say, No.

"Mahi Jaat,' he turned to me, "how did you first conceive of your groundbreaking scatback magnet-powered aircraft -- ?"

"No one calls it a scatback –" I answered. "And the sleds are nothing that special. We just needed a quicker way to get around the Farm properties."

"Well, does your magnetic aircraft float? Like a zeppelin?"

"No," replied Saanvi.

"Is it a balloon?"

"No," said I.

"Is your aircraft similar to engine-powered flight?" asked Dhruv.

"Not in the least."

"Then it must be a jet plane, like the Mitsubishi A63 Zero or a Messerschmi -- "

"No, it has nothing in common with those aircrafts."

"Okay," continued our friend, "is your flying dinghy contraption a brother to the X-1 rocket jet, with exploding chemicals?"

"Obviously not."

"So," concluded Dhruv, "what you're saying is, you've come up with a new principle of flight. Magnetic flight. Admit it."

Suddenly a big, ear-shattering Primary System Alarm shattered the air in the HQ.

Pulsing lights flashed, and an audio reminder of 'System Failure' sounded.   Saanvi and I looked at each another. This had never happened.

"Gotta go!" I called out --

"I'll come with you," volunteered Dhruv. "An exciting day in the life of our young heroines -- "

"Suit yourself." I warned him to strap in tight and keep his head down.

When the EMP sleds bank those first turns out of the compound, the tilt is something wicked.

We climbed into the sleds.

2. EMPTY CURVED SPACE

There is nothing in the world except empty curved space.

Matter, charge, electromagnetism, and other fields

are only manifestations of the curvature of space.

    —   *John Wheeler*

We're all victims here, A-Train.

    —   *Anne Cofell Saunders*

In fixed-wing aviation, the first problem to solve was speed.

This took two thousand, five hundred years.

The Meissner effect – the upward-lifting properties of air flowing over a wing -- only kicks in at about forty miles per hour.

Once the Wright Brothers figured out propulsion and speed, the only remaining issues were control and more speed.

Aviation advancements after 1905 addressed two questions: a) how not to crash, and b) how to go faster, higher, and better.

Our sleds addressed a slightly different question: how can you fly without air moving over wings? How can you drop the Meissner effect from the flight equation?

* * *

We took a wide, wicked curve over the pastures and settled into a straight swoop over the corn fields.

We cut close to the cliffs as we rounded the stacked air filters at Acre 9.

Saanvi's sled swooped right beside us, on our port flank.

Not like flying in a plane.

"This is magic!' cried Dhruv as he clutched the restraints and watched the multicolored rows of Vavilov white-wheats and dwarf maizes whip by below us.

The Botanicals kingdom on Saraswati is scattered. We planted wherever we possibly could, and some of our most productive gardens were far-flung from the Botanicals HQ. at the other end of the Colony. We climbed high over the colony floor, among the fans and utilities and drone nests. We were headed north and west, along the Irrawaddy, the fake-river bed.

"I didn't know it was like this," called Dhruv over the open-door rushing air. "How is this even possible?"

"Superconductors tend to repel magnetic fields," I told him.

"I can't handle this," wailed Dhruv. "I'm gonna throw up --
"

"Don't you dare," I told him. "What are you, *Tibetan?*"

We emerged into a dramatic vista of the Colony floor, its alternating stripes of glass and farmland.

I levelled us out over the fake (real water, artificial bed) Irrawaddy.

I brought us low enough to see the fish swimming.

"The big isolation transformer throws a heavy magnetic field onto the Colony's interior," I explained to Dhruv. "The entire Colony is like an electromagnetic lake. We are just taking advantage of it.

"We lined the sleds with superconductors, until we had enough pushback. Re-pulse. When a magnet *is placed above a superconductor, the repelling force can be stronger than gravity. The* magnet levitates. Fake flight."

"What's in the superconductors?" he asked.

"Lead, mercury, barium, calcium, tin, encased in wool. It looks like a thick electric blanket. We lined the sleds with them, and laid cable below. Lots of cable."

We approached the Colony's industrial manufacturing block, in the Colony's middle section, to allow for minimized gravity for some manufacturing processes.

We banked right, to avoid the gyroscope towers which keep us centered on La Grange points I and L

"It doesn't ride like an airplane," commented Dhruv, "more like a water slide. How do the brakes work?"

"You just cut the invisible connection. Certain metallics can block EMP's. Copper. Chennai figured it out, mostly."

We rounded the bluffs at Red River.

The low sprinklers were on over the fields of Acre 3. We bounced upward to avoid the array of high sprinklers which followed, in sequence.

I was careful to dodge the drones which circulated in Colony airspace.

"Orchard Ten," said I, pointing as we approached. "Berryland."

Now the sled was running sluggish. I couldn't tell why ...

I tilted and slowed, making a long, safe approach.

Focus, I told myself.

We touched down smoothly on the barrow road alongside the grape trellises, a road which acted as our runway.

Saanvi botched her landing, as usual, almost went

sprawling, and then caught herself in the doorjambs.

We exited the sleds.

We climbed steps and ladders to Level Seven, Section Blue Four, Row MM to see what the impediment might be. "Orchard Ten," said I.

We could see the blinking track lights alerting us to a disturbance, all the way to Shelf 77.

I was guessing one of the big hawks had crashed into the lettuce beds ... Why did we want all these birds in a space colony, anyway?

We stood on a platform between the rows.

That's when we glimpsed the sleeve of a shirt sticking out from the lettuce rows.

Saanvi pulled the foliage back to reveal a human corpse.

The arm was only slightly stiff.

The man had been dead for only a short time ...

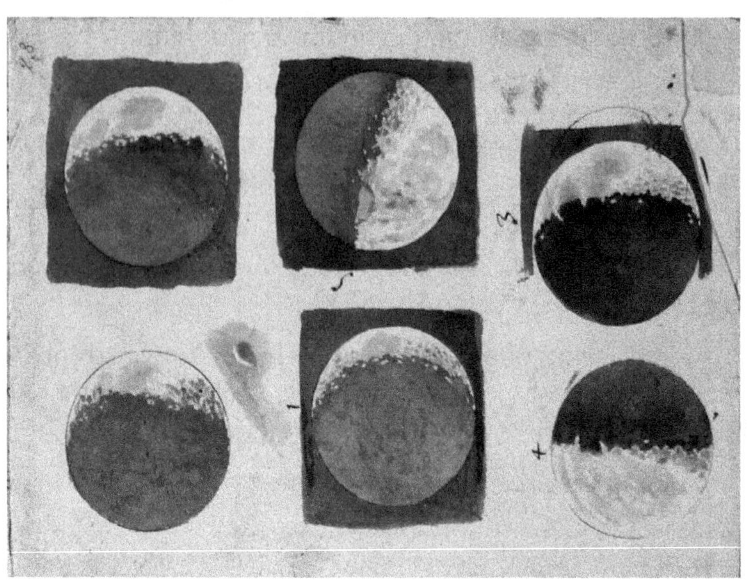

3. DEATH IN THE HANGING GARDENS

"Who shot him?" I asked.
The grey man scratched the back of his neck and
said: "Somebody with a gun."

— *Dashiell Hammett*

The gods grow jealous of too much contentment
anywhere, and they show their displeasure all of a
sudden.

— *R. K. Narayan*

Saanvi called out her ID number in a solid voice, then commanded:

"ISRO! Please call an ambulance! Orchard Ten, Station 3. We have a dead man in the rows.

"This is a Level One One emergency. Repeat. A Level One One emergency.

"We are calling for an emergency quorum. As soon as possible -- "

Dhruv recoiled from the dead body, clutching his stomach.

I repeated what Saanvi had said, as loudly and firmly as I could manage. Procedures call for two voices to request a quorum.

ISRO confirmed.

The big circular roof lights on the high panels began flashing with the news:

Death in the Hanging Gardens.

I signaled Saanvi over. I pointed to the dead man's shoes. Red-orange dirt tinged the boot soles.

She looked at me sharply.

"*What?*" called Dhruv, from across the way. "*What have you got?*"

Saanvi shook her head.

She was thinking the same thing I was.

This is bad ...

* * *

As we waited, I was having a hard time pretending that the presence of death did not disturb me.

We buried my grandmother when I was a kid, but that was different. We had known it was coming. She had been dressed up for the funeral like she was part of a family performance.

This was sad. Sad and sickening, but mostly sad. Who would call this guy's parents? His kids? Who even was he? How did he end up in our orchards? It was all too intimate. Too personal.

We are built to live. Every molecule, every atom within us, is wanting to live, to thrive, all the time. We all want to experience the world, freely, safely ... but here was a reminder: This is what's waiting.

The body was sprawled, but face-up.

It didn't seem right ...

There were blue veins in the pale skin around his eyes.

We couldn't see blood or any marks around his head, or throat ...

"Don't move him!" said Dhruv. "Forensics!"

"Why would someone stash him here?" asked Saanvi.

"I'm not sure he was stashed," said I.

"Look at the way his torso is twisted," said Dhruv.

"*Sick*," said Saanvi.

Saanvi shoved the surrounding lettuce back so we could get a clearer look.

The face was somewhat visible.

"That's crazy ..."

Dhruv reached way up on his toes and took a photo of the dead man's face. He showed us the photo.

"I don't know him ..." muttered Saanvi.

"Why would you?" asked Dhruv.

"Is he *deshee*?" I asked. "He doesn't look *deshee*."

"Look! Look here!" cried Saanvi.

Now we saw that the wrist that was showing was turned slightly, revealing an insignia – a little globe on a blue background with the atom symbol.

"Eff! He's *Russian!*" said Dhruv, as if we couldn't see that. Unlike us, the Russians wore uniforms.

"What's a Russian doing out here?"

Dhruv loaded the photo he had taken on the facial recognition app. It dinged.

"Here he is.

"Grigor Metchnikoff."

"Who?"

"Metchnikoff. Gri-gor Metch-ni-koff."

"Never heard of him. Is he one of their Botanicals?"

"It says here he's *Ubiyitsa*."

"What's that?" asked Dhruv. "I don't know any Russian --"

"*Security*," I answered. "He's on their police force."

This information seemed to send up a little mushroom cloud that hung just above the three of us, somewhere between the lower carrot balcony and the radishes.

Under some stretch of the imagination, there might be a

reason for a Russian Botanical team member to be all the way out in our sector.

But a Security officer?

"He has a history, too," said Dhruv. "Racketeering ... "

"Where are you getting this?" I asked her.

"I'm using the newspaper network. That gets me to the Earthside databases.

"Imprisoned for embezzlement," he continued. "Racketeering ..."

"This is bad," repeated a grave Saanvi.

"This is *bogus!*" said an angry Me.

"This is an intergalactic incident," said Dhruv, "is what it is."

We could hear the ambulance's approach. Everything had changed, and in a moment.

"Go ahead and file your article. Then sign off the network, Dhruv-ji," said Saanvi. "It's monitored. Someone could trace you to this location ..."

4. QUORUM: THE MYSTERY DEEPENS

I happen to have discovered a direct relation between magnetism and light, also electricity and light.

The field it opens is so large and I think rich ...

— *Michael Faraday*

Talhatra, the eccentric Keeper of Botanicals and our team leader, was the first to arrive.

Tal was older than us, in his early thirties. His voice was raspy and familiar. He looked like a schoolteacher on vacation.

Aarev Reddy was the second to arrive.

And we had our quorum.

Aarev Reddy was a pushy type, shortish, with a round head and a slight overbite. In most organizations, Reddy would carry the rank of Second in Command, or Lieutenant Governor. But Moon Colony Saraswati eschewed ranks. That was the whole point of everything. That's how we built the first, largest, and most productive colony mining the Moon, at a price almost half of what the Americans spent.

Flat organization. No hierarchy.

No frills.

Performance first.

All team members are equal. All ideas are equal.

The smartest ideas win. The best practices win.

* * *

The careful members of the ambulance crew were as shaken by Grigor Metchnikoff's dead body as we were. They took plenty of pictures. They gingerly loaded Grigor into the back of the ambulance on one of those folding wheeled carts.

Murder does not happen on a Moon Colony.

We retreated to the far side of the platform to consult while the medics dealt with the body of Ubiytsa Officer of the

Third Order, Grigor Metchnikoff.

"Five? Five, is it? E -e-enough for a quorum, have we?" asked Talhatra. "Ah. Ah. Aahhhmmm ..."

A quorum of five was the ground-level decision-making body on Saraswati.

The five of us would decide on what the next step would be. A plenum, a council of ten workers, would come next.

"*Murder*, you know," remarked Tal. "This sort of thing is ay, ah, you might say, EEeeyyyyyyyuu-un-precedented."

In his ongoing war with spoken language, Tal typically interjected with long pauses so he could claim the floor, so no one else could speak, this followed by a rush of words which no one could follow.

"I wonder uunnhhhhh, I wonder." He took a breath. "Iftthereareeven proceduresforthissortofthing. Mmmm? Hmm?"

"I say we run the investigation," offered Saanvi. "Ourselves."

"Hold on -- "

Aarev didn 't like the sound of that.

"Isn't Rule Five 'Initiate," I argued.

"'Don't wait to be asked'?" challenged Saanvi.

We were leaning against the balustrades and sitting in folding chairs on the little cement platform. Saanvi remained standing.

"Look," I said. "This guy – whoever he is, whoever he *was* – is dead. In our sector. It must have *something* to do with Botanicals."

"Someone out there knows what happened. That person is still walking around out there, in the Colony somewhere."

"Yes, ah, uh," stammered Tal, "ach, me, ach, it, it, it is precisely-all-the-more-reasonforustoturnthedamnthingover--"

The ambulance rolled down the wide path decline and onto the main road. We could hear the tires running over pebbles and asphalt.

"This goes up the chain of command. To Security," ordered Aarev.

He stood, as if to signal the meeting was over.

"Write up a report," he told me.

No one spoke. No one moved. No one looked in Aarev's direction. I plucked a blueberry from the shrubs and rolled it over my fingers.

"*What?*" exclaimed Aarev. "Oh, I see. I'm outvoted no matter what I say. The three of you -- "

"Your ideas are as good as anyone's, Aarev," I told him. "But we vote. You don't give orders."

A solid I-truly-don't -care-what-you-think tone in my voice caught Aarev off guard. He looked startled for a split-second, as though just now realizing that, between the pair of us, Saanvi and me, I might be the worse.

"We know his name and his detail," I told Tal and Aarev.

"Grigor Metchnikoff. Russian. *Ubiytsa.*"

"Umum, um. Unh. *Ah! Ah!*" Tal went into a mini-frenzy at this news. "Russian! You don't say! *Tutututtuttt --* "

It also seemed to surprise Aarev.

"Ah! Me! Then! Now!" continued Tal. "Th-th-this *news* is

cc-cc—certainly worthy of Security-Level-One, ah, ah, *tttttttreatment!* Shshshshurly thematterisnowinterGALACTIC, as it were. Yah! So to say, and ah, as, as, as such *out-of-Botanicals'-hands --* "

"All right," I said. I was out of patience for this runaround.

"How about this.

"The docs will examine the body.

"I forward a case report to all parties.

"Captain Gautam and the Colony Police will make inquiries.

"And we reconvene at Security HQ. Twelve hundred hours."

"Eleven hundred hours," said Aarev.

"Okay. Reconvene at 1100. With Security."

"All in favor," I said.

The resolution passed, three to two.

An open investigation, two teams authorized to make initial inquiries, at least for another 90 minutes.

5. THE FIX IS IN

The key to sustaining life on Mars is an extremely intensive, closed loop, efficient food system.

— *Lenore Newman*

"Okay. Why didn't we tell Tal and Aarev all that we

know?" demanded Dhruv as soon as they were gone.

"About Grigor. Just now."

"I'm not sure why," I answered carefully. "This whole thing seems ... creepy."

Saanvi nodded. "Something's up."

"The fix is in!" announced Dhruv. "I've read about this. The higher-ups are hiding something. This exact same thing happens to Vish Puri," he added, like we had asked.

"And who is 'Vish Puri'?" I inquired.

"My favorite private investigator," replied Dhruv. "I've read all his books. "He follows the money. He uncovers the crooks.

"What do you think is happening, Mahi?" Dhruv asked me.

I paused.

"You might not want to be here, Dhruv-ji," said Saanvi.

"What?"

"Things are gonna get gnarly," I said.

"Are you kidding? 'Murder in the Moon Colony'? 'Girl Genius Aviators turn *police detectives?*'" Dhruv was almost shrieking now. "Wait till my editor hears this!! It's *beyond incredib --* "

"Okay, okay," said Sanvi.

"Eat a peach, dude," I urged.

"I'm staying," insisted Dhruv. He drummed his fingers on the table.

"Copy that," I replied.

"You didn't mean 'Eat a peach.' That's T.S. Eliot," said Dhruv. "You mean 'Cool your jets.' Or 'Put a lid on it.' Not 'Eat a peach.'"

"Well, we're going to be breaking a few rules. Just so you're warned."

"Roger," said Dhruv. "Roger that. I'm in!"

I looked at Saanvi. She nodded.

Saanvi began changing the security codes for all our communications.

I switched us from the Colony mainframe to the private server we had rigged. Our own network. We needed to be invisible.

"Dhruv," I said, "you've got to stop drumming your fingers all the time. It's like a doomsday clock. Gives me the heebie jeebies -- "

"Once again, wrong reference," corrected Dhruv. "'*Heebie jeebies*' originally referred to -- "

"Oh, my God," I replied. "Cool your jets."

* * *

"Okay," I said. "Here's the plan. I'm gonna make tea. Then I'm gonna batten down all the hatches for the morning. Get all the sprouts' water levels right.

"Then we can pick up Chennai for the Plenum. Forty minutes, say."

"Sounds like a plan," nodded Saanvi, a phrase which was actually high praise, coming from her. "When I'm done with these sequences, I'll check the CCTV tapes -- "

"We need to *follow the money*," said Dhruv. "That's one of

Vish Puri's mottoes. Maybe I can look into the dude's bank recs."

"We don't have that kind of access," I said.

I looked up at the wall tv. It was Earthside News. Food riots. New bombings targeting American and British investment banks, mainly in Punjab.

My mind was swimming.

6. THE CHUTES AMONG THE MINING CABINS

Every surviving civilization is obliged to become spacefaring ... we have a basic responsibility to our species to venture to other worlds.

— *Carl Sagan*

Strawberries are extra complicated.

— *Elise Finch*

Little Harp, the mining camp, resembled a Yukon mining cabin on the rugged slopes of a Jack London scenario.

Chennai's family occupied a cluster of cabins on a clearing among the high bluffs, where the Moon's natural geology was encased in sheaths of curtain, so the drills and bulldozers could get to the ore.

As kids, we had visited Chen's family often, back when we were all in school together.

Above, haul trucks and graders criss-crossed the mountain slopes. Conveyer belts and flumes and draglines scaled the high walls of cratered terrain. Mankind sought platinum, gold, magnesium, iridium, uranium, and more from the Moon's storehouses. Rock flumed Earthward, sorted by density, through the downward throat of the Chutes at ten thousand tons per hour. It was apportioned among the Moon Colony nations, per years-long negotiations.

Below, you could see through the glass barriers to the procession of carts and haulers and rail cars hauling and dumping their loads into the great maw. Following the Urio Tinto and Ulaanbaatar designs, an array of piston-driven fixed-screen jigs processed the tonnage even as it fell. Gravity separated the nickel from the iridium, and the iron from the palladium. An arc gate on the end of the lip shuttled the minerals into apportioned trays far, far below.

The nearness of the Big Void, the deadly vacuum of space was never so vivid, so present so immediate, as it was at the Mines. It attracted sightseers, sitting in folding chairs along the high ridges and trailheads. Nothing lives among the stars. That infinite airless graveyard was separated from all of us on Saraswati only by several layers of plexiglass.

* * *

"Brought you some of the *Fregaria*," I presented to Mme. Sidhu, a stout, good-natured woman. The strawberries were in a basket, on a folded checkerboard dish towel, the way she does it herself. "I planted these from bare root crowns," I told her. "Super sweet." She smiled and nodded. Everyone loves good food.

"Black pearls," I said to Mr. Sidhu, offering him a clean

white ceramic plate with five ripened berries, bright red, plump and glossy, freshly washed.

"We found a dead body in the lettuce," I told them. "This morning. Must have happened last night."

They both stopped and stared at me.

I explained everything.

"We're investigating it," I told the Sidhus. "The three of us. Aarev and Tal don't seem to care."

"It's weird," added Dhruv.

"We're hoping Chennai can join the Plenum," said Saanvi. "At noon."

"He's over to Barrow Wing," answered Mrs. Sidhu. "He'll be back in an hour."

We heard the muffled boom of a cluster of detonations and involuntarily ducked.

Mr. Sidhu had not touched his strawberries.

"Before we leave," I said to Chennai's Mom and Dad.

"Is there anything you want to tell us?"

In the electric and intensely uncomfortable moment that followed, I could feel Saanvi and Dhruv snap their heads to look at me. We had not discussed this.

The question of mine was most discordant, most out-of-place, most presumptuous, no matter how nicely I had tried to say it.

"Why was rust-colored soil on the dead man's shoe soles?" I asked.

"It's gonna come out," I told my friend's parents.

"He was here, wasn't he?

They would not look at me. "Look, I continued, "the Moon is airless, and the red dirt on his shoes was hematite. Rust that requires oxygen and water.

"Like you have here."

We – the five of us – had arrived at one of those hinge moments in life, when the cat could jump one way or the other.

"Yes, Mahi," replied Mrs. Sidhu. "The Russian man, Metchnikoff, was here."

Saanvi and Dhruv stared, open-mouthed, at Chennai's parents.

"He tried to blackmail us!" she continued. "Him and his associates -- "

"Associates?" I asked.

"Yes. A young man. Tall and thick. Also, there was a woman. Hair in a bun."

"Crooks!" declared Mr. Sidhu.

"They accused us of tampering with the data."

"What data?" I asked.

"The Chutes. The ore -- "

"Tampering! What do you mean?" asked Saanvi. "How could they --

Alarms sounded on our phones, reminding us that the Plenum started soon.

"We gotta go. Chennai should join us if he can," I said to his parents.

"Mahi, *what the hell?*" wailed Dhruv bitterly as we climbed down the slope towards the sleds.

"What else did you two notice that I didn't? What else are you hiding?"

"Not hiding," corrected Saanvi. "Suspecting.

"I'll tell you after the Plenum."

"Effing eff!" exclaimed Saanvi, shaking her head in disbelief.

"The Sidhus met the dead Russian!" exclaimed Dhruv, with gusto. "This is getting *nuts* ..."

"*Eat a peach!*" he exclaimed, at a loss for words.

7. PLENUM

It's a murder inquiry. Sir. There's nothing

that wouldn't be of interest to us.

— *Colin Dexter*

"What do you mean, *you don't know?*" I asked, allowing a dead tone into my voice.

Doctor Yadav cleared her throat and repeated what she had said, glancing at me and Saanvi as she spoke.

"The exact cause of death is yet to be determined," she repeated.

"We've sent for the American coroner. He will have the requisite equipm -- "

"Equipment?" I interrupted. "You're kidding me, right?"

The Wise Men of the High Frontier had wanted to give the colonists as many familiar living and working spaces as possible. The conference room at Security HQ was one such place. It had a wooden door in a doorway, door handle with knobs, wood-paneled walls, lamps on side tables, seats around a table.

"No., I'm not kidding. He is arriving on the 2:30 shuttle from Jefferson Station."

"What are your preliminary findings?" Saanvi asked Captain Gautam, head of the Colony's Security Force.

A dignified, thick-set man, Gautam gave an air of calm and control. He seemed British. This, in modern Indian culture, is a two-way sword.

"We'll know more tomorrow," he answered. "We are limited by the scope of our information on this man. We need the rest of today to track -- "

"That's not factual," I commented. "Sir."

In the vivid hush that ensued, we could hear the soft sounds of air conditioning circulating.

"What, is that a polite way of calling me a liar?"

"Yessir. It is," I answered.

He glared at me, assessing me, assessing just how it was I thought I could speak to him that way. Then he looked at Saanvi, then back at me.

"Captain, do you have any experience with suspicious deaths?" challenged Pryanka, Dhruv's editor, who sat at the table, a member of the Plenum.

"With murder?"

"No," he replied, "not as such. But our procedural training includes all phases of police work.

"These things take time," affirmed Ashparti, a young

sycophant police lieutenant. "As you must know, our police contingent is small. Very small. Our budget -- "

"So what do we know?" asked Dhruv. "Three hours after a dead body is found in our lettuce patch, what do we know?

"Well, w-w-w-we we can certainly confirm," stuttered Tal, "ah, that the dead man is indeed, ahem, *RRRussian*."

"You better know his name, rank and occupation," said Saanvi. "We do."

"Yes," reported Captain Gautam. "Grigor Metchnikoff. He has a record of petty crimes. He serves on their *Doska* -- "

"What was he doing here?"

"I don't know."

"Yeah, you do," I said. "You have access to all the Level One CCTV feeds. All of White Fox. You know just where he went."

"He and his associates," added Dhruv. Aarev reacted to the reference to Russian 'associates' ...

"Listen, you little -- " The Captain was unused to being spoke to thusly.

Tal tried to moderate, to avoid the smash-up that was fast coming ....

"Ah, not-not-not-not ... to ... ahhhh, not to, ahhh, dis-*parage*, no, no, that is, not to *pre-judge*, you see, ah, good Mahi Jaat, ah, but let us not neglect to mention, that is, alltheresponsibilitiesofyourvaluablework ah ha -- "

"Tal's right," Aarev jumped in. "We can hardly expect you two to *abandon* your *Botanicals* duties. Your genetics are even in demand Earth-side, apparently."

"Not to worry, Aarev," said Saanvi sarcastically. "I think

we can handle it ..."

"I sh-sh-shudder to conjure g-g-grapes dying on the vine--"

"Are you KIDDING ME Tal?" Saanvi lost it. "We found a *dead body*! And you're saying we sh -- "

"I-I-I-am-of-course-saying-only-that, ah, I'm saying *Thank You*." Tal nodded in his seat. "The two, the two, the two of your *prompt attention* to this 'death' matter will trigger the colony's best practices -- "

"Okay." Saanvi tried to calm down.

"The procedures are clear," stated Aarev.

"No, they're *not*," I countered.

"They call for each division to review -- "

"We've *read* the bylaws," I said, "and there is zero contingency, not a single word, that addresses protocol for a murder investigation."

"—And to pass along a *review* of the case with their particular level of expertise," continued Aarev, completing his thought.

"We can have this discussion ALL DAY, Swami -- " said Saanvi.

"Don't call me that," said Aarev.

"Sorry," Saanvi apologized. "I lost my temper."

"This investigation is stalled," I announced. "We're taking the lead. Everyone else can stay out of it."

"You canNOT be serious-- " Aarev exclaimed. Captain Gautam had also come alive.

"Are you a stander-upper?" I asked Aarev rhetorically, using the ISRI *samaanata* lingo as a weapon. "Or are you a sitter-downer? Don't you want us to take some initiative?"

This was not a casual mention on my part. The entire Moon colony effort, the entire existence of the ISRI Space agency is founded on the rock of *samaanata*, a term which means 'democracy' but a whole lot more. *Egalite.* Flat Org. Shared decision-making. The ethos of taking responsibility. Togetherness. It is at the heart of Indian culture's success over its rivals, NASA's Jefferson Station and EuroGalactic and Roscosmos.

Israelis call it *Rosh Gadol.* No hierarchy. Best idea wins. No complaint is raised without pointing out a solution. No request is made that does not clearly account for the effects on budgets, and personnel. *Samaanata* suggests the opposite of bureaucracy corruption. Invoking *samaanata* is a direct reference to the Mission. We all take responsibility. Everyone acts.

"I've heard enough," said Aarev. "Amateur *speculation* of this sort is NOT the same as a proper Police examination.

"You are prevented from further efforts in this vein -- " ordered Aarev.

"*No, we're not—*" protested Dhruv.

"The investigation will be handled by the Colony Police. It is their *job.*"

Aarev sounded convincing, but he had no such authority.

"Everyone here needs to decide," I warned him. "This is all being transcribed. Recorded. Distributed. This question goes to the heart of the Colony.

"*Let's vote,*" said Saanvi. "I called the Quorum. Now I put the proposal to this Plenum:

Botanicals takes the lead investigating the Russian man's death on

Botanicals turf.

"Yes or No."

Hands were raised.

"I have no love for these plant girls," declared Parvati, Dhruv's editor. "They're rude. But they're right. I vote Yes."

Doctor Yadav also raised her hand. I'm not sure she was following our logic, but she did not want to miss the chance to stick it to the high-handed trio of Tal, Aarev, and Gautam.

"Make it a joint effort," suggested the Captain. "Dual responsibility."

Six to four. The motion passed. The Case of the Corpse in the Botanic Gardens would proceed along parallel lines of investigation. We would reconvene in 12 hours.

"I have no love for the plant girls," declared Parvati, Dhruv's editor. "They're rude. But they're right."

"All right." Aarev was extremely displeased. "You'll have to deal with the Russians, then."

* * *

We had not mentioned Chennai's parents.

"Where's Chennai, anyway?" asked Saanvi as we left.

"What the heck is with him -- "

"What?" asked Dhruv. "Are you guys suspicious?"

Saanvi and I both knew that Chennai's absence, like the Plenum's stonewalling, meant something.

And that would not be something good.

"Eff," Saanvi murmured to me. "We might've called down the thunder on this one."

"Roger that," I replied.

8. THE RUSSIAN ASSISTANT

The soup is hot, the soup is cold.

Antony is alive, Antony is dead.

— *Carlo Maria Franzero*

"Good morning," said the face.

"I am Matthew Wroblewski. Special Assistant first class to Minister Balakirev," said the face on the screen.

"Good day, Matthew Wroblewski," said Saanvi. She introduced herself.

He was young and anxious. He looked smart, but in a limited, dexterous way, like a low-level tech or a data-entry drone.

"The Minister has asked me to facilitate a portal. You need access to certain personnel files. For your... investigation."

"Ten four," said Saanvi. "How is the weather on Roscosmos?"

Matthew laughed nervously. "I – I—it's fine.

"I am presently forwarding you files. Now. Let me know if you receive --"

"Yes," said Saanvi. "Coming through. But you know what might be easier is if you just include the block."

"How would that work?" asked Matthew.

"Just send that whole -- you know what? Just give us that third-from-the-top sequence. The 12-digit *kielbasa.*"

He laughed.

"Your name is Polish," Saanvi explained.

"Yes, yes it is.," said Matthew. "Perhaps, perhaps I can do as you say ... patch that in ... I'm concerned, really, whether my clearance allows me -- "

"Limit it, if you like," said Saanvi. "Limit our access. That will bypass the protocols."

"What do you mean?"

"Twenty-four hours," replied Saanvi.

"Oh! I see. Well, in that case, I would have to -- "

"Six hours."

We heard a pause.

"Okay. I can do that ... let me code it ..."

We watched him working, on the split screen.

I held my breath.

"Got it," said Saanvi. "That should do for now. Please tell your boss we will be working hard.

"We will report back to him as soon as know more."

Happy to have fulfilled his assignment, Matthew signed off.

We waited until long after his face had blipped off, and all we saw was a dark screen. I triple-checked to make sure our microphones were off.

Dhruv did his happy dance.

Saanvi leaned back in her chair, shaking her head.

"I can NOT believe that just happened," I said.

9. BOTANICALS

The future is botanical.

— *Richard Pallardy*

Plants see you. They know if you're

wearing a blue or a red shirt.

— *Daniel Chamovitz*

The history of Botany is mostly looking at plants, classifying plants, and describing their properties. Thirty centuries of taxonomy.

And then came Gregor Mendel. 1862.

Boom ! Botany met genetics.

While the Americans were fighting their civil war, Mendel was changing scientific history. He took pea plants and gave them certain traits. His work signaled a huge turn in the road

-- that humans can 'improve' plants. Alter their DNA. Mendel, an Austrian monk, discovered the laws of inheritance, how genes determined a plant's characteristics.

He paved the way for people like Norman Borlaug and Janaki Ammal and the whole Green Revolution crowd. Super wheats. Champion-yield strains of rice. Plant breeders could create new crops with new gene combinations, new properties. Frog cells; light resistance; wind resistance; square tomatoes; anything we can think of.

Now, on space colonies like ours, we use zero-grav and moon soils to enhance the genetics. We are changing plants yet again.

Normally -- that is, on Earth – gravity informs the plant as to which way is up, which way is down. Gravity serves to break the water column in the plant stem. But in the half-gravity of Saraswati things are different.

So, Saanvi and I ran our own workshop within the plant kingdom. We used lunar conditions to boost the yields. We had enjoyed some successes, far beyond what the other colonies were doing. Now their Botanists requested our visits, asked us to share our best practices. New Delhi's Department of Agriculture, back on Earth, had noticed, too. Compared to the blights in Punjab and Uttar Pradesh, our crops looked healthy.

There are 30,00 species of algae. Mendel used pea pants, Saanvi and I used these hurried-up algae cycles as trials for our new seeds.

Sharing data and procedures with a Wisconsin botanist named Simon Gilroy, we had our biggest success with the land races. The older seeds, the legacies. Finding ways to develop hardy new lines legacies in zero-gravity was very promising. Our new legacies needed no expensive fertilizers or greenhouses or harvest machinery. They did not collapse at the first sign of blight. We were applying the ideas to almost all plant life – fruits, grains, mazes, vegetables. It took a ton of work. It took an intense amount of concentration on our part, Saanvi and me, which explains (partially) why nobody could tell us anything.

Winter wheat yields spiked, also spinach, kale and of course algae. These were not small improvements but sizeable yield improvements – 19 per cent, 17 per cent, in the case of the Hokkaido cherries, 24 per cent, year on year.

The New Delhi aggies, the geeks at Ministry of Agriculture and Farmers Welfare, were most pleased. They announced each new strain and variation announced like a military triumph. They asked for our crop rotations, row by row. They were obsessed with our hydroponics. The other Moon colonies stacked up messages for us every day, so they could farm with similarly efficient yields as ours.

And all of these new seeds, we gave patent-free to the people of India.

Hence the Punjab riots.

The farmers refused to pay the high fees for seeds and fertilizers from the Americans.

10. DEEP ACCESS GAINED

The clock is ticking. Nancy Drew knows too much.

— *Jessica Sharzer*

—

We always want to look in the dark, scary spaces,

when all the important stuff is stuck under a desk.

— *Maggie Trinrud*

Matthew Wroblewski had, without meaning to, given us access to *saphed lomri*. White Fox. The moon colonies' executive network.

Originally used for administration, the White Fox network served the earthside governments of all three space colonies. Off-limits to workers, it provided access to all CCTV feeds, all audio surveillance, all profit-and-loss calculations, supervisor memos, everything. We eventually discovered passenger logs, personnel records. The modest-looking portals which Matthew had allowed us to download provided access (through the Russian system) looping back to the official sublevels of our own Colony, Saraswati.

It took Saanvi less than thirty minutes to copy and re-code the dozen portals we needed.

We transferred this new content to our laptops.

We blanked out our own server. Our tracks were covered -- for now anyway.

We retreated to the Barns with our laptops.

Less than twenty minutes after we did so, a night-prowler drone glided down over the Botanicals offices we had just vacated. It seemed to hover, and dip this way and that, and then move on.

* * *

We camped out on the roomy second floor of the Barns.

Smikle, the good-natured manager of the Barns, knew us well.

We were unaccustomed to working with the White Fox architecture and procedure. It took all three of us all experimenting for hours to figure out how to download the many Saraswati CCTV locations ... and audio archives.

"C'mon, Saanvi," I heard her say to herself. "Work smart, girl."

Once we understood the OSI framework, it went quickly.

* * *

I had fallen asleep when Saanvi announced:

"Mahi!! You gotta see this!"

We scrolled through the footage.

"Unbelievable," I whispered.

"I *knew* it," said Saanvi.

"Fol-low the MON-NEY! *Yes!*" Dhruv did a little dance. "Ow! I *knew* it. This detective stuff really works -- "

We kept going. Several familiar faces appeared on the grainy CCTV feeds.

Then we scrolled through the memos.

"*Egalite*, commented Saanvi with a slightly bitter laugh.

"*Egalite*," I responded.

* * *

By midnight, we had traced all of Metchnikoff's actions, whom he met, what he said. Who was with Metchnikoff when he died.

"I can NOT believe this," said Dhruv.

By two o'clock, we undeerstood how all this connected to us, our work, and to the Punjab riots.

Saanvi found scores of memos alerting all colonies to Russian criminal gangs and their many rackets. Gautam had known exactly who Grigor Metchnikoff was, all along.

We saw the preliminary cause-of-death report.

And more.

"Trouble ahead," said Saanvi in a low voice.

That would prove to be an understatement.

II. MIDNIGHT RAID

Put yourself in the here and now, Paul.

— *Gia Gionfriddo*

You have to make sure they've stopped swinging at the pinata before you dive for the candy.

— *Meredith Stiehm*

In the shadow of the Moon, music rose over the sleeping plant beds.

It was the overture to von Flotow's opera *Martha*.

The orchestra's slow, darkish A-minor introduction changed to an A major theme.

The intruders came towards the Botanicals HQ from the south this time, along the Broccoli Shire trails. One, a male, was tall and thick. The next silhouette was that of a woman, wearing her hair in a bun.

An extended French horn solo accompanied the figures sneaking over the rise.

The darts rose silently from their underground perches. No one noticed.

The opera's forest theme was re-stated by the woodwinds.

The small band of Russian intruders paused. The leader made sharp signals with arms and fists –

The darts fired. Designed to immobilize rabbits, raccoons, and deer, the darts were much more powerful on this particular night. I had doubled the doses of tetrodotoxin.

Amid cries, groans and cursing, the intruders fell, wounded and half-paralyzed.

The sprinklers came to life.

Martha's peasant-girl theme from Act One returned, accompanied by triangle and string punctuation, then full orchestration.

Despite some dark beginning passages, the opera would end happily.

12. ENTER CHENNAI

The magnetic force is animate.

Earth itself is a giant magnet.

> — *William Gilbert*

A new study reveals how the diminutive Moon could have been an occasional magnetic powerhouse early in its history, a question that has confounded researchers since NASA's Apollo program began returning lunar samples in 1969.

> *-- Alexander Evans*

At dawn, I texted Chennai and told him to get over here, ASAP.

We made breakfast.

Chennai arrived, looking like he had not slept in days. His usual upright posture was compromised.

We played him the first report.

* * *

"The subject died of brain trauma, brought about by *barutrauma*," replied Dr. Yadav, on the monitor screen.

"Improper procedures for maintaining safe levels of blood pressure inside the brain. From the Russian shuttle."

"*What?*" Chennai exclaimed. "He died of *what?*"

"Decompression sickness," continued Dr. Yadav patiently. "The blood vessels in his brain burst because he did not decompress properly. A little like the Bends when you're diving.

"The difference in atmospheric pressures among the Colonies is significant. Shuttle passengers need an hour to give the nitrogen time to clear from your blood. Otherwise, it's like your entire insides are a carbonated drink.

"The Russians consistently fail to enforce a reasonable Oxygen Protocol. We monitor them."

"So nobody slammed the Russian's head with a shovel -- " said Dhruv.

"Grigor Metchnikoff," continued Dr. Yadav's recorded face, "had susceptible blood vessels. We've seen his medical records. He was probably told that heliox would help. It doesn't."

"We've warned them a hundred times about incidents like this. Their shuttle does not conform to OSRI standards.

"We warned them."

* * *

Once he saw and understood the full implications of this data-A-bomb, Chennai seemed close to panic.

"Mahi!" he practically grabbed me. "You can't let this get out!"

"You can get ahead of it, brother," said I, "but you can't quash it -- "

283

A new and even worse thought seemed to occur to him.

"My Dad! He thinks -- "

"What?" asked Saanvi, concerned at the wild look in Chennai's face --

He ran towards the garages.

"Don't report this!" Chennai called over his shoulder. "Not yet -- "

Just then the Wisconsin conference call came to life online. I explained to them that we would have to postpone --

"He's taking a sled!" yelled Dhruv. "What the heck -- "

"Let's go! cried Saanvi." We gotta catch him -- "

13. CHENNAI LEADS US ON A CHASE

mate eh mate
giss a light
says the dead to the dead
    — *Maria Stepanova*

Electricity and magnetism share a close relationship.

Electromagnetic power is simply the force that exists between two objects possessing an electric charge.

You possess an electric charge. So does a tiny photon.

All electrical flow produces a small magnetic field. A moving magnetic field produces an electrical current.

This force is invisible. It is universal.

Electromagnetic pulses extend to everything from a wire coil around an iron rod to a planet- shivering X-class solar flare.

* * *

Chennai was the best pilot among us – he helped build the sleds – so he was hard to catch.

Chen in Sled Three was listing badly, port-side, as he cleared the fences.

He banked high and wide around the Orchard Two waterfalls.

The sled regained stability.

* * *

You would normally need a series of very large chargers to do this with electrostatics. and non-uniform magnetic fields. But for us, since the entire Colony was like a EMP pool, the master magnet gave us all the varying voltages we needed.

It performed like superconducting. The rudder is attached to a bar magnet, and then positioned in 360 degrees. A wire shaft connects it to the reaction wheels. That way, you can control reaction, repulsion, and shear force top maneuver.

We crashed three of the experimental sleds trying to learn how to steer properly ...

* * *

"Hey!" called Saanvi. "What's he doing?"

Chennai was angling upward, taking Sled Three up among the water towers and the Crow's Nest, a complex of generators and whirring filters.

He went whizzing among the great blades --

We emerged into a vista of Van Gogh's tulip fields, only more so – a most amazing perspective of the Colony Saraswati.

An O'Neill colony design, as ours was (but modified), is a cylinder, of course, but you cannot tell that when you are inside, gazing down on a landscape of rainbow-colored meadows and alternating stripes of green crops and blue glass, with the fake River Irawaddy meandering through.

He kept his altitude high, so high I was worried we'd scrape the ceiling glass.

I knew what Chen was up to. To get to the Chutes, we had to traverse the suburbs, where the magnetic signal was weakest, or least-reliable. Chen wanted his sled to be high enough to glide home even if the speed lapsed.

The sled coughed. It started to slide out of its trajectory. We were a good fifteen lengths behind him when Chen's propulsion stopped. He must have somehow damaged or impeded the EMP connection during the descent.

The steering on our sleds did not use the liquid nitrogen and ionic wind, but a modified repulsor scheme. Electrostatics. Like a modified mag lev course. Like Osaka.

Chen tossed a seat out of the window. The sled righted.

* * *

It was like flying inside an Impressionist painting, specifically Van Gogh's field of tulips, or Matisse.

Sled Three lost balance again. Chennai began to falter ...

Again, he regained power.

We caught back onto the magnet stream and rose, entering the foothills and mining camps.

We skimmed the swimming pools and city parks.

We descended.

We dodged flocks of birds.

We flew low through rows of palm trees.

We almost scraped the roof of the Middle School.

Suddenly, we saw Sled Three, up ahead of us, blank. She lost power altogether. She began to tumble into a death spiral.

I pulled up along Sled Three.

The two sleds were almost touching. I couldn't hold to a steady course, and kept slamming into Sled Three. On Chen's far side, Saanvi in Sled Two tried to help, but could not.

My arms were shaking --

Chen popped the starboard hatch.

My sled wanted to clang against its brother sled –

I slammed the Zero gravity button and everything floated in mid-air for a moment -- just a moment --

The magnetic pull between the two sleds brought us close ... not close enough ...

I called out --

Chen jumped --

Dhruv slipped and then caught Chennai, ripping his sleeve but hanging on --

Chennai flipped into our doorway –

Sled Three fell away, in an arc – pretty, almost -- and crash-landed in the radish fields far below.

14. A MOMENT OF TRUTH

This case just got a whole lot bigger

than whatever we thought it was.

    – Cait Dunphy

I'm not afraid of anything anymore.

    – Kathryn Hammond

We arrived at the Little Harp compound.

Chennai stood facing his father. His father stood at the open entry to the Chutes, ready to jump.

"*Dad!* Listen to me! The Russian died of brain trauma! You didn't murder him!"

Dhruv replayed Dr. Yadav's report, holding his laptop up at full volume.

I felt like we were all part of a theatrical production, a play with each of us hitting our marks, speaking worn lines that only stated the obvious.

"*What?*" said Mrs. Sidhu.

Chen replayed it.

"The Russians effed up the air pressure protocols," said Chen. "Metchnikoff's brain exploded. Get it? No one could have helped him."

"Is this true?" Mrs. Sidhu asked me.

I nodded.

"We know he tried to blackmail you," said Saanvi. "And why."

"You were changing the ratios."

"That wasn't her doing!" said Mr. Sidhu, agitated. "I ordered her to."

"No, you didn't," said his wife. "No, he didn't."

* * *

"It's too bad you both have to keep *lying*," I told them.

This stung Chen's parents, seeing as how it came from one of their son's young friends. The social order was changing.

"It was a mad scheme," I told them. "Trying to divert a third of the gold and half the titanium to the Lands of Five Rivers."

"Our loyalty is to Punjab," said the father stubbornly. "The Punjabis."

"The Westerners always win," Mr. Sidhu added, with contempt. "House rules. The raga never changes. The game is rigged.

"Let the *deshee* get their share," he declared sullenly.

"Like no one would find out?" burst Chennai. "God! You are *hard-headed!*"

"Punjabis stick together," his father answered, cryptically. "Our children starve. The London bankers light their cigars. And your mother is magic with the data. She has a way to mask the revised distributions."

"*No, she doesn't,*" I said, but it wasn't like I was mad about it.

"Do you think OSRI is stupid?" I held up my hands like an exasperated schoolteacher. "You thought that you can *alter* their *system* without anyone noticing?"

I added some choice words to make my feelings clear on this.

"There are two more levels beneath these," I told them. "The geologists re-calculate all of the densities so they can revise all the distributions. It's *built-in.* Who gets how much uranium. A failsafe. It automatically adjusts any anomaly. They hold back the haulages at the bottom until the ratios are negotiated. Did that never occur to you?"

"Mahi might be right," said Chennai's Mom. "I could not seem to patch certain of the codes ..."

"The Russian saw what we were trying to do right away," she continued. "He came over on the shuttle and told us if we didn't pay him, he'd go straight to Command."

"So what did you say?" asked Saanvi.

"I read to him," replied Mr. Sidhu darkly. "From the book of loyalties."

"And what does *that* mean?" I asked him. I was sick of all his ping-pong talk.

"It means he set the guy straight," explained Chennai.

"British greed. India enslaved. Two hundred years of the Raj. *Gandhi.* All that."

"I scuffled with him," said Mt. Sidhu. "I am willing to pay for what I did."

"You didn't *DO* anything!" cried Chennai. "Don't you get it? No crime, no foul ..."

"Right?" Chen turned to the three of us, his childhood friends.

No one spoke. Three successive explosions boomed from over the hill, followed by rockslide. The bulldozers did their work. Volumes of water flushed through the pipes to sort out the different ores.

"Even if we fail," proclaimed Chen's Dad, "others, those who come after, will see that we tried."

Saanvi and I exchanged glances.

"We'll see," I told Chennai and his parents.

We turned to leave.

"*What?*" cried Dhruv. "Have we decided something?" he implored of Sanvi and me.

"Send me a draft," Chen called after us.

"No," I called back.

"Eat a peach!" shouted Dhruv.

We departed.

EPILOGUE

In the hydroponic garden at Arizona State University, John R. Meyers has grown forage under artificial 24-hour lighting, high ventilation, and controlled temperatures.

His yield: an astounding 15,400 pounds per acre per day!

— *T.A. Heppenheimer*

It's easy to lose sight of how hostile space is to Earthlings.

— *Kim Tingley*

Dhruv posted his profile of Saanvi and me on the Colony News site. We edited it heavily.

The world turned.

We filed our case report on the discovery of the corpse in the lettuce rows.

The CCTV footages we were able to access -- thanks to Matthew Wroblewski -- gave us a certain leverage with the Saraswati authorities.

Example one: the CCTV footage of Aarev visiting the Russian brothel on several occasions. It was a little grainy, but we cleaned it up.

Example two: Tal's gambling debts. These came to light during Dhruv's midnight shift. He was sharp-eyed enough to pick Tal out, and patient enough to retrieve audio. A natural investigative reporter, we told him.

Example three: Captain Gautam's collusion with the Russian black-marketers and smugglers. This included repurposing pharmaceuticals.

* * *

The Case of Metchnikoff's Dead Body in the Botanic Gardens was closed.

We had followed the money.

We had punished the guilty.

No one was guilty of Metchnikoff's death, actually, but we had jailed several very bad guys. They had crossed the Saraswati mission. They had embezzled and cheated and worked counter to the mission.

You can't do that.

We had done our job, me, Saanvi and Dhruv. The system had worked. We solved the mystery and expelled the threat.

The incompetents Tal, Aarev and Gautam were relieved of their duties and sent back to Earth, to be punished.

The extent of Russian corruption was exposed as out-of-control. Within the next year, the entire Roscosmos Colony was taken over by a joint OSRI / China task force.

We got Matthew Wroblewski a job on the American Colony, Jefferson Station, where he is much happier tending our new winter wheats and strawberries.

Rosh Gadol. The best practices won out.

* * *

Our video chat with Waugh, India's Prime Minister on Earth, was ... wincing.

"So, my girls. Magnetic flight, eh?"

"No and Yes," I replied.

"No, we are not your girls," I told him.

The Prime Minister chuckled good-heartedly at this, for surely he had been warned about our sass.

"And Yes, we use a couple of magnetic sleds to get around the gardens out here."

"Just EMP aircrafts," added Saanvi, hoping we could end this as quickly as possible. "They're nothing much."

"You have innovated *superconducting* aircraft! Most ingenious!" exclaimed Waugh, an engineer himself. "And at room temperature ...

"How glorious! A new method of flight! India! Only India!"

He said he wanted to visit soon, and test-fly the sleds. We discussed the Punjabi riots over grains and vegetables, and the land-race seeds that could resolve the food crises.

Saanvi and me, we returned to our plants. We showed Simon Gilroy in Wisconsin what we were doing with cell signaling, and he set us on the right path. Together with him, we churned out some highly decent new Saraswati space crops. One was a new genetic model for peas, strangely enough, the dual-purpose *Arka Apoorva*, that would go on to cause such a sensation.

We had no way of knowing that soon, we would find ourselves in a drama that would threaten to turn all of Botany upside-down, and alter the course of human history.

But that is another story.

\#\#\#

TOM'S STORY NOTES

My tendency, as you know by now, in each tale is to deliver to the reader certain selected passages in excruciating detail, in order to anchor my dialogue and plot progressions. This can become tedious for readers who are expecting and would prefer more of a single-storyline John Green-type propulsion along with S.E. Hinton-style brevity.

This natural tendency of mine was not appropriate for this story. Every blade of grass, every aspect of life has a backstory on a space colony. The research would completely overwhelm the storyline.

So, I tried to keep the focus on the two lead characters, the concept of magnetic flight, and the unexpected (I hope) inclusion of the Raj theme.

* * *

As terse as they are, the oblique comments of Chennai's Dad can be seen as representative of *Navdanya*, a movement promoting biodiversity conservation and farmers' rights in India.

Navdanya was founded by a remarkable woman named Vandana Shiva, once called 'the Gandhi of grain.'. She is a champion of native crops and community seed banks, and an opponent of patented, genetically modified hybrid crop systems sold to Indian farmers by foreign concerns.

* * *

Rosh Gadol is not equal to the thematic idea of *Samaanata* which I am introducing. They are somewhat similar.

* * *

It took me a complete draft to figure out that a first-person narration might be best for this ambitious and unlikely (for me) story. Few of us try to explain context and exposition in our daily speech. My narrator could add character value, bypass third-party setup prose, lend some color, and keep the reader off balance.

I really wanted the Moon Colony story to deliver high marks on pleasing the reader. My feeling is that the X-1 and Aloots stories, filled out to their proper contours, are very challenging for young readers.

My efforts had to be deliberate if I wanted to keep the story's internal logic straight. For instance, if CCTV can capture footage of the gardens, then it would also be able to do so for the protagonists in the Barn or at the Chutes.

The best stories, I think, work like little contraptions, mousetraps, with a surprise in Act Three that has (the reader realizes) been building since word one. That is why I need to spend a lot of time laying out a story's sequence of events. The trap – whether it is a thematic aspect, a phrase, an idea, a hidden-in-the-past element -- must be laid out for the reader honestly. It must grow authentically from a combination of characters, setting and underlying ideas.

Here is an example. I knew I needed a big sky-chase for the Moon Colony action climax, immediately following the unveiling, or moment of truth. But why were the sleds in a chase? What was the rush? Were they chasing someone? If so, how would that person know how to pilot the sled? Until I could provide the reader sound answers for those questions, the chase could not take place.

* * *

Abraham Lincoln loved the aria *M'appari tutto d'amore.*' The song was one of his favorites. It's easy to hear why.

Himself a figure of great triumph and great melancholy, Lincoln no doubt shared the beautiful agony of young Lyonel. He requested to see the entire *Martha* opera at his second inaugural.

Who does not have such a heartbreak in their lives?

* * *

Murder mysteries have their roots in Victorian Britain. The trouble comes when you can't see through your neighbor's façade. Society itself is never in question – far from it, the fruits of imperial society are closely described and enjoyed. The detective story, on the other hand, is more American – these are existential narratives of suspicion, tales of fear of the city. Here, society itself is very much in question.

A true murder-mystery writer's talent is in scattering the puzzle pieces wide, and then re-assembling them in a way that delights the reader. Agatha Christie is the pinnacle. She had a strong wind at her back -- the cultural juggernaut of British High Empire. This same high tide of national destiny enriched a wave of writers around 1890-1945, including Rudyard Kipling, Kenneth Graham, and James Barrie. George Orwell came right after, to begin the process of sweeping up after High Empire.

I don't have that murder-mystery gift. A true parlor mystery seems like artifice to me, a phony exercise in High Empire. This may well be just sour grapes on my part, since I lack that skillset.

COMMENTARY by Professor Cameron Smith

Tom's story "Murder on Moon Colony Saraswati" takes place an 'O'Neill Cylinder', a prominent design for space habitats, but one among many.

If such habitats are built, they will result from tremendous energies expended in the making real of a concept from its origins simply in the imagination of one person; physicist Gerard K. O'Neill, who in the 1970's thought deeply about the shapes and sizes of habitats for tens of thousands of people living beyond Earth.

O'Neill sketched out the essential rotating cylinder design after considering all kinds of other shapes; spheres, donut-like 'toroids' and so on. The cylinder was the easiest to build and quite efficient in terms of the amounts of raw materials needed, compared to other possible shapes.

These materials were mainly metals for large parts of the cylinder, but also vast quantities of glass (derived from lunar dust) for enormous 'sky windows,' miles across, to provide sunlight for planet crops, forests, and, of course, people. Day and night can come and go, as on Earth, by careful coordination of the windows with the sun, and the use of giant floating mirrors outside the Cylinders. And The Cylinders themselves would sit largely in place (though rotating on their long axis) at 'Lagrangian Points' throughout the solar system. At these locations, the gravity of the sun and nearby planets and moons all 'canceled out' attraction to an object like an O'Neill Cylinder, so that it could remain in place for centuries with just one fuel: inexhaustible laws of gravity!

Once built and set in their endless spinning motion, the Cylinders would be populated by thousands of space colonists, not like crews on a submarine or a ship of exploration, but as regular people, families and communities. Kids will go to schools, parents will go to work, people will vacation -- sometimes on the Moon, sometimes back on Earth

-- and they will come home, happy to be home 'back in the Cylinder'.

The view would be that of life inside a gargantuan cylinder. Back On Earth, people stood on the outside surface of a rotating sphere. In an O'Neill Cylinder, people will stand on the inside surface of a 25-mile long tube, five miles across, spinning slowly on its long axis, like a cardboard tube rolling along a floor. This rotation will give half a million people--and their plants and animal companions—a similar pull of gravity, as on Earth.

THE IDEA OF ELECROMAGNETIC FLIGHT

The idea of an electromagnetic 'flying carpet' is a marvel of imagination. In this case, however, the principle of flight isn't magic, as it is in ancient tales. Here a new mode of flight is proposed by considering the unique electromagnetic features inside an O'Neill Cylinder. The combination of reduced gravity down the length of a Cylinder, at its core area, combined with the electromagnetic fields generated by the Cylinder stabilizing towers, is wonderfully creative. I want to know if it works, and I want to fly one!

CONCLUSION

In my Anthropology classes, students consider the many ways that humanity has adapted to so many environments on Earth. Cultures are often a close reflection of their environments, because they were designed and adapted to such landscapes as the Arctic, the Sahara, or the Congo Basin.

What shapes will human culture take in such exotic circumstances as living in an O'Neill Cylinder?

The need to relieve Earth of a lot of people and their

demands on the planet's resources is real. Even with conservation and clean energy, this generation is going to have to give these ideas a great deal of thought. Stories like Tom's are a good place to start.

As he imagines a new method of flight, Tom also throws out ideas about new forms of society for us to consider. History tells us that the national rivalries and incidents of corruption that emerge in his story have always been part of the social fabric. For me, one of the main questions posed by 'science fiction' is, do we HAVE to repeat history?

COMMENTARY (ASTROBOTANY) by Elaine Swanson

Consider any spacefaring adventures you've indulged in through sci-fi stories. Ever wonder how characters, human or alien, sustain themselves? These days, it is easy to take for granted the necessities of life (i.e. eating and breathing!) here on Earth. But in the vastness of space, where resources are scarce and environments hostile, basic survival becomes a constant challenge for characters. The science of astrobotany investigates how to make plants thrive in these harsh conditions. The primary objective of astrobotany is to then develop techniques that harness the adaptability of plants for integration into bio-regenerative life support systems (BLSSs), so our characters can thrive as well.

By mimicking Earth's ecosystems, BLSSs aim to reduce reliance on imports, increase crew autonomy, and enable long-duration space missions beyond Earth's orbit. These systems make our beloved sci-fi stories possible. However, if you're not planning on stepping into a lunar habitat tomorrow, you might not think that astrobotany or BLSSs have much to do with you.

Fortunately for us, this science isn't solely about interstellar exploration; it has terrestrial implications too. The purpose of BLSSs are to take the incredibly complex components of life on Earth that allow for human existence, and package it all into a payload. To make this work, it is crucial to establish a respectful and in-depth relationship between us, researchers and our subject matter: the world around us. With our human population climbing past eight billion and food demands escalating amidst erratic climate patterns, nurturing and exploring such a relationship becomes imperative. Yes, astrobotany offers a new and exciting path to start investigating how we can grow food in extreme conditions, but it can develop into a profound understanding of the agricultural resources readily available to us here on Earth.

Consider Mahi's and Saanvi's innovations in Saraswati's Botanicals. Not only did they advance the adaptability of their crops and communicate their findings to terrestrial agricultural researchers, but they also advanced their method of maneuvering through the Botanicals with magnetic flight. The crux and ultimate success of Mahi's and Saanvi's story is a deep-seated commitment to viewing themselves as integral components of a larger system. Their approach to movement, action, and management is as crucial to their success as the crimes solved and innovations introduced. These skills aren't only reserved for our favorite sci-fi characters.

If you're drawn to innovation, exploration, and the

safeguarding of our food future, astrobotany could be your gateway to a new realm. Explore this further by examining various programs at NASA, such as the work led by Dr. Gioia Massa, the project scientist for food growth production, and Dr. Alyssa Whitcraft, Director of NASA Acres, who spearheads food security initiatives in the United States.

7. Ruby and the London, Paris Air Race

The dawn of the Aviation Age is celebrated in an international competition. Rupa is recruited by Lloyd's of London. She meets the pioneer aircrafts.

Murder, sabotage and dark intrigue shadow her in this twisty tale. War looms. She must prevail to save her family, and Europe.

In the end, Rupa faces an impossible choice.

(London, 1909)

PART ONE

PROLOGUE

Now, can we stop pretending?

—   *Destin Daniel Cretton*

It was so cleverly done. No one noticed.

The Aldersgate station hit a lull in late morning, after the commuters and before the lunch crowd. Few passengers dotted the station's expansive floor.

The anarchists' first explosion was sudden, loud and fearsome.

Kathoom!

Glass shattered outward, shards skidding across the pavement. It was a piercing, intrusive sound, a noise that was disdainful of human decency, so complete as to seem the avatar of some new, lawless state of being. A tool shed was blown apart by the shockwave which followed the initial blast.

Then, everything stopped. That first explosion was muffled, stuffed, truncated in mid-blast.

Then a single gunshot rang out – a very different, precise, personal sound.

Then, after a ghastly pause, a second explosion sent flame and smoke billowing upwards, above the Barbican steps. Pedestrians shouted "No!" in disbelief. Smoke, flash and fire filled Aldersgate. More colorful, even louder, the second explosion was in fact harmless, like fireworks.

Later, the team from Scotland Yard found remnants of what the Orientals once called a "wind and dust" bomb – simply gunpowder in a tube, cased in a ceramic shell. No fragmentation, limited in range. Beyond one fatality – a young man from Croatia – the two bombs caused no injuries. A toolshed in a corner of the station's garage was lost, a westbound train was delayed, nothing more.

Oddly enough, the Croatian youth had been killed not by bomb shards, but by a single bullet to the temple. The bullet had been fired by a Bergman No. 5 pistol, a weapon favored by certain squadrons of the British Army.

* * *

In St. Andrews Square, pedestrians saw the colorful artwork and stopped.

Businessmen in their long grey coats and busy shoppers and baby carriages all crowded around to see the unusual illustration, and read the announcement

The big poster inside the glass box had appeared overnight on the public notice boards on the black wrought-iron gates which surrounded St. Andrew.

The poster showed a Voisin Biplane flying gracefully in an azure sky over Herndon airfield. The aircraft was tilting, jaunty, almost smiling. Bright white, gold-limned clouds framed the Voisin. Giant red letters announced:

Air Race

London to Paris, Paris to London

(L)10,000 to Winner

To Be Held ... October 27, 1909

Sponsored by the Times Observer

Applicants contact Goddard Manley,

Chesterton, Marlborough

Application fee: (L) 1,000

The illustration showed in glowing, flat colors a collage which featured a representation of a Blierot X1, one of the loveliest of aircraft, soaring gracefully over a blue sea. Her happy pilot waved invitingly for you to come and join in the flight ...

A crowd gathered within the minute. Londoners leaned in to read the details of the Air Race.

The news spread quickly.

Flying machines!

I. RUPA

Look well to each step; and from the beginning

think what may be the end.

— *Edward Whymper*

"Thank you for an outstanding semester!" Miss Sharma, the City & Guilds College Engineering Instructor, called out to the night-time class.

Rupishana Lal Pyradhakrishnan clapped, along with her fellow engineering students. Miss Sharma was one of the College's best professors, one who spoke clearly and knew the pulse of her classes. She was committed to her students.

"Good luck on your exams," Miss Sharma continued.

"I know you'll do us proud. You're ready -- well, not you, Sanderson." This brought a laugh, since Sanderson was the most disciplined and industrious among them.

Rupa's loyal cousin, Vandar, stood leaning against the back wall.

"Two things," said the Engineering Instructor, "as we part.

"One. *Integration.*

"All of the disciplines we've studied have an impact on one another. Electrical and structural. Chemical and Industrial. Brunel and Stephenson. Kinetic and potential."

She joined her hands and interlaced the fingers, like a little bridge.

"Today, we need to keep *aerodynamics* in mind if we are to properly design an office tower! Could da Vinci ever have imagined?"

Miss Sharma paused, to let that idea sink in, thoughtful teacher that she was.

"Two. *Details matter,*" she concluded.

"Never forget. Tay Bridge. South Fork Dam. Quebec Bridge. These were engineers in a hurry.

"*Not us.* Never us. Get it right."

She gave a bow, to honor her students.

"This is an era like no other. It is fast becoming a modern world. You are the ones building it."

She gestured, arms out, to dismiss the class.

"My door is always open."

* * *

"What was that she said, in the beginning of class, about *compressed air?*" Vardan asked his slightly- younger cousin, Rupa, when they were seated on the top row of a Number 24 tram.

"You can't *compress air!*"

"Yes, you can," replied Rupa.

"Oh, really? With what? Your hands? A pair of *pliers?*"

"Bellows," she replied. "Piston-based bellows. Or, a wheel-blowing cylinder."

She reached into her satchel and removed a graded exam. On the back, she began to draw a diagram.

"As the density of air increases, the pressure increases ... " she explained as she drew.

Vardan looked closely at her sketch ... a cylinder with gauges, now with pipes added, and pumps, and now he studied Rupa's calculations for clearance volume.

Horse hooves clopped on cobblestone. The tram made its way down Hampstead Heath. Traffic was light at this time of night.

Vardan turned the diagram it this way and that.

The No. 24 tram made a wide, slow turn onto Pimlico.

Rupa yawned as she reached into her satchel and emerged with a sandwich. She carefully unwrapped it and gave three-quarters of it to Vardan. Lost in consideration of the realities of compressed air, he bit and chewed the food absent-mindedly.

He grunted at the diagram. He turned it upside-down.

They were the closest of friends.

2. SATURDAY MORNING FAMILY CAUCUS

If the family were a boat, it would be a canoe that makes no progress unless everyone paddles.

— *Letty Cottin Pogrebin*

The Pyradhakrishnan family tended to caucus in odd places.

In kitchens, in carpeted hallways, in laundry rooms, aisles of food markets, the pantry at midnight (in robes and slippers, sleepy pets in attendance), the family members tended to clump together, chatting, theorizing, comparing notes.

On this sunny Saturday morning, seven of the garrulous clan walked along sidewalks and front lawns and park benches and street crossings in the familiar neighborhood of Little Mumbai in the Croydon sector of London, where the family was well-known and well-loved.

"No," said Father. "*Bilakul nahin!*"

'Yes, way," retorted Surat. "Rupa loves you."

Among them, they carried a week's groceries. A rolling cart and two wagons were included in the parade. Youngest brother Eshaan had outfitted the family dog with saddle bags for the fruits.

"I know that!" retorted Father. "Did you think I didn't

know that?"

He guided a cart laden with groceries while carrying two bags.

Rupa wanted to buy the Dane's tug for Father.

"Here is how it works," Father explained. "The father does for the child. For all his life. All fathers do for all children.

"Children do not do for Fathers. That would break the natural order. The stars would fall from the sky."

He waved to his friend Mahit, mowing his lawn.

Since the recent events at Balliol College, Oxford -- those memorable events, in which she and the young police agent Daniel Summerscale had solved 'The Case of the Shy Mathematician' -- Rupa had been promoted. She now served as Associate Partner in her engineering firm, Childress and Associates. As such, she earned shares of equity in addition to her salary, a growing sum which she placed each month in the family's savings account in Barclays Bank.

And now she could buy her father a boat. The old Dane's tug boat.

Which Father refused.

"Didn't you vouch for Grandpa Parminder when he lost his house ... ?" argued Surat.

"That's different --" said Father.

"Not really," said Mother. She shifted the bag she was carrying from one arm to another.

"No gifts!" insisted Father. "No handouts."

"That's good, that's a good rule," said Rupa, exasperated, "because it's NOT a GIFT! *AAaaggh!*"

"Call it what you like -- "

"Yes! I am calling it an *investment!*" she continued. "A family investment!"

"It is a fine boat," said Mother to her husband. "You yourself said so ... "

"With such a boat, Vardan can build his future," said Rupa. "Uncle Banjeet can put out fires all along the shores. Full employment for the extended Pyradhakrishnan family!"

"*Own!*" argued Rupa's sister, Surat, to Father. "'*Own, never rent.* Own a business. Buy a house. Acquire equity! Do not settle for working for wages.' Isn't that what you always tell us?"

"For India!" said Rupa.

Having no answer to all this invective, Father hefted the bags of groceries he was carrying and split off from the group, to enter the family home through the back door.

* * *

Mother linked arms with her eldest daughter.

"Listen, Rupa. You must have a serious talk with Vardan. Lilavani asked him to attend Diwali with her."

Rupa tilted her head, not understanding.

"He declined," Mother clarified.

"And Mahit says Vardan was almost late for his shift yesterday," added Rupa's sister, Surat. "Because he wanted to make sure you were safely home from your classes."

Mother smoothed the fabric of her saari.

"I have told him a hundred times -- " began Rupa.

"Enough is enough," concluded Mother. "Talk to him. It's time, Rubydoux. Cut him loose. He is a man, not an escort service.

"We," she continued, "we have taken the liberty of drawing up a rotation of escorts for you."

She named several friends and neighbors, older males from the neighborhood.

"But these men all have jobs, families," protested Rupa.

"Your investment in the tug is not unseen by Little Mumbai. A high tide lifts all boats. Your neighbors are eager to support your career."

Rupa nodded. She must now think of how she can talk to Vardan without hurting his feelings ...

* * *

The women stopped to collect the day's mail.

Mrs. Pyradhakrishnan opened an envelope.

"Ah! Your great-aunt Radhiyaa is making the Crossing, on the *White Star*, two months from now. Huh. The day before Diwali."

"Radhiyaa is a terrible gossip," commented Rupa.

"Aye. She leaves chaos in her wake."

They paused at the front door.

An engine noise in the sky caught their attention.

What on earth?

They looked up, squinting. There, among the low clouds ...

was it some sort of mechanical bird?

"What is it?" asked Mother.

"An airplane," answered Rupa.

"What is that?"

Rupa explained.

"So there is a person inside that contraption?"

"Yes. Probably a French person," remarked Rupa. "That's a Blierot. You can tell them apart, you know."

3. THE TUGBOAT DEVI GANGA

The Thames shouldered its way past Blackfriars Bridge, impatient with the ancient piers ... a rush of water that had scented the open sea and was ready to make a run for it.

— *J.G. Ballard*

"She is a most homely-looking boat, *priy*," said Mother to Father. "Is she not?"

"She is." Father nodded with pride.

Mother swung the bottle and let go.

The rope swung wide and the bottle shattered on the tug's nose, exploding in foam. It was the cheapest brand of champagne available.

Cheers rose along the wharfs.

The christening of the tugboat newly named *Devi Ganga* was a significant affair. Navvies, dockworkers, relatives, friends and neighbors -- eager to work their shifts on the tug -- all gathered.

The *Devi Ganga* rested on her little patch of the Thames, at the end of Wharf 7, Slip 21 of the Tilbury docks. She nestled safely in its slip, secure in her moorings, nets neatly folded and properly stored along the gunwales.

She was a good boat, a solid boat. Well-built in the Dutch shipyards at Vlissingen, driven by an almost-new 2,500 kW Hausley engine.

She had been immaculately maintained. All the dockworkers said so.

The new owners had added a water cannon. The Thames River Authority looked favorably on vessels and pilots who pull through for the collective during fires and other emergencies.

A high, celebratory arc of water shot upwards from the cannon. The arc seemed to dissolve even as it climbed, making for a pretty shower. Eshaan and the other children laughed and clapped.

A trio of swiveling klieg lights made the tug useful for night rescues for the Thames Port Authority.

The tug was indeed an unpretty thing, in its facade of grays and brown- painted panels and mud-streaked nets. Yet there was beauty in her proportions, in the way she owned her water-level, in the curve of windows of the pilot's cabin, in the slight tilt of her smokestack.

Mother 's sister, Miss Deepa, lit a candle and said a prayer to soften the arrival of the inevitable disasters which always follow today's joy.

This good fortune, they knew, would at some point be offset by a terrible calamity, a calamity currently unseen.

* * *

Rupa and her cousin and companion, Vardan, were not able to attend the tug's ceremony.

This night, they exited the darkened office of Cheswell and Associates, Civil Engineers.

It had been a long day.

Boarding the mostly empty trolley, they held hands, briefly, as they had done since they were toddlers.

They took their seats in silence. More than fatigue hung over them.

The trolley paused at the corner and then took up again, passing the Londoners who walked the lantern-lit night.

They disembarked at Twickenham, at the northern corner of the Little Mumbai neighborhood.

"Mother says that Lilavati invited you to the *Diwali*," said Rupa as they strolled homeward. "And that you declined. Is that true?"

Vardan looked away.

She stopped walking.

He stopped walking.

He turned sideways to Rupa, as though hoping her words might zip past him, and not count at all.

"*Vardan*," she said, in a voice pooled with compassion.

"*I know*, Rupashana ... " said Vardan.

He was one of three people (all of them family members) who called her that.

"Your family has recruited other escorts for you," he acknowledged. "As it should be."

They had both known this day was coming.

They had both avoided the topic.

Rupa and Vardan had been inseparable since they were toddlers. Vardan had protected her on the family's crossing from India, twelve years prior. She had taught him to read. He had chaperoned her to her engineering classes, and around London, any time of day or night, and all of her schooling, all her success, was only possible because of him. They had their own language. They had shared a thousand adventures, large and small.

But now they were young adults.

They were cousins. They could never marry.

They needed to move forward on their own paths. Her engineering career was taking her into new circles, far from home. Vardan needed to devote himself to his future family, to his own career on the docks, with the other men of London and India.

Rupa found that she could not deliver the speech she had prepared. Instead, the message of those words was conveyed in her face, in her kind expression, in the teary glance that passed between them.

Vardan nodded.

"We're good, Rupa-ji."

Vardan turned to walk away. His family's house was five doors down from hers.

"All good."

He turned back to show her a thumbs-up. She choked back a torrent of tears. Vardan looked so forlorn, in the light of the lamp-post ...

He did not sulk. He did everything to signal that she was blameless for being the one to bring it up.

Just like him! she remarked to herself.

* * *

Rupa sat on the edge of her bed, facing the window, looking out to the moon and stars, in the darkened bedroom she shared with her sisters.

"You've been working too hard," said young Surat. "You've been saving your lunch money. Going hungry. You think that no one notices."

"It's not easy, being the family's tent pole," Surat told her older sister.

"Money's tight," replied Rupa. "Dad worked three shifts last week."

"I know."

Silver moonlight lit the contours of the pretty London plane tree growing outside their window.

"Will the tugboat work out?" asked Surat.

"I think so," replied Rupa. "I keep going over it. All the paperwork has been registered, except for the insurance license. Until that goes through, we can only do scut work ... which doesn't pay enough."

"What's the worst that could happen?" asked Surat.

"That we can't cover the loan. "It could bankrupt us... if we can't re-sell the tug."

"What is that book you carry with you?" asked Surat. "The one Daniel gave you?"

"*Bayes Rule.*"

"Yes," said Surat. "What does that say?"

"It says not to be afraid to start fresh. Start *everything* fresh. Think new, according to new information."

"Well, then. Tomorrow is new. Tomorrow, there will be new information."

Young Surat walked to her dresser and dug around in the bottom drawer.

"I want some equity, too." She handed Rupa a carefully folded stack of pound notes.

"What is this?"

"My babysitting money. The Batra twins. They are horrible little people. But if I teach them to read, I get a bigger tip.

"Eleven pounds. Spend it on yourself, Ruby-dew."

Rupa drew up a Certificate of Equity with stars and a crescent moon across the top, like a letterhead.

"Now I, too, am an owner.," smiled Surat, admiring the paperwork.

3. REVERSAL OF FORTUNE

All is emptiness: your own self, the flashing sword, and the arms that wield it. Even the thought of emptiness is no longer there.

  — *Takuan, The Unmoved Understanding*

Two weeks later, the ceiling caved in on the Pyradhakrishnan family.

"The insurance application has been rejected," announced Mother, standing just inside the front door, with letter and opened envelope in hand.

They could re-apply in two months.

Calamity had arrived in full force.

The tug *Devi Ganga* had been refused an insurance certificate.

No explanation was given by the Thames Port Authority. Suspicion lingered in Little Mumbai that the real reason had to do with race.

Names of lawyers were circulated in the Gujarati community. Tongues clucked at the news of the attorneys' hourly rates. Mahit's wife had a brother in Southall who had worked as a paralegal ...

Rupa again calculated the cash flows under various lowered expectations of maritime income. The family savings account would be empty in thirty days, under the most favorable assumptions. They would have to pay lawyers to supervise the bank reclaiming of the *Devi Ganga*.

All would be lost. It would happen quickly.

"We'll be fine," said Father.

* * *

Desperate, Rupa paid a visit to the Foreign Services Office in Whitehall. While she despised asking anyone for favors, the tug would soon be lost without the insurance policy, and her family's house along with it.

When she inquired for Daniel Summerscale, the receptionist said he no longer worked there.

As she exited, the well-known Minister whom she had met that one day, a year earlier, with Daniel, came barreling down the corridors, surrounded by a gaggle of aides.

Recognizing Rupa, he slowed down long enough to convey his assurances:

"Our boy is in the field. Doing good work," he murmured in her ear, adding, "No new visits from the *fraulein*, I trust -- "

With a wave, he was gone.

4. LUCK

Not a breeze can blow in any latitude,

not a storm can burst, not a fog can rise,

in any part of the world,

without recording its history here.

— *London journalist, regarding the Underwriting room at Lloyds's (1859)*

The door swung open.

Melissa Childress strode into the offices of Childress and Associates, Civil Engineers.

"Ruby, dear, are you still looking for maritime insurance?" asked Melissa.

She was the resourceful wife and caretaker of the personable, well-connected young alcoholic, Rupa's boss, Andrew Childress.

"For your tug, I mean."

"Yes, we are," replied Rupa, looking up from the Rotherhithe plans spread across her twin desks.

"Well, we may have an answer for you. Are those the tunnel elevations?"

Rupa nodded. "We have a meeting with Brunel this afternoon."

"Ah. In any case," continued Melissa Childress. "Andrew and I attended an event last night at his Club, the Porcellian, and we ran into one of his Charterhouse mates. A chap named Harry Minton.

"Your name came up. Harry heard about you through your friend. Daniel Summerscale. High praise.

"Harry is partner in Lloyd's, and it seems they have a pressing need for a tertiary report. Risk assessment. A third opinion, from an engineer they can trust.

"Andrew volunteered you.

"Lloyd's vendors all qualify for private policies,, you see. That is, if you work for them once, you are in the family. You are guaranteed coverage.

"You could get insurance for your family's tug-boat."

"That would be most welcome!" said Rupa.

"It's the least we can do, my dear. You are the reason we are solvent, after all."

"Harry awaits your visit. This very morning. Cornhill, at Threadneedle. With luck, you can still make your Rotherhithe appointment."

Tom Durwood

* * *

The offices of Lloyd's of London, the Western world's best-known insurance underwriter, sat within the grand neo-classical structure at **Bank Junction**, in the **Ward of Cornhill** in the heart of the City, flanked by Cornhill and Threadneedle Street.

Rupa made her way briskly up the sandstone steps.

Lloyd's of London made possible the British Empire. Great Britain had figured out how to share risk.

The British East India Company and its ships would never have sailed without it being at risk. No single entity can take on such risky enterprises as a war with France or the colonizing of the Indian subcontinent without sharing that risk. Lloyd's syndicated, or shared, the bold explorers' investment – issuing slivers of risk, that is, on open markets, so that all Englishmen could buy bonds and help shoulder the danger of shipwrecks and native massacres (and share in the rewards as well). Lloyd's was not so much a contained company as it was an open bourse, an organized market.

Rupa entered the wood-paneled universe of Lloyd's – open halls of clerks scribbling at their desks, very high windows, slanted sunlight, and glass sky-lights. She was led through libraries stacked with tomes and maps and ships' logs. Rupa could pick out the circles of the semaphore alphabet which decorated the walls of paneling – nautical figures, flags, flag colors, and flag positions.

She was led to a tall-ceilinged office, all high windows, wall maps, and leather chairs.

"Harry Minton." The pleasant young man rounded his desk and shook her hand warmly. "Thanks for coming."

"You come well-recommended, Miss Pyradhakrishnan. Did I pronounce that correctly?"

"We need to file a third opinion. Backup. A tertiary risk assessment, if you have the time and interest.

"We already have a primary and secondary. Quite thorough. But we lost a good deal in the San Francisco earthquakes, as you may have read. So, our directors want us to err on the side of caution.

"On a fast turnaround, I'm afraid."

"I see," said Rupa. "And what risk is to be assessed?"

For an answer, Harry Minton slid across the table a colorful poster featuring a Blierot X1 aircraft, her pilot waving cheerily from the open cockpit:

The London, Paris Air Race

5. THE PATENT OFFICE

If all men are brethren, why are the winds

and waves so restless?

— *Emperor Meiji*

"I hope you won't mind."

Rupa stood in the doorway, holding an armful of heavy notebooks.

One hour later, Miss Sharma seemed pleasantly surprised to see her pupil Rupa Pyradhakrishnan in the doorway of her

City & Guilds College faculty offices.

"Ah!" replied the Engineering Instructor. "You come *laden*. Let me help -- "

Rupa explained the task which Lloyd's had set out for her. Miss Sharma listened carefully. After they had reviewed all of the Lloyd's notebooks, they concluded that 9 first-tier aircraft and 3 of the second tier were to be assessed and rated for risk.

"Penrose works part-time at the Patent Office," said Miss Sharma, naming one of Rupa's classmates. "That should be our first stop."

* * *

They found Penrose on the third-floor library of the Chancery Lane Public Records archives. An ungainly young woman who wore too much makeup, Penrose turned out to be a thoroughbred researcher.

Furious legal squabbles marked those pioneering days of aviation. The Curtiss team suggested that the Wrights would sue anyone who jumped in the air and waved their arms. As a result, each aircraft designer filed for patents on every conceivable innovation he could claim.

By noon, Miss Sharma had concluded that two of the aircraft were not in evidence, apparently never having applied for patents.

Another classmate, Stevenson, appeared and was recruited to help. They enlisted the guidance of a deputy record -keeper, and by the end of the day the four of them had assembled preliminary profiles of eleven of the nineteen aircraft.

By five o'clock, the Lloyd's Air Race tertiary report had

begun, in earnest, driven by not one but four engineering minds.

As night fell, the quartet carried the notes and applications and supplements to one of the Archive cells, where they were set aside for Rupa's future use.

Stevenson insisted on escorting Penrose and Miss Sharma to their respective bus lines, and then Rupa on the Twickenham Line home, to her doorstep.

6. VOISIN

There's more going on here than you're aware of.

— *Morten Tyldum*

The box camera which Rupa carried on the bus to the Herndon airfield was bulky to carry and temperamental to operate. The rotary shutter worked when it felt like working ... but the images the camera produced were striking, if you could get the light and shadows to contrast properly.

* * *

"Don't you miss Vardan?" asked Surat as they rode on the bus. "You two were always together."

"Yes," said Rupa, at length. "I think of him. Often."

"Didn't you think you'd marry him?"

Absently, Rupa joined her hands as they rested on the camera box and interlaced the fingers, like a little bridge.

She pulled them apart.

She re-joined them.

Rupa did not answer the question.

* * *

"The Voisin is a most elegant little aircraft," began Rupa's fourth report.

"A thing of beauty, most graceful. Flying in it is a life-changing experience.

"But it is not sturdy enough to make such a long trip as this. The Channel winds blow thirty per cent faster than the breezes of Umbria.

"Roll control is very much on the Americans' mind, very little on the French. Overlooking this flaw as it pertains to the Voisin will prove costly. The overhaul of the wings and rigging with dihedral will lend some lateral stability (but not enough).

"One-quarter box-kite, the Voisin is an awkward craft. The wheels I witnessed beneath its v-struts were pretty but fragile and will fail after five landings. A more powerful engine than the 50 hp V8 Antoinnette would make the craft more nimble, and increase the durability.

"At the Polygon de Vincennes (this past February), the lower booms supporting the tail failed on lift off. On 16 March, upon lift-off, the engine torque drove the Voisin's left-hand wing onto the ground, ending the attempted flight. Ballast corrections should solve this problem.

"Once the aircraft reaches 40 miles per hour or so, it begins to lift. But a low-pressure area forms along the vehicle's rear, trying to suck it backwards. If he could build in slots, aft, along the craft's curve, compressed air can then create a positive pressure. To offset, that is.

The images ... were striking, if you could only get the light and shadows to contrast properly.

"One note: the Voisin's mechanics know more about it than the engineers do. Normally, this state of things would be fine. Here, the engineers do not acknowledge it and therefore cannot be trusted to keep the aircraft aloft. I am mindful of the Sopwith engineer who sought to protect a wealthy sponsor by adding a metal bottom-shield, and in doing so ruined the aerodynamics and crashed the plane.

"Aerodynamically, this is brilliant. Structurally, it is suspect. These engineers have designed an elegant craft which will never survive high winds over Dover. Until they re-make it, using stronger material ....

The Aero Club of France is to be congratulated on this ingenious, eye-pleasing design -- congratulated but not trusted, not for a flight of such distance, and difficulty.

"The brilliant Voisin does not understand the basic issues of successful manned flight – lift, stability, control – and is concerned only with speed. This will lead to disaster.

"Revisit him at a later time, perhaps for the London, Paris Air Race of 1914."

7. Nulli SecUndus

Once you have tasted flight, you will forever walk the earth with your eyes turned skyward. There you have been, and there you will always long to return.

> — *Leonardo Da Vinci*

Phaeton, the son of Helios, having yoked the steeds in his father's chariot, because he was not able to drive them in the path of his father, burnt up all that was upon the earth, and was himself destroyed by a thunderbolt.

> — *Plato*

"Are you serious?" asked Rupa.

The craft below them was half a city block long and three stories tall ... and filled with flammable gas.

She had read much about dirigibles, but she had never seen one.

"Whatever madman first devised such a thing ..."

They stood on a catwalk in the high platform constructed at the top of the vast Aerodrome hangars.

The *Nulli Secundus* dirigible was moored to its pole,

They carefully climbed aboard.

Rupa boarded the airship near the passenger section of the cargo hold, tucked beneath the vast balloon. An iron framework composed of triangular lattice girders was marked by small lights along the railings. The long under-carriage held sleds that could be used as a boat if the vehicle was forced to land in water. The dirigible was designed to be driven by three propellers and steered with a sail-like aft rudder. Internal ballonets -- giant inflated panels -- could be used to regulate lift.

Rupa walked the wooden platforms and metal ladders and light-steel railings.

A dirigible has a rigid framework covered by an outer skin or envelope. The interior contains one or more gasbags, cells or balloons to provide lift. Rigid airships are typically unpressurised and can be made to virtually any size.

The engines and crew were accommodated in "gondolas" hung beneath the hull. Driving propellers were attached to the sides of the frame by means of long drive shafts.

Additionally, there was a passenger compartment (its alternate use was as a bomb bay) located halfway between the two engine compartments.

Zeppelins, she knew, proved to be terrifying but inaccurate weapons. Navigation, target selection and bomb-aiming proved to be difficult under the best of conditions,

From Rupa's Notes:

"The Zeppelin is unique among aircraft. She operates on an entirely different theory of flight than the other, heavier-than-air, propulsion-driven aircraft. She floats like a gigantic balloon and is propelled by a set of small fans. It pretends to be lighter than air, by virtue of the gas captured within. It is a hybrid aircraft, half balloon and half bicycle, driven by winds.

"The question of risk in a helium dirigible is hard to calculate, and is subject to many variables. The presence of helium makes a zeppelin un-insurable. A disaster waiting to happen. The engineers have no tangible design answer, and in many cases refuse to even acknowledge the explosive reality.

"So much about our assessment of the dirigible depends on the gas which, trapped within its airframe, gives it buoyancy. On one hand, hydrogen is cheap, renewable, and has more lifting power than helium. However, it is highly flammable. Only a madman would knowingly ride in a zeppelin or dirigible filled with hydrogen.

"On the other hand, if helium is used instead of hydrogen, everything changes. Helium is a stable gas, one not prone to exploding in a massive fireball. Helium is not as buoyant but is far safer than hydrogen because it does not burn."

From her Footnotes:

"They say that every aircraft is an idea. Filled with hydrogen, the idea of the dirigible is, apparently: *Enjoy a Pleasant Flight Before Your Ship Violently Explodes and You Die.*

"Under a helium balloon, the idea of a dirigible is that of the tortoise of Aesop's fable: slow, steady and dependable wins the race."

8. WRIGHT MILITARY PLANE

If we worked on the assumption that what is accepted as true really is true, then there would be little hope for advance.

    — Orville Wright

"*Insurance,*" said the guard flatly. "I don't know what that means."

"Of course.," said Rupa patiently. "I beg your pardon."

She spoke through the bars of the entrance gates. "I should explain."

The Northolt facility was being constructed on the grounds of a military school in Ruislip. Still in its infancy, the airfield had not set procedures for visitors.

"My firm is underwriting -- that is, we are here to *assess* the risk -- "

"Ah! Miss Prya- pash-wana!" shouted a voice.

A tall, red-cheeked young man, hair flying, came down the path.

"Pyradhakrishnan," said Rupa. "Rupashana Pyradha-krishnan."

The young man stopped, pleased that he had intervened in time, and bowed.

"I am Rupa. This is my sister," said Rupa, "Narinder, and this young lady is my cousin, Surat Ramakrishnan. They are accompanying me on the tour. On behalf of Lloyds of London.

"We have just come from the train station."

The gates opened.

"Of course!" replied the cheerful young man. "Lloyd's told us to be expecting you.

"Please let me -- " He took the box camera, holding it respectfully, by both latches,

"Sorry about that. It's the Wright team. The Americans are a bit paranoid. Patents, you know. Never get involved in a lawsuit, by the way. The damn things have a life of their own.

"Can I just get the three of you to sign this waiver, then I'll give you the Grand Tour."

* * *

From Rupa's Note.

"The Wright Military Flyer is a serious aircraft.

"Eight feet tall, 30 feet long with a wingspan of 37 feet, the Wright weighs 735 pounds. The biplane is wire-braced. Substantial wood construction with a muslin fabric covering. The engine is a 30-40 horsepower vertical four-cylinder engine driving two wooden propellers.

"Sprocket-and-chain transmission system. No wheels; skids for landing gear. Natural fabric finish; no sealant or paint of any kind.

"It is easily assembled and disassembled, so that an army wagon could transport it.

"It is able to carry two people with a combined weight of 350 lb., and sufficient fuel for 200 km. The Wright reaches a speed of at least 64 kph in still air. It can land without requiring a prepared landing strip. It should be able to ascend in any sort of country in which the Signal Corps might need it in field service.

"Built to satisfy specific requirements by the U.S. Army, the plane reflects design and manufacture of a high order.

"If any aircraft deserves a high rating for dependability and performance, it is this.

"Wright himself drives the entire enterprise, and he does not delegate. I'm not sure there is a second-in-command. If Wright falters, remove all support.

9. COMMISSION COMPLETED

Its natural waterways, long buried,

are coming back to life.

— *Dana Priest*

"Four days ahead of schedule," laughed Harry Minton.

The offices of Lloyd's were extra- busy. Multiple disasters developing in far lands needed to be assessed.

"Complete with photographs." Minton was most pleased at the heft of Rupa's report. He leafed through it.

"I thank you, Rupashana. This could not have been easy."

He handed the report to a scribe.

"The partners will read it today. With great interest."

* * *

The Pyradhakrishnan family gathered in the front yard, waiting for the mailman.

Rupa would soon arrive home from work. Today she was on-site at the Kew Gardens, a job she very much enjoyed, because the architect, Borgo, was ill, and she was acting as virtual project head. And now there was talk of her firm bidding on a prestigious botanical gardens project in Kolkata ... a sort of Indian corollary to Kew Gardens.

Rupa stepped off the red London City bus.

A satchel heavy with papers was slung over one shoulder, as ever.

All watched as Rupa opened the mailbox.

A manila envelope was inside. The crested seal pronounced "Lloyd's of London."

She opened it methodically, to Mother's exasperation.

The handwritten note on watermarked linen stationary said this:

A remarkable document. Most useful. We appreciate diligent work like this.

Footnotes most amusing.

-- Harry Minton, Junior Partner

Also enclosed was a Bank of England cashier's checque made out to Rupishana Pyradhakrishnan.

In addition, she found an executed insurance maritime policy for the tugboat *Devi Ganga.*

And lastly, a bonus award of a thousand pounds.

Mother fainted.

Uncle Banjeet held his forehead while murmuring a lengthy prayer of thanks.

Narinder held the bonus checque high, so all could see.

Eeshan danced a jig with the dog.

Deepa and Surat made their way to the kitchen. Tonight's dinner would be most special.

None noticed when Rupa retired to her bedroom.

When the door had closed, the Pyradhakrishnan's eldest daughter, pride of her family, collapsed on the floor in a heap.

Rupashana could not seem to draw a full breath.
Her hands would not stop shaking.

PART TWO

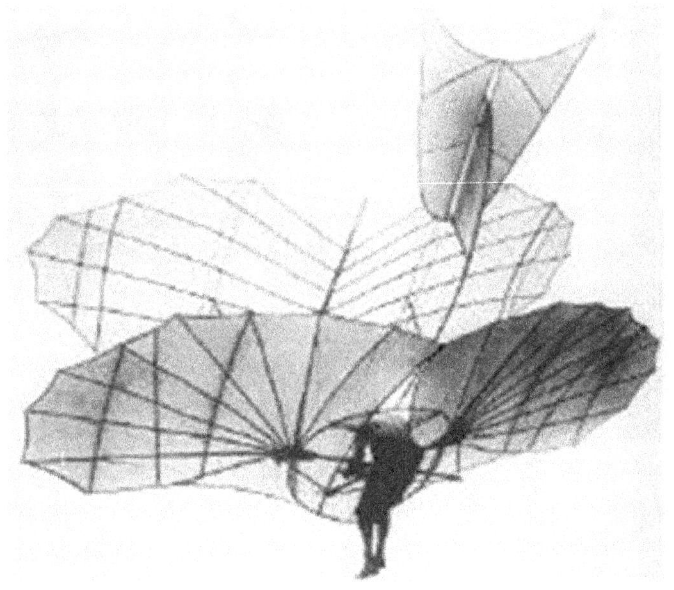

12. THE TUNNEL AT ROTHERHITHE

Our most basic instinct is not for survival but for family.

— *Paul Pearsall*

Eupalinus apparently trusted that any surveyor would have the knowledge required to assure that the two adits would meet in the middle of the hill.

— *Fred Roeder*

"Narinder. Surat. Get your jackets," said Mother.

"We're in the middle of the algebra workbooks -- " explained Narinder.

"No sass. You two are going to accompany Rupa today. She has an assignment in Guildhall.

"Can't Vardan -- " protested Narinder.

'Bring your workbooks," ordered Mother.

"Escorting Rupa is Vardan's job -- " protested Surat.

"*Was*," clarified Mother. "Was his job. No longer."

Narinder and Surat stopped and looked up at these words.

"Mahit and Gundar are both sick," Mother explained. "Everyone else is on the water."

"I've packed food," Miss Deepa clapped her hands in the kitchen.

"*Jaldee*," urged Mother. "Rupa can't be late."

* * *

The Rotherhithe Tunnel which Rupa's firm was helping to successfully excavate would be the fourth tunnel beneath the Thames, the eleventh crossing if you count bridges as well.

A massive undertaking, the tunnel actually started at the entrance arches two blocks into the park. The arches were 30 feet across, and marked a gradual slope to the cut-and-cover trenches.

The detail-oriented chief engineer Edward Tabor and the contractors, Price and Reeves, had insisted on shields and safety protocols. The dig's alignments were constantly recorded and circulated.

They had contracted with Rupa's firm, Childress and Associates, to oversee the various surveyor teams as well as the mining men who manned the shovels and drills and picks. The men brightened to see Rupa on site.

Many are the decisions to be made, large and small, on such a job. Rupa was unafraid to make them. She understood all of the numbers, and what the calculations meant.

Gargantuan fans spun methodically in the perpetual job of venting the tunnel shafts. Food and drink vendors offered their wares from stations along the narrow walkways lining the tunnel walls.

Lanterns held high, Rupa and her two charges picked their way carefully among the load-bearing wooden shafts and underpinnings and concrete rollers.

They stepped past the giant rotors of the excavators.

A vast cylindrical tunnel shield – a cast-iron structure with three levels and twelve sections per level -- protected workers from cave-ins. Surveyors and quality-control supervisors ducked among the wooden scaffolds and brick piles of the permanent support structure.

It was the surveyors whom Rupa targeted this day, roaming pairs of yellow-jacketed topographers who kept the work on its proper and exact course.

Surveyors are minor royalty, in such a project. When they err in their work, bad things happen. All engineers carry in their memories the cautionary tale of Eupalinus of Megara, a Greek engineer whose tunnellers chiseled away at solid rock for months, only to find that they had missed one another by twenty feet in the vertical and three in the horizontal.

Now Rupa and the two girls passed a boisterous, mutton-chopped Welshman miner who sang a lively work song so his diggers could keep a rhythm:

> *I remember the face of my father,*
> *As we walked back home from the mine.*
> *He'd laugh and he'd say, that's one more day,*
> *And it's good to feel the sunshine.*

As they approached the next surveying station, three things happened more or less at once.

Rupa glanced up to recognize a slim, henna-haired, narrow-shouldered figure among the hot-chestnut barrels. It was a woman. She was moving away. Rupa had seen that silhouette once before ....

Simultaneous to this, Rupa felt a note being slipped into her hand.

She looked down and read three lines written in pen and ink, in a handwriting she well knew:

$$P(A \mid B) = P(B \mid A) * P(A) P(B)$$

The Game is Afoot.

Stack 5 now

At almost that same moment, a loud flash-bang went up among the meat vendors.

Shouts and hot chestnuts and coals went flying. A whistle sounded.

A girl in each arm, Rupa walked through a large puff of smoke towards Stack 5.

Stack 5 was one of the giant vents. But Stack 5 was well west ... towards the middle of the mighty Thames, its seaward currents strong and swelling.

The trio moved along the railings. Workers made way, recognizing Rupa.

They reached the fans of Stack 5.

A second detonation went off, behind them. They heard shouts in several dialects.

Rupa pulled both girls up and then climbed up to follow them.

Behind, someone crashed the chestnut barrel, sending hot charcoals scattering. In the smoldering and smoke, Rupa heard shouting in different languages. She smelled fabric burning.

Now hands pulled them clear of the tunnel vent and into a paddle steamer.

It was the mutton-chopped Welshman.

The man pulled off his moustache and beard and facial disguise. He discarded his hat to reveal the smiling, familiar face of her good friend, Daniel Summerscale.

13. WORLD ON FIRE

"You mean *Nasr-ed-din*," he said, still munching crumpets.

– *Greenmantle*

It struck me that Albania was the sort of place

that might keep a man from yawning.

– *The 39 Steps*

A light rain started up.

In the boat, going north on the Thames, Daniel sang a second verse of the miners' song over the noise of the paddles:

Take me home, to my family,
Take me home, to my friends,
Take me home where my heart lies
And let me, let me, let me sing again.

They passed Cheyne Walk. Rupa guessed they were in the

Chelsea Embankment, neighborhood of merchant mansions, but she could not tell. The paddle boat slowed.

They docked in a slip. They walked up a hidden stone path winding its way among the sprawling homes.

Daniel held the door.

In the mud room of the mansion, servants offered the girls towels, cardigan sweaters and hot tea.

The spaces were more like that of a cathedral than a private home.

Daniel called Surat and Narinder by name, for he had met them before (*see the Epilogue to "The Case of the Shy Mathematician").

"I need Madame Rupa for an hour, no more," he told them. "Then we'll have you all three home.

"Tell the cook what she can put together for you ... her rarebit is outstanding."

"Ah! Here comes my sister, Amelia." He made introductions. "She cheats at cards," he warned Narinder and Surat.

* * *

Rupa and Daniel took seats in the cavernous library.

Piano playing and Surat's laughter floated in from the parlor next door.

Daniel poured them tea.

"Where have you been all these months, brother?" asked Rupa. "And what happened back there, in the tunnel?"

"I have been to Buluwayo," Daniel answered. "Kut. Umvelos. Points East. For a time, I was deep in the Rooirand, among the Bakhtiari.

"I have been known by other names. Ah! English tea. It has been too long..."

He removed more of his disguise with a towel. He looked more like a version of the young diplomat she knew. Unruly hair fell over his collar.

"The Sheikh-ul-Islam is neglected. The Kaiser proclaims a Holy War. Karolides' rise in the Balkans is causing a bloody uproar. God.

"Two of my mates were lost in Mesopotamia. May they rest in peace.

"The Minister's efforts – all of our efforts -- have been to bank the fires that threaten to enflame Europe.

"This next century will be one of the most violent since Alexander made war on Persia.

He took off his miner's vest and replaced it with a cardigan.

"All the Western empires are in decline.

"All native peoples seek Home Rule, as they should. Algeria, central Africa, Ireland, India. The Zionists. The native races must own their own destinies.

"Yet the empires resist. They want to stay in the game another century. They are convinced that the heritage of the dominant world races is to protect the lower castes from themselves. The anarchists will blow up half of England to make their argument against that very ev--"

He removed a heavy object from an inner pocket. A Bergman No. 5 pistol.

"What? So you just *kill* them?" asked Rupa.

"No! Why no, of course not -- "

Absently, Rupa joined her hands and interlaced the fingers, like a little bridge.

She pulled them apart.

She re-joined them.

"The Minister's idea is to make a peaceful transition to that new world. The anarchists are in a bigger hurry.

"The bombing in Aldersgate was a first shot in the new war.

"Our German friend, Emmaline Krauss – that was her you saw, back in the tunnel. She stokes the fires."

A sheet of rain made a swishing sound on the mansion's roofs.

"The little puff in the Rotherhithe was her work. A rehearsal. For a much larger, more deadly attack."

"What is it she seeks?" asked Rupa.

"War," replied David.

"The war of all against all."

* * *

Daniel poured a second cup of tea. Two kitchen servers passed through to deliver covered steaming platters on silver trays to the girls in the parlor.

"Miss Krauss and her employers will provide the weapons.

"The naïve anarchists whom she presently uses as

accomplices will not survive. They are a reckless, dangerous crowd.

"And right now, you impede her. She has not forgotten that night at Oxford. The chase across the lawns."

"You have heard of the American Canal at Panama," Daniel continued.

"Yes," replied Rupa. "We studied it at City & Guild."

"Now, a young engineer, Saul Dubinsky, has come up with a device he calls a synchronizer. He has fixed all of Schildhauer's problems. It is reportedly a wonder.

"The Krupps think it can improve any number of their arsenal."

"What does it do?" asked Rupa.

"It allows two systems to work in conjunction. Electric and mechanics. Engine and horsepower. I believe he devised it in Brooklyn, originally. As part of the Cincinnati clock commission.

"Now, I will mention three items in specific. Straight-running torpedoes. Bomb sights. And a poison gas called phosgene."

"That's where you come in," he said ... "England needs you once more, my girl."

"Airplanes and their capacities will figure in these. The Air Show is but a showcase. It has been targeted by the anarchists and weapons-makers. Half the aristocracy of Europe will be attending.

"That's where you come in."

Rain was coming down in earnest now, in sheets, loud on the waves and shutters of the tall windows.

Next door, Narinder was playing the Chopin piece that Mother forced them to practice, the Nocturne.

"England needs you once more, my girl."

14. THE RACE

British engineer Robert Whitehead invented
the self-propelled torpedo in the 1860's, with the
hope of ending war.

— *Edwin Gray, The Devil's Device*

The most difficult thing is the decision to act.
The rest is tenacity.

— *Amelia Earhart*

The Tower Bridge and St. Catherine's marina form a sort of cove and amphitheater on the northern banks of the Thames, across the way from Butler's wharf. It is sometimes called the Pool of London.

On this sunny morning, families of Londoners had gathered on the docks and piers to see the Air Race contestants on their way to the finish line at Nelson's statue at Trafalgar.

Civilian aircraft had come out to join the show. Amateur and experimental aircraft helped celebrate the joys of flight.

Garrick's, a private restaurant, featured a balcony and patio with bleachers. A windowed, multi-tiered dining room with expansive views of the little harbor had been set up across the channel.

Rupa watched from an observation balloon floating above the cove's southern section.

Daniel rode the dirigible.

* * *

It was the triplane which carried the torpedo.

The Fokker DR (*Dreidecker*, or triplane, that is) was an updated and modernized German version of the original British triplane, the Cayley, with three stacked wings above the fuselage and a separate stabilizing tail (with fins). Rupa well knew that such a large and glide-friendly aircraft needed plenty of low and horizontal airspace in order to make its approach -- and lay down the torpedo in the waters, aimed for its target.

Seeing the Triplane duck under Tower Bridge northward and then take its slow, inevitable turn, Rupa unfurled the giant banner.

The banner dropped over the side of the observation balloon, as strong and clear a semaphore as Nelson gave at

Trafalgar ("England Expects that Every Man will Do His Duty") and Burnside at Elk Mountain.

At her signal, the array of seven barges swiveled into their positions, near the eastern shoreline, facing the Thames. Roughly in unison, ropes and ties were cut -- letting fall the chain mesh curtains which held the dredges. In an instant, they formed an underwater curtain to protect the shoreline.

Blithe to this defense, the Triplane made a long and careful approach.

Closely recorded by of Daniel's photographers and scribes stationed on the quays and piers and in observation balloons, the Fokker descended in a graceful straight line aimed at the stadium stands of onlookers, so that she almost skimmed the water's surface.

The Triplane let loose four torpedoes from its metal talons.

One of the metal cylinders immediately detonated, sending up a sharp spray.

Then one of the synchronizers must have failed, for a second torpedo went wayward, veering off course, only to stop in the water altogether, then sinking out of sight.

The remaining two metal fish detonated against the steel-chain latticework which guarded the wharfs. Their shards fell to the bottom, joining the shoes, bottles, anchors, tobacco pipes, Roman pottery and other sad artifacts which lay abandoned in the mud and muck of the Thames river-bottom.

The barges rocked in place, irritated, no more than irritated, by the torpedoes' detonations.

* * *

It was the dirigible *Nulli Secundus* which harbored the poison gas, phosgene.

In the spacious *Nulli Secundus'* undercarriage, a pair of violin players serenaded onlookers.

The dirigible floated, lazily above the Pool of London, like a beneficent character in a children's fantasy book.

When the Nulli Secundus was high over the bleachers, its bomb-bay opened, three bags of phosgene fell out.

They had been too high, and two of the bags fell into the river. The bomb sights had been corrupted by Daniel's agents. While phosgene in its gaseous form is a potent poison, phosgene in water is harmless slush.

One bag of the noxious gas did manage to land half-wet and half-dry on the patio of the Garrick -- populated not by flesh and blood Londoners but by mannequin decoys. The gas was immediately administered by a half-dozen men in gas masks, abetted by powerful fans and large safety bags.

* * *

It was the Etrich-Rumpler Taube which carried the synchronized, front-firing machine guns.

As they crossed paths over Tower Bridge, the amiable young Voisin pilot waved at his brother pilot in the cockpit of the birdlike Etrich-Rumpler Taube on such a fine day, on such a jolly occasion.

In response, the Taube pilot fired a barrage of bullets from the front-mounted Maxim gun. The Dubinsky synchronizer allowed the bullets to fly out through the airplane's rotors, as if by magic.

Fortunately, the bullets missed the *Voison*. The tactics and details of aerial warfare had yet to be invented.

The Taube revved its engine and turned sharply.

Rupa knew just where it was headed,

Rupa unfurled a second banner, this one on the west-facing side of the cove.

At the signal, a tugboat sent a stream of forced river-water arcing high into the air, almost as high as the bridge.

A second column of water shot upwards.

The Taube could not maneuver wide enough to dodge the twin arcs of pressurized water.

The hoses on the tugboat *Devi Ganga* tracked the Etrich-Rumpler Taube aircraft as it shook this way and that, catching it square.

The motor was soaked. The engines stalled.

The synchronizer's perfection was ruined.

The Taube aircraft coughed and choked.

It dropped like a stone, barely managing to pull out of a ruinous dive and land on water sleds, into the waiting arms of the Thames Water Police.

Rupa waved to the crew of the *Devi Ganga*.

Rupa turned to wave at Daniel Summerscale, on the deck of the dirigible.

Much had been learned today. No one had been harmed.

As to the race itself, the contest was won by the *Vuia 99*, nicknamed *Liliacul* (the Bat), a pioneer aircraft designed and built by the oddball Romanian inventor, Traian Vuia.

Contestant #9, the French-built *Spad CR*, ended up in a Pas-de-Calais beet-field, near a farmhouse, in the rain.

The pilot of the SE 5A Scout contestant landed on the Champs Elysee in an act of sheer exuberance.

Overall, the London, Paris Air Race proved an extremely profitable venture for Lloyd's, with high premiums and low payouts, mainly the damage inflicted by the damn torpedo.

Their tertiary risk-assessment had proven most accurate.

EPILOGUE

Secret agents are such bastards.

— *Graham Moore*

Claridge's tea room was an establishment of white gloves, linen napkins, and chamber music. The Mivarts Bar section of its dining rooms, where Rupa was seated, were not visible from the Brooke Street elevation.

She had been surprised to receive the lunch invitation from Daniel. His thanks, she assumed, for her help in the Air Show.

A figure slipped into the seat across from Rupa.

It was not Daniel.

"First, I didn't poison Warinder," said a female voice from behind the menu.

"I know that's what you think."

Rupa looked across the table to see a woman of slim figure in a crimson dress with exaggerated shoulders. Sharp eyes, henna hair and a narrow, aristocratic nose.

Fraulein Emma Krauss.

"If Nignon is still chef here, the salmon should be top-drawer," commented she.

Rupa glanced left and right. She could identify the German woman's henchmen in the restaurant, watching her closely.

"Daniel Summerscale is likely to get you killed. You know that, don't you?"

Miss Krauss lit a thin black cigar.

"Ask him to tell you what really happened at Aldersgate ..."

"Just who do you think y-- " began Rupa angrily.

"Ah ah. You have angered some very powerful parties," her luncheon companion continued. "They mean to make a great deal of money from a condition of war.

"Yet you keep thwarting them."

Miss Emma Krauss took a drag on the cigar ...

"A contract has been put out on you, dear. I argued against it. But you have embarrassed certain vain men.

"Did you really think there would be no recoil? You have forgotten Newton's Third Law, or perhaps just tucked it out of mind ..."

She extinguished the cigar in a tea saucer.

"You need to be on another continent."

"How *dare* you -- " demanded Rupa, half-standing ...

But she was too late.

The seat across from her was empty.

* * *

Diwali celebrations cover all the bases – costumes, music, colorful lit lanterns, food, dancing, neighbors of all ages, long toasts and in this case a cake in the form of a tug-boat.

The entire neighborhood was celebrating.

From Rupa's Engineering College, Miss Sharma, Stevenson, and Penrose were in attendance. Penrose took enthusiastic part in the circular *giddha* dance, women acting out the phases of village life.

Rupa was distracted. The singular conversation with the German woman in Claridge's was still on Rupa's mind when Daniel Summerscale appeared through the crowd.

"I can't stay," said Daniel over the music. "I just wanted to deliver this."

David handed her a small envelope.

"What is this?" asked Rupa.

She tore open the envelope. Inside was a stiff ivory card.

She read it but could not seem to grasp ...

"It's an invitation, my girl," said David. He took a glass of lemonade from a passing tray and downed it.

"To my family's place. Van Oss Hall. Sussex. For Hunt Week. You don't have to actually hunt," he added.

"My sister was taken with Narinder and Surat. Now my whole family wants to meet you. And your clan.

"You can all stay in the carriage house. It is entirely private. Your parents will have their own staff. Your sisters can ride any horse in the stables."

Rupa hesitated, not knowing what to say.

This was far more than it seemed.

A young woman, marriage age, meeting the family of an eligible Englishman ...

At that moment, Surat and Narinder arrived to fuss over Daniel. They insisted on borrowing him to premiere their new piano duet (Brahms, as abridged by Miss Deepa).

* * *

"What news, Radhiyaa?"

Father asked the question before Mother could stop him. It was later that same night, at the Duwali party.

The primary dinner table had been set up at one end of the patio, amid lanterns dancing, music, and patter. The *Devi Ganga* had brought Little Mumbai good fortune.

"Disagreements over the Bengal partition," answered the older woman, Radhiyaa. Her voice was loud and penetrating.

"And no one can pronounce the new Viceroy's name.

"Our youth linger on the street corners like ruffians. They are easily sucked into the whirlpool of Home Rule. A movement several decades ahead of its time, I'm afraid. It's all the men talk about.

"And Hutheesing, the Butcher's wife, died of cholera. In April," continued Radhiyaa.

"She left documents behind, confirming that our Vardan is her natural son. Her friend Sai adopted him. At birth. That is a very good friend, don't you agree?"

Everything stopped.

Sai was a well-known woman, and well-liked in Little Mumbai, almost as esteemed as hard-working, hard-headed Vardan himself.

"What did you just say?" asked Deepa.

Radhiyaa, like most gossips, pretended to be ignorant of her words' wider, often harmful consequences.

"Young Vardan," she said, innocently.

"He is *adopted*."

"Oh," she feigned. "I *am* sorry, Deepa-ji. I assumed this was common knowledge --"

Vardan, on the far end of the patio, dancing under the gently swinging strung lanterns with pretty Lilavani, stopped to glance over their way.

Had he heard his name mentioned?

How odd, thought Vardan. He saw faces around the dining table.

The faces had all turned towards him.

His eyes met Rupa's.

Rupa imagined that she heard the words '*You need to be on another continent*' being spoken out loud ...

\#\#\#

TOM' STORY NOTES

This story takes place at the height of early aviation experimentation ...that period when the future of aviation would be formed. I wanted to show the drastic difference among the designs.

As I came to understand the full extent of this story's connection to the Math Girls stories, a Rupa epic arc took shape, one to be continued in the next collection, "Science Girls."

To be avoided by me, to be avoided by all authors, is a large cast of characters. Readers cannot follow a confused or crowded narrative. One of Billy Wilder's rules for good writing is to develop a clean line of action for your leading character. I am always trying to de-clutter, to slim down the cast of characters. to keep the narrative line clean.

* * *

Bayes Rule, which Rupa applies to her cases, also applies in a small way to me and my writing.

I think that is why certain scenes took so long for me to write.

The Tower bridge sequence towards the end of the Air Race story is an example. It took the better part of a week for me to scheme it out. That was because my comprehension of not just that section but of the entire work was incomplete. I didn't really know why each plane was doing what it was doing. Working successfully through this sequence, in turn, establishing the deeper structure of the story, brought me to a new level of understanding. So, I needed to redo other scenes to fit.

As Bayes reminds us, every new piece of the puzzle, small or large, requires us to change all of our thinking.

Commentary by Jessica Ghilani

In "Ruby and the London, Paris Air Race," many early aircrafts help to bring meaning and historical context to the story through their mentioning and description. What you may not realize is that each inclusion of an early flight vessel comes from genuine aviation history. Often, the given names of these aircrafts are the same as the last name of the inventor(s) that developed them. And each of these technological marvels represents innovation, risk taking, trial and error, and ambition.

Nulli Secundus translates from Latin to "second to none," and on October 5, 1907, a military airship for the British Army made a pioneering flight from a balloon factory in Farnborough, England, to London. It took nearly three and a half hours for the aircraft to make the 40-mile journey.

The Voisin was named after Gabriel and Charles Voisin, European aviators considered to be pioneers in the field. The National Air and Space Museum in Washington DC contains a Voisin Type 8 in its collections, the oldest surviving aircraft designed as a bomber. Historians consider The Voisin 1907 pusher biplane to be one of the most important pre-WWI era flight technologies. Louis Blériot watched a trial of the Voisin-made floatplane glider in 1905.

The Blériot is an aircraft of early aviation named for its inventor, Louis Blériot. Between 1909 and 1914, Blériot made hundreds of these airplanes. The Blériot XI aircraft is depicted in the poster for The London Paris Air Race. A Blériot aircraft was used in 1909 for the first "heavier than air" flight that traversed the English Channel. This achievement brought Louis Blériot fame and recognition.

The Wright Brothers referenced humorously for their alleged litigiousness are central to the history of aviation. The legal considerations for inventors pursuing early flight made it necessary to file patents to protect their inventions. Orville and Wilbur Wright, usually referred to as The Wright Brothers, are credited as having created the first heavier-than-air powered aircraft, moving forward the story of aviation technology. The Wright Flyer from 1903 can be seen today at the Smithsonian Institution's National Air and Space Museum in Washington DC. Interestingly, prior to their work in aviation, the brothers owned a printing company and a bicycle business. Their prior experience from working with the printing machinery and as bike mechanics helped orient them to important aspects of engineering and invention. Their hometown of Dayton, Ohio is also said to have been significant in positioning them for this work. The National Air and Space Museum profiles of the brothers mention that in the late 1800s. Dayton was a hub for industry and manufacturing.

The history of early flight encompasses more than just a few names and

inventors. My brief overview intends to situate the history and pursuit of flight and aviation technology during the turn of the twentieth century, when "Ruby and the London, Paris Air Race," takes place.

Commentary by Tim Grove

Tom's story about Rupa and the London, Paris air race captures a little of the excitement surrounding the early days of flight. Many people had been trying to figure out a way to fly, then in 1903 two brothers in America, Wilbur and Orville Wright, succeeded. When Orville flew the Wright Flyer 120 feet in twelve seconds, he flew the world's first powered, heavier-than-air machine to achieve controlled sustained flight with a pilot on board. The principles of flight suddenly clicked in brothers' minds when they solved three specific challenges needed to fly. Lift addressed the type of surface (wings) that would carry the vehicle off the ground and keep it there. Balance and control allowed the pilot to direct the machine's movement. Propulsion provided the power to keep the machine going.

The work of the Wright Brothers immediately inspired a generation of inventors everywhere who used those principles to build their own flying machines. Gradually more and more people around the world began to spot flying machines in the sky. At first, no common term for them existed, but around 1906 someone first designated them an "airplane" (based on the French word "aéroplane," which comes from a Greek word, aeróplanos, meaning "wandering in air").

A Brazilian by the name of Alberto Santos-Dumont made the first public flight in Europe in 1906. Not until 1908 did a Wright plane carry its first passenger. That same year the Wrights traveled to Europe and made a series of demonstration flights. The world's first air race took place in Reims, France in 1909 between American Glenn Curtiss and Frenchman Louis Blériot. The American won in a close race. Forward thinking people saw the potential of air travel and soon began sponsoring races and demonstrations, offering large cash awards for the winners. These spurred more innovation as more and more people tried to invent faster and safer airplanes.

Amazingly, the first airplane fatality did not occur until almost five years after the first flight. In September 1908 while demonstrating the Wright Military Flyer for the United States army, Orville lost control and crashed it, causing the death of his passenger.

With all of the wacky flying machines built by all kinds of tinkerers, it is understandable that flying was risky, even downright dangerous. Soon pilots were doing loops and many spectacular stunts, such as wing walking where people walked on an airplane's wings while it was in flight. Yet it was a time of adventure and the sky really was the limit.

\#\#\#

8. The Price of Flight

Strong-willed Isoke meets her match.

An odd couple learn the hard way what is what.

I. BANISHED

We are humans ... because of the way
we affiliate with other organisms.

    — *E.O. Wilson*

I deeply regret the necessity.

    — *Marshall of Canyon Gap*

The tribe's Chieftain, the woman Obioye, returned from her failed hunt to find that a girl of the village had built something special.

At the river's edge.

It was a *shadoof*, one of the gently-moving water pumps, such as the Nile tribes fashion, which serve to bring water to the shore in a constant manner.

This one was shoulder-high, big enough to supply a steady stream to a small basin. A brief length of aqueduct then carried the water from the basin to the lower terraces of gardens, where the tribe grew herbs and vegetables.

"See how it pumps!" exclaimed Imani, second Aunt to the girl Isoke, pride of the Atakora tribe. Isoke, gifted in designs and ingenious with tools, was excited to surprise the Chieftain.

"Isoke chose special trees," narrated Imani. "She cut the planks and smoothed them all herself, with her hatchet."

These praises for the skinny girl with big ideas did not please Obioye ... they only made her angrier.

"The water feeds all 36 rows of the lower gardens," continued Imani. "Isoke thinks a water wheel might be nex-- "

"Enough!" exclaimed the Chieftain. She held up one hand high.

All this celebration for Isoke grated badly on the Chieftain Obioye's nerves, particularly so in the wake of her own hunting failure.

She preferred to be the center of attention.

She preferred to do the unexpected, and to rule by cruelty.

This episode represented a deeper threat. This new 'water pump' signaled a new age for the tribe, a new direction which featured clever devices that she, Obioye, could not control. And Obioye's counsel – and permission – need not be sought, apparently.

This water pump was only the beginning. The tribe's

identity was changing.

So, as often happens, decisions were made for all the wrong reasons ...

"*Kufukuzwa!*" declared Obioye with a stamp of her royal walking stick.

"No!" cried Simtho, Isoke's brother.

"Banished!"

"My chieftain!" protested Imani. "You cannot -- "

Obioye stamped her brightly colored stick again, ending the matter.

"But I can! And I do! Isoke failed to ask my permission!"

"But just look at the beets," insisted Simtho. "The moringa! See! Isoke is a peacock, Great One, just spreading her wings--"

"Then this bird is grounded!"

The Chieftain turned to Isoke.

"Isoke, you are banished from the Atakora."

Once spoken, the command could not be reversed.

A thick silence had fallen over the tribe, like a cloud.

This interchange meant something. Isoke had done nothing wrong, in thought or deed. She had acted only to improve the lives of her people.

"A fortnight!" ordered the Chieftain. "Shunned. Cast-out."

Obioye glared.

The girl Isoke said nothing.

With the ice-cold, wounded look of one who has been badly betrayed – one who would seek revenge -- she turned and walked away, slowly.

2. THE CLIFFSIDE WAY STATION AT DAKSURI

Truth and beauty, Tony. Forget everything else.

— *Bill Evans*

The lone figure entered the Valley of Wedeme from the east, walking with purpose towards the far cliffs.

The station at Daksuri is one of the better-preserved stations along the Tintenou range.

A wayside shelter for travelers, overlooking Vale Wedeme, Daksuri is almost impossible to find unless you're looking for it (and even then ...).

A day's hike south and partly east, the trailhead revealed itself to the banished girl Isoke. The unmarked path wound across the valley floor and then slanted upward, towards sheer rock walls, then turned abruptly to transform into a narrow stairway curling up the obscured-by-trees cliffside.

Spear and bow and quiver of arrows strapped to her back, Isoke moved carefully up the final steps to the way station. Her hand unsheathed a long knife from her belt. One of the short-handled hatchets was tucked in the back.

She called out a greeting.

The way-station was empty.

The travelers' station at Daksuri was a broad stone ledge overlooking the valley. Covered by treetops, the retreat was safe from pursuers, and the wolf- and stoat- and hyena-packs which forage the valley floor for meat.

Journeyers past had stamped a floor of grass and dirt on

the broad ledge, with low benches and a ring of stones for a fire.

The ivy-covered mouth of a cave beckoned along the cliff wall, beyond the ledge. Isoke took inventory, and found it was well-stocked with flint and kindling and rabbit traps. A coil of hemp rope hung on a wall, beside a pair of leather straps. She found straw for beds, strips of cloth, jars and bowls.

Those who came before me have been thoughtful ...

Torches along the wall indicated that the cavern cut deep into the mountain. Perhaps there would be mysteries to explore. She wondered what they might have been like, those travelers, and from what shores they had come to visit the Tintenou.

At the mouth of the cave was a bubbling stream. The creek-bed had been engineered, its path diverted from its natural way to the sea.

Isoke built a fire.

After a dinner of berries and dried fish, she sat at the edge of the stone perch, looking out over the valley. She replayed the events of the past week, just to make sure they were clear in her mind, and in her memory. Early-evening patterns of sunlight filtered through breezy curtains of leaves, moving and shifting.

Night fell. The dome of stars was friendly and familiar. The lonely girl picked out constellations.

I'm never going back, Isoke vowed.

* * *

So humiliating, so complete, so cruel – *and disrespectful!* --

had been Obioye's reprimand, so enraging, that it had lit a fire within Isoke. It changed Isoke's theory of herself.

She had worked many days on that shadoof, and solved many thorny problems along the way to success. And that success had been rewarded with banishment.

Is this who I actually am?

A creeping possibility crept into Isoke's mind: that she was not in fact a visionary at all, but an indulged child, making trivial contraptions that led to nothing. Regardless of her own opinions about herself, this appeared to be the conclusion of the tribe at large ...

She would not stand for that.

At some point between dusk and dawn, among the eternal stars and the shooting silver comets and the rich night sounds, a more specific decision was made.

I can marry the Mundari boy.

The two had met at a council of the tribes of the plains when they were children, and they had kept in contact since. When Mundari strays wandered off from the cattle herd, it was always he who retrieved them, along the southern fences.

His intentions were quite clear.

He had promised to pay her family three cows for Isoke to become his wife.

* * *

The next morning, before her departure, Isoke had made sure she left the station better than she had found it. She had swept the clearing, fortified the rock walls of the fire-pit and added to the piles of kindling.

Now she would seek her destiny with the Mundari.

A large, warlike and thoughtless tribe, the Mundari might welcome her talents. They might not.

Isoke ran her fingers along the knife handle at her waist. She adjusted the bow slung over her shoulder.

We'll soon see.

But as she placed her foot on the first step down to the valley floor, Isoke heard a rustle and a clumsy *Plop!* in the shrubs.

Something had fallen from the trees.

She followed the sound.

There, cradled in a blackthorne shrub, lay a dead bird.

A falcon.

The lady hawk was young. Her wings were outspread. Her eyes were closed. Her breast was motionless.

The loser in some aerial combat, no doubt...

Isoke looked up but could see no nest, either in high branches or along the face of the cliffs.

An eagle glided away, in the high breezes, in the western sky.

Isoke stroked the falcon's breast with her thumb.

To see such a fine creature up close--

Looking closely, she saw where the barred, stone-grey and white feathers of adulthood were growing in. Like Isoke herself, the young she-falcon was on the brink of adulthood.

This must be a lesson, sent to me by my ancestors, thought Isoke.

How short life can be ...

The falcon fluttered.

It opened its eyes.

3. WHAARIKI WALKS

They must have done it, knowing

that it was part of a sequence.

— *Robin Swicord*

Isoke took the helpless bird back to the stream at the Daksuri cave's mouth. She gently washed the wounds – across the neck and along the plane of one wing, which was broken.

She carefully removed the thorns which had lodged in the bird's plumage and breast muscle.

She fashioned a bed of straw for the bird.

The helpless falcon watched her caretaker. The orange eyes blazed like pieces of coal.

"I will stay with you the night, my girl," she murmured to the bird.

Isoke searched until she found a thin length piece of wood among the kindling. She fashioned an indentation at one end and used it as a spoon, to feed the falcon water and bits of crushed berries.

"I can catch a rabbit for us. Get you on your feet, at least."

Too weak to resist, the bird glowered. It opened its beak to protest, but no sound emerged.

* * *

"Who did this to you?" asked Isoke.

At the third day's dawn, Isoke was speaking to the falcon as she might speak to a sister, or close friend.

All night, both nights, Isoke had stayed awake to tend the she-falcon. Lain on a bed of straw at the cave's mount, the bird could gaze up at the stars and the clouds in the skies.

"Was it that eagle I saw?" asked Isoke.

"Let's kill him."

The girl had been able to insert a thin brace along the front of the broken wing. It seemed to be a preliminary fix. The bird was livid at being handled in such a fashion ... but too weak to resist.

"My arrows can reach far," planned the tribal girl. "If only we can lure your foe close ..."

Isoke applied a poultice of her own making, herbs and roots -- cissus, malva roots, acacia, baobab, river pumpkin -- similar to ones she had made for her people. It had taken Isoke the better part of a day just to gather the ingredients.

"Death to all eagles!" She unleashed a string of searing oaths at the absent villain.

"Are you with me?"

The falcon stared balefully back at Isoke.

Every wild particle, every feral aspect, every feather and mote of the bird seemed to agree with Isoke's murderous call to action. This was a creature who lived for violent moments and mortal battle. She was built for it.

Shaking with anger, the she-falcon seemed to blink.

"Fine. We agree," assented Isoke.

"All one."

"So now we need to fix your wing. You must fly again."

* * *

By the morning of the fourth day, the falcon was strong enough to stand.

With encouragement and an assortment of treats, she made her way from the perch to the stream, to drink.

"Is that how you walk?" Isoke demanded, even as she egged the bird on.

"That's *pathetic*."

The falcon hopped, then triple-hopped – instead of flying -- to cross the flat space clumsily.

"This is just ... embarrassing."

In response, the falcon made a clicking sound, showing her impatience, at the back of her throat.

"You are *royalty* among the Bedouin."

The falcon dipped her beak in the running waters.

"Fie!" said Isoke.

* * *

There was a wood-handled hatchet alongside the slim Arab knife which Isoke carried in her belt, in the back.

She used the hatchet to carve a series of short steps into the squat, fat trunk of an ancient Iroko tree, so that one could cross up the steps and without effort over to the stone ledge, or sill, which oversaw the valley. The wood was hard, and it took most of the morning, but when she was done, the bird had a staircase to her own private platform, tucked into the foliage surrounding the lowest branches of the Iroko.

Now the she-raptor could see clouds as they floated and changed shape, wafting up the valley. She could smell the exotic odors in the updrafts.

"If you're thinking the wing is getting better on its own," warned Isoke, "it's not."

Each step in the little staircase was low. Isoke took note of the falcon's sad, slow progress up the staircase, crawling and half-dragging herself by beak and foot and one good wing.

"No, that must not be what you're thinking since YOU DON'T ACTUALLY THINK -- "

Once the bird had made its way up the tree, she sat scowling at her captor from her fine new perch.

* * *

"Hold still, you *five-clawed ferret—*"

Isoke had distracted the she-falcon with food while she slipped a knotted leather cord over its foot. The leather cord had been tied to a long coil of hemp rope, ending at a stake in the ground. The bird could move freely about the grassy shelf, but it could not fly away.

"I have tied your foot," gloated Isoke.

The falcon bit at the hemp, but it was too strong. She flailed and bated and yelled at her captor.

"You can hate me, that's fine."

Again and again, the bird bounded upward and fell, until her primary feathers looked like a crow's. She kicked and complained and took to the air in these brief, sloppy, unstable arcs, always ending in a heap on the ground.

"You'll kill yourself, for all your 'bravery.'"

"You don't know what you're doing."

"You're a walker, for now. Welcome to the ground."

* * *

The wing did not heal.

The bird insisted on shredding every brace and bandage which Isoke attempted. She seemed to tolerate a poultice on her wounds, so they did not become infected, so that was something.

"I can't fix your wing," Isoke informed the falcon.

"I can strengthen it. You have to let me."

For several days, the girl had been trying to insert a newer and stronger brace – longer -- one which she had carefully carved, after many trials and errors. The brace would help the wings catch and hold air currents, and could at least glide, if not maneuver, in the atmosphere.

Isoke tried waiting until the bird was asleep, and overfeeding her, to make her drowsy ... but nothing worked. Isoke worried that she could cause further harm if she held the delicate creature down.

* * *

"Did you know that I can build a bridge?" challenged Isoke one morning as they sat together, watching the clouds.

"Aye. Across the Sota," she added, for clarification. "The big river down there. Do you see it? Look. Look where I am pointing! See where it takes a turn, and narrows? That's where I'd place the bridge."

"I know how to curve the supporting arches beneath the platform. That which holds the wood planks.

"I know how to cut and stack the stones. I *measure*. I know the shapes of *ijiyomethri*. I use the Arab systems. You'll see. I'm not bragging.

"I mold wood onto the stone foundation. Mortar, *defari*. Mortar and correct shapes and strong hands. Clay. Mud. Tar. *Believe* it."

The falcon tensed --

There, far below, in the valley's lower stratosphere, a flock of swifts spread out, in a unison so perfect it was almost magical.

After a beat, they all tilted, innocently, to catch a breeze and fly away. The falcon flexed her talons, to see such perfect prey and yet be prevented from hunting.

"A crossing like that would save my tribe three hours," said Isoke. "Every day!"

"Then I could build boats, like the Phoenicians," continued Isoke, "only smaller. The Navigator told me so, last year. The Portagee.

I know the shapes of *ijiyomethri*. I use the Arab systems. You'll see. I'm not bragging.

"If I can build a bridge," Isoke ruminated to her stoic companion, "I can build a shelter. A house."

"Oh, yes. I saw one at the fair, last year. I saw how they did it. I just don't know how they fastened the wood, at the joints.

"Once I figure that out ..."

Isoke caught herself, remembering now that she would never be back among the Atakora.

Silently, the bird turned her and her companion's attentions to the skies, where a new set of shapes gathered to be observed, and interpreted. Perhaps the clouds could provide them with a sign.

If only they could know the future.

This new flank of clouds looked like billowing water descending a mountainside.

Or was it a pair of ocelots? Or a gigantic ostrich's head, its eyes wide and questioning ...

* * *

The pair spent mornings together walking the upper valley trails.

"Hear that?" Isoke asked the falcon, on one such outing.

She did not mean the trickle of the brook, water streaming over rock-bed, or the buzzing of insects, but something other.

"That frog's croak. Hah! It's not a frog at all! It's not a frog, it's a mallard. You didn't even *know*!

"Now! *Shush*! That sound -- the thrushes click like snails."

Isoke made a show of stopping to listen.

"That bachelor thrush wants a mate in the worst way, does he not? Ugh! Love. Croon on, brother!

"Those crackling seeds – those are finches. *Hooroo!* I know so much!"

The falcon, of course, knew all of that, and more. She knew each bird's song, and their foraging spots, their flight paths, and the habits of every species, each genus, each crawling thing.

All prey, to her.

"Hold a moment, Good Companion. Hold, I say."

The falcon cocked its head.

"Do you hear that? That two-note call, smooth and then raspy – it is a crow assembly call.

"An assembly! For what? Is it war? A funeral? To mount an assault on the red ant-hills, perhaps. Who can say?"

The falcon relaxed her talons' clutch on the perch of Isoke's shoulder and listened.

The bird watched the bush on either side closely as they moved though the branches and shrubs and smaller trees.

"Have you been told what happens when you marry?" Isoke asked the she-falcon.

"I mean, that first night."

The bird bated – displayed her wings, that is, as if to show them off -- and then lifted each of her feet and re-clenched her talons on the thick leather, permitting the thrum and buzz and gurgle and caws of the valley around them to absorb all else.

"I thought not," said Isoke.

4. FLIGHT SCHOOL

Evolution has created a far more complicated

flying device than we have ever been able to engineer.

– *Samik Bhattacharya*

That afternoon, Isoke gathered all of the pelts from the rabbits she had caught in the traps. She trimmed each, and smoothed them on the flat rock, and baked them in the sunlight. Then she beat them with an edged rock, scraping all fur and creases and burrs away. She washed them in the stream.

If you saw Gazal, perhaps you would understand.

She rinsed them dry and flattened them, and pounded them again, and repeated. One pelt she cut carefully into thin strips. It was an ancient process, fashioning leather from the hides. It required Isoke to rub and scrape the skins with a sharp rock-blade, then rinse them in the stream. She used different shapes and weights of rocks, so that each one could smooth in its own way. She laid out the pelts. She thinned the strips so she could wrap them around her wrists and forearms.

Twice she was careless and let blood stain the pelts brown, so she did them all over again.

She dried them.

The pelts were now leather.

She held her leather-wrapped arm out.

She walked twenty paces away.

"Fly!" she demanded.

"Fly to me, *defari* -- "

"Yes! Now!"

All she got was a furious stare.

It took two days. Finally, the falcon's hunger won out.

She flew resentfully and landed on Isoke's leather-bound outstretched arm. She struggled to stay aloft. She was rewarded with squirrel meat.

* * *

The two of them took a close viewing of the bumblebee, its massive torso somehow being held aloft by the intense working of absurdly tiny wings.

"Look at that."

Isoke tossed the bee from her hand, returning it to the air.

Both girl and falcon watched as the bee regained its balance.

The falcon snapped its beak and ate the insect.

"Dammit!" cursed the girl.

"Why did you do that?"

* * *

Isoke had taken to studying different creatures of flight, so as to inspire her reluctant patient.

"How about gliding?" she asked.

"It seems fairly easy. I once saw a lizard do it."

* * *

"Use the last downstroke as the trigger to bring up your legs. To land on your perch. Of course. See? See how I am using my legs -- to land squarely --"

"Are you even listening? You need to fly in a new manner. You must compensate for your damaged wing."

"I cannot fix it, Mighty One. It is thus. It is as I say. Without flight, you are doomed."

The falcon, disapproving of all this theory and all this dancing around, turned her attention to grooming the handsome coat of fore-feathers along her right wing. She fluffed the feathers, to examine them.

"Fine. Ignore me."

"You are good at what you do. What you once did. Hunting. Flying.

"But you are terrible at everything else.

"You'd better learn a new way to fly. On the ground, without me, you won't last a day."

5. DEATH STALKS THE GLEN

"I am a daughter of Gazal," she answered.

"If you saw Gazal, perhaps you would understand."

— *Robert E. Howard*

As dawn broke, Isoke slept heavily. Her fire burned low.

Through the bush, mostly hidden amongst the trees and shrubs, the hungry predators approached.

A pack of hyenas had been stalking her for some time.

Now they wanted more than to say hello.

Spotted hyenas are big, as big as boars, with short torsos and sloping backs.

Hunger showed in their bared teeth, in their tensed postures and too-careful footsteps. Death gleamed in the hunters' eyes.

Isoke snored. She shifted beneath her blanket.

But the falcon had heard them coming. She watched them tiptoe towards the sleeping girl.

With a shriek, the falcon launched --

She soared and faltered -- betrayed by the bad wing – but managed to land on the back of a smaller hyena, near the back of the pack.

With a swift and savage slash of her talons, she slit the beast's throat.

Red gushed forth --

The throat-slit hyena howled and cried and staggered, slumping to the ground, open mouthed, already bleeding to death --

Isoke awoke and grabbed for her axe and her bow--

With a single motion and a shout, she sunk her hatchet blade in the skull of the first-most hyena.

Three of the girl's hastily-fired arrows (five shot, two missed) helped convince the hyenas that easier game waited elsewhere.

The hyenas fled.

Hyenas are among the most successful of predators, and they do not seek a fair fight. They do not seek feisty prey.

"I am a daughter of the *Atakora!*" screamed Isoke as the beasts ran away, adding a choice list of gerunds, in several dialects.

"You don't KNOW!" She waved the bow.

The falcon hopped up and down, twice. Three times. Four times. *Mighty is the warrior.* Let the world hear.

* * *

Rhadamanthus, learned King of Crete and later Judge of the Dead, once ordered his citizens to swear oaths to particular animals of their choosing.

The animal's spirit would inform the human, when the path is lost, when the signal is weak...

This deep bond between human and beast, he felt, would strengthen each citizen's sense of belonging, and ground them in the natural world as all connected -- a common herd, or flock -- and in the end accrued to the benefit of Crete, overall.

The animal's spirit would inform the human, when the

path is lost, when the signal was weak, when the purpose was proving evasive.

So it now was, with Isoke.

6. CAVE DISCOVERY

*He that would bring home the wealth of the Indies
must carry the wealth of the Indies with him.*
— Samuel Johnson

Dark rainclouds gathered over the lands of the Wedeme.

In the distance, the girl Isoke and the falcon could see thunderheads gather in phalanxes. They heard the rumblings.

The bird shook her feathers into place and looked up at the sky. A rift in the clouds sent down a shaft of sunlight that spun and vanished.

Rain fell in drops, big and heavy.

Now rain fell in sheets on the glades and avenues below and all the underbrush and fallen logs and glades in the valley. The creeks swelled to rivers.

The gale buffered the falcon's perch and bent the thickest of branches.

Isoke came to get her.

Together they retreated to the cave.

The falcon reluctantly allowed her human caretaker (or perhaps her servant) to lead her into a great stone maw or entrance in the cliffside with a ceiling, something she had never seen.

Isoke narrated as they entered the cavern. "These are the traps left by others. You see, brave one."

She took a torch from the wall and lit it.

The bird stood on her toes, there on Isoke's arm. She craned her neck at the ceiling.

She did not care for the torch, and stayed as far away as she could.

These new sights…

She stared hard at the torches along the wall.

But the circle of rocks, traps, pottery, piles of gathered kindling, flat stone benches -- these things held neither meaning nor use for her. She quickly lost interest.

"Come, *asampate.*"

Had the falcon but known the Igbo tongue, she would have remarked on the use of that particular word, for it signifies great affection.

"Let us look further -- "

The pair began to examine their surroundings in detail.

"We are not alone, Winged One."

She prepared a meal for the bird, in a bowl.

"Never alone. Those who came before are with us."

Isoke prepared a meal for the falcon, in a bowl.

The bird watched her companion prepare food. She stared long and close at Isoke, to see if she had changed in the new light.

The hungry bird devoured her lunch.

The she-falcon fluttered, and ducked her head twice,

making a low growling sound. She seemed to regain some measure of patience.

A small waterfall dropped into a spring-fed pool that ran as a stream through the outer cave.

Isoke held the torch high. The falcon hopped behind her, tilting its head.

What is this …?

Against one wall, hidden in shadows, Isoke saw a children's bench.

She picked it up and held it under the light.

It was a small, smoothed-wood three-legged stool.

The legs were attached by man-made wooden joints.

Mortis and tenon, so the Phoenicians call them.

Isoke had never seen one.

On each side, the carved pieces of wood were bound fast at the point where they needed to meet permanently. The thirty sarsen stones of Stonehenge were dressed and fashioned with such joints.

Carefully, she coaxed apart the three legs from the base.

She could see now that the maker had fashioned a wedged dovetail held by a fastened groove. She carefully disassembled the stool, and then re-assembled it.

A pegged technique kept the thing sturdy. The maker had cut two mortises into the edges of two planks, while a separate tenon was then inserted in the two mortises. The assembly had then been locked into place by driving a dowel through holes in the mortise side wall.

Isoke hummed as she put the joints back together again, seeing, trying to understand, how and why it worked.

Ah! This changes everything ...

It meant she could permanently fasten together the planks of a bridge across the river. It meant she could build her water wheel, and a set of feeding troughs for the livestock. It meant she could fashion a corral fence, and after that a series of boat-hulls ....

The falcon chuffed twice and displayed, signaling that she preferred to leave now.

7. A NEW COURSE

The breeze at dawn has secrets to tell you.

Don't go back to sleep.

> — *Rumi*

The night told Isoke something imperative, so that by dawn, she was packed and ready.

"We must be honest," said Isoke to the bird.

"We must speak of things as they are."

The falcon fluttered on her perch, standing and then sitting back down on her haunches.

"I should be chieftain," said Isoke. "Even as young as I am."

A morning chorus gathered and grew in the valley below. Creatures awoke after the rainfall.

Isoke took the bird down from her perch. She removed the leather straps, so she could carry the bird on her shoulder.

"My designs will grow. They will help our little tribe survive. Resist Queen Nala's new taxes. Sidestep the Zulus.

All the rest.

"But I never will be chieftain. As we see.

"I have been banished from my own tribe. And no stampede has arrived to invite me back.

"No one is coming. I am alone with my 'gifts.'"

The creek gurgled with the rain's runoff.

"You were once queen among hunters. Now you hop like a frog."

The hatchet and the Arab knife were tucked in Isoke's belt, in the back.

The little stool was strapped to her back. The way station had been stocked and cleaned ...

"Yet life is worth living, *defari*.

"I will find a way to build a bridge across the Sota. More structures will follow. I can see the designs already taking shape, my friend. I see them in my mind's eye, as surely as I see you.

"We will strike out on our own. We'll find you a mate! A handsome tiercel.

"I have strong arms, and long legs. Sure feet for climbing rocks and fording streams.

"There is a little grove I know, not far from the river, a safe place. I can build a proper perch for you. With steps, and a shed for me. As many rabbits as you can eat! Fish, too!

"I will hunt for the two of us, *Whaariki*. As long as I breathe. It is my promise."

Isoke took and gripped her walking stick in one hand. "We should be there by sunset.

"It is a fine morning. We can pick out the different bird songs. I myself can sing as we walk. I have a beautiful voice.

"Huh! We two. Many adventures. Come. Ride on my shoulder, as you so hate to do --"

She removed the tether that held the bird's legs, so she could perch the bird on her shoulder.

Suddenly Isoke's blood was chilled by the unmistakable sound of an eagle's screech --

Freed momentarily from her collar, the falcon hopped, then ran directly at the ledge and launched off, spreading her wings wide and full --

"*No!*"

Isoke dove, realizing too late that the leather straps that bound the falcon were free --

The she-hawk leapt off the ledge.

Isoke missed, skidding half off the cliff herself --

Looking down, she saw the eagle gliding, its long wings spread.

Then she heard the sound she had dreaded --

Eechup! Kik-kik-kik!

The war cry of the falcon.

She watched, prone, heart-broken, as the falcon's swirling, crooked glide took her downward, to face her nemesis.

Treetops hid what happened next.

Why?

The falcon's swirling, crooked glide took her downward, to face her nemesis.

Why? answered a voice within Isoke. *You always knew how it would end ...*

She asked the question out loud, but she knew the falcon's answer:

Because it is better to die, having flown.

Isoke rose. She dusted off her skirt.

She once again strapped the stool and the weapons on her back.

She set off down the cliffside staircase.

That bridge over the River Sota would not build itself.

Tom's Story Notes

My readers may be familiar with Isoke's stubborn ways and blossoming geometrics from the story "The Architect" in last year's collection, *The Adventures of Ruby Pi and the Geometry Girls*. This story takes place two years before her eventful first encounter with Queen Nala of the greater Benin empire, an encounter over engineering.

This falcon story's original ending had loyal brother Simtho arriving to fetch his sister with the news that odious Obioye had been ousted from the tribe and Isoke voted in as the new chieftain ... but as the true meaning of the story emerged, this ending seemed more and more bogus. Isoke triumphs to the extent that she sets out to fulfill her own difficult destiny, not because anything is given to her.

With *The Price of Flight*, I wanted to give my readers a simple-premise, straightforward, two-character study. My longer stories -- particularly *My Korean Sister* and *Gia Finds a Love* -- tend to feature big casts, lots of names, and multiple storylines.

* * *

I wrote this story in the shadow of one of the finest books I have ever had the pleasure of reading, Helen MacDonald's *H is for Hawk*. Her writing is so good I almost gave up on mine.

* * *

After this episode, Isoke continues to hone her design and engineering skills. She guides her little tribe with vision through the Benin Wars of Succession (among the larger and more warlike tribes). In the end, she partners with the German would-be Navigator prince from *The Colonials*, in an epic battle with the Mad Queen and her host.

9. My Korean Sister

The daring X-1 reaches to break the sound barrier.
An autistic girl proves her worth among the Lost Boys
of Muroc.

PROLOGUE

When flowers bloom, the wind often blows.
This is the way of things.

— *Cheong Yogyong*

"That?" I asked.

If ever a human fell in love with a machine, it was my Korean sister with the Bell X-1 experimental rocket jet plane.

"You think *that* can fly?"

The X-1 looked like a giant bullet.

Stubby, rust-colored, fixed-winged, the unadorned one-seat test aircraft had been built to its own set of rules, true to its mission of speed in its every aspect.

The X-1 did not seek to please or inspire, looks-wise.

The X-1's insanely high-performance capacity was a secret kept by its humble exterior.

I had heard all about the X-1, of course: the mysterious and futuristic aircraft which the U.S. Air Force had developed and designed specifically to break the sound barrier. I was expecting something a little bit grander. Bigger. Flashier. I had spent time with many of the personality planes of the era, as well as seeing others up close in aviation museums ... and whatever "It" was, the X-1 did not have it.

My sister disagreed.

She circled the X-1, all 30 feet, 9 inches in length, and ran her hands along the tiled surfaces and thin, back-slung wings. The cockpit looked tiny. She was a little hypnotized by its presence, like a religious follower or something.

Yi Tai-jo, herself, was outwardly unremarkable -- maybe that's where the affinity between her and the X-1 lay. By her bright eyes, you knew she was smart. By her mouth and by her expressions, you knew she couldn't care less what you thought about her. By her posture, you could see she was unpredictable, and ready.

Like the X-1, she was trying to look plain and normal outside while containing a fiery explosion on the inside. It was an explosion that would take place in its own time.

There was never an aircraft that meant so much as the X-1.

There was never a person who meant so much, who tried so hard, or felt so deeply, as Yi Tai-jo.

The story of how my Korean Sister and the X-1 fell under one another's spell during those desert days and nights in Summer, 1957, is an epic tale. Much happened in those eventful weeks. More than I am able to tell you here.

Here are those parts of it which I remember.

I. IN THE PRINCIPAL'S OFFICE

The Bell X-1 is one of the most significant
aircraft in the history of aviation.

— *Nathan Cluett*

"I'd appreciate it if you didn't use that term," said Dad.
"'Radio head.' That's mighty rude."

"I *didn't* use the term," Principal Mays sought to clarify.

"I said that is what Yi Tai-jo was called by one of her
classmates when your son Charles chose to break that
classmate's arm. Good grief."

Principal Mays was choosing his words carefully.

Dad was looking sharp in his dress uniform, hat in his lap,
as the four of us sat in the Principal's office – Air Force Pilot
and First Lieutenant Dad, me, Principal Mays, and my Korean
Sister.

Yi Tai-jo was wearing blue culottes and a white blouse,
which is pretty much what she always wore.

"Gary asked me if I had transistors in my skull," she said,
just to clarify things. She repeated what Gary said, in Gary's
voice.

Yi Tai-jo has a mimetic memory. She can reproduce
anything she heard, even if it was years ago. She replays it, or
echoes it, in the exact same voice as she heard it, cadence and
accents and all. She goes through anxiety spells, where she

clams up and refuses to look at anyone. One doctor in Long Beach called it Childhood Disintegrative Disorder, which sounded like a catch-all to me, another called it Kenner's Syndrome. Today you would call it autism.

I had heard Gary, one of the Senior boys, making fun of her for this.

Fighting ensued.

"Well, sir," began Dad, using a phrase which usually signaled that he was really, really mad. "I've taught my kids how to defend themselves. And my little girl has one hell of a memory, is what. I'm very proud of her, and her memory.

"So anyone calling my daughter names is gonna tend to get an arm broken," concluded Pilot Captain Korean American Dad.

"*Non melior amicus, non nequior hostis,*" he added.

Dad only knew ten of those Latin phrases, all of them mottoes from some military regiment, and I'm sure he mispronounced most of them, but they always seemed to fit the occasion.

"I hope everyone savvies that. Sir," concluded Pilot Dad. "Because that ain't changin' –"

"We've suspended two members of the Senior class," answered Principal Mays. "But I don't think it will end there. These are unstable times.

By 'unstable times,' he was referring to the recent riots against Korean-owned liquor stores in Southern California. Also, to the recently concluded Korean War, about which many Americans were confused and conflicted ... regarding North and South Korea, that is, and which was actually which, and why they are not in fact Japan, and why America was involved in an Asian land war at all.

"Something to consider," Principal Mays continued, "might be the CEE program. California Equivalency Exam. You could have Charles and Yi Tai-jo tutored on one of the Air Force Bases. Then they take an equivalency exam. You just have to establish that it is a 'remotely staffed' situation."

"Here's the application form." He slid a brochure across the desk.

U.S. Air Force Pilot Captain My Dad unfolded the brochure.

So ended our stay at Long Beach Polytechnic High School.

* * *

Dad had decided that Yi Tai-jo and I would be spending the Summer with his friend Red Kearns, up at Muroc.

Pilot Squadron Leader Dad Sir was being sent on a joint training mission, a 90-day stint to Osan AFB, on the Korean Peninsula, to instruct young South Korean pilots on the American bombers and big jets. America was leaving South Korea, and we needed to defend our own skies.

The shooting war on the Korean peninsula was over. Now South Korea needed to bulk up its new fleet for a possibly long and smoldering peace with the North and the North's evil buddies, Russia and China. Dad called it "an effing grenade with the effing pin pulled."

That morning, what should have been a joyride on Dad's B-29 Superfortress was like a death march, for Yi Tai-jo and me.

"Say," I rallied, as we were all sitting in the cockpit, about halfway through the short flight north and east, to the desert.

"Isn't Muroc where they fly the X-1?"

"Roger that," Dad answered.

2. SUPERFORTRESS

It just blew my mind. First of all, its size,

and then its capabilities. And to think that

they could take an airplane, a bomber,

and pressurize it, so that we could feel the same

at sea level as we do at 30,000 feet ...

— *B-29 Pilot Robert Rodenhouse*

If you can walk away from a landing,

it's a good landing.

If you can use the airplane the next day,

it is an outstanding landing.

— *Chuck Yeager*

If you have ever seen a B-29 Boeing Superfortress touch down, you won't soon forget it. A thing like that can change how you think about the world. About what is possible.

A Boeing B-29 Superfortress starts as a speck on the distant horizon.

As it rolls down the runway towards you, big and loud with the bomber-bay windows in those distinctive patterns, the four thunderous Double Cyclone Wright jet engines at full blast, shaking the ground as it rolls, you wonder:

How can this mid-sized castle be flying?

It is the largest bomber in the fleet. Any fleet. It is the most advanced bomber in the world. It was the most advanced bomber in the world, in its time, with 2200 horsepower behind it and remote gun placements on all sides.

It wasn't that Dad was using the Superfortress as an air taxi to deliver us to Muroc, it was that the X-1 needed to be launched by a larger plane, to save its fuel for its own 12-minutes-of-hell flight. The B-29 was the X-1's mother ship.

Isolated, desolate, the Muroc lakebed offered 60 open miles of runways, each one 300 yards across. Flat, baked earth as far as the eye could see, rimmed by the distant Shadows Mountains.

Seeing the B-29 Superfortress land can change how you think about the world, about what is possible.

Vast, flat, many shades of brown and rust. During the Paleozoic era, the Mojave Desert was covered by shallow seas.

My Korean Sister took hold of my hand.

She did not like change.

Sitting in the B-29, looking down over the prehistoric desert lakebed, I could tell how miserable she was. One idea was dominating the mind, for both of us:

This is gonna be Topaz, all over again ...

3. WELCOME COMMITTEE

We were every card in the deck.

— *Timothy Liu*

Loading and coupling the B-29 and the X-1 takes two hours, so we left Dad and Red and their platoon gang of engineers, mechanics and rocket scientists to take a look at our new quarters. We would not be getting much goodwill from our peers, judging from the faces of our welcoming committee -- a tight gaggle of scruffy, mean-looking boys who were not pleased to see us.

Our new home, Line Shack Six, was a ramshackle cottage on the western side of the Muroc Air Force Base compound, across from the garages and Line Shack Six, the workshop.

It was a large storage shed with two cots and some sheets and blankets tossed in. Dusty but roomy. Sunlight peeked through slim spaces in the wooden planks of the walls.

Two bedrooms and a big spare room with shelves which looked like the final resting place of an assortment of military odds and ends – bayonets, maps, helmets, empty cartridges, a box of dog tags, funny-looking binoculars, riding crops with the Third Cavalry seal.

I checked under the beds and in corners until found what I was looking for.

A white canvas bag with writhing and squirming going on inside it.

I held the bag with a bayonet, at arm's length, warning Yi Tai-jo away.

I ran outside a minute until I was in among the shrubs and

prickly undergrowth off-property and emptied the bag, in a grove of Joshua trees.

The bag left in our quarters contained snakes and scorpions, like I figured.

Topaz all over again.

Welcome to Muroc.

* * *

I followed the sound of laughing voices and found the group of them huddled by the windows of the second-floor barracks, a big sunny room.

"Who did this?" I demanded.

No one answered, so I went to the biggest guy there and chucked the empty bag at him and slugged him.

Yelling and shouts rose when he straightened up, holding his jaw.

He took a powerful swing at me, amid jeers and catcalls --

The cheering died when I kicked the guy's legs out from under him and he slammed on the floor.

I jumped on him, landing hard on his chest.

It always worked this way.

I had caught him off guard. Sooner or later his size and strength would overpower me, so I had to get my licks in early.

I slapped him with my open hand. It made a loud sound.

I called him Korean names that I won't repeat here.

I struck him again.

That second blow would normally have broken his nose, but I was holding back.

He tossed me off – I went flying --

He stood.

He was advancing for the inevitable beat-down when a blue-and-white streak crossed in between us --

Yi Tai-jo snatched a small boy who happened to be standing next to the big one.

She crashed the little kid against one wall, knocking the breath out of him.

My Korean Sister shifted her prisoner and held the kid very tight, from the back, a thick leather holster belt around his neck.

She jerked him, hard, off the ground.

The kid tried to scream but could only make a muffled panic sound.

His blue-jeaned legs and P.F. Flyer sneakers flailed in the air. He could not get free.

Yi Tai-jo yanked on the leather belt, and not in any preliminary, '*I'm warning you*' way --

Yi Tai-jo did not hold back. His face, already crimson, was turning a deeper redder by the heartbeat. Blood flowed from his busted lip.

Yi Tai-jo was choking him to death ...

"Okay! Okay!"

Two of the onlookers wrestled the boy away from Yi Tai-jo's deadly grip --

"*Jeez!!*" they whined, and "*Frickin' A!*"

"So, you like to *dish it out*," I called out to the group in general. "But you don't like it much when someone *fights back...*"

The little kid wouldn't stop whining and pawing at his throat.

Yi Tai-jo wiped blood from her cheek ...

We had seen all this before, she and I.

I squared up with the big kid, who looked really mad now —

"I'm not giving up," I said, "if that's what you think."

Suddenly, from outside, from the unbounded Muroc desert landing strips, we heard the unmistakable whine and rev of four thunderous Double Cyclone Wright jet engines --

The X-1's test flight was about to start --

We all ran outside.

4. LINE SHACK SIX

You've been told, but none of you really understand.

— Kazuo Ishiguro

Right there on Runway 2, Dad's B-29 had been hoisted onto a raised platform, with the assistance of three cranes mounted on a freestanding tower. A derrick lifted the X-1 (3).

A network of hooks and straps held the X-1 shackled fast to the B-29's belly, like a papoose.

We waved to Dad, behind the B-29 cockpit glass.

They turned slowly and set up at the head of Runway 7. The bomber's mighty engines ignited. The conjoined aircraft sped down the runway.

Roaring and acceleration.

Liftoff.

We watched, shading our eyes, until the planes disappeared.

Soon after, Dad and the B-29 (out of our sight, now) banked and headed back south to Victorville.

We were not allowed into Mission Control – basically a corner of Middle Hangar Utah – so we all watched from the balconies as they monitored the flight.

Fourteen minutes later, we cheered as the X-1 landed.

Red and the others were not pleased. They went back and forth amongst themselves in a hubbub, asking urgent questions, pointing to the gauges, troubleshooting, concerned at the data they were seeing.

We heard the words 'fuel injection.' A contraption they called the oscillator seemed to be an object of attention.

* * *

At least Line Shack Six was roomy.

With a living room, kitchenette, a bedroom and two walk-in closets, the cottage that was to be our quarters had been most recently used as a storage shed.

Behind a large door, we found a washroom and sink.

The closets were filled with dusty odds and ends, mostly military stuff -- oversized compass, helmets that looked like they had been used at Normandy, a box of Navy medals and dog tags, a pile of leather belt holsters, boxes of Navy medals, dog tags. Behind a shelf of history books we found cartons of rocks and fossils.

The water to our cabin had been shut off. I found the main valves and opened them and flushed the rusty water. Yi Tai-jo discovered a hot-water heater in the closet. All the connections were loose, so I scrounged some tools and fixed them.

I went outside and ran into a good-natured young carpenter wearing a tool belt. He was working on what looked like new windows for the Infirmary expansion. I introduced myself. He said his name was Wally. He looked over the situation, lent me his tool kit, and sent one of his helpers to track down 3/4" valves and a lift pump. We had hot and cold running water by evening.

We cleared everything in the storage rooms, dusted it all off, and laid it out in the sunshine. We labelled everything we could. We cleaned the merchandise and re-shelfed it.

I found a model plane, well-assembled, mounted on a little pedestal. It was a DeHavilland Viper.

My Korean Sister hates dirty floors. I was able to fashion a broom frame and tied a piece of pumice stone tightly to a stick, so she could sweep in between the cracks of those board floors.

We heard a firm knock on the door of Line Shack Six.

It was Red Kearns, my Dad's pilot buddy. He looked tired.

He carried gifts of sheets, blankets, towels and soap.

"You did this plumbing? Wait 'till Wally finds out about you ..."

"We heard about the fuel injection," I said.

"Yeah." Red sat down on one of the beds. He lit a cigarette. "Once we hit 820, 830, she just won't behave ..."

"Is it safe?" asked Yi Tai-jo.

"It'll get safer if we can figure out why the damn sensors keep shorting out."

Red shook his head ruefully.

"We've done so much good work. It's a shame. But the thing just doesn't fly right. That last run ... nearly augured it."

In the Air Force gumbo of pilots, that particular verb – 'auger' -- is very, very bad. A word you do not ever want to hear.

"Really?" said Yi Tai-jo. "We couldn't tell -- "

"We checked the tail a million times," Red explained, "the suspension, the stabilizers --

"Problem is, we have no way of knowing what to expect, once we pass 800 or so. These speeds, these altitudes. We're just guessing."

"*Aut viam inveniam, aut faciam*," said I, invoking just about every military man's number one favorite motto. The quote is from Hannibal, being his response when told by his generals that he could not cross the alps with his phalanx of elephants. It means, "I will either find a way, or make one."

'Hah!" Red smiled. "That's just what your Dad would say. Only he'd mispronounce it."

"We're gonna run all the numbers again tonight. You can watch from the upper deck if you like. Then there's a Brit giving Rocketman Bob a run-down, you can sit in on that."

Red smiled and put out his cigarette in a gaudy *Welcome to*

Las Vegas ashtray on the end table.

"Glad you're here."

5. BREAKFAST WITH LEWIS

Even before the start of World War Two in 1939, engineers knew that propellor-driven aircraft had reached their limits ...

— *Mark Finlay*

The next morning, at breakfast in the Commissary, a skinny Lost Boy with an old Air Force jacket came over and sat at our table. He took off his wool cap and set down his tray. His plates were piled high with pastries, scrambled eggs (powdered) with some type of gravy, toast, hot tea, and a bowl of oatmeal.

He introduced himself. He said his name was Lewis. We told him our names.

"Sorry about the snake gag," he said. "That was lame."

"That was a *garden* snake," I replied. "And those scorpions were babies. You're not very good at intimidation -- "

"Check," replied Lewis. "Check that. I'm not sure the Lost Boys are good at anything. We run around like we're doing important things, but it's mostly phony."

He gobbled several spoonfuls of oatmeal from the bowl on the orange tray in front of him.

"But you can't really blame us for pranking you.

"First, you're Korean.

"Second," he turned to Yi Tai-jo. "You're seriously weird. Do you have mental problems or something?"

"Maybe," answered Yi Tai-jo. She tried one of the pastries on her tray. "My doctor in Long Beach thinks I show signs of Kanner's Syndrome. When I get nervous."

"Uh huh," nodded Lewis.

"And my memory is freakishly good."

"But are you like a witch or something? I get a weird feeling when I'm around you."

"No," she answered.

"You seem really smart," Lewis added, in case he had offended her.

He got up with an empty plate and returned with it piled high with half-cooked bacon and sausage and hash browns and scrambled eggs (powdered).

"That test run went real bad yesterday," Lewis told us.

"Apparently the fuel injection froze up at altitude. Forty thousand feet, that's what I heard Pomerantz say. Red says the whole project's gonna close down if they can't figure it out."

"Why?" I asked. "Who else is gonna break Mach?"

"Rudebaugh. The Warnock team. They're over at Fairchild. We see 'em sometimes at the night markets."

Lewis waved at a table of Lost Boys in the corner, motioning for his friends to come over. They stayed where they were.

"Was that ju-jitsu you used yesterday, on Michael David?" he asked me.

"*Subak*," I answered. "Martial arts. My Dad had us learn it when we were toddlers."

"*Wild*," nodded Lewis approvingly. "That is wild. *Ka-ra-te* stuff ... "

He drained his tea.

"That was your Dad piloting the Superfortress, right?" He scarfed three strips of bacon. "Boy howdy."

He drained the oatmeal bowl until nothing was left.

"Well, I can show you around if you'd like. Jolly Wally is installing new sinks in the Infirmary this morning. He says you're pretty handy."

"Yippee Ki Yay, you can check with the kitchen cooks, they always need help. Also the nurses -- "

"She stays with me," I answered. "And it's 'Yi Tai-jo.'"

"I dig, Big. Yee Tie Joan."

"Yi Tai-jo," my sister corrected him.

As we got up to clean our trays, we came face to face with the big Lost Boy from yesterday, the one I had punched.

This was the one whom Lewis called Michael David. Two small boys were trailing him.

"Hey," said Michael David.

"Hey," I replied.

"No, I mean you." He faced Yi Tai-jo.

"Stop looking at me like that," he told her.

I started to tell him he could stuff whatever it was he was trying to say back into his mouth, but Yi Tai-jo pulled me away.

"Why?" she demanded. "Why should I?"

"Because you're buggin' me! I mean it!"

His cheeks were flushed bright red.

"Huh," he added.

"Clever comeback, Heathcliff," Lewis told Michael David.

"What?" demanded Michael David. "Why did you call me that? Who is 'Heathcliff'?"

"You're just mad that I can see through you," Yi Tai-jo informed Michael David.

"Don't tell me what I *think*," said Michael David. This comment seemed to surprise even him.

"What is even your *name*?" Michael David asked. "None of us know your *name --* "

"It's *Yippy*. Yippy Yee *--* " interjected Lewis.

"Yi. Tai. Jo," said I. "That's her name."

"Don't say my name," my sister ordered Michael David. "Don't *think* my name. My name is off-limits to you. Got it?"

"No. I don't 'Got it,'" rejoined Michael David.

He stalked off.

"Whoa," exclaimed Lewis. "*Dutch tilt!*"

"What was that?" he asked Yi Tai-jo. "Do you and him already know one another, like from a previous life?"

"*Nauen yeogi issda*," said Yi Tai-jo defiantly to Michael David, even though he was gone.

I liked hearing her say it in Korean.

"*Nanuen nanikka.*"

"And what was that?" asked Lewis. "What did you just say?"

"'*I am here*,'" my Korean Sister translated.

"'I am me.'"

6. EPISODES

Trying so hard seems to have backfired.

— *Haku Inoa*

"Rocket ship" is a nice way of saying "barely-controlled bomb-blast."

The X-1 carried enough explosive fuel to blow up the Empire State Building.

Fuel for the X-1 is alcohol and liquid nitrogen (its temperature lowered to 297 degrees below zero). The liquid explosives boiled and steamed as they were injected – gallons and gallons and gallons -- into the plane's tanks. The engineers wore thick gloves and full-body suits and helmets with glass visors when they handled it.

Things behave differently when they are moving above 700 miles per hour ... it's just that no one knows how. Which things? How different? Different in what ways? The very air becomes the enemy, at the point where you're going faster than sound.

Such a thing as supersonic flight had never been done before. There is no precedent, no earlier data to which the rocket scientists could refer. Mankind is not built for this. The very air resists you, trying to stop the plane, not wanting it to move that fast, clawing at its skin to slow it down.

Once the X-1 entered the transonic zone – that band of the speed spectrum on the cusp of supersonic – the aircraft would buffet and shake and shimmy like crazy, forty or fifty different parts, in twenty different ways.

For a military-grade salary of $283 per month, the pilots were finding out the answers to all of these questions, on the fly.

In mid-flight, that is.

* * *

There were three versions of the Bell X-1, more or less indistinguishable except for their colors (1 was rust, 2 was rust-orange, and 3 was white).

The X-1 fuselage was jammed with pressure regulators, landing gear and 500 hundred pounds of flight-test instrumentation.

What happened?

Why did the test run go wrong, and just when the X-1 crossed the 900 mph line ...

Was that a coincidence? Was it the fuel injection? Was it the angle of the tail? Was there a flaw in the fuselage skin? Was the cockpit secure?

This morning they were taking a close, close look at the wings.

The wing of an airplane is shaped in such a way as to control the speed and pressure of the air flowing around it. Air moving over the curved upper surface of the wing will travel faster and thus produce less pressure than the slower air moving across the flatter underside of the wing. This difference in pressure creates lift.

"Overdesign," suggested Red.

"Well, sir," commented John Pomerantz. "That is as may be ..."

He was thinking as they looked over the readout. He ran his index finger down the paper, so as not to miss a word, or a syllable, or a letter.

"I'd rather be overly cautious than streamlined and dead."

"It ain't that, John," answered Red.

* * *

"You can sit in with the Brit, Dockley, if you're interested," Red had told us earlier.

NACA, the U.S. government agency which sponsored the X-1 tests, had a deal with the Brits that all data be shared.

So Rocketman Bob, low man in the hierarchy of engineers, was assigned to swap information with the British engineer, a very smart, well-spoken young man named Dockley. Sid, another would-be rocket scientist, was there, taking notes. Yi Tai-jo and I sat at the next table in the Commissary.

The English had lost the DH-108 in transonic flight, killing ("auguring," in Muroc airman gumbo) the pilot. So they were extra-cautious, preferring remote guidance to manned tests.

Dockley reviewed the Brits' latest luck with the crowded fuselage, the thin wings, fuel injection.

"And you might want to check your I Bars. Your O rings. All your rubber moldings," said the Englishman, Dockley.

"Synthetic rubber," he continued, "performs poorly at those higher speeds, anything over 900. Higher altitudes. Brittle, don't you know. We don't actually understand why. Brazilian rubber seems far more stable. Actual plant rubber.

"There you have it."

* * *

"You look more American than your sister," observed Lewis one dinner.

Yi Tai-jo was up getting seconds on vegetables.

"Yeah. We have different mothers. Her mom is Korean, so she's pure Korean. I'm half and half. My mom's from Orange County."

"What did that supervisor mean about 'Topaz'?" Lewis asked me. "What is 'Topaz'?"

"It's an internment camp," I answered.

Yi Tai-jo sat down.

"We spent time there, at the beginning of the war. Almost a month, then the Pilot sprung us."

"America had concentration camps?"

"Yup. North of here."

Yi Tai-jo abruptly rose to clear her tray.

"That's *whack!*" said Lewis.

"It was bad," I said.

Yi Tai-jo stood at the back of the cafeteria, at the tray depot, waiting for me.

"Maybe don't mention it around Yi," I told Lewis.

7. VISIT FROM SCHOOL SUPERVISOR

We're going through a period when

nothing can be left to chance.

– *Yasmina Khadra*

One morning, we saw Red running out of Bay Two. He was moving fast, wiping the grease from his hands on an acetone-soaked towel.

We all followed him to see what was going on.

Five people stood in front of four vehicles parked in the roundabout. The sprawling desert lay beyond. A big-grilled, dark blue Oldsmobile, a sturdy Ford Fairlane, doors open, and two long trucks with fenced-in rear cargo spaces. Paddy wagons.

The seal on the Olds read: *Muroc Unified School District*

The seal on the Paddy wagons read: *412th Test Wing Public Affairs*

Three uniformed officers stood behind a friendly-looking man in a suit.

He was holding a fedora to his chest, trying to be polite.

A woman stood at the front of the contingent. She wore a green ensemble and held a clipboard. She was not trying to be polite.

She was reading a list of names. After a moment, I recognized enough of them to realize she was taking a roll call of the Lost Boys.

"But you can't just *seize* them like this!" protested the nurse, close to tears.

"You can only ignore the State of California for so long," said the lady in green. "Without proof of schooling, they are wards of the state. Wards of the state. We're taking them."

"You knew this," she added.

"I thought we had until August," said Red, wiping his hands on a towel.

"August is the date for their arraignment," replied the woman in green. Your deadline to submit certification came and went."

"This's my fault," said Red. "What can we do?"

"Tell me what school they've been attending. Show me their transcripts. Their curricula."

"Look," pleaded Red. "These boys are Air Force orphans. Their fathers served bravely -- "

But she was done talking. The woman in green stepped aside and nodded to the policemen, who now advanced, handcuffs at the ready –

A loud and eerie new voice stopped everyone where they stood.

"You might look into a Hard-to-Staff Setting waiver," said the voice. "Under the Small Rural Schools Achievement Program. It's California *Education Code* Section 44865 ..."

The weird voice was coming out of Yi Tai-jo's mouth, but it belonged to Principal May of Long Beach Polytechnical High School.

The woman looked hard at Yi Tai-jo.

"You're that mimetic girl," she declared. "From Long Beach Poly."

"Yes, ma'am," said Yi Tai-jo.

"What she said is true," said the man in the suit cautiously. "They can apply for a Hard-to-Staff Setting status. Then take the equivalency exams."

The woman in green looked from Ya Tai-jo to Red, then back at Yi Tai-jo.

"It's a lot of paperwork," she said.

"Can you get them over to the New Vista Middle School?" she asked Red. "For the exams?"

"Yes," answered Red. "Yes, we can. And when is that?"

"July 14. That's three weeks away. Doesn't give you much time ... "

"We can do it," said my Korean Sister.

"All right," said the lady in green.

"You two were at Topaz," she said to Yi Tai-jo and me.

"Yes, ma'am."

She nodded.

She turned and walked back to her car.

"We'll mail you the forms, and a copy of last year's exam. You've got a lot of work to do."

The pack of vehicles drove off, trailing a plume of dust from the Paleozoic Era, suspended granules of stegosaurus and pterodactyl.

8. CLASSROOM

A half-civilised ferocity lurked yet in the

depressed brows and eyes full of black fire ...

   — *Emily Bronte*

"Today," announced the teacher, Miss Carlson, one of the base nurses. "The lesson plan is Compare and Contrast.

"This is going to be on your equivalency exam."

"*Sell it*, baby," said Lewis encouragingly.

"Quiet!" ordered Red impatiently. "She's here on her own time. Don't waste it." He was standing along the side wall.

"Does anyone know why Lewis calls Michael David 'Heathcliffe'?" asked Miss Carlson.

No one spoke.

"Somebody answer," commanded Red.

"It's after a character in an English novel," answered Yi Tai-jo.

"Correct," said Miss Carlson. "'Wuthering Heights,' by Emily Bronte."

"I did not know that," said Yi Tai-jo.

"Here is my point," continued Miss Carlson. "On the exam next week, you are going to be asked an essay question. They want to see that you can formulate a solid argument.

"So use what you know. Tie these larger themes to your own life. Examiners love that."

"Focus, boys," urged Red.

"I'm on it, Chief," stressed Aldhabi.

"You're not on it," replied Red. "She hasn't given you the topic yet."

"Take your pens," said Miss Carlson.

"Now. Compare and contrast two examples of love. One that we find in literature and the other from your own life. That's your topic today."

The classroom full of Lost Boys paused, wheels spinning. They each started scribbling. *Two hundred fifty words…*

Lewis raised his hand.

"Can I ask a question?"

This was met with groans.

"Frickin' A," said Red.

"Can you not?" said I.

"Yes, Lewis," said Miss Carlson.

"Ma'am, do you happen to know which Lady Blackhawk I'm in love with?"

"No one cares, Lewis," someone commented.

"Tell us, Lewis," said Miss Carlson. "Are there more than one?"

"There are three of them, ma'am. All equally pretty, as drawn by Reed Crandall," explained Lewis. "Zinda, Natalie, an -- "

"Well, why don't you use them as examples in your essay," said Miss Carlson. "Compare and contrast them."

"Use it," urged Red.

"Sit up straight, Ace," said Red to Wasson, smacking his

chair with a blackboard pointer.

"*Hawkaaaa*," affirmed Lewis.

"All right." Miss Carlson clapped her hands. "Five paragraphs. Just like we practiced. Two hundred fifty words. That's a page. We'll read them aloud.

"You have fifteen minutes."

"Fifteen minutes!" I protested. I am not skilled at essays.

"If Miss Carlson here isn't happy with your essay, you're doing laps." announced Red.

"*Hawkaaaa*," affirmed Lewis once more.

* * *

"Where were you, M-D?" called Lewis, in the Commissary at lunch. "You missed class."

Michael David was walking to the back counter, carrying his tray.

"I don't need your stupid 'class,'" he said loudly.

"Good!" responded Yi Tai-jo, without looking up from her plate. "You couldn't understand it anyway -- "

Michael David cleared his tray.

"Huh. You don't even KNOW what I understand."

"Not much, apparently," replied Yi Tai-jo.

He dropped his tray onto the pile of trays in the bin.

"You're *absurd*. Really," he told my sister. "You live in an *absurd* world. You're how I define 'absurdity.' Do you even *comprehend* that?"

She almost smiled at this last remark.

"Yeah, well ..."

The Commissary doors swung shut. M-D was gone before

she could finish the thought.

Lewis and I exchanged glances.

He raised his eyebrows, but kept the rest of his face expressionless.

9. NIGHT DESERT AND DROP BOXES

It was an age when the limits of time,

space, and the imagination were being

dramatically expanded.

— *James Young*

Sometimes we couldn't get to sleep.

Yi Tai-jo found this stressful, so she and I would tiptoe out of Line Shack Six and go fossil-hunting out in the near desert, across from the airplane bays.

We were armed with experimental starlight scopes, liberated from the Line Shack Six storage closets. These bulky, photocathode contraptions strapped on your forehead and gave a low-degree moonlight image. While they were only marginally effective, we liked wearing them.

During the Paleozoic era, the Mojave Desert was covered by shallow seas.

Yi Tai-jo looked like a big, happy bug.

* * *

Only Runway Three was properly lit, like a fully-loaded landing strip should be, with parallel sequences of runway lights. Airfield lighting systems and taxi beacons are complicated things, integrated to the base's entire grid. The last time the Oscillator and Wind Tunnel had been in use, the runway lights had set to flickering. Those same electric drop boxes also controlled the West Hangar lights. You did not want those misfiring. The job of the breaker box is to distribute power throughout the system, in the branch circuits, and to disconnect power from the incoming feed when needed.

So Wally asked me if I could help him to check all of the connections of the airfield lighting system – beacons, transformers, the couplings, the drop boxes – the whole shebang. I know more about plumbing than electrics, but I was happy to help.

Yi Tai-jo and Lewis tagged along, all three of us keeping our thick insulated gloves on throughout.

Lewis wanted to know all about the drop boxes, how they worked.

The wind cones were swiveling, the flag and banners were fluttering.

We were about halfway through the sub-panel circuit when Rocketman Bob called Lewis over. Lewis had a visitor.

We saw a black truck parked in the far curve of the driveway. Lewis and a man were sitting on the running boards, sharing a soda.

Wally squinted in their direction.

"That's a Department of Corrections truck," he concluded.

"That must be Lewis' dad. He's doing a stint in Lancaster. Got mixed up with gamblers, over in Las Vegas."

We checked the drop-boxes and found the loose connections. We guessed it was from one of the night-time critters, either that or the weight and vibrations of the Superfortress. Several of the drop-boxes, where an earlier electrician genius had solved a problem with duct tape (now frayed), featured wires that had been burned through. It's best to make a rule: never settle for a temporary solution.

We replaced all of the couplings. We re-wrapped them, tightly, and made sure each was properly welded. Nocturnal visitors and Superfortress vibrations would not soon dim those light strips.

Wind cones and flags were flapping on the poles and parapets of the slim control tower. We shaded our eyes in the bright sunlight.

"Say," said Wally. "The internment camp. Topaz. Was you there when that garrison guard got killed?"

"I don't know about that," I replied.

"Heard it was a real bad actor who got it," said Wally. "A killer. Someone did us all a favor. Garroted, wasn't he?"

I shrugged. I undid and rewrapped one of the couplings.

Lewis looked upset when he came back. He didn't say much when Wally asked how his Dad was.

Cumulous clouds scudded across the sunny sand-flat skies.

9. A CARD-TABLE MEMORIAL

The word 'happy' would lose its meaning
if it were not balanced by sadness.

  – Carl Jung

Our eleventh night in Muroc was the date of our *gijesa*.

This is the ceremony Koreans hold on the night before the anniversary of a loved one's death.

We held the ceremony every year, Yi Tai-jo and me and Dad, in honor of Yi Tai-jo's mother, Iseul Iseul. It was also to honor our ancestors as a group, as a family.

Yi Tai-jo always inserted a few mentions of the women of the circle -- that is, the circle of those Topaz women who had taken my sister in like she was their own daughter, and been repaid with a fierce devotion on her part.

They had formed a lifetime bond in those dark, dark days.

Those Topaz women lit a fire burning inside Yi Tai-jo, and I knew that at any time of day or night, they were close to her.

My own mother, the controversial second Mrs. Lieutenant Chui Yoon, was still very much alive, living in St. Louis with her boyfriend and wanting nothing to do with me.

I also have an American sister. She is five years older than me, also wanting nothing to do with the Korean side of the family. Last I heard, she lives in the Quad Cities, either Moline or Rock Island, I forget.

But enough about that.

* * *

The *gijesa* ceremony honors our departed.

At midnight, we set out the little folding-table shrine beneath a set of night lamps, on the south patio, outside the Commissary.

We set a framed picture of Iseul Iseul beneath a paper screen facing north.

We set out six of those squat, slow-burning candles around it.

We recited the long prayer for ancestors. The first part tells of their honorable deeds. The second part deals with our own shortcomings and our appreciation of their wisdom in our lives.

I forgot my lines during the middle section, so I substituted (in Korean) the lyrics for "Fly Me to the Moon." I asked (in conversational Korean) for our ancestors to help Yi Tai-jo since she had fallen in love with a flying machine. This won a smile from my sister.

"*Ko ma wo, nae joseng,*" we said, together. We bowed our heads.

We looked up to see that one of the Lost Boys had placed a photograph on the table beside our photo of Iseul Iseul.

The new photo was of a teenaged girl. She was skinny and pretty, with a sweet smile and curls of light hair framing an impossibly young face. She seemed to have no clue whatsoever to the kind of dark twists, the snakes and scorpions, that life has in store. She was holding a baby.

We didn't turn to look, but the Boy, whoever it was, had knelt behind us and listened while we recited the ancestor prayer:

Ulineun ilh-eobeolin ideul-eul jongyeonghabnida.

This is old-fashioned and corny, but it fits.

One by one, more Lost Boys came out and silently placed photos and mementos of departed ones on the card table. Each Boy moved the candles a little, so that light shone on his picture. Each boy took a place facing the table. I lost count when it reached ten.

Michael David, I noticed his arrival. The photo he set down must have been of his dad. A pilot, his features were almost identical to M-D, except that he was smiling.

Yi Tai-jo and I repeated the main prayer, venerating beloved ancestors, every time a new photo went up.

Then we ran out of prayers.

Then we gave up, and sat there on the patio in silence.

We listened together, all of us, to the sounds which the desert night gives off.

In highly-charged, wordless moments like these, other senses come to the fore. I could hear different breezes in the twisted miniature trees. Now I could discern what I was sure were chattering gray foxes, and critters improving their nests of sticks.

Was that a squadron of wild bees?

Yi Tai-jo started crying. She couldn't help it.

That table with the little candles and all those pictures of actual people, actual people, all of whom had departed -- it was so, so sad.

I thought of Iseul Iseul. I knew her, while Yi Tai-jo never did. I remember those little dances she would make up in the kitchen, and her cooking those really good fruit *yakgwa*, serving them fresh out of the oven. She was always kind to me. Pregnant with Yi Tai-jo, Iseul Iseul had always tried to put together American-style sandwiches for me and Captain Lieutenant Pilot Mister Dad.

Dad loved Iseul Iseul very, very much. That's why he doted on Yi Tai-jo.

Yi Tai-jo was weeping openly now.

Sorrow is always with us, I think, and sometimes it just needs to make its presence known. You can't resist. So much sadness, and such a strong dose of it, had moored itself in our pool of light, right there, where we were, on the patio in Muroc, at the edges of the frickin' desert. I couldn't handle it. Where was all this sorrow coming from?

My sister was trying to stop crying and stay quiet, but that only made it worse. She prayed in Korean that she be allowed to stop crying.

My sister stopped crying.

Sorrow is always with us, I think. Sometimes it just needs to make its presence known.

At length, beneath those upper layers of noises, rose the sounds of tiny burrows being dug. Billy owls gossiped in the night. Lizards scuttled across the sands. Skunks scratched at shrubs.

Gradually, I heard, or imagined that I heard, waves lapping in the ancient inland sea that the Mojave had once been. The vast dolomite flats were producing impossibly low and subtle night-sounds, groans and low cracks. Maybe it was the Moon tugging at all those buried fossils, restless, fitful, dreaming of emerging once again, to retake their rightful place beneath the star-splashed skies.

10. TURNAROUND

Water has bubbled in caverns under
this desert for thousands of years.

— *Scott Wilson*

The next morning, a knock on our cottage door woke us.
It was early dawn.
I opened the door to a billowing of mists.
Buried beneath the Mojave sands lies an aquifer – an underground reservoir – the size of Rhode Island. Moisture from this vast underground lake rises to the surface during the night and can produce a brief, but most excellent, light fog in the early mornings, among the night-cooled sands and the day-heated rocks.
Three figures stood in the mist.
Two were horses, standing patiently behind the third

figure, which was Michael David. He held two bridles in hand.

M-D was wearing jeans and a plaid work-shirt, his dark tousled hair crammed under a baseball cap.

He saw Yi Tai-jo behind me. He took off his cap.

"Got a filly," he said to her.

One of the horses pawed the ground, ready to go. I think it was an Appaloosa, but I might be making that up.

"She won't let any of the boys ride her," said Michael David.

"I thought you might have better luck."

He held out a set of reins, hopefully.

11. TEST RUN CRASH

It's *always* that bad.

   — *Alexi Hawley*

In the tracking station, we could hear them talking back and forth over the land-to-air sound system.

We could hear all of the spoken exchanges over the intercom speakers.

> **John Pomerantz:** Red, swing to the right sharp, clear down on the edge of the lake bed.
> **X-1 pilot Red Kearns:** I'll be down over the South track there in a minute, down to 7,000 feet.
> **John Pomerantz:** Roger.

Once again, the B-29 carried its strapped-on X-1 cargo

down the runway.

At 24,000 feet, the pilot climbed down a ladder into the tiny, crowded-with-wiring cockpit.

The flight engineer climbed down to slam shut the cockpit door.

At 26,000 feet, the B-29 went into a shallow dive and pulled up, releasing the X-1.

> **X-1 pilot Red Kearns:** Flaps coming down.
> **X-1 pilot Red Kearns:** Source pressure still 1600.
> **X-1 pilot Red Kearns:** I'm a little bit fogged up – not too bad.
> **Sid:** Red, swing to the right sharp, clear down on the edge of the lake bed.
> **X-1 pilot Red Kearns:** I'll be down over the South track there in a minute, down to 7,000 feet.
> **John Pomerantz:** Roger.

Red set off the four rocket chambers, one by one.

The surge of the rockets slammed him back in his seat.

The plane rose at a 45-degree angle, just as called for in the flight plan ...

At about .87 Mach, the buffeting started ...

> **X-1 pilot Red Kearns:** Windows iced up –

"What? How'd *that* happen?" murmured Sid off-mike.

X-1 pilot Red Kearns: Flying blind ...

Sid: (Expletive)

John Pomerantz: What cylinders are on, Red?
X-1 Pilot Red Kearns: #3 coming on now. Start.
X-1 Pilot Red Kearns: Cylinder seconds on 250 right now.

He had taken the ship up to 108,000 feet after cutting in the rocket engine at 60,000. The atmosphere was so thin there that the reaction controls worked. This was temporary -- an illusion of control that the plane would not retain for long.

Once the rockets kicked in, the angle of ascent steepened to 50 degrees.

The nose pitched up. The next thing that would happen would be going into a spin, then dropping like a stone. We heard the thrusters push the nose right down again.

At 40,000 feet, Red cut in the afterburner.

The X-1 stalled.

John Pomerantz: NO, no, no --

The X-1 had stalled at the top of a round-out.

This was fatal.

It had paused in the high in the stratosphere, in the bright sunlight, for a long moment, then toppled backward and over in a full aileron. Red hit the opposite rudder and managed a Dutch roll which simply delayed the inevitable.

The X-1 plummeted like the giant bullet it was, graceless, gaining speed as it fell, 50 thousand feet in 70 seconds.

X-1 Pilot Red Kearns: Push over.
John Pomerantz: 20 seconds.
John Pomerantz: Got him in sight, Sid?
Sid: No, he's going out of sight – too small.

X-1 Pilot Red Kearns: (Inaudible – gasping) – I'm down to 25,000 over Mojave. Don't know whether I can get back to the base or not.
John Pomerantz: At 25,000 feet, Red?
X-1 Pilot Red Kearns: Can't say much more, I got to (blurry) – save myself.
X-1 Pilot Red Kearns: I'm – (illegible) – (Christ!)
Sid: What say, Red?
X-1 Pilot Red Kearns: I say I don't know if I tore anything up or not but Christ!
John Pomerantz: Tell us where you are if you can.
X-1 Pilot Red Kearns: I think I can get back to the base okay. Boy. I'm not going to do that anymore.

John Pomerantz: Red, stretch. You gotta stretch it --

Sid: Red, listen up. The main engine is overheating from the exertion of the climb ...

X-1 Pilot Red Kearns: Roger. Done.

Sid: Drag's too high ...

John Pomerantz: Nope.

X-1 Pilot Red Kearns: Done ...

Sid: No, sir! No! Not done!

X-1 Pilot Red Kearns: Iddnat right?

John Pomerarantz: Red.

X-1 Pilot Red Kearns: Ah ... ah jes' ...

Silence.

Red had conked out.

"Around 12,000 feet, the oxygen content of the air should bring him around, Sir ..." said Jolly Wally, but he didn't sound too sure.

"Holy Hell," said Sid, softly, but not like he was mad. More like "I did not actually think this could happen," a sort of transitional comment, now that we had entered the Realm of the Unknown.

This was bad.

I went cold inside.

Yi Tai-jo gripped my hand.

X-1 Pilot Red Kearns (reviving): *Ugh! Hey!* There she--

John Pomerantz: Red!

Sid: Don't code on me now, Chief --

Silence.

We glanced at the diagram boards in the tracking station, then at the blinking red light on the sensor board –

This was all wrong.

"He's not supposed to be where he is," remarked Rocketman Bob.

> **X-1 Pilot Red Kearns:** (mumbling): Happy Trails, boys --
>
> **John Pomerantz:** Just line it up, Red ....
>
> **X-1 Pilot Red Kearns:** Fuse-out.
>
> **John Pomerantz:** Hey!
>
> **Sid:** Altimeter's spinning --
>
> **John Pomerantz:** Red, you're falling 150 feet a second--
>
> **X-1 Pilot Red Kearns:** Burzappibairnrelo –
>
> **Sid:** Pull up, Red!
>
> **X-1 Pilot Red Kearns** (groggy): Okay! Can do --

But it was too late.

The X-1 was failing on all three axes – roll, pitch, and yaw.

Spinning out of control yet still hurtling forward at near-Mach speed--

> **John Pomerantz:** Red, the thrusters aren't working.
>
> **Sid:** We got to get that nose up ...

"Nose won't budge, Sir," narrated Rocketman Bob off-mike.

X-1 Pilot Red Kearns (rallying): Short wall. Short wall. Five in --

The intercom went dead. Only a flat buzz remained.

With 16,000 pounds of thrust, the poor X-1 slammed into earth's bedrock, the hard surface of silicates and limestone, dolomites, diorite and gabbo from the Precambrian Age.

* * *

Red had crash-landed at the far end of Lakebed Runway 18.

Michael David was already on his horse, galloping at full speed to where Red had ended up.

Horse and rider were a blur against the silhouettes of Joshua trees.

The X-1 had come to rest shoved up against a shallow box canyon wall, among the boulders and twisted pine trees.

We followed in a Jeep.

One of the X-1 wings had dragged, cutting a jagged trail sliced in the former ocean floor.

The plane's landing gear had failed at such high speeds.

The bouncing Jeep made a skidding stop.

We saw Michael David arrive at the crash site and leap from his horse and sprint straight towards the broken plane.

He ignored flares of orange fire and the wires shorting and popping sparks --

Nnngh --

With a grunt, he yanked the crooked cockpit canopy from its hinges and tossed it --

The X-1's fuselage was busted open. A fine stream of fuel sprang from one section of the piping, forming a rainbow-crested arc before hitting the hot sand.

Yi Tai-jo jumped from the Jeep and ran towards Michael David --

Flames flickered higher and higher in the smashed cockpit. Our pilot Red hung half-out of the cockpit. He looked unconscious.

Black smoke swirled and rose in thick clouds.

I had seen how much fuel had been loaded onto the Ex. I knew what was coming.

I was just counting the seconds before the rocket detonated.

Yi Tai-jo sprinted headlong into the flaming, smoking wreckage and emerged, clutching Michael David, who had somehow lifted Red up and over the transom, and now would not let him go.

The pilot and his uniform were smoldering ...

We clambered back into the Jeep and sped back to base.

In the shifting light of the flames and headlights, I had seen the serrated edges of a very thin line along the X-1's lower section.

Someone or something had scored the aircraft's skin, with a screwdriver.

* * *

In the Infirmary, Yi Tai-jo would not leave Michael David's bedside, except to sit with Red.

I set up cots for the two of us.

"*Nanuen yeogi issda,*" she told Michael David that night, even though he had passed out. I can tell you that this was about as true a statement, deeply true, and true in as many ways, as any you will ever hear.

"*Naneun nanikka,*"

This last declaration was unnecessary. We all knew who she was.

12. A SECOND MIMETIC EPISODE
THE ALL-NIGHT OSCILLATOR

The NACA X-1 procedures and personnel ... helped lay the foundation of America's space program in the 1960s.
The flight data collected by the NACA in the X-1 tests then provided a basis for American aviation supremacy in the latter half of the 20th century.
   — *Dryden History*

What you are seeking

is seeking you.

   — *Jalal al-Din Muhammad Rumi*

Various tests and theories about why the X-1 had crashed

proliferated.

I told John Pomerantz and Sid and Wally about what I had seen. I was not sure the first two took me seriously, but Wally did. He installed a movie camera in the corner of each hangar, so we could see if any funny business was taking place.

The idea of sabotage on the Muroc grounds was hard to believe. Everyone on the base was family. It must have been something else – an accident, one of the gardeners' wheelbarrows scraping up against X, or maybe that raised ladder platform on stilts that's so heavy.

I tried to put it out of my mind.

***

"What's 'inertia coupling'?" asked Yi Tai-jo through her bedroom door late one night. We were both awake, staring at the ceiling.

"Red and John keep talking about 'inertia coupling' ..."

"I don't know," I answered. "I'm pretty sure it's bad.

"I think it's loss of stability. Like when the wings and fins are too small to support the weight of the fuselage ..."

A breeze wafted the curtains in the moonlight.

"What's wrong with X?" asked Yi Tai-jo.

The night lanterns along the walkways cast a second, alternate scheme of shadows on our walls.

"I don't know."

* * *

I woke with a start, about an hour before dawn.

I couldn't hear Yi Tai-jo breathing. I got up to check on her. Her bed was empty.

I put on my bomber jacket and went outside.

I found her in Hangar Bay 3.

Donny N., the lamplighter who doubled as a night watchman, was reading a newspaper in the corner of the Hangar, listening to a big radio console.

The radio was replaying one of the old Mystery Theatre shows, *The Shadow*. I could hear Orsen Welles' distinctive voice.

And there below, I saw a familiar slender figure in blue and white. She was patiently, thoroughly mopping the white tile floor of Bay 3. She wanted the X-1 to enjoy a very clean nest.

"What is she doing?" asked a yawning voice next to me.

Lewis appeared beside me.

"I guess she can't sleep," I replied.

"Uh huh."

Echoing in the big bay was Orson Welles' big voice explaining that the Shadow had the power to hypnotically cloud the minds of those near him, to make himself invisible.

"Does she think the floor is dirty?" asked Lewis.

"What's wrong with X?" asked Yi Tai-jo.

"I don't know," I answered. "Once, In Victorville, she got it in her mind that if she could clean the kitchen floor, perfectly, then no one will die."

"What, like no one, ever?" asked Lewis sleepily. "No more death?"

I did not know the answer.

One thing about Yi Tai-jo is, she can go long stretches when she's acting like anybody else. Then something like this pops up. It's like a compulsion, something she has to do, and cannot explain.

A second thing is, while she was eccentric before, the serious weirdness started after Topaz.

"Well," said Lewis. "Can't hurt, I guess."

Lewis went down the staircase to join Yi Tai-jo in her mopping.

I followed. We found mops and buckets in the gigantic utility closet. We filled the buckets with water in one of the big sinks.

Orson Welles reminded his radio listeners that the secret identity of the Shadow was Lamont Cranston, wealthy young man-about-town.

Lewis and I found mops and buckets and filled them at the oversized utility sink.

We began to mop small sections of the tile floor near Yi Tai-jo, in concert with her. A space that big, you want to be careful to focus on one square space at a time.

Aldhabi came in, watched, and then joined. Three more sleepy Lost Boys figured this was something.

"Each of us is capable of the deadliest of deeds," explained Lamont Cranston to West Hangar 2. "To save those we love, perhaps ..."

The group of us mopped and cleaned quietly. One of the moppers would hum from time to time. While words were not exchanged, much was shared.

Yi Tai-jo got on her hands and knees to clean with sponges the tiles beneath the X-1.

She spoke to the aircraft, perhaps not realizing I could hear.

"Be careful," Yi Tai-jo warned the sleeping aircraft. "That which makes you great is the very thing that can bring your downfall ..."

She reached up to touch the X-1.

"Tell me," she said to the X-1. "Maybe I can fix it."

She carefully wiped clean the precise spot where her hand had touched the plane's skin.

"Tell me," she said to the X-1. " Maybe I can fix it."

She finished mopping carefully around the X-1's under-carriage and wished it Goodnight.

"Who knows what evil lurks in the hearts of men," laughed Orson Welles, as The Shadow, as we continued with our mopping.

"The Shadow knows! *Mwahahaha ...*"

9. MOMENT OF TRUTH

Girls aren't fearless. Girls are terrified.

— *Mattie Kahn*

Among the group of mechanics and engineers, all the men trying to solve the X-1's problem, Sid was the first to see her.

"Hey, sweetheart," he said, "you shouldn't be here -- "

Yi Tai-jo stood at the edge of the Mission Control area, so that everyone could see and hear her.

"*And you might want to check your I Bars. Your O rings. All your rubber moldings,*" said she, in the Englishman Dockley's precise voice and inflection.

Sid and Red stopped and stared at her like they were seeing a supernatural being.

"*Synthetic rubber,*" she continued, still in that eerie voice borrowed from the Englishman, "*performs poorly at those higher speeds. Anything over 900. Higher altitudes. Brittle, don't you know.*"

All the others turned to look --

"*We don't actually understand why. Brazilian rubber seems far more stable, actual plant rubber. There you have it.”*

Sid, Jolly Wally and John Pomerantz all gaped at her, then at one another.

All hell broke loose.

“It's the rubber! Frickin' A!”

“Why didn't we think of that?”

“God *dammit*, Bob, that wasn't in your notes –

“Yes it was!”

“Well it certainly wasn't starred -- ”

“Can you say that again, sweetheart? The whole thing about the I bars -- ”

“Get us the written transcript of that entire British session! Damn, Bob --“

“Don't blame me! Wally was there, too -- ”

“Where is that report? Who has -- ”

“Hell, she can recite everything he said for us, from A to Z.”

“Is that true, sweetheart? Can you?”

On it went, until Red and John Pomerantz organized things.

* * *

The first thing was to hunt down all the natural rubber we could get our hands on. It resists abrasion and oxidation and is more resistant to heat and cold, and retains its elasticity longer than the vulcanized rubbers.

Rubber doesn't melt down so you can re-mold it, like lead or gold. We needed sections of Brazilian or rubber-tree rubber that we could cut down to fit the X-1 eye-bar seals and valve O Rings. Like those which edge the cockpit or those which seal the junctures of the tail structure's moving panels.

Natural rubber is a monomer, synthetic rubber is a polymer. So John Pomerantz and Wally devised a test which could detect sulphur, which is NOT present in natural rubber.

While words were not exchanged, much was shared.

We started with the Schwinn tires in the bike shop, all synthetic. John Pomerantz took off for the Chrysler dealership in town. Air Force Bases Victorville, Beale and El Segundo came up blank because the U.S. Army hates the Air Force for being superior, superior in every way. Joint Task Force Los Alamitos came through with three crates of rubber hoses but those had been painted and glossed. The Coronado Navy Yard slow-footed it until a call from Senator Proxmire's office lit a fire.

Yi Tai-jo got the word out to Miss Thak, one of her Topaz group of friends, up in Sanger, up near Fresno. Miss Thak's husband arrived the next night after dinner, driving a green pickup truck with a payload full of rubber scraps of every size and shape. We all of us unloaded him in a hurry. He had to make it to a job in Muscatel by dawn, and that's a seven-hour drive. Red gave him gas money, but he wouldn't take it.

11. NIGHT WATCH

Open the door, open it wide

As fast as you can, and leap outside.

The dogs are fierce when they get untied.

    — *Dafydd Ap Gwilym*

We were fossil-hunting with our night-vision goggles while the mop patrol finished up when the lights went out.

All three hangars went dark.

Yi Tai-jo and I were the only ones who could see.

I heard a sound and caught the glimpse of someone on the far side of the X.

After a count of twenty or so, white panels of light -- the backup, or emergency circuits – cut in.

Now, I heard a scuffle.

I took off the goggles and ran around the fuselage to find Yi Tai-jo, still wearing her goggles, strangling Lewis.

As I got close, I could see that she had fashioned a garotte with a thick wire she must have grabbed from Red's table. Lewis was struggling mightily, kicking and jerking to either side. Panic filled his eyes.

Lewis had about six seconds to live –

Michael David and I wrestled them apart. With repeated tries, we broke my sister's hold around Lewis' throat.

Her captive fell to the ground.

Yi Tai-jo took off her goggles. Her face was ice-cold. She

flexed her hands and rubbed one forearm, where the wire had cut into her. Blood appeared.

She glared at Lewis as if she really, really wanted to finish what she had started.

A screwdriver lay on the floor.

"Lewis was trying to sabotage X," she said. "I saw him."

I looked and, sure enough, you could run your hand along a stripe or thin gash halfway down the length of the aircraft's carriage.

"What?" I confronted Lewis, who was still choking.

"You rigged the lights so you could do this?" I demanded. I was furious.

"What the hell, Lew?" said Michael David.

Once he could get his breath, Lewis tried to explain. His voice was raspy.

"The over/under on Rudebaugh and the Warnock team," he said, "is up to 1500. My dad has all his money on it.

"Dad told me we just needed -- "

"It doesn't matter what he told you," said Michael David coldly. "You could have killed Red -- "

"Naw, naw man," protested Lewis. "Red would have caught it. Or I would have told 'em. It's an easy fix. I would have told 'em. It would just delay the flight, so -- "

"What, so Rudebaugh would be first to break Mach?"

"Check," assented Lewis. "Dad had a parlay -- "

"Get out," ordered Michael David.

He pointed to the desert.

"Brother! The closest town is twenty miles away."

"Go now, Lew," said Michael David.

"Can I at least get my kit?"

Michael David shook his head.

"I'm *bleeding* here, man -- "

Michael David turned his back. He picked up the screwdriver from the floor.

"What is this, *Lord of the Flies*?" Lewis croaked piteously. "EmDee, I ... I'm *sorry*...

"Hey! Can't we -- "

But no pity could be found among the Lost Boys of Muroc. They watched silently as one of their own trudged into the dark and shallow seas of the Mojave.

13. MACH

The aircraft climbed to an altitude of 45,000 feet over Rogers Dry Lake in the Mojave Desert and achieved a level flight speed of Mach 1.05, officially flying faster than the speed of sound for the first time.

— *Mark Finlay*

X-1 Pilot Red Kearns: Just reached 900 –

Sid: You're haywire, Pilot.

X-1 Pilot Red Kearns: Ejection signal -- what was that?

Sid: False alarm.

John Pomerantz: Red, did your suit blow on you?
X-1 Pilot Red Kearns: No, it never did. I opened the – uh – it got up to about 43 thousand and I opened the windshield defroster and it went back down. I think I busted the canopy with my head. I don't know.

Sid: Metrics returning to normal. Headers … (unintelligible)

X-1 Pilot Red Kearns: Sid, got me in sight yet?
Sid: (unintelligible)

X-1 Pilot Red Kearns: Huh?
Sid: Negative.
X-1 Pilot Red Kearns: Came down to 12,000 feet on a right-hand downwind leg over the end of the East-West runway in the sound end of the lake.

John Pomerantz: Try to tell us where you are, Red.
X-1 Pilot Red Kearns: I'm (gasping) – I'll tell you in a minute. I got 1800 lbs [nitrogen] source pressure.
Sid: Chuck from Murray, if you can give me altitude and heading, I'll try to check you from outside.
X-1 Pilot Red Kearns: Be down at 18,000 feet. I'm about – I'll be over the base at about 15,000 feet in a minute.
Sid: Yes, sir.

X-1 Pilot Red Kearns: Now I'm venting both lox and fuel. Leaving hydrogen peroxide alone.
Sid: Roger.
X-1 Pilot Red Kearns: I cut it, I got – in real bad trouble.

X-1 Pilot Red Kearns: Seals may be compromised.

John Pomerantz: Hold tight, Red. Those seals will hold.
X-1 Pilot Red Kearns: Ice forming. Can't see --

Sid: It should clear any second ...

X-1 Pilot Red Kearns: Ice is clearing. Those guys were so right!

X-1 Pilot Red Kearns: Source pressure is still 15 seconds, I'm getting OK now.
Sid: I have you.
X-1 Pilot Red Kearns: Does everything look okay on the airplane?
Sid: No breaches. I'm still catching up to you.
X-1 Pilot Red Kearns: Going to do a 360 here to the left.
John Pomerantz: We don't have you, that's a T-33.

X-1 Pilot Red Kearns: Over the base right now, Sid, at 14,500 feet.

Sid: Crank it Red!! For Chrissake --

X-1 Pilot Red Kearns: Likewise --

X-1 Pilot Red Kearns: Hang on. Here we go !!

X-1 Pilot Red Kearns: (unintelligible)

In the skies overhead, we all heard the very loud, very distinctive and brand-new thunderous, shearing *CrackCrackWham!* of the X-1 breaking the sound barrier.

It shook the windows and several burst, from the sheer joy of it all.

Cheers rattled the hangars' tin roofs. Much jumping on

chairs and pounding of garbage-can lids. John Pomerantz stood at the console, his head buried in his hands. Rocketman Bob was on his knees.

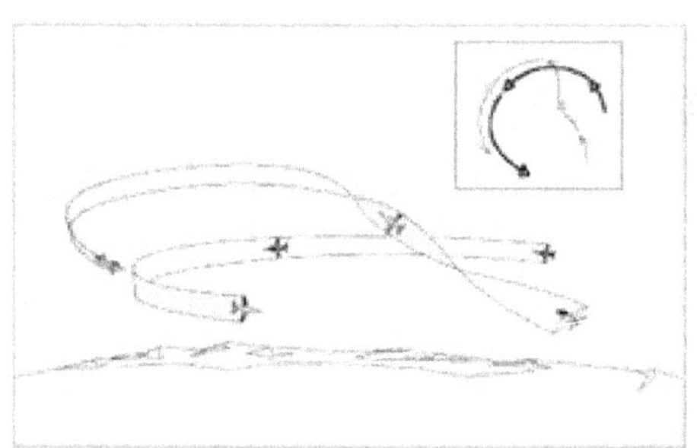

EPILOGUE

You've never been lost until you've been lost at Mach 3.

— *Paul F. Crickmore*

When it became clear that the next generation of X-1's would lead to monkeys sitting in phony rocket "cockpits" to fly missiles to the moon, I set my sights elsewhere and ended up in flying F-100D Super Sabres with the 416th Squadron.

The F-100 is a thoroughbred plane, sleek and silver with elegant, slanted wings. In Vietnam, the F-100 was painted green and asked to descend into the swamps of Southeast Asia. We watched over the 3rd Battalion, mostly air-to-ground stuff, which was a shame for such a fine aircraft. We didn't encounter Colonel Tomb much, except for once over Phuc Yen.

Half of all the missiles our planes deployed in Vietnam misfired, by the way. Colossal FUBAR. Did you even know? Not many people do.

But enough about that.

** * **

Yi Tai-jo and Michael David were married in 1960, in the Legion Hall at Dana Point.

She was never so happy.

My Korean Sister died in 1971, at Kusan AB, with the 3rd Tactical Fighter Wing. She was helping oversee the PACAF assumption of host-unit duties when a T-33 Shooting Star sideswiped the C-47 Skytrain she was riding in.

She left behind two Korean nieces. Any time of day or night, either Michael David or Lieutenant Captain Pilot Sir Dad or myself, one of us, is no more than ten steps from those girls.

Neither of them has Yi Tai-jo's gifts. Both of them have her eyes, and her mouth. Ready for anything, that's what they are.

The Bell X-1 remains revered in aviation legend.

Apollo 13 was nothing more than a really, really big version of the X-1.

X-1 Model (1) is in the Smithsonian. Model (2) was never rebuilt after Red's crash. Model (3) is on the East Coast, in Washington D.C., at the National Air and Space Museum. I visited it once. It's like seeing a formal version of the aircraft I knew, but dolled up to look nice for a party.

The X-1 (3) is a prettier orange than it ever was in the high desert.

I'm writing this in May, 1976. Moon landings. Skylab. Now a rocket-powered shuttle. *Ooo-rah.* All good. But people have forgotten that the X-1 opened that door; the door to space. Mercury and Project Gemini and those flashy numbered Apollo flights and virtually all of the NASA rockets owe their existence to Red Kearns and John Pomerantz and Jolly Wally and the whole Muroc crew, and what they achieved, together, that summer, to reach Mach 1.

* * *

Riding your bike at Muroc, every once in a while, your tire would hit a zillion-year-old fossil, a crustacean or three-spine stickleback or camel-skeleton, or some such thing.

The past has a way of forcing itself into your present mind.

My life now is like that. If I see a short, squat candle, or a white-headed mop, or a leather holster belt, or if I hear a radio mystery drama ... it takes me back. And once I'm in the past, all roads lead to her.

None of us knew it at the time, but we had a secret weapon in our corner when we went up against the Sound Barrier, up against Nature in all her complexity, up against the G-forces and the bad O-rings, all the buffeting, all the doubt, all the inertia, the smoke and flames, our own ignorance, the desert, and the endless perils of invading the stratosphere.

We had an Ace in the Hole. We had a thing to help us overcome the scores upon scores of elements of man and physics which stood against us launching that most excellent aircraft at the speed of sound.

A secret weapon.

The love of Yi Tai-jo.

Non melior amicus.

TOM'S STORY NOTES

What was always so exciting for me about the story which became "My Korean Sister" was the chance to center a YA adventure directly at the moment at which powered flight became space flight, and jets became rocket jets, with droll pilots recklessly launching themselves into the unknown.

The notion of placing a mildly autistic heroine into that drama was just too good.

I have pushed back the timeline concerning the development of the X-1, from 1947 to 1956, for story purposes. Knowledgeable readers will note that the Muroc goings-on which I depict actually took place earlier. Similarly, I have pushed forward on the timeline with the liquor-store troubles which roiled the Southern California Korean-American communities – these actually took place in the 1960's.

What was so challenging about "My Korean Sister" was that both the X-1 itself and the Muroc setting brought many, many aspects with them. I needed to build these different aspects gradually. A data dump is highly undesirable to readers. Therefore, I needed to design the storyline of Charles and Yi Tai-jo as a gradual build, so as to maintain a balance between character development, historical context, and setting, and the deeper themes which grow out of that mix.

The two kids are the story (especially her). Everything needed to be run through them.

I feel that this adventure, as it is written now, contains close-to-enough narrative pull, or reason to read. When the dark incident at Topaz occurred to me, it seemed like a strong and authentic mystery element ... 'authentic' to me in the sense that it grew out the research, and authentic to the character in that it provided an explanation or trigger for her latent autism (I'm not sure that concept is entirely accurate). The revelation that it was Yi Tai-jo who garroted the evil camp guard at Topaz who was victimizing her friends is, I hope, both surprising and 'logical.' Again, that is not quite the right wording.

Lewis was a pleasant surprise.

I needed a way to connect the protagonist and the aircraft, so I made up the term 'mimetic memory.' Eidetic memory is photographic memory, based on visual images, and is of course not at all the same thing.

* * *

The eccentric aviator (and inventor, and film-maker) Howard Hughes tried to capture the excitement of an aerial dogfight for his 1930 film "Hell's Angel." He amassed an armada of vintage planes, pilots and mechanics to film hours of daring aerial maneuvers. But the footage fell flat. No one cared. In the sky, there is no foreground and no visual field for context, so the action does not 'read.' Hughes had to re-shoot it over and over, mixing the small-objects-in-clouds sequences with ground-anchored scenes.

Something similar faced me in the X-1 story: namely, how could I portray the historical sound-barrier-breaking flight. I was getting nowhere with descriptions and adjectives of a lone rocket-jet in the empty skies ... so I tried capturing the emotions and technical movements of the episode in dialogue. The transmissions in my story are based on the actual transmissions of Chuck Yeager's historic flights in the X-1.

COMMENTARY by Anne Millbrooke

Tom's delightful stories in "The Aviation Girls" span ancient ideas about flight through the Golden Age of aviation to the age of Rocketry.

People have dreamed of flying since ancient times. The Greek myth about Daedalus and his son Icarus is evidence of this. They escaped from captivity on the island of Crete by making wings and flying away. But Icarus flew too close to the sun, which melted the wax holding his wings together. He fell into the sea and drowned. The evidence of this myth comes from oral tradition eventually written into the historical records.

Leonardo da Vinci's notebooks and manuscripts contain evidence of the early scientific and engineering study of flight. Working on the Italian Peninsula centuries before Italy became a unified country, Da Vinci produced a codex (a handwritten manuscript or book) on the flight of birds in the years 1505-1506. He also drew hundreds of pictures as he explored the design of mechanical aircraft. His written words and his design drawings reveal what he did centuries aircraft were built and flown.

Joseph-Michel Montgolfier and Jacques-Étienne Montgolfier, brothers, achieved flight as a human activity in 1783. For their first public demonstration of balloon flight, an unmanned hot air balloon was used. They then tested the effect of flying on animals by sending a sheep, a duck, and a rooster aloft in a basket hanging from balloon. Testing then involved a tethered flight with Étienne Montgolfier in the basket.

Pilâtre de Rozier as pilot and François Laurent d'Arlandes, as a military observer, made the first free flight in a balloon on November 21, 1783. In 1784 a Frenchwoman named Elisabeth Thible became the first female to go up in an untethered balloon flight. Illustrations, newspapers, letters, and other manuscripts document these early developments in aviation history—and the flights of men and women flying balloons today.

Aviators had over a hundred years of flying experience before kite experiments led to practical airplanes, heavier-than-air craft. The Wright brothers, Orville and Wilbur, carefully documented their experiments, flights, exhibitions, and company. Earlier exhibition flyers such as Bessie Coleman, who had African and Native American ancestors, and Katherine Stinson, and later Amelia Earhart, attracted much press attention, and left letters, contracts, and other documents as evidence of their aviation activities. Anne Morrow Lindbergh won National Book Awards for her books about flying, *North to the Orient* (1935) and *Listen! The Wind* (1938).

The history of rockets date back to ancient China. From then to now, rockets have been launched during displays of fireworks. The word comes from the Italian word "rochhetta" that means a bobbin or small spindle, a reference to its shape. The modern history of rockets dates to experiments in the United States and other countries in the 1920s, most notably to Robert Goddard's 1926 liquid-fuel rocket with its hypersonic jet of gas. The Russians test-fired solid-fuel rockets soon thereafter. In the 1930s experiments used rockets to assist the take-off of aircraft. The Bell rocket X-1 became the first manned vehicle to break the sound barrier. In

Germany in the 1940s, Hanna Reitsch became the first woman to fly a rocket‑ powered plane. Female engineers contributed to the development of rockets and testing rocket‑ powered aircraft and spacecraft, including the rockets that launched the Apollo spacecraft on its 1968 moon landing mission.

Tom's "Aviation Girls" have a base in history!

CREDITS

Main cover art: White Rabbit Arts at The Historical Fiction Company

Page 1: Tasneem Amiruddin. Commissioned for "The Aviation Girls."

Page 3 ... Meeting d'Aviation, Nice, April 1910, by Charles Leonce Brosse

Contents page illustration by Dugald Walke

Page 17: Curtiss Aeroplane diagram Wikimedia Commons

Page 26: Bird in Flight by Eadweard Muybridge (circa 1896)

Page 47: Artist David Cheney. Commissioned for "The First Manned Flight."

Page 182: Thach Weave diagram: Wikimedia Commons.

Page 195: Art by Timothee Mathon. Commissioned for Aviation Girls.

Page 252 ... Phases of the Moon by Galileo

BIOGRAPHIES

TIM GROVE

Tim Grove believes the past is filled with amazing stories waiting to be told. He writes from twenty-five years of experience as a public historian and museum professional, working at some of America's most-visited history museums. His career memoir, *A Grizzly in the Mail and Other Adventures in American History*, highlights some of the fun projects he has worked on. More recently, he has been writing history-focused nonfiction books for ages 10-14. His book *First Flight Around the World* was a finalist for the 2016 YALSA Excellence in Nonfiction award. He is also the author of *Milestones of Flight*. Besides telling stories from different perspectives, he seeks to help all ages understand the historical process and to see that the past is vitally relevant to our world today.

SEZAI ADIL

Sezai Adil is an academic with fifteen years' experience writing and editing scientific manuscripts, books, and grant proposals. His specialties include Biodiversity, Ecology, Biology, biological control, ecology and also education sciences. He holds a BS in Biology, a Master's degree in Zoology, and a PhD in Zoology.

PAUL GLENSHAW

Paul Glenshaw's lifelong passions over several disciplines all fuel the same goal: storytelling. In addition to being an instructor and lecturer for the Smithsonian Associates, Paul is co-director, writer, and producer of the just completed documentary *The Lafayette Escadrille*. He is a frequent contributor to the Smithsonian's *Air & Space* magazine, and recent drawing projects in crude work with the Folger Shakespeare Library and the National Museum of Health and Medicine. He is also a writer and producer for the theater, radio, museum exhibits, interactive media, and STEM education. He lives in Silver Spring, Maryland and is a graduate of Washington University in St. Louis.

MICHAEL QUETTING

Michael Quetting is a laboratory director and ultralight pilot at the Max Planck Institute for Ornithology, which gives him a unique opportunity to combine his love of flying with his love of birds.

Among his works are the book *Papa Goose: One Year, Seven Goslings, and the Flight of My Life* (Greystone Books).

JESSICA GHILANI

Jessica Ghilani, PhD is an Associate Professor of Communication at the University of Pittsburgh, Greensburg. There, she teaches and studies the history of technologies, primarily in media. Her interests in aviation came from examining military recruiting advertisements in the archives of the Smithsonian Institution's National Museum of American History, which led her to the impressive expanse of the Steven F. Udvar–Hazy Center at the National Air and Space Museum. This airplane hangar located in northern Virginia displays numerous early through present aviation technologies for museum visitors to inspect and admire.

She has written extensively about the use of technologies in military recruiting and public relations. Her work has been published in academic journals and edited volumes. She has been recognized with numerous grants and awards, most relevantly a 2009 Smithsonian Institution Predoctoral Fellowship and in 2020, the Aviation Space Writers Association Award given by the National Air and Space Museum. She is a mother of two bookish girls who love to invent and learn about history, so she is delighted to contribute to this collection.

CAMERON SMITH

Teaching human evolution and prehistory since 1999, Cameron Smith studied at the University of London's Institute of Archaeology and then Durham University (UK) (BA Joint Hons), with two field seasons at Koobi Fora, Kenya; he then earned an MA (Anthropology) at Portland State University, and a doctorate in Archaeology at Canada's Simon Fraser University in 2004.

Dr. Smith's books include *The Fact of Evolution* (Penguin Random House 2011), *An Atlas of Human Prehistory* (Cognella 2019), and *Evolution and the Drake Equation: An Anthropologist's Estimation of the Probability of Intelligent Life in our Galaxy* (Springer 2023).

ELAINE SWANSON

Elaine Swanson is a second-year master's student in applied computation at Harvard. Elaine's experiences as a farmer, combined with her bachelor's degree in mathematical biology and botany from Oregon State University, inspire her to develop algorithms aimed at addressing food insecurity resulting from population growth and shifting climate patterns. Elaine is also an artist committed to youth education and teaching the dynamics of astrobotany and mathematics in nature and art. During the summer months, she runs Math in

Nature daycamps for K-5th graders and NASA STEM programs for middle school aged girls.

ANNE MILLBROOKE

Anne Millbrooke is a historian educated at Boise State College (bachelor's degree), University of Wisconsin-Madison (master's degree), and the University of Pennsylvania (doctorate degree). She used to manage the archives for Pratt & Whitney aircraft engines, Sikorsky flying boats and helicopters, and Hamilton Standard propellers. She taught history at several universities. She wrote the award-winning *Aviation History* book published by Jeppesen and the National Register Bulletin: Guidelines for Evaluating and Documenting Historic Aviation Properties published by the National Park Service.

....

TOM DURWOOD

Tom Durwood is a teacher, writer and editor with an interest in history. Tom most recently taught English Composition and Empire and Literature at Valley Forge Military College, where he won the Teacher of the Year Award five times. Tom has taught Public Speaking and Basic Communications as guest lecturer for the Naval Special Warfare Development Group at the Dam's Neck Annex of the Naval War College.

Tom's ebook *Empire and Literature* matches global works of film and fiction to specific quadrants of empire, finding surprising parallels. Literature, film, art and architecture are viewed against the rise and fall of empire. In a foreword to

Empire and Literature, postcolonial scholar Dipesh Chakrabarty of the University of Chicago calls it "imaginative and innovative." Prof. Chakrabarty writes that "Durwood has given us a thought-provoking introduction to the humanities." His subsequent book "Kid Lit: An Introduction to Literary Criticism" has been well-reviewed. "My favorite nonfiction book of the year," writes The Literary Apothecary (Goodreads).

Early reader response to Tom's historical fiction adventures has been promising. The stories have won nine literary awards to date. "A true pleasure ... the richness of the layers of Tom's novel is compelling," writes Fatima Sharrafedine in her foreword to "The Illustrated Boatman's Daughter." The Midwest Book Review calls that same adventure "uniformly gripping and educational ... pairing action and adventure with social issues." Adds Prairie Review, "A deeply intriguing, ambitious historical fiction series."

Tom briefly ran his own children's book imprint, Calico Books (Contemporary Books, Chicago). Tom's newspaper column "Shelter" appeared in the North County Times for seven years. Tom earned a Masters in English Literature in San Diego, where he also served as Executive Director of San Diego Habitat for Humanity.

Bonus: Tom interview

https://www.circumlocution.net/2021/08/interview-with-thomas-durwood.html

AWARDS

TOM'S HISTORICAL FICTION

Moonbeam Award (Silver)
Celebrating youthful curiosity, discovery and learning through books and reading.

Pre-Teen Fiction – Historical

Gold

Operation Overlord: A Tommy Collins Adventure by Francis Moss (Self-Published)

Silver

The Adventures of Ruby Pi and the Geometry Girls by Tom Durwood (Empire Studies Press)

Bronze

Molly Shipton Secret Actress by Sheri Graubert (Clear Fork Publishing)

Presented by Jenkins Group and Independent Publisher Online, the Moonbeam Children's Book Awards are designed to bring increased recognition to exemplary children's books and their creators, and to support childhood literacy and life-long reading.

2023 Purple Dragonfly Book Award Winners

The Purple Dragonfly Book Awards recognize accomplished, up-and-coming, and younger published authors in the field of children's literature.

The Incipere Awards, sponsored by Entrada Publishing, recognize exceptional writing across multiple genres with particular focus on works that have been published by small, independent, and academic presses.

First Place - Anna J Walner - *Saltwater and Driftwood*
Second Place - Tom Durwood - *The Adventures of Ruby Pi and the Math Girls*
Third Place - Frances Schoonmaker - *Sid Johnson and the Phantom Salve Stealer*

The Historical Fiction Company

"Ruby Pi and the Geometry Girls" by Tom Durwood receives 5 stars and the "Highly Recommended" award of excellence from The Historical Fiction Company.

Firebird Award

Two judges from a select panel of 27 read each book and independently score each entry. Only entries with the highest scores are awarded the coveted Firebird. **The Firebird Book Award judging panel includes a diverse group who represent a cross-section of ages, cultural heritage, races, religions, gender, and experience.**

The Literary Titan Book Awards are awarded to books that have astounded and amazed us with unique writing styles, vivid worlds, complex characters and original ideas. These books deserve extraordinary praise, and we are proud to acknowledge the hard work, dedication and writing talent of these brilliant authors.

SPR BOOK AWARDS FINALIST An unexpected love note to mathematics, this collection of stories is an allegorical plea for young girls to pursue and discover the wonders of numbers. The marketing potential for empowering young girls could make this a sleeper hit.

CHANTICLEER AWARD
Congratulations on your work advancing to the FINALIST position of the SHORTS Book Awards for Fiction Series, a division of the 2022 Chanticleer International Book Awards (the CIBAs)!

The Adventures of Ruby Pi and the Geometry Girls

A robust entry into the YA field, this first "Ruby Pi" collection of adventures tells of brave heroines fighting tremendous odds, using the one tool that can save them – mathematics.

From ancient India to World War II, from Sputnik-era Moscow to the Benin Kingdoms and the Jim Crow South, clever girls overcome huge odds to save their families.

Few works of fiction truly transport the reader to another place and time, and even fewer give that reader something they can take back home afterwards. 'Geometry Girls' achieves both, breaking down barriers in educational literature and making mathematics not only interesting, but a matter of life and death. **Tom has done his homework ... this work will be a treasure of school libraries everywhere in years to come.**

Written with a skillful hand and with the kind **of attention to detail** that will grip an ambitious teenager.

The MLK story ... an excellent story with a crucially important message for young people in modern Western society. **The mathematics is simple but elegant.**

-- Graham Van Goffrier, third-year PhD candidate (Theoretical neutrino physics)

www.themathgirls.com

The Illustrated Colonials Trilogy

A new perspective one on of history's most fascinating moments. This richly illustrated trilogy captures some of the global thrill and tumult caused by the American Revolution. The epic tale follows six young rich kids from around the world as they join the cause, finding love and treachery along the path. Unique entry into the robust YA.universe.

A deeply intriguing, ambitious historical fiction series.

– Prairie Review

Clever .... Durwood's deeply realized characters are sketched with precision and care.　　　*- Books Coffee Reviews*

www.mycolonials.com

The Illustrated Boatman's Daughter

An Egyptian girl fights intrigue and corruption for the completion of the world's greatest man-made waterway. Illustrated edition of a young-adult novella with 40 original color pieces. An attention-getting story featuring multicultural characters and settings. Classic adventure starring a smart, strong heroine.

"A true pleasure. The richness of the layers of Tom's novel is compelling."   *-- Fatima Sharrafedine, in her Foreword*

"Uniformly gripping and educational ... pairing action and adventure with social issues."   *--The Midwest Book Review*

www.boatmansdaughter.com

Kid Lit: An Introduction to Literary Theory

There are twin premises to Tom Durwood's "Kid Lit: An Introduction to Literary Criticism." The first is that literary theory is for all of us, and the second is that students can develop marketable lifetime skills when building critical thinking regarding their favorite stories.

Tom is a teacher and it is quickly evident in the clarity of his writing. He poses a simple question – for example, *What makes a good villain?* -- and then draws you into a comparison between Captain Ahab (apocalyptic evil) and Dr. Octopus (simple greed). This then flows into a consideration of evil in all literature. You are then invited to formulate your own theory of good and bad by following his clear illustrations.

This is literary criticism at its least formal and most lively .... It will definitely challenge you and your students.

-- Todd Whitaker, author of "What Great Teachers Do Differently"

My favorite non-fiction book of the year, by far.   *-- The Literary Apothecary*

www.kidlitcrit.com

Empire and Literature

Tom Durwood's supplemental-text e-book *Empire and Literature* promises to be an invaluable tool not only for students following his courses, but also for anyone interested to explore the deep relations between literature and empire.

Durwood brilliantly argues that literature and the workings of empire are deeply connected.

An exceptional pedagogical tool, clear and concise exposition.

-- Andrei Ionescu, PhD in Languages/Literature and Psychology, University of Padua

Durwood has indeed given us a thought-provoking introduction to the humanities. Teachers will find much here that is imaginative and innovative. I hope his book will receive the attention it deserves.

-- Dipesh Chakrabarty, The University of Chicago, from his Foreword

www.empirestudies.com

NON-FICTION HISTORY

Teddy's Tantrum

A Case Study in Empire and Literature

This new account revisits a little-known 1906 incident in Teddy Roosevelt's administration and finds an epic "lost" story of intrigue, combat, politics and redemption.

On November 5, 1906, Roosevelt dismissed 167 members of the 25th Infantry in what historian Lewis Gould calls "one of the most glaring miscarriages of justice in American history."

Sixty years later, a journeyman writer named John D. Weaver, the son of a clerk at the 1906 hearings, embarked on a campaign to exonerate the soldiers. His book produced a small measure of justice: in February of 1973, the U.S. Army issued an apology to the men of the 25th Infantry and awarded the sole surviving battalion member (Dorsie Willis) back pay.

This is the first chronicle of the entire Brownsville story, treating Weaver and the troops' exoneration as an equal part of the narrative. Author Tom Durwood scratches the surface of "Teddy's tantrum" and finds a confluence of rich characters and enduring themes. It is a story of military heroism and redemption, loyalty and betrayal, presidential influence and the power of narrative. *Teddy's Tantrum* seeks to set the neglected episode in its historical context.

'Teddy's Tantrum' takes a period of history and shines **new light on it** ... Tom pulls out the grander themes of the tragedy and triumph. **The true stuff of history.**

-- Tim Pritchard, author "Ambush Alley"

www.teddystantrum.com

Printed in the USA
CPSIA information can be obtained
at www.ICGtesting.com
CBHW061919101024
15670CB00007B/65